JOURNEY
OF
THE SCROLLS

AN HISTORICAL NOVEL

By ED STRUM

REMDUST PUBLISHING
Journey of the Scrolls, Copyright © 2010 by Ed Strum
All Rights Reserved
ISBN 978-0-9913897-5-9

Although referring to actual historical figures or locations, this novel is a work of fiction. Journey of the Scrolls is based on the Merovingian Cross written by this author and contains significant additions and extensive revisions to that book.

Books by Ed Strum

THE CONNOISSSEURS – A Play

MONTOBA: THE PRINCESS OF ÉLEVÉ – A Novel

JOURNEY OF THE SCROLLS – A Novel

JOURNEY OF THE SCROLLS – SPECIAL EDITION

THE BURROW – A Play

<u>Acknowledgements</u>

I wish to extend my thanks and appreciation to Leslie Brown, Heather Couthaud, and Jim Jacobs for their reviews of the drafts, and their many comments and suggestions that helped immensely in the creation of this novel.

Thanks also to Sandra Geist for her research and Tom Clemo, Brad Strum and Tyler Strum for their comments.

Special thanks to Jim Jacobs for his ideas, and development of illustrations, and Sean Jacobs for his technical help.

JOURNEY
OF
THE SCROLLS

CHARTS AND MAPS

ILLUSTRATIONS

Charts, Maps, and Illustrations by James Jacobs

COVER DESIGN by James Jacobs

TABLE of CONTENTS

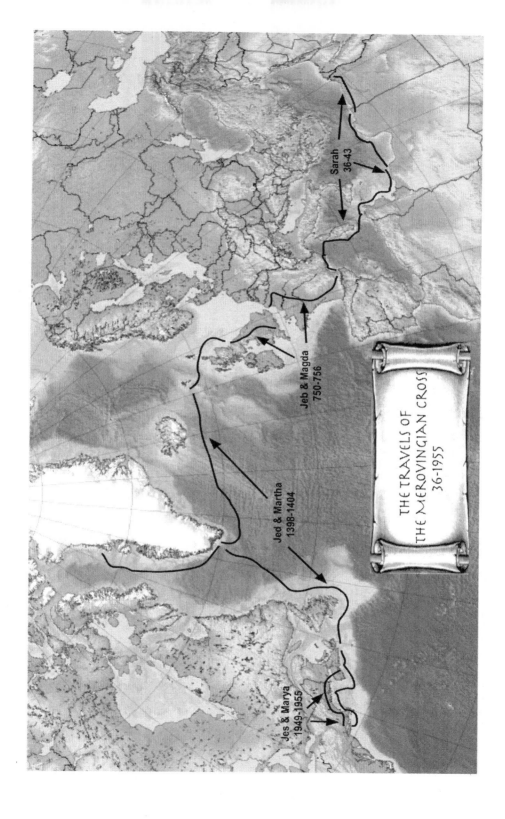

THE TRAVELS OF
THE MEROVINGIAN CROSS
36-1955

Sarah
36-43

Jeb & Magda
750-756

Jed & Martha
1398-1404

Jes & Marya
1949-1955

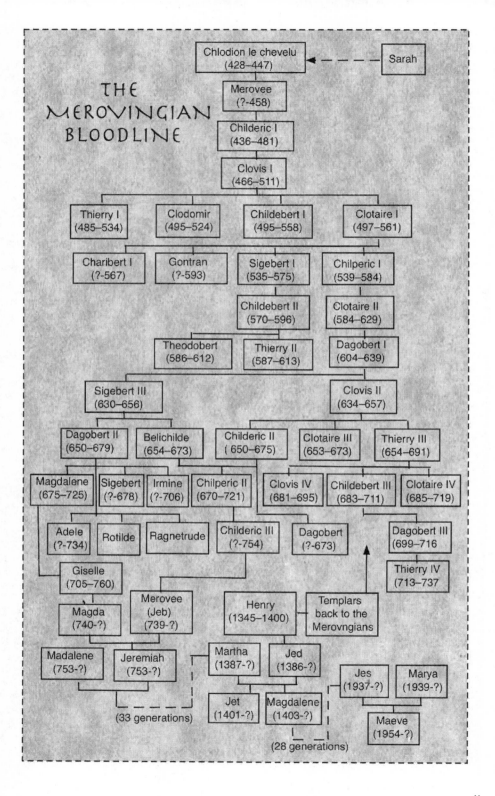

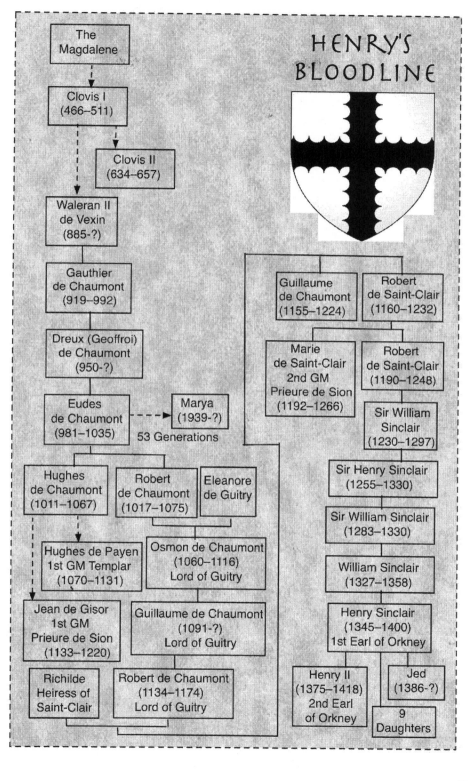

HENRY'S BLOODLINE

The Magdalene

Clovis I (466–511)

Clovis II (634–657)

Waleran II de Vexin (885-?)

Gauthier de Chaumont (919–992)

Dreux (Geoffroi) de Chaumont (950-?)

Eudes de Chaumont (981–1035)

Marya (1939-?)

53 Generations

Hughes de Chaumont (1011–1067)

Robert de Chaumont (1017–1075)

Eleanore de Guitry

Hughes de Payen 1st GM Templar (1070–1131)

Osmon de Chaumont (1060–1116) Lord of Guitry

Jean de Gisor 1st GM Prieure de Sion (1133–1220)

Guillaume de Chaumont (1091-?) Lord of Guitry

Richilde Heiress of Saint-Clair

Robert de Chaumont (1134–1174) Lord of Guitry

Guillaume de Chaumont (1155–1224)

Robert de Saint-Clair (1160–1232)

Marie de Saint-Clair 2nd GM Prieure de Sion (1192–1266)

Robert de Saint-Clair (1190–1248)

Sir William Sinclair (1230–1297)

Sir Henry Sinclair (1255–1330)

Sir William Sinclair (1283–1330)

William Sinclair (1327–1358)

Henry Sinclair (1345–1400) 1st Earl of Orkney

Henry II (1375–1418) 2nd Earl of Orkney

Jed (1386-?)

9 Daughters

iii

JOURNEY OF THE SCROLLS

CHAPTER ONE

Flight From Aegyptus

Northern Coast, Aegyptus
Spring, 36 AD

Sarah looked up at the clear night sky and noticed three bright stars in a row.

"Mama," she pointed, "Do those three stars have a name?"

"They form the belt of the Hunter." The answer came from the man called Joseph, riding next to Sarah and her mother on one of the six dromedaries he had obtained for their journey. "The Hunter is called Sah. If you look closely you can imagine his right arm raised with his sword in his hand while his other arm holds a curved shield. The scabbard that holds his sword hangs from his belt."

Sarah stared hard with her dark brown eyes and could just imagine what Joseph described. Even at her young age of five, she knew she had exceptional night vision. She sat high on the top of the dromedary in a special chair and looked up at the many stars above. Her mother Mary rode behind her and her aunt Martha rode another dromedary next to them.

"The Egyptians considered Sah to be a god," Sarah's mother whispered. "When a Pharaoh died, they sometimes took the form of Sah in the afterlife."

Joseph and Sarah's uncle Lazarus rode near them on two other dromedaries and a Bedouin guide rode at the front, leading the way. Two other women rode together, and on another rode a man who kept his cloak tightly around his face so that only his penetrating dark brown eyes looked out at her. The eighth dromedary carried the parts of a portable boat along with food, tents, and other supplies. Each dromedary carried a pair of large goatskin sacks filled with water slung across their backs.

Sarah looked north to her right and saw the stars reflected on the vast sea that stretched far into the distance. They twinkled and glimmered and glowed across the slight waves for as far as she could see. Sarah had realized that they were traveling along the seacoast as closely as they could. With the remains of a huge dried up lake to her left and the sea to her right they seemed to be following a narrow stretch of land.

"Why do we travel at night?" Sarah asked Joseph. Her Aunt Martha turned to answer.

"It is cooler at night, Sarah," she spoke quietly, "and, besides, we can travel unheard and unseen by others."

"Are we afraid of someone that might see us?"

"We are traveling on a little used path," Joseph answered, "but there is still the chance we might be seen by a group of Roman soldiers and we want to avoid that. We camp away from the main route for the same reason."

"It's beautiful to look out at the sea but why do we pass so close to it?"

"For the same reason, Sarah," added her uncle Lazarus, "Most people and soldiers are camped inland."

"How much longer before we get there?" Sarah persisted. Before anyone could answer, the Bedouin guide announced, "We approach Taposiris Magna." He slowed the pace, seeing a fast approaching dromedary with a lone rider. The man saw the guide and motioned him to follow. As dawn arrived, they came to the edge of a Bedouin camp and set up tents under a large date palm tree. Sarah shared a tent with her mother and Aunt Martha. She was given goat's milk mixed with wheat and dates in a beautiful goblet her mother always carried with her. She laid out her soft woolen rug and covered herself lightly with her cloak. As the hot sun rose, she drifted off to sleep and woke up listening to the soft voices of her mother and aunt.

"We should visit the tomb of the Queen here," Martha murmured, "We may never get another chance."

"Yes, I agree," Sarah's mother responded. "The temple is at the west end of the lake we have been traveling along. I will ask the Bedouin to take us there. I understand it is becoming difficult to go into the tomb next to the temple since the sand has just about covered it. It will soon be gone and lost forever. Antony is buried with her, they say."

"Yes, that is so." There was a moment of silence. "I hope her tomb is lost forever and her relics never found," Martha spoke angrily. Sarah had never heard her speak that way before.

"When I die," her mother responded, "I hope no one ever finds my remains. I would like to be left in peace. But I suppose I won't have anything to say about it." Sarah could tell her mother was trying to keep a sense of humor about dying but she could not quite manage it.

"I feel the same way," replied Martha.

Suddenly Sarah heard the soft voice of a man.

"No one will ever find my remains. I can assure you of that."

She thought it must be the voice of the man with the deep brown eyes since it didn't sound like Joseph or Lazarus. Sarah thought his voice was gentle and beautiful.

It was deadly silent for a moment. No one spoke and then her mother continued. "They say she was very beautiful."

"She must have been since she charmed both Caesar and Antony," Martha added. "She was charming, intelligent, and had a great wit as well. And they say her voice could beguile anyone."

"No doubt she had the beauty and charm of youth when she met Caesar." Sarah's mother spoke softly.

"I've heard it said of her," Martha continued, "that 'Age cannot wither her, nor custom stale, her infinite variety'. She must have been remarkable."

There was another long moment of silence. There was the soft shuffle of disappearing footsteps as if the mysterious man was leaving.

"Mama," Sarah called through the tent opening.

"What is it, Sarah?"

"I heard the soft gentle voice of the man with the deep brown eyes. Does he have a name?"

"He is called Joshua, and you are correct: he does have a beautiful voice." That satisfied Sarah. He had a name.

Then the Bedouin yelled, "Dromedaries approaching."

"What's happening, Mama?" Sarah called again through the tent opening.

"There are two men on dromedaries racing toward us from Alexandria."

"One looks like Mark the Evangelist," Martha said, "and the other appears to be a Roman soldier."

As they approached, Mark yelled. "You are being followed by a group of twenty Roman soldiers on horses. You must hide."

"Mary," Joseph said. "Take Sarah and go into the middle of the Bedouin camp. They will hide you in one of their tents. We'll stay here." He then turned to their Bedouin guide.

"Take the dromedary carrying the portable boat and hide it. It will draw too much attention and suspicion."

"I'll go with him," said Joshua, the man with the deep dark eyes and soft voice.

"Follow me," ordered the Bedouin guide. Joshua climbed onto a dromedary and followed the guide out of the camp. He was followed by the dromedary with the boat parts and supplies.

"Stay hidden until we come to find you," the soldier called. "Where will you be?"

"Inside the walls surrounding the temple," the Bedouin replied. "They won't look there."

Sarah and her mother were ushered into the center of the camp by one of the Bedouin women and crawled into a tent. The Bedouins also suggested the rest of the group move within their camp, and with their help, Joseph, Mark, Lazarus, and the soldier moved tents and food from

3

the edge to the middle of the camp. They tethered the remaining seven dromedaries with the Bedouin dromedaries, Martha and the other two women stayed in a tent, and they all awaited the arrival of the Roman soldiers.

As they waited in silence, Sarah whispered to her mother. "What will happen to Joseph and the others when the soldiers come? I'm afraid, Mama."

Mary replied, "Don't be afraid, Sarah. We will all be protected. The Bedouins are looking after us."

The silence was slowly filled by the steady rumble of approaching hoof beats growing louder and louder until they suddenly stopped. Sarah clung to her mother and strained to hear but it was deadly silent outside her tent.

CHAPTER TWO

The Last Merovingian King

Francia
Early Winter, 750 AD

Jeb's father was Childeric III, the King of the Franks, or Merovingians.

"I thought we'd gotten an early start but it looks like winter came sooner than I expected." He turned to his kinsman Clotaire and pointed to a small opening in the side of a hill. "That looks as if it might be a cave. If it's safe, let's make camp there before it gets too dark."

They'd left Stenay in the north two weeks before, attempting to reach Rhédae in the south before the onset of winter. It was clearly too late. At first they tried to make use of the old Roman roads going south but found most of them either heavily overgrown with wild thyme and mint, or going in the wrong direction. However the beautiful old stone arched Roman bridges were still intact, and even though they too were overgrown with brambles, they used them a few times to cross over rivers. Jeb was curious about how they were built, especially those that had several spans with pillars set in the riverbed.

"Clotaire," Jeb once asked, "some of the rivers are very deep. How did they build those pillars going into the bottom of the river? It's amazing that they are still standing after all these years."

"Jeb, the Romans were astounding architects. They perfected bridge building long ago. They used something called opus caementicium to secure the pillars supporting the bridge. I know it contained volcanic ash. I'm not sure how they got the pillars placed solidly and precisely in the river bottom but they did. Then of course they built the stone arches to hold the road bed. Would you like to build something like that?"

"I would like to learn how but I am not sure I would like to build one. It would take a long time."

"You would be the architect, the designer, and a team of men would actually build it under your direction."

Jeb smiled. "That wouldn't be too bad."

They had avoided the highest mountains to the east but they still had to cross a mountain range in the latter part of the journey as well as several deep gorges. Climbing the mountain range was difficult but they were able to go through several passes which saved time. Traversing the deep gorges was another matter.

They had to work their way slowly down the steep zigzag trails descending into the gorge and then find a way across the rushing water. Once, they had to stretch a rope across a wide chasm and traverse it holding on to the rope with their hands while dangling in the air. One man was nearly killed when he lost his grip and fell onto a ledge. They threw him a rope and he managed to climb up.

With the snow steadily falling and covering the steep paths rising up out of the gorge the going was treacherous and slow. They balanced very carefully following the narrow switchbacks to avoid falling down the steep incline. A foot of snow was already on the ground and more was coming down. Jeb thought *it will be a very long cold winter*. The wind was very strong and he was afraid a tree might fall on them in the dense forest.

The cave his father pointed out was huge and surrounded by thick growths of oak, elm, and beech trees, snowberry and honeysuckle bushes, and went deeply into the hill. Clotaire said he could see very well in the dark and would go first.

Jeb stepped in front of him. "I can see even better than you in the dark, better than anyone. Let me go first."

Clotaire smiled and let Jeb go ahead but then asked, "What if there is a bear living in there? Maybe I should go first."

Clotaire's smile grew wide but Jeb faltered only slightly and kept going. He led Clotaire slowly into the cave. It was over six feet high, nearly thirty feet deep, and about twenty feet across in the middle. The rock ceiling was rough to the back of the cave with dirt in crevices, most of which had fallen to the floor over time. The walls were rough rock except in places where they were smoothed out by countless previous inhabitants to allow carvings and a few paintings of animals. The floor was smooth dry dirt with the remains of an old fire pit in the middle. Water seeped through and down the walls, washing out parts of paintings.

After carefully searching to make sure no bear was occupying the cave, they helped the men build a big fire at the entrance to keep animals away and to cook their meat. Jeb pulled back his long blonde hair, walked slowly into the surrounding forest, and started to fill his arms with wood when he heard a high grating sound *krri-krri-krri-krri* and looked up into the branches of a beech tree. He saw a very large black woodpecker with a red crown and stopped to watch it drum loudly. Then he filled his arms with dry fallen wood. When he heard rustling in the thick underbrush and saw fresh bear tracks, he dropped the load and quickly ran back. His blue eyes were wide as he reported to Clotaire.

"I heard noises and I saw bear tracks." Jeb was breathing hard. "They looked fresh."

Clotaire just grinned. "Don't worry," he tried to calm Jeb, "we'll take care of the bear. Wolf tracks would be a different matter. A pack of them could be a problem."

Jeb recovered his breath. "I also saw a big black woodpecker high in a tree. What kind is it?"

Clotaire laughed. "Strangely enough it's called a black woodpecker. It's our largest kind. You're lucky to see it. We're almost out of its range."

Dinner was simple that night as it often was, but they had a special treat. Usually it was dried salted meat with a little dry bread, but tonight it would be fresh game. In the late afternoon Clotaire had an opportunity to shoot a deer with his powerful bow and arrow. He had not missed and the group carried it with them until they stopped at the cave. Jeb thought *this fresh meat might have had something to do with Father's decision to stop earlier than usual.*

While waiting for dinner, Jeb found a place for himself in the back of the cave. Even at the age of ten he had to carry his own bedding: a gunny sack and a warm fur skin. The gunny sack served also as a pack with the fur rolled up inside together with a pair of breeches, a spare shirt, and his warm weather shoes. In the cold winter Jeb wore a coarse woolen pair of long breeches and leather boots with thongs that wrapped around the lower part of the breeches. When the trail was not too rough or when it was warmer he switched to soft lightweight flat-soled leather walking shoes made of a single piece of deerskin. Now he wore a warm woolen shirt with a leather vest and a leather cap with his hair tucked in. He waited to eat until he was invited to join the circle of men. He did not have to wait long.

"Come join us, Jeb," called three of the men.

He was looked after by all of them. They knew he would be their King one day.

Jeb was almost eleven and his father thought it was time Jeb prepared to become a man. *One has to grow up quickly in this world*, Jeb thought. He had liked being a child but knew he was destined for something special. Jeb was descended from great Kings like Merovée and Childeric I and Clovis and Dagobert I. At the age of twelve Jeb would automatically become a King as with all Merovingians of royal blood. Because Childeric was King of the Merovingians, Jeb knew he would be the one to succeed him.

One day when Jeb was putting on his shirt he noticed the strange mark in the middle of his chest and asked his father what it was.

"Jeb," Childeric answered, "That is the birthmark called the Merovingian Cross, a red cross in the middle of a white circle. All Merovingians of royal blood have it. You should never show it to anyone. It is the mark of your heritage and your destiny. The Merovingian Kings, and that includes you one day, as blood descendants of Jesus and Mary, have a special destiny and responsibility. When we have time I will tell you about other Merovingian Kings and explain the history of your birthmark."

"And another thing, Jeb," his father added, "You should never use your real name, Merovée, when you are traveling in strange country. Always use your code name, Jeb."

Jeb felt it was dangerous to be a Merovingian king and especially the son of the King of the Franks but it was not something to spend time thinking about. It would be better to think about all the dangers in the forest that every other man or woman or child had to worry about. There were dangerous animals like bears and wolves to worry about, and thieves and bandits that preyed on travelers. With a group of twenty four they need not worry too much but they always had to be on guard.

During the night Clotaire and two of the men had to go out to chase away a bear.

"It was probably," Clotaire told Jeb, "the same bear whose tracks you saw. I didn't see any sign of wolf tracks so you should be relieved. It might take all of us to drive off a pack of hungry wolves."

After that Jeb slept soundly and awoke to a small blizzard with snow piling up all around the entrance to the cave. Jeb thought it was exciting and very beautiful in the forest. The wind was blowing the snow in circles and creating huge drifts. He could hear the wind whistling in the tree tops. The snow would accumulate on branches and the wind would bring it down in huge sheets which would blanket bushes and small trees underneath. Then the wind let up briefly though the snow continued to fall. Jeb went out to a winter wonderland. He trudged through the heavy snow that was above his leather boots and half way up his breeches. He circled around several hundred feet from the entrance of the cave looking for fresh tracks of animals. He saw bear tracks that came toward the cave but then made large leaps away into the forest. He thought *this bear must be the same one they chased away and decided to keep his distance.* The wind picked up much to Jeb's delight and the blizzard continued. Jeb returned to the cave entrance for a breakfast of dried meat, cheese, bread, and water.

He was the only one that was excited by this unexpected storm. It meant a delay to Childeric and the others that they could ill afford. They were traveling south at the start of winter because a messenger from Rhédae had arrived to report a possible attack on the castle there and the sooner they reached Rhédae the sooner they could help fend off the attackers. In Jeb's entourage were some of the best archers and fighters from the King's forces. Childeric also had many fine warriors in Rhédae, and could not afford to lose them.

"My father," Jeb mentioned to Clotaire, "seems to know this trail we are following very well."

"Most of us have travelled this route many times," Clotaire explained to Jeb.

But the relentless weather took its toll. Under the best conditions the trip took three weeks of hard travel; now they could lose as much as another week. After the second day, the blizzard suddenly stopped. They continued on but had to move slowly in the deep snow. The King was frustrated at the slow pace but also afraid because of the tracks they were leaving. An enemy could follow them with no trouble.

To prevent an attack or ambush they split into two groups, the main body and a flanking group, and created two sets of tracks about one hundred feet apart. This made it difficult for an enemy to figure out how many of them there were and if the attackers saw only one set of tracks, they might be detected by the flanking group before they could launch an assault. Jeb followed in the tracks of the flanking group, thinking this was the safest. He noticed his father was leading the main group. He thought this technique worked very well.

Jeb had to stop for a break to relieve himself and told the man in front that he would catch up, but one man dropped back to keep Jeb in sight. Jeb was tying his breeches when he looked back. In the distance he saw a sight that made him freeze. A group of thirty or more men had figured out their plan and were silently stalking them, one half following the main body and the rest the flanking group. The leader was closing in on Jeb. He ran as fast as he could, caught up with the man who had dropped back, and together they raced to the group ahead. Jeb screamed as loud as he could.

"Clotaire," Jeb yelled ahead, "we are being followed."

Clotaire immediately signaled the two groups to come together to form two lines. The men crouched down and prepared for attack. Jeb hid behind Clotaire who slipped behind a tree. When the approaching band was in range, Clotaire stepped out and fired a single arrow at the leader. It struck but did not kill him. He yelled and hid behind a tree. The first line of Clotaire's archers stood up and fired a deadly volley of arrows. This was immediately followed by the second line stepping forward and firing another wave of arrows. The first line had reloaded but it was not needed. The double assault killed or wounded many of the attackers and the rest turned back.

"Who were they, Clotaire?" Jeb asked.

"There are many groups of roving bandits that prey on travelers. This group will not bother us again."

None of the King's warriors were wounded. From then on they traveled at a relentless pace to make up for lost time and soon outdistanced the snow on the ground. They resumed traveling in two parallel tracks since they still feared attack. Jeb barely kept up but somehow managed to stay with the men. He had to show he was as tough as the others. At the end of each day Jeb was exhausted and hungry but never once faltered or complained. He would gobble his dinner and go straight to bed. The others smiled because they too were tired, and understood.

Jeb felt, as each day went by, he was gaining greater respect. He saw it in the way he was now treated. The men would walk with him and converse with him as an equal.

"Hey, Jeb," one of the men called to him, "you're doing great. You set a strong pace. I don't know how you feel, but I'm looking forward to the end of the day and dinner."

"Me too," answered Jeb, "and sleep."

The man laughed. Another walked alongside and replaced the other man.

"I know you're tired and so am I, but you don't show it at all. Keep it up, Jeb." The man moved away.

He had always received respect as the son of the King but now he even seemed to be admired for his toughness and willingness to endure everything that the others had to endure. He saw the men had developed a special fondness for him. *I will never let them down,* he vowed, *I will keep up no matter how hard it is and I promise never to complain.*

ROSLIN CASTLE

11

CHAPTER THREE

Danger From The South

Roslin, Scotland
April 1, 1398

Jed was eleven and would be twelve in early summer. He loved Roslin Castle. Built on a massive rocky promontory that perched high above the north bank of the River Esk, the castle was partially cut out of the rock. All four sides consisted of sheer cliffs. The river surrounded it on three sides and a wide moat lay far below on the fourth side, making access impossible except across the drawbridge with stone arches spanning the moat. The Castle was two hundred feet long and ninety feet wide with walls that were nine feet thick. Entrance was at the fourth level where the large courtyard was surrounded by a wall. The dining room was at the fourth level and Jed's bedroom was above on the top level. Below the main area of the dining room the servant's quarters occupied the third level. They were above the bake house with the kitchen and dungeons below them.

On a clear day Jed would climb to the rim of the wall around the courtyard and watch the birds fly above or speed past him. He could see in the distance a stone arched bridge across the Esk. He could see golden eagles soaring high above the castle looking with their mighty eyes at the ground far below. A rare sight was the swift flight of the goshawk zooming by below him in search of small birds he would catch in mid-flight. Jed would watch the twists and turns of the small bird trying to escape but usually it was in vain. The goshawk would snatch it out of the air. Once he saw the glorious red kite floating overhead peering down at him, his red color almost matching the color of Jed's own hair. The kite drifted down and turned his head, looking at Jed, as he went slowly past and then circled and came back for an even closer look. Jed held his breath in awe. He thought the kite was just curious about him. Then it silently drifted away in the slight wind. It was an amazing experience that Jed never forgot. He marveled at this beautiful intelligent bird.

On other days Jed would run across the drawbridge and pretend he was being pursued by enemies on horseback. His unkempt red hair hung to his broad shoulders and the top of his leather vest. He carried a bow and arrow and would turn and fire his arrows and bring down his imaginary attackers. He would explore the gatehouse and keep and the bartizans, the towers on the corners of the castle designed to protect it. Each tower had many long narrow slits aimed in all directions to allow the archers to fire down at attackers attempting to scale the walls. He would run along the walkways and the corridors, and go into the monks' cells and the scriptorium where he would look through some of the old manuscripts. He was so glad he had learned to read at an early age. He read every manuscript he could find. He went down to the bake house and kitchen and then down to the dungeons which were the most exciting. He explored every nook and cranny on all five floors.

One day he was in one of the dungeons and noticed an unusually shaped rock in the wall. It was of a different color than the others and seemed to be loose. He pried it out and saw a deep cavity behind it. He reached in and felt some kind of parchment. He pulled it out and realized there were two sets of scrolls rolled together. Each set consisted of several scrolls, one of which was much older than the others. He unrolled them and realized they were ancient bloodline charts: the older one detailed the descendants of Mary Magdalene and Sarah; the others showed the Merovingian Dynasty and the many generations of descendants to the present day. He ran to look for his father, Prince Henry Sinclair, to show them to him. Jed raced up to the level of the drawbridge and saw his father with two of his men, lowering it to allow a lone rider to enter. The rider dismounted and approached Henry.

Jed's father was tall and lean, with a thick red beard and blue eyes that squinted slightly and gave the impression of piercing what he was looking at. He wore a fine linen white shirt with a soft black wool vest and a red cape around his shoulders. His blue beret perched jauntily on his head. He was a refined and well-bred gentleman of the nobility.

Jed was close enough to overhear the conversation. The man was waving his arms in an agitated manner and pointing south.

"My Lord," the man said, "There is a large army of more than one hundred armed men on horseback headed in this direction. They are within a day's ride. I raced here as quickly as I could."

"Thank you," Henry responded calmly, "I have been expecting this. Go inside. My men will take care of you." Henry spun around and walked toward Jed. Henry saw the scrolls in Jed's hands.

"I see you found them."

Jed was about to speak but his father held up his hand.

"Keep them safe," his father smiled and spoke gently, "because now you are in charge of them."

"What do you mean?" Jed asked.

"You're going with us on this next journey. But never under any circumstances mention the scrolls. That must be our secret."

"I think I understand." He paused. "I overheard what the man on the horse said. We are in danger?"

"Indeed we are. Sadly, I have been expecting this news. We have little time. Now you can understand the reason we are going on this long sea voyage."

"A long voyage? Where are we going?"

"I can't tell you that yet."

"When do we leave?"

"We sail at dawn. Be ready, very early."

That was all that his father said.

CHAPTER FOUR

The Blizzard of '47

Southern New England
December, 1947

Jes woke up shivering in the cold of the winter night. The wind whistled around the corners of the house and rattled the windows. It was dark in the upstairs bedroom but he was glad his night vision allowed him to see even in the darkest of nights. The clicking of the wind driving the snow against the windowpanes seemed like music to Jes with a rhythm of its own. He imagined what the countryside looked like at night, and pictured the windswept pastures with snow piled against the fences, the sides of the barn, and the farmhouse. The tops of shrubs and bushes would be barely visible under the high drifts. He was sure the horses and cows and lambs were nice and warm in their barn, and he imagined the barn owl huddled in the rafters. He visualized the many pastures and corn fields and barns for miles around, bleak and barren in the dim light from the moon and the stars trying to break through the clouds. His mind wandered through the orchards behind his house and the woods in front and the frozen brook down the hill behind the outhouse. He pictured the great horned owl hunkered down on a branch looking for a meal. And then he stopped dreaming and returned to more pressing business.

Why do I have to go to the bathroom now, he thought? He decided he couldn't wait for daylight and reached for a small flashlight next to his bed in case he needed it. He found his slippers and crept as quietly as he could down the old uneven stairs trying not to make a squeak, and stepped into the dining room. The huge fireplace in the middle of the house no longer crackled with warmth. The fire was almost out and only a few glowing cinders remained. *No wonder it's so cold,* he thought.

He sighed then crossed over to the kitchen, tiptoed past the even larger kitchen fireplace, and put his hand on the handle of the back kitchen door. He glanced at the empty Dutch oven next to the fireplace and pictured warm fresh bread cooking in it. He wished he had not left his boots and coat out in the vestibule. At least the outside door had not been blown open by the gusts of wind. He took a deep breath, opened the door, and dashed out into the cold small space of the vestibule, grabbing his heavy coat from the hook and pulling it on. Then he exchanged his slippers for his highest boots and steeled himself.

The snow had begun the day before, on Christmas, and had continued to come down all day and all night. It was really only the beginning of winter and already the snow was piling up. He recalled his father's comment at dinner. The weatherman had projected a very cold winter with lots of snow. It certainly had started that way.

Jes opened the door and stepped out. The snow pelted his face and the wind swirled the flakes around, covering any tracks made during the daytime. He picked his way to the right around the vestibule, and followed the trail to the outhouse past the apple tree and the stone well on his right and the sour cherry tree on his left. Jes had always been intrigued with the different sounds made by walking on snow. He loved the crunchy sound of walking on packed snow but tonight he listened to the squeaking he made on the light powder. The snow on the side of the path was above the top of his boots and the wind blew some of it inside them. The cold snow on his feet woke him up and propelled him at a faster pace.

Jes crossed the hundred feet of buried pathway, wrenched open the door, turned on the flashlight in the pitch black outhouse, and put it on the floor. He pulled up his coat, and sat on the icy seat. He shivered but steeled himself. His unruly brown hair fell over his forehead and he tried to brush it back. It was not that long but he felt he had some that was too long and he vowed to cut it when he had a moment. The flashlight on the floor created an eerie dim glow in the outhouse. His coat fell open and he looked down at the strange pale mark in the middle of his chest just below the tip of his sternum. His mother had told him once that it was a birthmark and that it was special to have. He'd not thought about it again but this time he looked at it carefully. It was in the shape of a red cross within a white circle. *Very strange*, he thought. *It must be my imagination.*

Jes pictured the hill behind the outhouse and the little bridge he had built over the brook. He was sure the snow had covered the ice on the brook and the bridge as well. He imagined the water flowing under the ice and under the stone bridge on the road, and the little waterfall splashing below the bridge. Then he made the mistake of looking up at the tangle of spider webs. Some of the spiders were enormous. Jes's heart pounded beneath his birthmark, and his brown eyes opened wide. He imagined he could see the giant spider's beady little eyes looking down at him wondering how he could make him into a big meal. Jes finished his business as fast as he could and dashed out again into the snow.

He knew he would have another nightmare about being stung and wrapped up in a sticky web by a giant spider. He vowed to come out one day with a stick and broom and knock down the webs.

Jes made his way back along the trail. Once inside the outer door he exchanged his boots for his slippers but decided to keep his coat with him as he made his way back upstairs. He curled up in bed but could not sleep. He thought about the day when they would have running water. His father and uncle had told him it would take another year or two to finish the plumbing in their spare time. He wished they had money to hire help but it was not to be. He did not mind going out to the well to lower the pail for water but he felt he could not take this long walk to the outhouse with the spiders much longer.

Jes finally dozed off. He woke up a short time later just as the dawn light shone through the window. He heard his dad downstairs making a fire in the big kitchen fireplace and quickly got dressed in warm corduroy pants and a heavy red cotton shirt and went down to join him. Jes liked to help his dad when he didn't have school and though it was Christmas vacation now he was sure school would have been cancelled anyway.

"Can I help, Dad?" he offered.

"Sure. Put your boots on and fetch a few more logs from the woodshed, would you? Thanks."

Jes went out again to the vestibule, put on his boots and heavy brown coat, and went around the side of the kitchen. The snow swirled all around him. The wood was stacked up against the side of the house under a sturdy woodshed to keep it dry. He had helped his uncle build the woodshed during the summer. He grabbed a few logs and carried them back inside.

"Couldn't we have a stove somewhere? Wouldn't that make the house warmer?" he asked his dad.

"We'll have one soon. We have the stove on order and the pipe as well. We'll use the small fireplace in the den for the pipe to go up the chimney. Do you know, Jes, this house was built in the 18th century? It gives you an idea of what it was like living way back then. This large kitchen fireplace with the pot hanging on the swinging hook and the Dutch oven next to it were common in houses like this one."

Jes thought about the shape of the house. A small fireplace in the den sharing the chimney with the huge dining room fireplace was seldom used. Besides the fireplace in the kitchen and those in the dining room and den, there was also a fourth in the living room which was never used. There were six rooms downstairs. The dining room and den were in the middle. The kitchen and a room next to it used as a spare bedroom were at the back end of the house. The living room and study at the end facing the road, and the hallway to the front door between them were never used in the winter. The stairs down to the cellar, which still had a dirt floor, were just off the dining room.

The stairs to the four upstairs bedrooms were also off the dining room. That didn't make sense to Jes to have stairs off the dining room but then he realized they had to be above the cellar stairs. He tried to imagine a better arrangement but couldn't come up with one and wondered what it would be like to design a house. His uncle told him once that he should be an architect when he grows up and he thought that was an interesting idea, to design buildings. Then he thought about the upstairs layout. He reasoned that the top of the stairs ended in the middle of the floor so they had access to all bedrooms. Jes mused, *we usually seal off all the downstairs rooms in the winter except the dining room, den, and kitchen. And we usually keep all the heat downstairs and seal off the stairs to the bedrooms.* Jes shivered involuntarily as the fire his father was building slowly took off.

"Jes?" his dad called, "Would you fetch a pail of water? We need some for cooking."

"Sure," Jes responded. "Be right back."

Jes was happy he could help his father. His dad worked such long hours and he would normally be getting ready for work but he had Christmas vacation as well. Out again Jes went with boots and coat and a woolen hat and warm leather gloves lined with soft cotton, and trudged through the snow to the well which was close to the woodshed. He lowered the pail with a rope attached to the handle, clanging against the stone sides until he heard the familiar splash. Then he hauled it slowly. This was one of his chores of which he was very proud. It was hard work to pull up the full pail without spilling it and without banging the pail too hard against the sides of the well.

Just as he was about to carry it through the snow into the kitchen, he looked up and saw a man one hundred feet away, crouched in the deep snow. All Jes could see was a long black beard and cold dark eyes. When he realized Jes had seen him the man turned and disappeared down a snow bank. Jes shivered, turned, and headed back to the entryway. His arms were shaking but he managed to carry the pail in without spilling a drop.

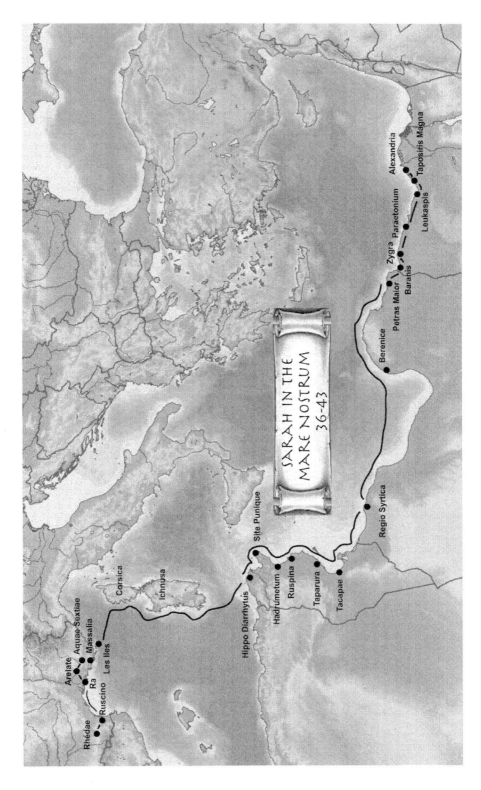

SARAH IN THE MARE NOSTRUM 36-43

Taposiris Magna
Alexandria
Leukaspis
Paraetonium
Zygra
Baranis
Petras Maior
Berenice
Regio Syrtica
Tacapae
Taparura
Ruspina
Hadrumetum
Site Punique
Hippo Diarrhytus
Ichnusa
Corsica
Les Îles
Ruscino
Ra
Rhédae
Arelate
Aquae Sextiae
Massalia

19

20

CHAPTER FIVE

The Sign from Heaven

Northern Coast, Aegyptus
Spring, 36 AD

Sarah clutched her mother tightly, listening for any sound. She heard footsteps of a man approaching the edge of the camp. He seemed to be asking questions of someone. His voice was calm and then he paused. She heard Joseph's voice. Another man approached and asked a question. Sarah stayed inside the tent with Mary listening to the voices and gradually relaxed her hold on her mother. The voices were not raised in anger but the conversation was steady. She could identify the voice of Joseph and sometimes of Mark but the other voices were strange to her. There was a slight pause and then she heard the voice of a woman. She did not recognize it and decided it must be that of a Bedouin. Then the voices stopped and she heard the footsteps of men walking away followed by hoof beats gradually growing faint. Then she heard the sound of a dromedary leaving the camp.

A short time later Joseph opened the tent and smiled.

"It is safe now," he told them, "you can come out. The soldiers have gone."

Mary and Sarah came out into the dim light of dusk. Sarah was given goat's milk with honey, mixed with wheat and figs, in the beautiful goblet she loved to hold. She looked up and saw the familiar shape of Sah on the horizon and then heard the sounds of approaching dromedaries. It was the Bedouin guide, the man called Joshua, and the dromedary carrying the portable boat. With night approaching she went back into her tent and curled up listening to her mother and the others.

Joseph greeted them with a smile as they rode into camp. "Welcome back. Mark and I convinced them to travel south."

Sarah heard her mother's voice. "What did they want?"

"The three of you of course." Joseph said.

"I believe we have an informer in Alexandria." Mark added.

"And how, may I ask," spoke Joshua, "did you convince the group of soldiers to leave and head south? What story did you concoct?"

"They know me as a tin merchant." Joseph replied. "I said I was traveling west for that purpose with my companions. And then one of our Bedouin friends came to the rescue by casually mentioning that a woman with a child had stopped briefly for water and was in a hurry and seemed to be traveling south."

"South?" Mary raised her eyebrows. "What does that mean?"

"Well," Mark spoke hesitantly. "She implied you were traveling to the oasis south of here."

"You mean Parva? That is over one hundred miles. Why would they believe that?"

Sarah heard Joshua speak again. "People will believe anything if it is in their interest to do so."

"No," Joseph interjected. "We mean Arsinoe. That oasis is much closer. It is noted for figs and grapes, olives, rose trees, and sheep. Not a bad place to escape to."

"I see." Mary paused. "The Bedouins said we were in a hurry. Perhaps we should be in a hurry and leave here in case they get suspicious and return."

Joseph had the group up before dawn and on their way. The Bedouin guide was in the lead, followed by Joseph and Lazarus on their two dromedaries. Martha had her own, Sarah and Mary rode another, and the two other women were on a sixth. Dromedaries carrying Joshua, Mark the Evangelist, and the Roman soldier, followed behind. The last dromedary carried the portable boat, and many supplies. The Bedouins wished them well and they set off at a good pace before sunrise.

"How long will Mark travel with us?" asked Martha.

"He said he would go with us at least to Leukaspis and possibly all the way to Zygra, but then he must return to Alexandria." Sarah's mother replied.

"I hope he stays with us until we assemble the boat," Martha wished. "And I hope the guide goes with us as well. Perhaps Joseph can convince them."

Sarah peeked out and could see both of them in the morning light. They still wore their dark cloaks. Martha had short dark brown hair and dark eyes. Her mother had long reddish blonde hair that she wore hanging loose to her waist. Her deep dark eyes sparkled in the dim light. Sarah loved to watch her mother. She thought she was very beautiful and she wanted to look like her when she grew older. Sarah thought her smile was the most beautiful thing about her. Aunt Martha was shorter. Sarah always thought of her as much more lively compared to her mother who was usually very quiet, and seemed always to be thinking about something.

"Mama," Sarah called out. "Will we keep going again tonight when it is dark?"

"I will ask Joseph what he plans," she answered, "but I think we will continue on along the sea."

Sarah became aware of the wind starting to blow. It rattled her tent and she could hear the low rumblings of the group of dromedaries and the bleats of the two goats that huddled with them. Suddenly she became aware of excited voices calling out.

"Sirocco!" yelled Mark. "The beasts. Tether them!"

"No need," she heard the Bedouin guide reply. "They have seen this before. They will wait it out."

Her mother reached in and told Sarah to stay in the tent and wrap up in her cloak.

"Keep the opening closed and you will be all right. I will help make sure our food and supplies are safe."

Sarah heard her mother and the others running around to secure the tents, the food, the supplies, and the parts of the boat. The wind grew stronger and stronger, blowing dust and sand north toward the sea. It went on and on for several hours. *My mother was right*, thought Sarah, *my tent is surviving the wind*. The sand made a sharp pinging sound as it bounced off the sides. Late in the day the wind decreased and finally stopped altogether.

Sarah's mother reached in and handed her some goat's milk and a few figs and grapes. The milk was again in her mother's beautiful goblet of shimmering silver. Sarah knew it was a very special cup.

"It will be dark soon," her mother told her. "Joseph and the guide say we should keep moving. The next sirocco could last for days and we want to reach the Roman town Leukaspis as soon as possible."

At dusk, Sarah resumed her position in her chair and watched as the entourage loaded the dromedaries with tents, food, and the boat. She found it fascinating to look at the different beards of the men. Mark had a short black beard to match his short black hair. His dark eyes were partially covered by the hood of his cloak. Lazarus had a short blonde beard, light brown hair and brown eyes and Joseph had a long white beard, white hair, and blue eyes. They all wore cloaks that covered their heads and hung down to their knees. The Bedouin guide had a short gray beard. Sarah could not see his hair beneath his Keffiyeh which protected him from sun, dust, and sand but she thought his eyes were blue.

They moved at a fast pace as they rocked from side to side, the dromedaries moving their legs in pairs on alternate sides, causing the rocking motion. The group reached Leukaspis in four days and camped near a Bedouin camp. The guide took Sarah and her mother and aunt to see the Roman tombs in the necropolis, the theatre, and the basilica with the round columns.

"This big city is the center of the olive, wine, and wheat trades," Joseph told them. He had brought a small supply of tin pots and utensils which he traded for water and wheat. Sarah ate grapes and dates and figs and flat bread made from the wheat they acquired. It was covered with honey. She drank goat's milk again, also with honey in it.

"Mama," Sarah asked, "you always give me milk in this beautiful cup. I know it is very special. I am always afraid I will drop it. Where did this cup come from?"

Her mother paused. "Yes, Sarah, it is a very special goblet and was used for a very important purpose. But you are very special too. I am not afraid that you will drop it and you should not worry either. It came with us from Judea and I will always cherish it."

"We came from Judea as well? I don't remember that."

"We left Judea when you were very small and came to Alexandria."

"Why did we leave? Did we have to?"

"We were in danger there, Sarah. We fled quickly to safety in Aegyptus."

"And we were in danger in Aegyptus so we had to flee again. Why? What have we done?"

"We have done nothing, Sarah. It's not what we have done but who we are."

Sarah was not content with this answer and wanted to know more but decided not to ask more questions. However, she did not worry about the cup after that. She mounted her dromedary at dusk as they left the Bedouin camp. She was content to ride high and look at the stars and the sea in the distance. The sirocco winds did not arrive those days and nights. Sarah began to observe the others in the group who rode behind silently.

The two women who rode together never spoke. The man called Joshua with the deep brown eyes had a full dark brown beard that had a little red in it. The Roman soldier was called Petronius and seemed to be a friend of Joseph. When they stopped, Joseph and Petronius would go off together to talk. There were ten people altogether besides herself. She wondered about the identity of the two women who seldom spoke.

"Mama," Sarah asked as they rode together, "who are those two women riding behind us? They never say anything."

"They are friends of ours. They will go across the sea with us. They will help look after you if needed. They are both called Mary just like me."

"I like Joshua. His eyes seem to look right through me."

"I'm glad. He likes you also." Sarah's mother answered softly. "He is very quiet but a very nice man."

"And that Roman soldier? Why is he traveling with us?" Sarah was curious about everyone.

"His name is Petronius. He is our friend and a special friend of Joseph. He also is a friend of Joshua who was able to cure his sick son. He will stay with us for some time to make sure our journey is a safe one. He feels it his duty to look after all of us. We are in safe hands. I think he will leave us when we put to sea, and he will return with Mark."

That seemed to satisfy Sarah for the moment.

The group left at dusk after resting at Leukaspis for two days. They made sure the dromedaries had water and rest before leaving and loaded up with water bags themselves for the long journey to Paraetonium.

"How far do we have to go this time?" Sarah asked her mother. "Will we see Sah the god every night?"

"It will take another few days but the time will go quickly." Mary smiled. "Let's see if we can find the belt of Sah."

Sarah realized her mother also had great night vision and could often see the small stars in Sah before Sarah could. "I see the stars in the shield," Sarah called out.

Her mother nodded. "See if you can count all the stars in Sah."

Sarah started counting but lost track of the number and fell asleep before she could finish counting. She woke up when they stopped for the night. She tried to help put up the tent she slept in, then curled up and fell fast asleep. She woke up with the wind roaring and the sand pelting the sides of her tent. This time it did not stop. When daylight came she could not tell it was daytime since the wind covered the sky with dust and sand. She became very hot and was glad her mother managed to bring her water and figs or dates now and then. Once her mother gave her a pomegranate which she loved to eat. Another time she was given cherries which were a special treat.

The wind continued for two days. Once she looked outside and saw the dromedaries sitting quietly waiting for the storm to end. They were protected from the sand by hair around their eyes and nostrils and ears.

When the windstorm stopped, the group dug out the parts of the boat and other supplies covered by the sand. The Bedouin guide thought they should start out as soon as night arrived. The two other women named Mary came over and asked Sarah if she was all right. She said she was and they smiled and told her she was a brave little girl to come on this long journey. Sarah felt a sandy grit on her face from the fine sand that got into her tent.

And then a surprising thing happened. The mystery man called Joshua with the soft lovely voice, came over and looked at her. This time his dark brown eyes twinkled and he smiled. He did not say a word but Sarah had a warm feeling and felt good that the man had smiled at her. He left to help get ready for the next phase of the journey.

They arrived at Paraetonium at dawn after traveling one more night. Again Joseph traded some tin goods for more water and wheat and dates. It was very warm during the day but before it became too hot, Joseph took Mary and Sarah and Martha to see the temple of Rameses II.

"Who was Ramesses II?" Sarah asked Joseph.

"He was a very famous Pharoah who lived over 1200 years ago. He was called Ramesses the Great and was considered the greatest, most celebrated, and most powerful Pharoah. This is one of his temples."

"Isn't there also a palace of Cleopatra here?" Martha asked.

"Yes, but we won't be able to see it. I believe it is submerged now."

Sarah was happy when dusk came. Just before it became too dark her mother asked if she would like to bathe with her and take the grit off of her face. She agreed eagerly. They walked down to the white soft sands and calm clear waters. The bay was protected from the high seas by a series of rocks that formed a breakwater. They dropped their cloaks and linen garments and waded in. Sarah noticed that her mother had a rolled up scroll she kept tucked into the sash around her waist. When she removed her undergarment she tucked it under the pile of her clothes. Sarah watched her mother dip into the water and she again thought how beautiful she was.

"Mama," Sarah asked quietly, "will I look like you when I grow up?"

Her mother smiled. "Yes, Sarah. You will have a womanly body like mine when you get older. You are a beautiful girl now and I am sure you will be lovely when you grow up."

Before Sarah put her clothes back on, she noticed the small mark in the middle of her chest. Her skin was dark but this mark was white and round.

"Mama," Sarah called, "why do I have this mark on my chest? Is something wrong with me?"

This time her mother had a serious look. "Sarah, that mark is very special. It is a sign from heaven. You are the only one that has it and you are indeed very special. Do not show it to others."

Sarah still did not know where it came from but felt very special nonetheless.

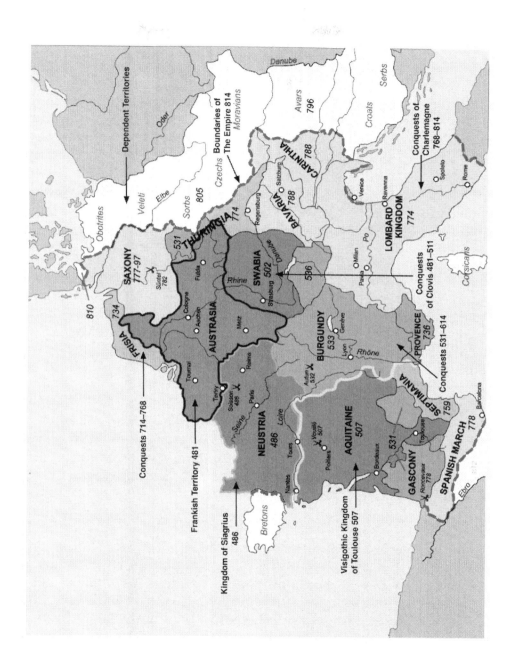

Dependent Territories

Boundaries of
The Empire 814

Conquests of
Charlemagne
768–814

Conquests
of Clovis 481–511

Conquests 531–614

Conquests 714–768

Frankish Territory 481

Kingdom of Siagrius
486

Visigothic Kingdom
of Toulouse 507

Obotrites

Veleti

Sorbs

Czechs

Moravians

Avars
796

Croats

Serbs

Danube

Oder

Elbe

810

734

FRISIA

SAXONY
777–97

Süntel
782

Fulda

Cologne

Aachen

THURINGIA
531

774

SWABIA
502

Regensburg

Salzburg

BAVARIA
788

CARINTHIA
788

596

Danube

Rhine

Strasburg

AUSTRASIA

Metz

Reims

Tournai

Terffy

Soissons
486

Paris

Seine

NEUSTRIA
486

Tours

Nantes

Loire

Poitiers

Vouillé
507

Autun
532

BURGUNDY
533

Lyon

Genève

Rhône

AQUITAINE
507

Bordeaux

531

GASCONY
778

Carcassonne
778

Toulouse

SEPTIMANIA
759

PROVENCE
736

SPANISH MARCH
778

Barcelona

Ebro

Bretons

LOMBARD
KINGDOM
774

Milan

Pavia

Po

Venice

Ravenna

Spoleto

Rome

Corsicans

CHAPTER SIX

Dagobert's Legacy

Southern Francia
Early Winter, 750 AD

Jeb realized that his father, Childeric, and Clotaire had chosen the most direct route going south which had the advantage of avoiding difficult river crossings but also had the disadvantage of having to cross mountains. They had been lucky until they crossed the mountain range where they had encountered the cold winter weather and the beginning of snowfall. Nevertheless, after four weeks of travel from the time they left the castle at Stenay, they finally reached the outskirts of Rhédae. Jeb's father sent a three person party ahead to report back on the situation at the castle.

Childeric had been watching the growing toughness of his son and the respect he was gaining from the men. He'd always loved Jeb but for the first time he had come to develop a genuine admiration for him. While waiting for the return of the scouting party, the King told Jeb about the struggles of a Merovingian King named Dagobert II who spent almost his entire life regaining his rightful position as heir to the throne.

"Dagobert was a very important King in our history," explained Childeric to Jeb. "Dagobert's father died in 656 AD and Dagobert became the rightful heir when he was only five years old. He was spirited off to Hibernia where he was raised in a monastery in Slane, near Dublin. He grew to manhood, left the monastery, and married a Celtic princess in 666 AD when he was fifteen. Then he moved to Britannia where he had three daughters but no sons. As fate would have it, his wife died in 670 AD giving birth to their third daughter. He was only nineteen years old. He was still considered a monarch but a king in exile."

"If Dagobert didn't have a son," asked Jeb, "how did the Merovingian Kings continue?"

"He did have a son but who never became King. That passed to our line of the family. Be patient, Jeb," his father cautioned, "There's more to the story. Through the influence of his mentor, Wilfrid of York, who had his own agenda on behalf of the church, Dagobert married Giselle de Razès in 671 AD. She was the daughter of the Count of Razès and niece of the King of the Visigoths. He'd returned to the mainland by then and they were married in Rhédae, joining the royal bloodline of the Merovingians with the royal bloodline of the Visigoths. This formidable alliance produced two more daughters and finally a son. Sigisbert IV was born in 676 AD. By this time Dagobert was King."

"But why was Dagobert so important?" inquired Jeb.

"Dagobert had bided his time from 671 AD onward," continued Childeric, "but after a few years he declared himself King. He had the support of the church in the form of Wilfrid and other prelates such as the Bishop of Sion as well as his mother and her family and his wife's family. From 676 to 679 AD he established control and order, acquired considerable wealth, and because of his marriage, acquired vast territory. Finally here was a worthy successor to Clovis the ancient Merovingian King."

Childeric paused, listening for the return of the scouts but heard nothing.

"Who was Clovis?" Jeb asked, "And why was Dagobert considered a worthy successor to him?"

"Clovis was a powerful Merovingian King who lived a few hundred years ago. He conquered and united all of Gaul under one King: himself. Dagobert was also a very powerful and influential King who amassed a great fortune but also created enemies amongst the Church."

"Why did he create enemies?"

"The Merovingians," Childeric explained at length, "as blood descendants of Jesus and Mary, know the truth about their ancestors and know that the Roman Church has stolen their birthright, usurped their role as leaders of the True Church, and co-opted the idea of Christ to create a fantasy, a fictionalized version of the Messiah. This was done to further their own agenda of secular and spiritual world domination, to subjugate the masses, and to achieve vast amounts of money and power. The Church is built on false grounds and the Merovingians know this. If the Church could arrange the death of Dagobert they thought they would extinguish this threat forever."

"Did Dagobert know about this threat from the Church?"

"He certainly did," Childeric answered, "He knew he had several things to worry about. First of all he had to protect his wife Giselle who was connected to the powerful Visigothic family and then he had to make sure his only son and heir, Sigisbert IV, was also protected from these threatening forces. Finally he had amassed enormous power and territory as well as a vast treasury, and he had in his possession incriminating documents against the Church, evidence of their corruption and moral decay, and most significantly, documents going back to the beginning of the millennium showing the true history and genealogy of the ancestors of the Merovingians."

"Wouldn't these documents you mention be extremely valuable?" Jeb asked.

"Yes, which must be protected and hidden at all costs."

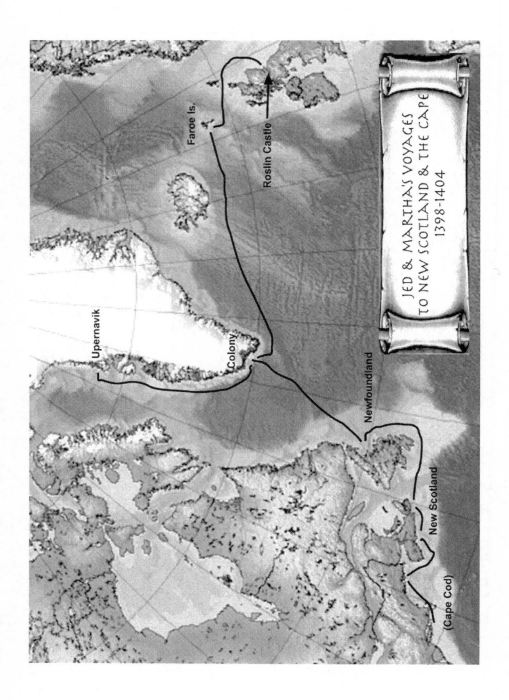

Faroe Is.

Roslin Castle

Upernavik

Colony

Newfoundland

New Scotland

(Cape Cod)

JED & MARTHA'S VOYAGES
TO NEW SCOTLAND & THE CAPE
1398-1404

HENRY'S SHIP

31

CHAPTER SEVEN

The Stowaway

Roslin, Scotland

Jed was so excited he had trouble sleeping. Before dawn he had packed up his belongings including a spare pair of leather breeches, a linen shirt, and his fur skin and put them in a gunny sack along with the two sets of scrolls and some food. The food stuff included dried bread, salt, dried beef and mutton, and a few carrots and onions. He wore his warmest woolen breeches and a leather vest over a woolen shirt. He kept his cap in a pocket of his vest and put it on when he went outside. He knew it would be cold on the ship journey. When he was called, he followed his father and the crew. This was his first long ocean trip. He knew it would be dangerous but he knew Prince Henry had taken many such voyages in the past, and was considered the finest navigator and ship captain in the land, possibly in the entire world.

The fleet Henry commanded consisted of thirteen small ships, two of which were powered mainly by oars, although they had a small sail on a short mast. The rest were sailing ships with one or two masts, and a bowsprit extending in front of the bow. All of the ships were square-rigged, with square sails perpendicular to the keel. They made good time downwind, but often struggled upwind. Henry's ship was the flagship and one of the biggest with two masts. Jed thought it was between eighty and one hundred feet long while the smaller ships with one mast were only sixty to eighty feet in length. Sir James Gunn, Henry's trusted friend and second in command, was the captain of a ship comparable in size to Henry's. These larger ships put up several sails.

"How many men do we have, Father?" Jed asked.

"We have about two hundred and fifty men all together, but to be honest I don't know the exact number. I guess I should but I know we have an average of about twenty men on each ship. Because ours and Sir Gunn's are larger we have a few more on board."

Henry's quarters were in the stern section and included a large stateroom which also served as a dining room. There were several smaller cabins adjoining these rooms and several storage areas. The men occupied the space below in the hold. Next to them at one end was a separate section with several dozen chickens, most of which were laying hens. Jed was glad of that since he looked forward to eggs for breakfast now and then along with dried meat and bread, usually with cheese. At the other end was a larger section where Henry hoped to put sheep and hay for the voyage. All the ships had a similar arrangement but most had less space for cargo and smaller cabins for the captains.

The fleet sailed out of the Firth of Forth and north up the eastern side of north Scotland. They would sail through the Orkney Islands and the Shetlands. Henry planned to stop first at Faroe Island where they would take on provisions and water in exchange for salt and other goods. Jed learned they would then sail to Iceland and then onward to Greenland. As Jed watched from the bow of the flagship, they sailed out of the Firth and headed north into the upper North Sea. They were headed into a strong northeast wind. The waves grew higher and deeper and soon were crashing over the bow. Jed did not yet have his sea legs and flew back and forth across the rolling deck. The wind carried the mist from the splashing waves high overhead and created a fine salty dew on his face.

Jed loved the feel of it on his face, but when the wind became too strong and the waves too high and he began to crash into railings and trip over ropes on deck, Jed decided it was time to return to his cabin. He was given quarters in a very small room next to Henry's. He entered it to a very big surprise. There, curled up in a corner, was a young girl. She had short dark hair and brown eyes and wore a fine blue woolen dress which came down to her knees. She held her finger to her lips.

"Don't say anything. No one is to know I'm on board. Only you and your father know." She pulled him inside and shut the door.

"Who are you?" Jed challenged.

"My name is Martha. I'm to share this little room with you."

"I'm Jed. How are we both going to fit in here?"

"Oh that's no problem. We'll just lie this way." Martha indicated the width rather than the longer length. "We can just curl up and have more room that way. It's wider."

"That's all right for you because you're short but I think I'm too tall and big to fit that way."

"I'll give you most of the room if you want. And, besides, you can curl up a little, can't you?"

She wasn't asking for an answer and talked in such a decisive manner that Jed had nothing to say. Then he thought about her having to hide in this room all the time. If he could convince his father to let her out of hiding they could explore together. That would be loads of fun. He explained his plan to Martha.

"Maybe if you dressed up as a boy he would let you run around with me. We could explain that you were one of my friends and we brought you along to keep me company. What do you think?"

"I don't know." She didn't look too pleased.

He couldn't understand her hesitancy. Maybe she liked being a girl and being cooped up. First he had to convince her and then Henry.

"Wouldn't it be fun to explore this ship together?" That convinced her finally. "Wait here until I talk to my father. Then we need something to make you look like a boy."

When he explained his plan to Henry it was not too difficult to convince him. He didn't know where his father had found them but they had the clothes in their little room within a couple of hours.

Martha's woolen dress was replaced by baggy leather breeches and a woolen outer shirt over a linen shirt that concealed her developing shape. She was given a cap to conceal her hair. Fortunately her hair was not that long and this outfit would work perfectly on her. Jed gave her the name Mark and she laughed. He knew they would get along famously. He was sure they were going to have loads of fun.

As they were about to start their adventures they felt the ship rocking. They went up on deck and saw they were being hit by huge waves at the bow. The strong wind had turned into a major storm and Jed estimated the waves to be twenty feet high. He watched as the small boats with manned oars prepared to turn about and head back. Before leaving they transferred most of the men to Henry's ship and Sir Gunn's. They were able to do this despite the danger by being downwind of the other nine ships. The men came across to the flagship with long boats. The remaining crews on the two ships put up sails and flew back to port. The fleet was now down to eleven ships.

With such fierce weather Martha and Jed started to feel sick and went below. He dashed into his room and grabbed some of the bread he had stowed.

"Eat some of this," Jed ordered.

They both ate a few pieces and that helped. After an hour of rocking and rolling the storm let up and the rocking decreased. This would be fun after all. They staggered around the deck looking over the sides and then the bow and finally went aft where the wind was not as strong. The waves decreased, and now and then one of the men would wave at them but were usually so busy they scarcely noticed Jed and Mark. Then they went below deck, sliding back and forth as they peered into every corner and every room. Most of the crew stayed on deck or in the rigging, keeping the ship headed into the diminishing winds, and the storm was over.

At dinnertime Jed took the food for the two of them to a quiet nook. This time it was a simple meal of cured beef and eggs, boiled onions, preserved cabbage, and dry bread. Henry thought it best that they eat separately from the men. There were questions about who this other boy was and Henry had nonchalantly mentioned to the men that he had decided to bring Mark, a friend of Jed's, so that Jed would have companionship on the long voyage. None of the men thought more about it since it seemed a natural thing to do. But Jed himself wondered why Martha was on board.

"Why did you come on this voyage anyway?" he asked her as they munched their dinner of beef covered with eggs, and a cup of cider. "It could be dangerous for a girl."

"I don't think it's any more dangerous for me. Besides, it's probably more dangerous back there than it is here on board."

"What do you mean?"

"Maybe I came for the same reason you came." She let that thought sink in. "Your father thought it would not be safe if I stayed back there in Roslin."

Jed had not thought of that at all. In fact he had thought the only reason he had come on this journey was to give him experience at sea. *After all, he reasoned, how else would I become the great navigator and explorer that my father was known to be?*

Jed had known that there was some unknown danger lurking back in Roslin but didn't know exactly what it was. Martha seemed to know more about this danger than he did, but he decided for now not to ask any more questions. He had a hunch he knew the answer already but he would ask his father about it when he could.

They finished their dinner and the sea stayed calm as night approached. They went out on deck and looked at the other ships sailing beside them and behind them. Jed loved the sea at night with the hundreds and thousands of twinkling stars and the vast sea all around. The smells from the dining room drifted out to the deck and mingled with the smell of the salty sea mist carried by the wind.

"I love the feel of the salty wet air on my face," Martha said and Jed agreed.

The bow waves made by the other ships pushed out and created white caps. Dolphins and porpoises liked to ride these waves, staying just ahead of the bow. Jed could hear flying fish hitting the water all around him again and again and the regular rhythm of the waves splashing against the bow. In the distance he could hear the cries of seagulls but could not see them flying high in the sky.

Finally he and Martha turned in. They had a candle lit for a short time and talked. She told him about her family and where she lived and how excited she was about this journey and that she was not at all afraid of any danger at sea or where they were going. She just knew it was important that she go. This gave Jed a chance to resume his unanswered questions.

"I'm still not sure why you came on this voyage. Do you know?"

Without uttering one more word Martha flung off the fur skin covering her body. She had removed her woolen shirt and linen as well. Jed stared. Her breasts were well developed and she had dark hair down between her legs. Jed was speechless. Martha pointed between her breasts into the hollow below her ribcage.

"This is what I'm talking about." Martha's voice was imperious as she pointed to her birthmark.

Jed's green eyes were as big as saucers. He finally took his eyes off of Martha's breasts and hair and noticed she had the royal birthmark, a white circle with a pale red cross in the middle of her chest just where the hollow of her ribcage was. Now he understood why she came on this voyage. She was also one of the few left with this indication of royal blood. It was unmistakable. He pulled off his own fur to uncover the same identical birthmark in the same place in the hollow of his chest.

"I have one like that too," he said.

They were both silent for a moment. They realized why they had been put together on this long journey to the west.

"My father says there are very few of us left," Jed continued. "In fact only a few on board this ship have the birthmark and they are not to reveal it. Legend has it that all of the Merovingians had this mark. My father says that royal blood is becoming extinct. We are both descended from the Merovingians."

CHAPTER EIGHT

The Black Bearded Stranger

Southern New England
December, 1947

His arms stopped shaking before Jes entered the house. He could not explain what caused his fear of the stranger. Perhaps it was the cold eyes. He could not explain what he saw and what he felt so decided not to mention the bearded man. He put the filled pail on the table.

His father used some of the water to fill the heavy cast iron pot which hung on the iron support arm attached to the side of the fireplace, and pushed it in over the fire. This hot water would be used for washing up and the remainder would be used to make porridge.

When Jes was not in school he often fetched half a dozen pails of water a day. And today was not a school day so he would be fetching many pails. It was just as well it was vacation because all the cars and buses and trucks would be having lots of trouble in the deep snow. He turned on the radio to listen to the reports. In a few minutes the news crackled forth. They were starting to have blizzard conditions. The report said that the roads were heavy with snow and all vehicles were having trouble getting through. Jes liked to go to school since it was easy and fun for him but he also loved vacation time especially with weather like this. He had been given a toboggan for Christmas and was hoping he and his friends could slide down the hills but it was looking less likely all the time. The snow came down hard all day long. The strong wind blew the snow around and piled it up into even higher drifts. If this became a blizzard it would be the first Jes had ever seen.

The house gradually warmed up and finally his mother came downstairs.

"Jes?" she called, "Would you help me start breakfast?"

Jes also liked to help his mother. He knew it must be difficult to do all her chores without having running water. Besides the cooking and washing up, she laundered the dirty clothes by hand, put them through the rollers to get the water out, and hung them outside to dry. In this weather she had to hang them inside. He helped by getting a pot and pouring water into it from the pail. He also lit the gas stove for her. *Even if we don't have plumbing yet,* he thought, *at least we have electricity and lights and a gas stove for cooking*. He was very hungry and looked forward to the porridge.

"All set, Mom," Jes said. Then his father called for help.

"Sorry Jes, to ask you to put boots on again, but I could use some help with the snow."

He went out with his father to try to keep the pathways clear but it was very difficult with the winds swirling all around them. Jes tried to help shovel the snow but found it very tiring. Finally they both went inside for the hot porridge. Jes liked to put brown sugar and cream on his. His dad had coffee and Jes had hot chocolate. But within an hour after finishing his breakfast, his father called him outside for another shot at shoveling snow.

Their first priority was to clear a path to the outhouse and then to the well. Both of these were essential. Then they turned and cleared a path to the left of the vestibule past the gardens to the driveway and the corn house. Jes pictured the gardens as they were in spring and summer with beautiful peonies, irises, and roses. Now they were being covered with a foot or more of snow.

"Dad," Jes asked during a pause while they caught their breath, "will the rose bushes and irises freeze with all this snow covering them?"

"No, Jes, the rose bushes go dormant in the winter to survive the cold weather and the irises are bulbs under the ground and safe from the cold. They'll all be fine. In the spring the rose bushes will bloom and the iris bulbs will sprout and grow."

As the day wore on the snow was clearly winning the battle and was getting deeper and deeper. It was difficult that night for Jes to sleep with the incessant roaring wind shaking the windows and doors. Sometimes it seemed as if the whole house was shaking.

Jes woke up the next morning to a winter wonderland. The snow was so deep it covered all the bushes. It was up to his neck and even higher in some places. Jes was considered tall and lanky for his age but he could barely see over the snow drifts. The wind had stopped but the snow continued to come down silently although it was much lighter snow. He helped his father again clear the path to the outhouse and the well. Next they cleared the one to the driveway and corn house and to the garage. The hardest part was making a path over one hundred feet long straight past the corn house to the chicken house where he fed the hungry chickens. Jes yearned for longer days when the chickens would start laying again. From there he made a small path fifty feet down to the barn and fed the lamb.

As Jes returned to the vestibule, he looked at the high snow drifts covering the large asparagus bed of twenty by fifty feet behind the house. They had an equally large bed of raspberry bushes behind the well, and next to it, a magnificent catalpa tree that Jes loved. He and his friends would pretend the long bean pods that grew in the fall were cigars. He pictured the asparagus coming up in the spring and the lush raspberries in the summer. It was Jes's job to cut the asparagus stalks an inch or so below the surface and pick the raspberries when they came in season.

"Do the asparagus plants and raspberry bushes also go dormant in the winter like the rose bushes?" he asked his father.

"They all are much the same. Even the trees go into a dormant state to survive."

"That means all the apple trees in the orchard too. If I ask her, maybe Mom will make apple sauce from the apples wrapped and stored in the cellar." When apples were in season, Jes would help his Mom with the cone shaped metal strainer, and the cone shaped wooden roller or masher they used to make apple sauce. After she cooked the green apples which were best for apple sauce, she would add the apples to the strainer so that Jes could mash them with the wooden roller. The sauce would go into a bowl and the skins and pits would stay in the strainer. He liked brown sugar and cream with the apple sauce and loved the apple pies and baked apples his mother made occasionally.

"Stop dreaming Jes," his father called. "Let's get to work."

He helped his father shovel the snow down the long driveway in case the road was plowed later on. Where the driveway ended, the road to the left was at the top of a hill that went down and over the stone bridge. It was paved but the road that continued to the right was packed dirt. They felt lucky because the town plow stopped just at the top of the hill. The neighbors along the dirt road that continued on for half a mile had to share plowing amongst themselves.

"Dad," Jes finally said, "I have to take a break now. I'm getting tired." His dad nodded.

The blizzard continued for another day and night before it finally stopped completely. The next morning Jes walked along the deep pathway his father had finally completed and had to stand on his tiptoes to see across the snow. Their "outside" cat named Giblet hid under the floor of the corn house. Their Irish setter Mike normally loved to play in the snow with Jes and his friends but this deep snow was too difficult for him so he ran up and down the pathways until he finally gave up and went inside.

Ten days after the blizzard ended Jes went back to school. Each day he would have a warm breakfast, usually porridge with bananas, grab his books and lunch, and start down the long road, sometimes with the other kids in his neighborhood following him. One younger boy lived a few houses up the dirt road and two boys lived just below him on a farm at the bottom of the hill. Their father was the caretaker of the farm owned by a rich man, who was seldom there.

The walk from his driveway was one mile down to the bus stop and he would whistle all the way. On this first day back to school, Jes walked down the hill, over the stone bridge, and down the hill. Halfway to the bus stop, he looked to his right into a group of trees, and saw a man crouched down behind a bush, watching him. He was sure it was the same man he'd seen before: the man with the black beard and dark piercing eyes. He stared at Jes for a moment and then disappeared from sight. Jes shivered as he had when he had first seen the man.

At the end of the day the long walk was uphill and he didn't feel as much like whistling. He looked into the woods and was glad he didn't see the man with the black beard. Once he could see his house he usually started whistling again. None of the other boys could whistle as well as Jes could. He was very proud of being able to whistle fast intricate tunes and even learned how to double whistle with two notes at the same time.

The snow stayed on the ground for weeks and then another smaller snowstorm piled up the snow again. Jes thought another blizzard would be fun and was just what he wanted but it didn't happen, though two things did happen before the winter was over. He turned eleven years old and his grandfather came to live with them several days later.

Two days after his birthday he was alone in the field between the driveway and the barn. The field sloped down from the corn house to a large maple tree just above the dirt road. There was a little snow on the ground and he was making a large figure eight with his boots when he had the feeling he was being watched.

He looked down toward the end of the driveway. Standing behind the maple tree was the same man he'd seen twice before. He had a black full beard, dark piercing eyes, and was dressed all in black, black shirt and pants, and a black coat. His dark eyes peered out from under his black hat. He was staring intently at Jes and Jes shook uncontrollably as he moved across the driveway toward the house. As soon as he realized Jes had seen him the stranger disappeared down the embankment on the other side of the dirt road and into the thick woods. He'd not shown any sign of harming Jes so Jes decided not to mention it to anyone, at least for the moment. But somehow he knew he'd see him again.

CHAPTER NINE

Dagobert's Demise

Rhédae, Southern Francia
Summer, 679 AD

Dagobert knew that he and his family were in danger. His marriage to Giselle and the connection to her powerful family, the Visigoths, had raised some eyebrows, but the power and substantial treasury he amassed after he became King began to cause some concern in the eyes of the Church. This growing threat did not go unnoticed.

When he used his growing power to curb the attempted expansion and power of the Church, he knew that he had better watch his flanks. By 679 AD he had acquired considerable enemies. He did not know from where the threat would finally come but there were several possibilities. He feared the Church the most, but he also feared his own mayor, Pepin the Fat.

Dagobert was an imposing figure. He had long black hair and a black beard, and his eyes seemed to penetrate one's very soul. He was tall and powerfully built with thick strong arms that he displayed by wearing a heavy leather vest over a coarse woolen sleeveless shirt. He carried a sword around his waist hung from a wide leather belt with a huge brass buckle that had his emblem on it.

Dagobert decided to leave Rhédae and go to his other royal palace in Stenay with its sacred Forest of Woëvres. But he felt that if his entire family went with him this would create a very large target. He realized that he also must protect his wife and children, especially his young three year old son, so he arranged for them to travel in disguise and follow a circuitous route to the protection of the Visigoths, Giselle's family in the south. The focus would be on him and perhaps no one would pay attention to their whereabouts. If anything happened to him at least his wife and son would be in a safe haven.

"Giselle, I don't want you to worry," he said, "but if I am attacked and killed you should stay hidden for several years since the enemy forces will look for you."

After seeing his family safely off under cover of darkness he decided he must hide his vast treasure in the event an enemy did surface. In the very short time of a few years, Dagobert had accumulated chests filled with gold and silver coins and chalices, ornate goblets, jewelry, cups decorated with jewels, elaborate religious crosses acquired from the Church, as well as the artifacts, cups, and a precious scroll from Egypt that had been passed on to successive Merovingian Kings. This treasure he had carefully hoarded but now he faced a dilemma. He could not carry it away but did not want to leave it and let it fall into enemy hands if they came looking for him at Rhédae.

The first thing he did was to find the best possible place to hide the Merovingian scroll showing the genealogy of the Merovingians from their origins several centuries earlier to the present day. This scroll had Dagobert's special mark on the back. Dagobert also had in his possession ancient cups and artifacts and a scroll that dated back well over 600 years. It had been carried to Egypt, then across the sea to the southern coast, and then to the ancient city of Rhédae. Dagobert muttered out loud, "It must never under any circumstances fall into the hands of the Church."

Dagobert decided the two scrolls should be buried together since they showed the origins of the Merovingian Cross and the complete genealogy from Judea and Egypt to the present day. The oldest scroll identified the birth of Sarah to Mary Magdalene and Jesus, her family history from then on, and the origination of the Cross. She married into the earliest ancestors of the Merovingians and the Cross was perpetuated thereafter. It was indicated that she was the first person known to have the Cross.

Dagobert found a small crevice in the undercroft of the church of Sainte Marie-Madeleine in Rhédae and hid the scrolls behind a small marked brick. Then he created a small diversionary treasure trove in a support structure under the church. He knew that if anyone was seeking treasure they needed to find something, so he would make it easier and more likely to find this small treasure than the scrolls. Perhaps they would be satisfied and stop looking. He also knew that almost no one knew of the existence of the scrolls since they had been carefully guarded by the Merovingian Kings. He selected this location far from the place he had planned to hide the main part of the treasure. He made sure to leave some gold and silver coins and chalices and other valuable and ancient objects dating back to the first century in this large hollow space under the church.

Then he took the remainder of the huge treasure he had amassed and the ancient cups and artifacts from Egypt and hid everything deep in the back of the largest cavern of Rhédae, buried in the bottom of the cave under what appeared to be fallen rocks. He had dug a huge hole and emptied all the chests, keeping out all the documents which he wrapped in oilskin and buried separately. Dagobert was used to hard physical labor and was able to do this heavy work without help. He was satisfied when he was done and wiped the sweat from his brow. He believed and hoped only the wisest and most deserving future Merovingian would find it.

Dagobert travelled rapidly with a small entourage along a route that was not well known just in case he was followed. He felt he would be much safer in Stenay and the Forest of Woëvres that he loved. He was able to reach the palace in Stenay with little trouble and began to relax thinking his plans were working. Dagobert loved to hunt and was in the heavily wooded Forest of Woëvres at the edge of the Ardennes when he made his fatal mistake.

He had let down his guard and had fallen asleep in the forest after hunting all day. Dagobert was awakened by a noise and the last thing his mortal eyes saw was a tall massive figure in a black cape and hood leaning over him wielding a blade that glinted in the dappled sunlight. By order of Pepin the Fat and supported by the Pope, Dagobert was assassinated under a tree in the Forest of Woëvres.

CHAPTER TEN

The Royal Princess

Rhédae, Southern Francia
Winter, 750 AD

"What happened after he was murdered?" Jeb asked.

"The assassins immediately went to the palace at Stenay to murder the family but did not find them," Childeric explained, "they raced to Rhédae but found no one. Then they carefully approached the Visigoth domain in the Languedoc, and under disguise as troubadours, attempted again to find the family, all to no avail. Some weeks later a messenger arrived and reported the death of Dagobert II to the Visigoths."

"What happened to Giselle and the children?" Jeb pressed.

"Giselle was much smarter than Dagobert and did not follow his advice since she figured sooner or later assassins would come to the Languedoc. She spent two years traveling to the west coast with her family and the one person she could trust, the Visigoth warrior named Alaric." The King paused to remember. "She traveled slowly by boat north to Bretagne and remained in hiding there for two years. When it was considered safe by her family she returned to the Languedoc under disguise with Sigisbert and his sisters."

"And what happened to Sigisbert? Did anyone ever attempt to kill him?" Jeb persisted.

"No. Sigisbert IV grew to manhood and married Magdala. He later became the Count of Razès and had a son Sigisbert V who will succeed him as Count. He is still alive and lives there still. There was no attempt to kill him because he is not considered a threat as we are, and also he is well protected. He never became the King of the Franks, but he helped continue that branch of the Merovingians."

Childeric paused again to listen. This time he heard noises. The scouting party had returned. It had been less than an hour. They rushed to King Childeric bringing with them a man they'd found, hidden in a small room inside the castle. He reported what had happened and the King realized the situation was much worse than he had expected. Rhédae had been attacked by a small force of armed men and had barely been able to repel the enemy. The King was told it was a conspiracy by Pope Zachary and Pepin III to usurp the rightful throne of the Merovingians. Fearing the return of a much greater force, almost all of the inhabitants who survived had fled far and wide to escape slaughter.

The King swept into Rhédae and searched for other survivors. His men found signs of the battle including several swords and spears on the ground and blood from those that had been wounded or killed but there were no bodies and they found no one else there. While they were searching the entire area Jeb's father told him to go to the church of Sainte Marie-Madeleine, go down to the undercroft, and look for a special brick with a small symbol of a cross.

"Pull it out, remove the two scrolls, make two copies of them, and then return one copy to the hiding place. You have very little time, Merovée," Childeric told him, "so you must hurry to complete this."

Jeb suddenly realized why he had worked so hard under the direction of the monks. All those hard study lessons learning to read and scribe were very valuable. As the King's son he was one of a very few receiving the special education and therefore one of a very few that could read and write.

He looked in the offices of the church and found a roll of parchment, a quill writing pen, and ink. The parchment was old and the pen was primitive but he was sure it would do. He rushed down to the undercroft, and faster than he imagined he might, he found the special brick. He reasoned, *if you know what to look for, it's a lot easier*. He pulled out the scroll and the other document and carefully made a complete copy of each one first in case he didn't have time to complete a second copy.

He was half way done with the second set when his father yelled. There was strong urgency in his voice. He put the first copy of the scroll alone back in the crevice, replaced the brick, and dusted it with dirt to make it look as before. He wanted to make it even more difficult to find. He dashed up with his scroll, the other document and the copies, pen and ink, and followed his father out of the church and away from the site. *When I find time later*, he thought, *I must finish the second copy.*

"Father?" he asked. "Why are we making these copies and leaving one here and taking the originals?"

"We have a report they are headed this way." This was all that his father said.

Jeb followed his father and the others to the outskirts of the town where they could find safety in the largest of a set of deep caverns. Childeric left a lookout behind to report when the enemy forces arrived to take the castle. The King's men had removed everything they could find that was of value but there was very little left that had not been taken by the others who fled. Soon thereafter the lookout came to report the arrival of the forces of Pepin.

"They were intent upon killing the remainder of our people," he said, "but when they found no one they left as swiftly as they had come."

While this information was being conveyed to the King, Jeb slowly moved into the back of the cavern to see how big it was. His blue eyes grew wider and wider as he tried to see. The cavern was twice as deep as the cave they had stayed in on the way there but very narrow. The ceiling was smooth as were the walls, and the floor was hard rock. He had trouble seeing even with his good night vision as he moved deeper into the back of the cave. Suddenly he heard a noise just ahead. It was a cry of a child. Then he heard another sound, a soft sob.

"It's all right. No one will hurt you," Jeb called out, "come here so I can see you."

Slowly three small figures appeared out of the darkness. Their leader was a petite slender young girl. Her long black hair was disheveled and her face was dirty. She peered at him with large dark brown eyes. *She cannot be more than 9 years old,* he thought. There were two boys dragging behind her, barely able to walk. She stepped forward unafraid while the other two cowered and sniffled. She stumbled but regained her footing.

"I told them not to be afraid and not to cry but they wouldn't listen." She shook her head with something akin to disdain. "Who are you?"

"My name is Jeb and I'm the son of the King," Jeb answered firmly.

"My name is Magda and I'm a princess of royal blood," she answered just as firmly, "and these," she waved her hand dismissively, "are princes. We hid while the fighting was going on and then we were all left behind when the others fled. So we came up here. The other children went somewhere else. They probably died. These are the only two left. We're very hungry and they're very weak. We haven't eaten for almost a week, only water from a little creek." She paused. "Do you have any food?"

"I'll get some for you."

Jeb led the group out and presented them to his father who seemed pleased to have found them. He asked Jeb to take care of them and give them food as soon as possible. Jeb gave them some bread. Then he went to help the men prepare dinner and asked if the young children could eat first since they had not eaten for days. His request was granted. Jeb waited until he was one of the last to eat. He felt the leader should make sure his men were taken care of first. *The children are now under my care,* he thought, *and the men would be one day as well.* The two young princes seemed too weak to travel. What would be done with them? The young girl was another matter. She must be very tough or very brave. He decided she was both. He liked her.

Jeb's father seemed to agree. "Jeb, I have an important mission for you," he said, "and I feel you're up to the task. You will head back up to Stenay and take Magda with you. You'll be accompanied by Clotaire and a dozen men to protect you but you'll take a longer, more circuitous route to the west and then cut across. I feel this route will be less likely to encounter trouble. The men will defend against animals and in the case of attack will lay down their lives for you," he said with gravity. Jeb knew he must look after Magda and by all means keep both of them from danger.

"What about you, Father? What will you do?" he asked.

"I'll stay behind," the King said, "We'll look after the princes until they're strong enough to travel. My men will also look far and wide for any other survivors. They must also be near starvation just as the young princes seem to be. We'll all return to Stenay in a month or two when the weather's better. I owe it to our people to find as many of them as possible." Jeb said he understood and made ready to leave.

He had completed the second copy of the scrolls before they began their journey. He was not sure why he made a second copy of the originals, and was going to bury them deep in the back of the cavern where Magda had been hiding with the princes. But he could not see any reason to hide this second copy so decided to keep it and take it with him.

They left early the next morning. Jeb was tall and quite muscular for his age and had become stronger from the journey south. He carried his own sack with the large fur skin, clothes, and food, including dried boar and rabbit, turnips, onions and leeks, radishes, beets and carrots, a sack and fur skin for Magda, and as much bread as he could fit in the pack. And of course he carried securely the original Merovingian scroll as well as the scroll from Egypt, and a copy of each. Magda was too small and weak to carry anything but she was dressed warmly with a long coarse woolen dress and high leather boots. She also had a leather cape over her dress and a large soft leather cap similar to Jeb's covering her long black hair which tumbled down her back. Her pack also contained a spare dress and soft lightweight flat-soled leather shoes which she wore in warmer weather. They set a slow pace at first until she regained her strength.

The countryside was mostly flat in the beginning of their journey, which made it easier for Magda. Their route veered to the northwest. They avoided the open spaces and stayed in the cover of the woods. Although most of the beech, chestnut, and oak trees had lost their leaves, they were so close together that they provided excellent protection from being observed by others. They were able to see rabbits scurrying through the bush, and now and then a fox. If they looked carefully they could see deer standing still and almost invisible. Jeb told Magda it was not as cold now as when they came down from the north.

"It's cold enough for me," she responded. "What will it be like on our journey ahead?"

Jeb turned to Clotaire for help and he told them it would probably be warmer as they traveled closer to the sea.

"We will avoid the mountains by this route but our big challenge will be the many rivers we will have to cross."

As they trudged on through the cold winter landscape, Jeb watched Magda carry on stoically and he admired her. *She is certainly a plucky little thing,* he thought.

CHAPTER ELEVEN

At Sea

Spring, 1398

Jed and Martha were both silent for a moment.

"Do you think we are the only ones on board with the Merovingian birthmark?" Martha spoke quietly.

"Probably," Jed answered.

"Why don't you take the fur off all the way?" Martha asked, "Are you shy? I'm not."

"I guess I'm still a bit shy. Maybe one day."

"You shouldn't be. Do you have hair yet?"

"Not yet. I'm not quite twelve."

"It will match your red hair."

"Your hair matches."

"I'm almost eleven. I'm a woman now. But you mustn't tell anyone. No one knows, not even my mother. They think I'm still a little girl. I never show anyone. You're the first. You promise?"

"Yes," Jed said firmly. He wouldn't dare tell anyone.

"Do you like me?"

"Yes," Jed faltered. "You're not a woman yet. You're still a girl and I'm a boy."

"I can have a baby now. When you're a man would you like to have a baby with me?"

"Let's go to sleep." The candle was fluttering and went out. This conversation unnerved Jed. He had felt like a man with the responsibility of the scrolls and thought he was also in charge of looking after a young girl. Now he felt much more like a boy again.

The next day Jed regained his composure and tried to get the vision of her body out of his mind. They continued to explore every corner and room and nook and closet all over each of the decks and up and down stairs, but they were careful to stay out of the way of the men and their shipboard duties.

Finally they settled on the bow, standing against the rail and looking over at the waves created by the other ships. The sea stayed calm and they made good time. As they sailed through the Orkneys and Shetlands, Martha would spot black birds with white on the wings and others with large beaks and point them out to Jed.

They often were the first to spot whales and dolphins. They could look directly down the side of the bow and see the dolphins clearly, playing in front of the bow waves and racing along the side or in front of the ship.

This would go on for many minutes and then they would suddenly disappear. The ships stopped briefly at Faroe Island to take aboard onions, turnips, and water, but then immediately continued on.

They headed out into the open sea. When a whale would appear in the distance off the front of the bow or sometimes off to the side, they would call out to the bridge.

"Whale ahead on port bow," Martha and Jed would yell, and point. They had quickly learned some of the boat language and were proud to call out. The men would look and smile and the word would spread. Jed and Martha were amazed at how many whales they saw. They imagined the ocean must contain thousands of them.

Henry decided to bypass the colony at Iceland and head straight for Greenland. After traveling for several weeks he called for Jed and Martha. "We are within a day or two of Greenland, so keep your eyes out for land. We are beginning to run out of food items such as meat and bread and I hope to replenish our supplies before going on," he explained. "A settlement has existed for some years on Greenland and I am waiting anxiously to see if they are still thriving. I hope they can spare some meat in exchange for salt, spices, and other cooking items I brought along for this purpose."

Jed noticed that each night Martha would sleep a little closer to him. At first he thought she was cold and then he thought she just liked to cuddle closer. After several nights she was right next to him under the same fur and pressing against his side. She still slept without clothes and eventually Jed got used to cuddling up with her to keep warm.

As each day passed Henry seemed to relax more and more until he found some time to talk to the two of them. He had exchanged his gentlemen's clothes he wore at the castle for seagoing garb. He wore a dark blue jacket with his coat of arms on the pocket, and long pants. He also wore a dark blue sea captain's cap with the coat of arms on the brim. He told Jed what Jed had suspected all along: that there had been several previous voyages to Greenland and even a couple to the west.

Henry explained, "The Norsemen originally created a colony on Greenland several hundred years ago but ran into some hard times. They were eventually forced to abandon it. During that first period they took at least one voyage to the west of Greenland. Later on they again established a colony and raised sheep and farmed to survive. They built several buildings out of stone. The winters were long and harsh and it was difficult to survive but they were hearty people and did prosper, at least for a time."

"How do you know all this, sir?" asked Martha in a quiet voice.

"I have taken a couple of voyages there myself. In fact, I helped establish the new colony on Greenland which we believe is still thriving. At least I hope so, since we need to trade for supplies and water for the rest of the journey. We also established a second colony further west up the coast of Greenland and I took a voyage about five years ago to the western lands so I have an idea what to expect."

"When we land in the west where will we stay?" Jed asked.

"If you mean are the buildings still there, the answer is maybe. There were only two some distance from the native village and they may have both been destroyed either by weather or by unfriendly marauding natives. The local natives will not destroy anything. They know I expect to return one day and will remember me. Besides, we can always stay in wikuoms." Henry smiled and paused.

"Father, what's a wikuom?" Jed inquired.

"A native dwelling. You'll see them when we first arrive. And this time we will build a castle on the hill in the middle of the island we call New Scotland. You will get plenty of experience in building, Jed. Perhaps you will become a true mason."

"Can I help too?" Martha asked.

"Yes, 'Mark', I'm sure you can help too." Henry smiled and she smiled back.

GREENLAND

52

CHAPTER TWELVE

Greenland

Late Spring, 1398

Henry's prediction came true. His estimate of when they would reach Greenland was very accurate. The next day, as they were watching the sea from the bow, Martha spotted land.

"Jed, look! Land ahead!" Martha called above the sound of the wind and the waves hitting the bow.

"Land ahead off the starboard bow," Jed yelled to the helmsman.

The crew came forward, looked, and cheered. It was only a matter of an hour before they approached the bay. They scanned the land for signs of life and they were rewarded by sighting a small band of men on the shore waving at them.

All eleven ships dropped anchor in the small bay. The land was bare and rocky and still covered with snow around the settlement except where the men had cleared the landing area. Half a dozen stone huts with wooden roofs surrounded a main building made partially of wood and painted a red color that had long since faded to a dull red. The first group went ashore with Henry and took salt and other provisions as a preliminary to trading. Henry returned after spending half an hour ashore and reported the news.

"It is indeed grim," Henry began. "Fences enclose empty space where the sheep had once been but they are long gone. The colony has lost its livestock but still is able to grow hay and grain. It's this they use to make bread which has helped keep them alive, along with fish, shellfish, and small game."

The occupants of the colony had not been visited by a large ship in years and had only small boats to travel along the coast. More than half of the colony had succumbed in the last couple of years to disease and cold and starvation and the rest were close to starvation as well. Instead of acquiring meat and other needed food items, Henry and his men would have to give up some of their own provisions. In short, Henry's plans had received a huge setback.

He consulted with those on shore and then with his own crew. Jed listened to this latter conversation with great interest. Henry explained to his assembled crew that the biggest problem now for everyone was going to be food since he didn't expect to find much meat when they landed in New Scotland. Jed watched as the crew nodded their understanding.

Henry quickly made a decision. He would send seven ships ahead to the west to look for a safe place to hunt and create a colony. They would be under the temporary command of Prince Henry's old friend, Sir James Gunn. Henry would join them after he helped this struggling colony. He would leave the two smallest ships with their crews in Greenland to help grow grain. It was too cold to grow corn but they could grow winter wheat, rye, and barley. Henry said he would take one ship with him to the northern colony. He would sail around to the west side of Greenland to see how the other colony was doing, and if they prospered, he would trade as needed and then return. After a brief break he would once again set out for the west.

The sailors on the four ships that would stay behind bid farewell to the sailors leaving for the west and the seven ships sailed away. The two smaller ships anchored and went ashore with all the provisions they had on board. Henry offloaded the chickens because he thought the colony could find better use for them. He and the Captain of the other ship made ready to leave. Jed and Martha weren't completely sure what would happen to them. They came quickly and quietly to Henry when he was by himself for a moment and asked if they could go with him. He thought about it and quickly answered.

"I'm afraid you'll have to go with me. I can't very well leave you here under the circumstances. We'll sail just as soon as I unload a few more provisions. Stay put."

When they were out of his sight, Jed and Martha jumped up and down with excitement as their journey took a delightful turn. As far as they were concerned, this adventure was getting more wonderful all the time. They had no thoughts of any great hardship that may be ahead of them. They were children having fun.

Henry kept a small crew on board and let the others stay on shore to see what they could find in the way of food and to help the inhabitants regain their strength. He hoped to return in a couple of weeks. They set sail under a fair sky and made good time. Within six days they approached the colony of Upernavik. They were delighted to see several people waving and running to the shoreline. They also saw many arctic terns flying overhead and a few arctic foxes in the distance. Seals and walruses floated on the ice flows. This time, when Henry went ashore, he was not disappointed.

This northern colony had been reduced in size but they had been able to raise enough sheep and grow enough wheat to sustain themselves. They even had a sizeable surplus they were willing to part with for salt, seeds of a new hearty grain, and various spices and other supplies that were hard to obtain including a few pots Henry had brought along. Henry loaded up both ships with as many sheep as he could find room for, and a small amount of hay to feed them. He promised the Upernavik colony he would stop by on his return journey from the west. He thought it might be in a year or two. He set sail quickly.

During this return journey to the southern colony, Henry spent more time with Jed and Martha and answered many questions they had. He told them about the early days of the Merovingians and the birthmark these early people all had. He explained the importance of the early scrolls.

"They show centuries of genealogy leading back to the early Merovingians." Henry explained, "Look at one of these charts and you see how each successive generation added to the scrolls after they found them. You will both be added to the scrolls as well." Henry paused for a moment.

"The special birthmark that each of you possesses shows that each of you is a direct descendant of…"

Henry paused. He found it difficult to discuss a subject he considered sacred.

"Of who sir," Martha persisted, "descendant of who?"

"Of The Magdalene," answered Henry softly.

Henry did not want to continue. Instead he switched stories and began to tell them about the Cathars and Templars.

Henry did not get very far before he was interrupted by a member of the crew. They were approaching the dangerous area of rocks and islands toward the southern end of Greenland and did not want to make errors at this critical time before they turned east back to the southern colony. The rest of Henry's story about the Cathars and Templars would have to wait.

Jed and Martha went to the bow for most of the daylight hours. Jed was slowly learning the basics of navigation as he watched Henry tell the others about the stars and currents and tides and how to read the ocean and what adjustments needed to be made not only for the current but also for the direction of the wind. He knew he was learning from the best navigator in the world. It was yet another important part of his education and he understood its importance. He found that he loved the sea. The rolling deck, wind in the sails, and salty mist in the air were now familiar to him and he felt at one with the sea.

Martha, on the other hand, was more interested in the mammals of the sea, the flying fish, the occasional kelp beds, and the different species of birds. She was especially fond of the terns that often flew overhead.

"Look, Jed," she pointed out. "They have forked tails, dark red beaks, and black crowns. How big do you think they are?"

"I think they are over a foot long," he answered, "and their wing span is more than two feet."

She explained to Jed that different birds appeared depending upon where they were in the ocean and she tried to understand the reason. "Perhaps," she said, "you could use the birds to help with navigation, to understand where you are, and to determine what weather conditions were ahead."

Time sped by quickly. Before they were aware of it, five days passed by and they were approaching the southern colony. Since Henry was ahead of the schedule he had projected, those on land did not expect him. When they saw the two ships sail into the harbor the men ran to the shore and yelled and cheered their arrival. The ships settled in to anchor and Henry had some of the sheep offloaded along with some wheat and hay. They kept on board just what they needed for the remaining sheep to eat on the rest of the journey. Henry anticipated this should only take a little over a week.

He was anxious to continue on as soon as possible because he feared the weather would turn against them. They loaded more water. Most of the men from the other two ships came back aboard but a few stayed behind in Greenland. In addition, a few of the colonists joined them for the voyage. They would help explore the western areas but would return with the ship on its eastern voyage in a year or two.

They set sail the next morning and the wind immediately began to pick up. Henry was concerned about these conditions because he felt a major storm would hit them before they reached their destination. Nevertheless he found time to resume the story of the Crusades and the Templars and the Cathars with Jed and Martha. The first thing he told them was the history of the Crusades and the reason for them. He extolled the exploits of Godfroi de Bouillon on the First Crusade and then began the story of Richard Coeur de Lion. But before he could continue he was interrupted. He was called to the bridge because of the rising waves.

Jed and Martha cuddled even closer together that night. Jed was beginning to feel it was the most natural thing in the world to curl up with her. That night her hand reached up to his chest and touched his birthmark. She gently caressed his chest with her soft hand. *Such a long time,* Jed thought, *but it's probably only been a few minutes.* Then she gently took his hand and placed it on her own birthmark. She put her hand on top of his and in a moment they both fell asleep.

They were awakened in the middle of the night by a crashing noise. They were being tossed back and forth in their small space, banging their heads against the wall. They quickly dressed and went to find Henry. They looked out over a roiling sea with huge waves battering the bow and splashing over onto the deck which was strewn with ropes and other gear that had not been fully secured. The roaring wind was deafening and so strong they had to hang onto the railing to keep from being blown toward the stern.

"What's happening?" Martha yelled to Henry.

"This is one of the worst storms I've ever encountered," Henry shouted. "I'm afraid we'll have to turn back. You'd better go below. It will be very dangerous in a moment."

"We'd like to stay here, sir." Martha spoke in a loud voice.

"How can I ever become a great navigator and sea captain like you if I don't learn how to handle storms like this?" Jed pleaded above the noise of the wind.

"I don't feel like such a great navigator right now," Henry replied, "but all right. You can stay. Just keep out of the way of the men."

"Don't worry, we will," they answered simultaneously.

They watched as Henry directed the crew to come about and run before the storm. Jed realized how treacherous such a maneuver could be. They had to pick up speed and come about at just the right time and the sails had to be handled quickly. Henry gave the order and handled the tiller himself as the men let out the sails to catch the downwind. They picked up speed and Henry managed to stay ahead of waves crashing toward the stern.

Jed realized why this was so dangerous. If a wave swamped the stern, it could easily sink the entire ship. Some water did spill over the stern but luckily they avoided being swamped and the ship raced back toward shelter. Jed and Martha hung on to ropes and whatever they could to keep from being tossed across the deck and possibly over the railing. They stayed out of the way of the crew dashing about as they handled the sails but were caught by splashing waves that carried high overhead. In a short time they were drenched and went below to dry out. They found this to be one of the most exciting moments at sea.

The crew did not eat until they were safely anchored in a small protected cove on the shore of Greenland near the colony. Then they all ate a hearty meal of dried bread, boiled beef, carrots, turnips, onions, and preserved cabbage. Henry decided to wait awhile before setting out again. He felt it would be wise to wait until they got much better weather. They would still have time this summer to establish the colonies in the west. The hundreds of men he brought with him would be located at a few places. He could accomplish this before winter and the ships could return to Scotland before encountering the severe fall storms which frequented the seas between Greenland and New Scotland at that late time of year.

While waiting for better weather to arrive they battened down their ship and went ashore to the comfort of the colony's stone buildings. These buildings were built to survive the winter winds and storms and to keep out wandering white bears. Henry chose a stone building with a stout door at one end and small windows high above. On the side was only a small window to look out but at least they felt safe. And then one night Martha heard a noise and the dogs started barking. She looked out the window and saw a white bear in the dim light from the stars. It was slowly approaching their stone hut.

"Wake up, Jed," she yelled. "It's coming this way."

"What is?" he mumbled, as he awoke from a deep sleep.

"A bear! It's right here." Martha looked through the window into the cold eyes of the bear. Then the bear moved to the stout wooden door and clawed at it. Henry and Jed were awake and on their feet. The bear kept hammering and banging to try and dislodge the door.

"Don't worry," Henry said to calm them. "We are safe here. It will go away. It's probably a bit hungry." The large bear persisted and it seemed as if he would finally rip the door off but then finally did give up and meandered away from the colony buildings. Martha let out her breath in a big sigh; she'd not realized she had been holding it.

"What would we do if the bear had ripped the door off?" Martha asked.

"I would have shot it," Henry said as he brandished the crossbow he'd brought with them, "but I don't think the bear can rip off the door."

"Why didn't you bring a gun instead?" Jed inquired.

Henry smiled. "I can load this faster than I can a gun. Just in case I miss."

"Would you miss?" Martha asked.

"No."

They all went back to sleep but slept fitfully the rest of the night. When they awoke a light snow was falling and dusting the ground with powder. It stopped after a couple of inches fell. Jed and Martha were cautious during this stay, and at the direction of Henry, tried to avoid being too involved with any of the colonists or crew. Henry felt this would avoid any of the questions he received now and then about the two of them. However, Jed and Martha did manage to explore the hills nearby. Henry told them to be on their guard for another bear but didn't think now they needed to be reminded. They did see several small arctic foxes on the low hills but Martha laughed. "I don't think I need to be afraid of them."

Even in late spring many of the hills still had several inches of snow on them but wild flowers were peeking through. Sometimes Henry would join them on these jaunts as they wandered over the hills of ice and snow and rocks and would tell them more about the Cathars, and how they were cruelly persecuted.

"Who were the Cathars?" asked Martha quietly.

"They were fellow Christians considered heretical by the Roman Church because they did not believe in Church doctrine and despised the Church because of its corruption and lack of pure motives. They believed one could commune with the True God through a spiritual experience they called 'gnosis'. They did not believe in the crucifixion or honor the cross.

They were also a threat to the Church because they had great wealth that was rumored to contain the Holy Grail."

"What's the Holy Grail?" Jed asked.

"That's a very good question, Jed," Henry smiled. "I'm glad you asked. It is rumored that the silver goblet used by Jesus at the Last Supper disappeared and was never found. It is considered to be a very sacred relic by many."

Henry continued, "I will tell you more about the Holy Grail after I tell you the rest of the story about the Cathars. The Church began to persecute them in the year 1209. Their last stronghold, Montségur," he explained, "was besieged in 1244. Three months before that the Cathars had taken the bulk of their treasure and hidden it in a fortified cave in the mountains. During the siege, four parfaits, or Cathar perfects as they were called, made a daring escape by lowering themselves down the walls in the dead of night. They brought with them the valuable documents and relics. These four took this treasure to one of the caverns around Rennes-le-Château, which was still under the control of the Knights Templar."

"What happened after that with the treasure – all of it?" Martha urged Henry to continue but he seemed tired.

"That will have to wait for another time. Then I'll tell you all about the Templars."

They returned to a warm dinner of cured beef with boiled cabbage, onions and leeks, beets and carrots, and a small amount of bread. Then they returned to their little stone hut with Henry. It was very safe but he did not want them to be too far from him just in case they were visited by another big white bear.

They had a long sleep during this spring night.

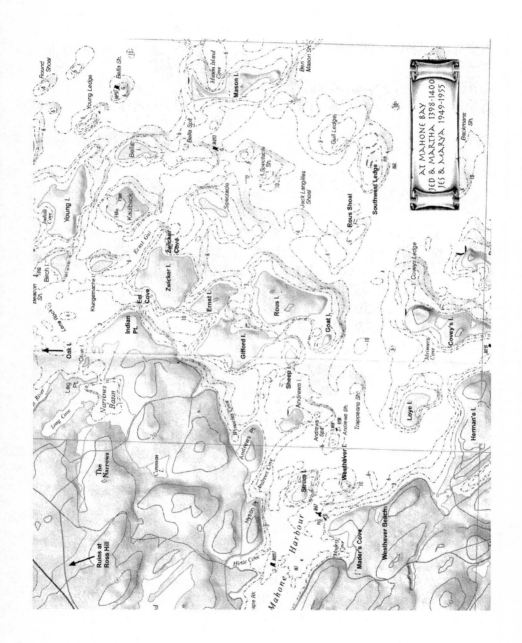

AT MAHONE BAY
JED & MARTHA 1398-1400
JES & MARYA 1949-1955

Frouard Shoal
Young Ledge
Bella Sh.
MPS7
Masin Island Cove
Mason I.
Ben Mason Sh.
Bella Spit
MPS7
Inch
Bella
Young I.
Inglis Cove
Kaulback
Spectacle
Spectacle Sh.
Gull Ledge
Southwest Ledge
Brant Gut
Zwicker Cove
Jack Langilles Shoal
Rous Shoal
ZINORON Sh.
Birch I.
Kurgematie I.
Zwicker I.
Eel Cove
Ernst I.
Rous I.
Covey's Ledge
Levi Rock
Indian Pt.
Gifford I.
Goat I.
Mistaken Cove
Covey's
Oak I.
Crow I.
Andrews I.
Sheep I.
Loye I.
Blackmans Sh.
River
Leg Pt.
Long Cove
Narrows Basin
Andrews Pt.
Hysons Cove
Andrews Spit
RGR - Andrews Sh.
Trappeares Sh.
Herman's I.
The Narrows
Common I.
Hyson Pt.
Westhaver I.
Strum I.
Ruins at Ross Hill
Hirtle Cove
Mahone Harbour
Maders Cove
Mader's Cove
Westhaver Beach
Cape RR

CHAPTER THIRTEEN

Grandfather

Southern New England
Spring, 1948

Jes's grandfather came to stay with them a few days after Jes had seen the stranger. His mother fixed up the spare bedroom next to the kitchen so he would not have to walk up and down stairs. He had lived all alone and was in poor health, so they decided he needed to be with them. He was a tall lanky man but quite thin at this point. He usually wore a bathrobe over his clothes to keep warm. Each day he would just sit in a rocking chair near the big fireplace in the dining room and rock back and forth, deep in thought. He would usually have a roaring fire going. Jes remembered the day the fire was so huge the chimney caught on fire. A neighbor called the fire department and they poured water down the chimney while he was rocking and he scolded them for getting water on the beautiful wide plank oak floors that Jes's father had refinished and pegged.

In the winter, Jes wore a warm shirt and a cap over his brown hair. Later, when the weather warmed up, he would wear a tee-shirt and go outside and sit in the door of the corn house next to his grandfather. Jes soon learned that when he asked, his grandfather was very happy to tell Jes the stories of what it was like to grow up many years before when he was a boy in Nova Scotia. As the days went by it seemed to Jes that his grandfather's health was improving rapidly. He gained weight and looked healthier and younger. Perhaps it was in part due to his storytelling.

As winter turned to spring, the crocuses bloomed and the daffodils followed. The peonies, irises, and roses bloomed and the asparagus began to sprout. The baby robins hatched and the foxes patrolled the grounds looking for fallen chicks. The rain came down and turned the ground to mud but the forsythia and lilacs still budded and the snow disappeared, and the skunk cabbage bloomed down near the brook. The raspberry bushes and cherry trees blossomed, followed by the pears, plums, and apple trees, and the land was filled with beauty and the perfume fragrance of spring. The coolness of spring turned to the warm long days of summer. Whenever his grandfather was in the mood Jes would listen to him tell many stories about the time when he was a boy. He told Jes how he had lived in Mahone Bay in Nova Scotia when he was Jes's age. Jes was enthralled hearing what life was like then.

"You know," his grandfather told him, "many of our ancestors lived in that area of Nova Scotia for centuries. There are islands and bays and coves and beaches named after many of them."

Jes was fascinated by these stories and dreamed about going to those places one day. He kept asking his grandfather to tell him more about what it was like growing up there.

"Jes," his grandfather told him, "there are so many islands and dangerous shoals in the bay that it takes an expert navigator and helmsman to maneuver through those treacherous waters. It's very cold in the winter and the tides and currents, winds, and snow make the bay even more treacherous."

His grandfather paused. "I loved the summers even though the water was so cold. Even in August we seldom went swimming. There was a beach near where we lived named Westhaver Beach. Yes, it was named after an ancestor. Sometimes my friends and I would dare each other to swim. No one else was ever in the water."

"Besides swimming," Jes asked, "did you ever fish?"

"Did we ever! We had lots of fun taking out a small rowboat and exploring some of the islands. There was a small island named after our ancestor sitting right in the middle of Mahone Harbor, and another one called Mason's Island way out in the bay. There was also Mader's Cove, named after another ancestor. It was next to the beach where we went swimming. We rowed into the cove and dropped anchor. Then we fished for hours. My friends and I were just about your age."

"You never told me about fishing. I love to fish. I'd love to fish there."

"Maybe we could someday." His grandfather hesitated. "When I get my health back, we will."

"I hope that's soon, Grandfather," Jes wished.

Grandfather paused in thought, then went on.

"My friends and I spent so much time exploring and rowing in and out of all the little coves and inlets I could probably draw a map blindfolded. We took every opportunity to fish that we could. Mader's Cove was the best place but we often went along the north shore to Indian Point. There weren't so many people back then. We would fish off the point and sometimes row around the big island close to the point called Zwicker Island. Yes, that was another ancestor from way back. When the weather was good we loved to fish the cove on the other side of Zwicker. And then there was another island."

He paused deep in thought. At first Jes thought Grandfather was tired but then he realized he was just thinking.

"What island?" Jes prompted him.

"It's called Oak Island. It lies close to the mainland several miles by water north of Zwicker. Once in a while we would take a canoe up there because a rowboat was too slow. Usually we would go at night and sneak on to the east end."

"Why did you have to sneak on?"

"Some strange things have gone on and still are. It's believed treasure is buried on the island. I'll tell you more about it some other time."

Grandfather would grow tired after talking for an hour or so. Jes could always tell. He would grow silent. Jes would leave him and come back another day. He wanted so much to hear about everything that happened long ago but he learned to be patient.

Jes also liked to learn other things from him. Grandfather had been a carpenter and builder when he was younger and taught Jes many things about carpentry. Jes had learned a lot from his uncle when they built the woodshed but learned much more just listening to Grandfather.

"Different buildings are constructed in different ways," Grandfather explained on another day. "Houses have a certain set of stringent requirements for people to live in," he said, "but building barns for livestock requires a different, less stringent set of requirements. We had to design them for the needs and sizes of different animals and had to consider hay barns and where to keep food for sheep and goats and pigs away from rats and mice."

"Then there are the chicken houses and the corn houses just like yours. Those are the easiest to build, but everything needs to be built solidly with plans that consider all aspects. They should be built to last."

Jes looked at the house and barn and corn house and chicken house in a different way than he had before. He was sure they would last a long time.

One day Grandfather told Jes about his own father and grandfather. "They were ship captains and spent many years at sea. They were extremely good navigators and could handle the tricky maneuvering required to move in and out of Mahone Bay. All the islands and shoals and hidden rocks made navigating extremely difficult. It was especially challenging to enter Mahone Harbor."

"They also knew how to handle the challenges of the many other bays and harbors along the coast. They were very familiar with the tricky tides and currents and, most importantly, they understood the weather off the coast of Nova Scotia and Maine, and Newfoundland as well. These areas have some of the most terrible weather in the world and they were experts at navigating these dangerous waters. Once your great grandfather saved a British ship at sea. He was sent a letter thanking him on behalf of Queen Victoria."

Jes was fascinated by these stories. "Why did you become a carpenter and not a ship captain like your father and grandfather?" he asked one day.

"I guess they inherited from someone the ability to be great ship captains and navigators," answered Grandfather, "while I inherited from someone else the ability to be a good carpenter. Inheriting things from ancestors is a complicated business. Perhaps your dad can explain. All I know is that the genes we inherit can be passed from generation to generation but can also lie dormant or something like that and not show up for several generations." He hesitated briefly. "Being a carpenter and ship captain are both in your blood, Jes, along with other very important genes." But that is all he would say.

Grandfather would sit for hours using his old jack knife to peel apples that came from their orchard. He would also use his knife to whittle shapes from old pieces of wood. He would come up with amazing figures that fascinated Jes and would tell Jes stories while he whittled.

One lazy summer day when Jes was sitting near him without a tee-shirt on, Grandfather asked him, "Have you noticed that unusual mark on your chest, Jes?"

Jes didn't know what to say except that it was a birthmark. Just then his father came by and overheard the conversation. He took Jes aside and with some gravity in his voice told him about the history of his birthmark and that he had inherited it from some ancient ancestors.

"Very few people have it," he said. "It's the only visible sign of your heritage and your destiny. You should be very careful with whom you discuss it and never show it to strangers."

"What about Grandfather?" Jes was puzzled. "Can't I talk to him about it?"

"Of course. He knows about the history of the birthmark but he may have forgotten." His father shrugged. "Perhaps it's better not to talk about it with him."

Jes was perplexed. He could tell that his father had not told him the whole story. The birthmark came from the Merovingians he had said. Jes wanted to know more but his father did not want to continue with the subject. Jes was very curious and wanted to know how the Merovingians got the birthmark. *What ancestor of the earliest Merovingians had the birthmark*, he wondered, *the gene of the birthmark had come from someone, but who?*

"One day I'll tell you more about the story of the birthmark but not today."

Jes knew not to persist when his father had this serious, ominous look. He had the feeling that some danger was associated with his birthmark and could not wait to hear more so he looked in all the books in the house including the encyclopedia for some discussion of the birthmark but only found an explanation of the Merovingians and their dynasty.

The summer was almost gone and Grandfather was improving rapidly. He would walk around the fields and orchard with the support of an old twisted cane. One afternoon Jes was playing in the field near the barn and the chicken house, out of sight of Grandfather who sat at the entrance to the corn house whittling wood with his knife. Then Jes saw the dark stranger with the black beard again. This time when Jes saw him peering out from behind the barn, the man suddenly darted out and ran swiftly toward him. Jes started to run away and began yelling but the man was too fast. He grabbed Jes and was dragging him toward the rose bushes and blackberry bushes between the barn and the dirt road. Jes thrashed as best he could trying to escape but it was no use. He was held firmly in the man's arms and continued to scream.

As he was struggling and waving his arms in vain, he looked behind the black bearded man and saw Grandfather racing toward them. He had no idea Grandfather could run that fast. He charged the stranger with his cane waving before him and swiftly struck the stranger on the back of the head. Jes fell to the ground and the man rolled away. Then the man jumped up and did not look back as he ran through the thorny bushes, across the road and down the embankment on the other side. Grandfather tried to chase after the man but could not get through the rose bushes and blackberry brambles. He turned back to Jes who had stood up and threw his arms around him in a big bear hug.

"Jes." Grandfather looked into his eyes. "I'll never let him hurt you again." Jes saw the tears in Grandfather's eyes. He had never realized until then how much his grandfather loved him.

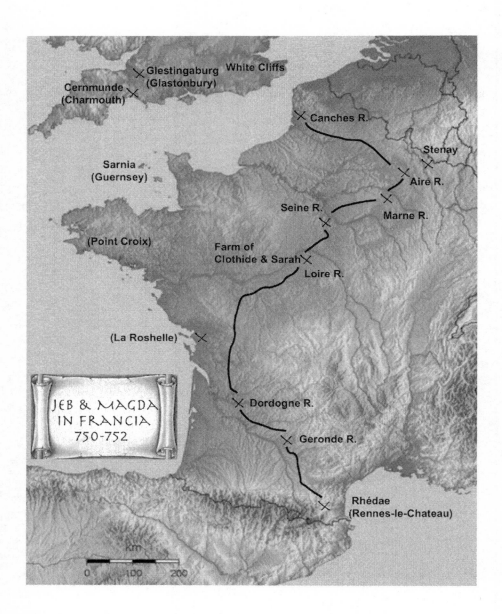

JEB & MAGDA
IN FRANCIA
750-752

Glestingaburg
(Glastonbury)

White Cliffs

Cernmunde
(Charmouth)

Canches R.

Stenay

Sarnia
(Guernsey)

Aire R.

Seine R.

Marne R.

(Point Croix)

Farm of
Clothide & Sarah

Loire R.

(La Roshelle)

Dordogne R.

Geronde R.

Rhédae
(Rennes-le-Chateau)

km

0   100   200

66

ROMAN BRIDGE

CHAPTER FOURTEEN

The Journey North

Francia
Spring, 751 AD

Jeb's blonde hair grew even longer and he thought he was beginning to look like the other men, all of whom had long hair. Magda's black hair grew down to the middle of her back. Jeb, with Magda in tow, was escorted by a dozen of the King's men with Clotaire in charge as they followed a long circuitous route back to the Stenay castle. Clotaire was the greatest warrior and most trusted man in his father's entourage. He was very strong in arms and legs, which were like tree trunks. He was tall with a massive torso and even his head was like a large craggy rock. He had scars on his face and arms from the numerous battles he fought and won, and yet to Jeb seemed as gentle as a lamb. He wore a sleeveless woolen shirt with a leather vest over it and had armlets on his powerful biceps. His hair was long and brown and he seemed to Jeb to have a constant smile. He always carried a long spear or axe and a bow and arrows.

Clotaire made the decisions about the direction they would take and the pace they would set, but always with deference to Jeb. Jeb usually supported Clotaire's decisions but once he politely suggested they go further upstream to cross a river where he thought it was shallow and they could ford without building a raft. Clotaire complied and was quite impressed with Jeb, not only for challenging him, but for being correct. They were following a long circuitous route as close to the coast as possible to avoid any large groups of marauding outlaws.

On this northward trip Jeb continued to gain respect and admiration from all the men. He seemed to have grown in stature even though he was only eleven. He often voiced his opinion to Clotaire and the others about when to keep going and when to stop. He showed strong leadership qualities in front of the men, and yet was very gentle with Magda. She in turn grew much stronger as they progressed.

They travelled through stands of oak and beech and even some chestnut trees. This gave them a chance to gather acorns, beechnuts, and chestnuts to add to their food supply. They also struggled through thick pine forests, and sometimes had to wade through or around thickets of yew trees and snowberry, honeysuckle and rosemary bushes. Their fragrances and that of the wild jasmine were often so strong that they were overwhelming to Jeb, but Magda said she loved the smells no matter how strong they were. They encountered many deer and a few foxes, and an occasional wild boar, but no bears or wolves. Clotaire explained that bears and wolves would generally avoid large groups of men on the march.

The few birds that they saw scurried away or flew up as they heard the noise. Jeb did see a few grouse and some smaller birds such as black birds and larger ones such as crows but he thought the birds were few in number. He once heard a woodpecker like the one he saw on the journey south. One day he saw a large hawk flying low as it tried to grab a thrush that had been foraging on the ground. Jeb watched as the thrush escaped into thick bushes.

"Clotaire," Jeb asked, "what was that big bird chasing the smaller one? It was very fast."

"That was a sparrow hawk, Jeb, and it doesn't usually miss. This time the thrush got lucky."

After they had traveled for a couple of days the weather grew warmer. The trail was well trodden too, so they switched to their soft lightweight leather shoes, giving them a silent footfall and more comfort.

"Jeb," Magda said, "I can carry my own fur skin and gunny sack if you let me."

Jeb let her carry her sack with her spare woolen dress and fur skin in it but he carried her boots along with his own.

"Let me know if it becomes too heavy," he told her, "you need to be strong enough to walk."

Each of the men carried an axe, a bow, and a quiver of arrows plus their fur and gunny sack for sleeping. Four of the strongest men also carried the parts of a portable boat they could assemble quickly. It could carry several men and had a shallow draft so that it could skim across the rivers if the water surface was not too rough. They also carried a sailcloth to cover the bottom of the raft that the men had to build at several of the rivers. The men would row across on the portable boat pulling a rope, and from the opposite shore, pull across the raft. Jeb and Magda were both curious about the boat.

"Clotaire, how is the boat built so that the men can assemble it so quickly?" Jeb asked.

"It uses a technique called the mortise and tenon joint. All the pieces are designed and constructed so that a fixed tenon made by shaping the end of one timber or plank fits into the correct mortise or hole of another. That way the boat can be assembled and disassembled very quickly."

"Where did that idea come from?" Magda wanted to know.

"It came from Egypt hundreds of years ago. They built portable boats of all sizes. Ours is only about fifteen feet long but some of the larger ones of seventy five feet or more in length were used to carry Pharoahs. We believe The Magdalene came across the sea from Egypt in a small one and landed on our southern shore."

"Do you know what the boat looked like?" asked Jeb. "It must have been a very dangerous crossing."

"From ancient myths we believe it had a high bow and stern to handle the high waves," Clotaire replied, "but we really don't know much beyond that."

Jeb and Magda were curious about this boat but asked no more questions. They joined the men and continued walking. All of the men carried a share of the food. This consisted mainly of dry bread, hard cheese, and meat, together with a few onions, turnips, and some preserved cabbage. Altogether it was not sufficient to last much more than a couple of weeks if not augmented. They carried some basic spices including salt to dry game when it was caught. The meat kept several days until it was cooked over an open fire. Jeb carried his sleeping gear and an axe which was slightly smaller than the one carried by the men. He also carried some food. Their concern about finding food deepened as they progressed.

"Jeb," Clotaire informed him, "we must be prepared to find food all along the way for at least two and perhaps three months. Winter is coming to an end but the snow is still on the ground."

The loads they carried were similar to those they carried on the direct southern trip, but the distance they would have to cover on this coastal circuitous route would probably be twice as long. And the pace was slower because of Magda's weakness and the swollen rivers.

"That means," Jeb stated, "we'll have to stop often to hunt."

Clotaire had been along this route in the past and knew generally what to expect.

"Yes, but the biggest problem we'll face will be the large rivers we'll have to cross. The rivers are much wider as they approach the sea than they are to the east. They're much fuller and raging in early spring from the melting snow."

Jeb asked, "Are there any bridges we can use to cross these rivers?"

Clotaire laughed. "Those stone arch bridges are magnificent, Jeb, but most of the time the Roman roads are going a different way than our route."

When they encountered the first large river, Clotaire said, "Do you remember the rivers we crossed on the way down?" Above the place where they were crossing, the river rushed over rocks, throwing up spray that felt cold on Jeb's face.

"Yes," Jeb responded, "they were much smaller than this one and the water level was much lower." Jeb now understood the difficulties facing them.

Clotaire took them across the Geronde early in this northern trip when the river was small. It was easy to cross now but would be much more difficult if it were later on when the river became swollen from snowmelt and rain. They used the portable boat and built a makeshift raft to carry the men and supplies across. Taking Magda across was not as difficult as they thought it would be.

She sat behind Jeb on the raft laughing and giggling as they crossed, seemingly unaware of the danger of falling in. She was as plucky as he had thought. He found out she had just turned ten years old in the same month he had turned eleven. When Jeb was not too busy, she would ask questions.

"Jeb," she asked quietly, "where are we going? What will it be like? Are we in danger from lots of wild animals? I'm not afraid. I just want to know."

"We are returning to our castle in the north, at Stenay," Jeb would explain. "I don't think we will see many dangerous animals. There are too many of us. But we could see a few wolves or a bear. Don't worry. We saw a bear on the way down but Clotaire and the men chased it away. The worst thing was being followed by a large group of bandits. Clotaire wounded the leader and the men killed many with a volley of arrows. The rest fled."

He wanted to sound more confident than he felt. She continued to ask questions about where they were and what would happen next. When he could not answer he would ask Clotaire who seemed to know everything.

They traveled northwest for some time along the north bank of the river. Clotaire explained they would need to turn in a more northerly direction and cross another river, the Dordogne, before it became too wide and dangerous.

It was only a short two day hike before they looked from the bluffs above and saw the wide river below. There were steep cliffs on both sides of the smooth flowing current which appeared to be at least two hundred feet wide. It did not have any visible rocks or rapids that they could see from above. They stopped while two of their men searched for the best place to cross. The river was so wide that the portable boat was of no use. This time it took longer to build a raft before they attempted the crossing. This one needed to be very sturdy and much bigger. Jeb was attentive to its construction.

He watched as they cut logs of equal length and thickness for the length of the raft and shorter, thinner logs for the width. They used thick vines to lash the logs as four men held them together as tightly as possible, weaving the vines over the short logs, then under the longer ones all along the length. Jeb marveled at how fast the men worked and still kept the logs tight together. They also made sturdy long poles to push the raft across.

This second crossing was a much rougher one and they all came out of it soaking wet. Magda thought it was very exciting and seemed to have no fear. She sat behind Jeb, gripping him with one hand and clasping the vines with the other. The current was very fast, causing rolling waves that splashed over them. Magda had to hold on very tightly to keep from being swept into the river but she could not help screaming with joy. When they were all safely across, they immediately built a fire to dry out and warm up.

From this point on they marched directly north. They then began to head in a northeast direction, crossing several other rivers with rafts. Once, one of the men thought there might be a Roman bridge a few miles to the east. He led them along the bank until Magda spied an old stone double span bridge in the distance with glorious arches soaring above the river. They crossed it and resumed their northeast direction.

CHAPTER FIFTEEN

A Warm Meal

Francia
Late Spring, 751 AD

As they progressed steadily northward, Jeb, Magda, Clotaire, and the men escorting them, would stop in caves now and then, building fires and sending out forays into the nearby forests to find game. The little amount of hard bread they had found at the castle and church at Rhédae was dwindling fast. They looked for edible roots, mushrooms, and berries to augment their diet which was primarily venison with a small amount of bread and cheese. They shot grouse and other birds when they could find them, and an occasional hare but that was not often, and finding an elk was rare. Providing food of any kind at this time of year was difficult so they often went hungry.

On one such foray, Magda and Jeb were searching for edible mushrooms and berries when they heard a loud grunting noise coming from behind thickets of yew and nettle trees.

"Jeb," Magda whispered, "there is something big in those bushes."

"Don't move, Magda."

They froze and found themselves face to face with a large brown bear. Jeb was reaching for his bow and arrow when he heard someone or something coming up behind them. The bear suddenly ran away into the brush. Jeb turned and saw Clotaire standing there with his spear in his hand. He was smiling.

"I guess the bear was more afraid than you were."

They resumed their search and then suddenly the rain came down heavily and they returned to the cave.

"I love the smells in the forest when it rains, don't you Jeb?" Magda said. "It is like perfume coming from the flowering berry bushes and trees. It is thick in the air when it rains."

The sound of the rain falling and making a light spatter on the leaves was the only sound Magda could hear that night as she curled up in her warm fur.

As they traveled, Clotaire would look for abandoned huts or old buildings for shelter. Once they stopped at a large dilapidated hut that was clearly abandoned but still had a large supply of grain and salt and other foodstuffs, including dried meat and cheese. It appeared as if the occupants had taken sudden flight or left to do battle. For whatever reason, they'd left all these supplies so the men loaded up with as much food as they could and made some flatbread to carry with them. They also used the wheat to make a kind of porridge each morning with water and salt.

"Take as much meat and cheese," Clotaire said to Jeb and Magda, "as you think you can carry."

This food lasted them for more than two weeks of travel. During this time they encountered many rivers of all sizes. When they came to another large river, Clotaire explained to Jeb that this one flowed into a huge bay at a place they called La Roshelle. They would not cross it at this point but follow it inland for a short distance and then cross. They then would travel north until they reached a big wide river called the Loire. They would follow this for many days and keep in a much more easterly direction.

"Clotaire," Jeb asked, "how would we make a raft to cross a larger body of water such as a sea that has waves and wind and currents but does not flow as a river does? We couldn't use poles because the water would be too deep."

Clotaire said he would explain when they stopped to camp for the night. He became increasingly concerned about encountering danger. He was not so worried about contact with animals such as bears and wolves but with tribes of men on the march. When he noticed the wide pathway had seen an increasing amount of recent traffic he devised a plan. They began marching parallel to the heavily traveled path. This made the going a bit tougher so he would look for small lightly used trails that headed in the same direction. Often these were runways made by deer so they had to walk in single file with one or two men scouting ahead. This strategy worked quite well.

In fact this plan had an added advantage. Because the trails they traveled on were frequented by deer, Clotaire and the men would lie in wait next to the trail in the early or late hours and shoot the deer with arrows as they passed. In this way they managed to have enough meat. Magda and Jeb had the job of searching for berries, mushrooms, wild onions and carrots, or any other edible food they could find. Clotaire had taught both of them which mushrooms were safe to eat and which were poisonous. Jeb also learned to look for certain roots that they could add to the meat. By following the rivers they need never worry about lack of water but the one thing that Jeb craved was bread. They had run out of the bread they'd made as well as the grain they'd found.

Following the rivers had another advantage. Jeb and Magda could bathe now and then. The water was extremely cold at this time of year, but they would find an inlet in the river, a place where the water was not moving rapidly, and was quiet and secluded. Clotaire would stand guard nearby while the two children splashed about for just a few minutes. They would not stay in the water very long.

These little breaks were the only time they could relax and have a little fun so Jeb looked forward to them and he knew Magda did too. When they were on the trail she was somber and quiet most of the time. She struggled hard to keep up with Jeb and the men and not complain, but during the times they were able to bathe, she laughed and giggled. He would help her wash her long hair and then she would splash water on Jeb and run or swim away as he chased her. She would let him catch her and giggle loudly. She clearly loved to be caught. They were both like little children. She was not at all shy nor was Jeb about being naked.

Sometimes the yelling and laughing alarmed Clotaire. He would come to see what was going on. Once he came up to them with a deep look of concern on his face.

"You must be quiet," he warned, "and not make any noise. It's dangerous now."

Later on Jeb learned that a large group of men were passing on the main trail. Even though they were some distance away, Clotaire was still worried about being heard. The group disappeared into the distance and Clotaire eventually relaxed. Jeb and Magda were careful after that when they bathed, playing and splashing quietly.

They had to deal with another delay when the rain started again. It rained for one solid day and they took refuge in a shed along the trail until it stopped.

They reached the Loire after more than two months of travel and they still had a long distance to go. Magda had grown much stronger and she was able to make much better time. She still carried her own little sack with a dress and fur in it. Still the pace was maddeningly slow. Clotaire realized the long hours, hard pace, and irregular supply of food, or even occasional lack of food, was beginning to affect the children.

To cheer them up, he said, "Soon we will approach the small farm of a kinsman and stop for some time so you both can recover your strength."

"Will we have a warm meal there?" asked Magda.

"I'm sure we will," he responded. "Let's hope they are home and welcome us."

In a few days Clotaire halted. The group followed him as he made his way off of the trail and traveled south away from the river. Soon they came upon a small farm and a makeshift wooden hut nearly invisible nestled in the thick woods. They approached carefully. Then Clotaire told them to stay out of sight and wait while he went ahead alone. He came back half an hour later with a big smile and waved to them. They came up to the small square house with a stone base four feet high and wood walls above. The thatched roof had a chimney at one end. Inside was a large room with a small woodshed attached to one corner and the kitchen equipment at the other end. Jeb noticed the pots hanging from an iron rack suspended from the ceiling. It was warm inside from the crackling fire.

They were greeted by a jolly heavyset woman who beckoned Clotaire and the children inside. The men stayed outside and rested quietly. Clotaire introduced the children.

"This is Jeb and this is Magda. They are in my care and we are headed east." He paused and said no more after that about their journey. "They are very hungry."

"Children, my name is Sarah. Clothilde, my husband, will return shortly. In fact, Clotaire, why don't you fetch him? He'll be in the barn across the field. He'll be glad to see you." She pointed in the direction to go. "Meanwhile, while I start dinner for all of you, I have a chore for the children, a nice chore."

She gave them mugs of beer to take to the men. The mugs were carved from hard wood by Clothilde. Jeb and Magda made a couple of trips back and forth and were cheered by the men as they brought this special treat. The men had not had beer since they'd left Stenay months before. This was a special moment for Magda and Jeb. They knew how much they owed to these men who had looked after them for months, and the journey was still not over.

Clotaire returned with Clothilde and they both helped Sarah prepare what seemed to be a feast for Jeb and Magda. They had salted pork and turnips and onions and carrots and beets and cabbage, and another vegetable that she called a parsnip. Jeb was even allowed a small mug of beer and Magda tasted it. She made a face and wrinkled her nose.

That night they all slept soundly. The men found hay to sleep on in the barn, and Jeb and Magda curled up next to the fire in the hut. They listened to Clotaire tell of their journey thus far but fell asleep quickly. The last thing Jeb remembered was the story of the first river and the building of the rafts. He had a dream about building a huge raft. It had sides to keep out waves and a floor to keep the boat from taking on water. It had a sail and two oars just in case there was no wind. It even had a closed space for storage to keep things dry. In the middle of the dream Clotaire appeared and laughed.

"You're building a ship not a raft. Where are you going?" he said. Then he disappeared before Jeb could answer. Jeb woke up and the fire was out and everyone was asleep. He looked at Magda who was sleeping soundly. He realized what a tough stoic little thing she was and how fond he was becoming of her.

The next day was spent helping Clothilde and Sarah to repay them for their generous hospitality. The men cut logs for a building Clothilde wanted to erect. They split wood. They helped plow up the field for planting, and the men also took some of this time to make additional arrows to replace the ones they had used for hunting. They had another wonderful dinner of mutton and cabbage, turnips, carrots, onions, and parsnips, and this time some of the men helped to prepare it. Even Jeb and Magda helped a little. And of course the wooden mugs continued to overflow with beer.

CHAPTER SIXTEEN

Sailing The Aegyptian Coast

Northern Coast, Aegyptus
Spring, 36 AD

After swimming in the sea, Sarah dried off and got dressed. She kept thinking about her birthmark and what her mother had said: that she was the only one with such an important mark. She still had questions.

"Mama, what is that rolled up scroll you keep with you? Is that important?"

"It is very important, Sarah," her mother spoke in low tones. "It is a record of our history, yours and mine, and others. I will give it to you when you are older to keep and protect. Now let's get back."

"Mama," Sarah continued, "I have one more question. Do I have a father?" There was a moment of silence.

"Yes, Sarah," her mother finally answered. "You have a father and he is a wonderful man."

"Will I ever meet my father?" Sarah spoke in a low sad voice, "I would like to have a father."

"Sarah, you will meet your father when he reveals himself to you. Meanwhile you must know he loves you very much and always will. You are very special to him as well as to me. Just be patient."

"All right, I will." Sarah was content with that.

They joined the others, loaded up the dromedaries, and headed toward Zygra, a Bedouin village that the guide knew very well having grown up near there. He introduced Joseph and the others to his relatives. Sarah asked her mother if they were also Bedouin.

"We are not but why do you ask?" Sarah's mother seemed surprised at the question.

"Because our skin is dark like theirs."

"We are from Judea. We have always been dark. But you may be right. Perhaps the Bedouin feel at home with us since our skin is dark like theirs."

"I like them. They are very friendly. They have helped us a lot."

"They think you are very special too."

"Will we leave here soon?"

"Yes Sarah. Joseph says we will go next to Baranis. There are some Roman wells there where we will fill up our water bags. It will only take one night of travel. It is another Bedouin village." Sarah's mother paused. "I think we will then go to another small village called Petras Maior."

They traveled along the seacoast that night. There was no wind. It was so quiet Sarah thought she could hear the footfalls of the dromedaries as they shuffled along. Sarah again spent much of her time silently looking up at the stars. They rested during the day. Sarah was awakened by the yelling of the Bedouin guide and then she heard a roar. The dromedaries began to bleat and snort in fear and tried to break their tethers. The other men joined the Bedouin and began yelling and banging pots and waving sticks as they tried to chase a big male lion away from the camp. Finally the lion retreated and the dromedaries calmed down. Sarah could not sleep after that. In fact the entire camp was disturbed and Joseph decided to get an early start. They continued on through the next night, reaching Petras Maior at dawn.

The next day turned out to be an important one. With the help of the Bedouin guide, Petronius and Mark assembled the mortise and tenon boat, fitting the parts together as marked. They filled the cracks with reeds and grass and covered it both inside and out with mud that dried and left a smooth surface. Joseph said this would make the boat watertight for the long journey ahead. The boat was about twenty feet long with a high bow and high stern where food and water were stored. The inside of the hull had a layer of timber with tents placed on top of it.

While they were preparing the boat for the long sea journey, Joseph traded seven of the dromedaries and one goat for more water, as much grain as he could fit into the boat, along with dates and figs, honey and nuts, a few avocados, and some camel milk for Sarah. He gave the other three dromedaries to Mark, Petronius, and the Bedouin guide for their return trip. While assembling the boat he also had the other goat slaughtered and the meat cooked and dried for their long journey. They bid farewell to the three men and set sail at dusk.

The winds were with them at first until they passed Berenice.

"It has a large Judean community," Joseph said, "but it is also a very large Roman city and we will bypass it."

Joseph and Lazarus took turns navigating while Mary and Martha and the other two women named Mary huddled down in the boat with Sarah. The man called Joshua who had smiled at Sarah also helped Joseph and Lazarus now and then. They had a sail set in the bow section which they managed deftly to steer the boat. Once they sailed past Berenice they headed directly west across the open water.

"How long will we sail before we stop on land again?" Sarah asked Lazarus who seemed to be the one navigating the boat.

"We will probably be at sea across this gulf for the night and the next day and another night." Lazarus answered quietly. "When we stop on shore we will rest for a day before we go slowly north along the coast."

"We will stop near a large town called Regio Syrtica," Joseph added. "It is along the coast going north. We will follow the coastline stopping several times until we reach a place called Site Punique, or Kerkouane, where we will rest before going across the wide and dangerous sea. It is the site of war between the Romans and the Carthaginians a few hundred years ago."

As they sailed the open water, Sarah stayed under the tent covering to stay warm and dry. Once, she looked out and saw the familiar stars including the belt of the Hunter. During the night Sarah awoke with the boat rocking and splashing. It seemed the bow would rise up and drop down. She looked out and peered over the side and noticed the seas were high and rolling. Lazarus kept the boat heading into the waves. Sarah realized this was to keep them from tipping over. The wind was coming directly at them and blowing so hard that Lazarus had to lean forward to stay upright, his cloak wrapped tightly around his waist and his tunic around his legs, whipping back and forth. Somehow he managed to stand upright even though he was buffeted violently.

Then the wind shifted and swirled around them, splashing the boat with spray which gradually accumulated in the bottom of the hull. Sarah realized the water was sloshing around underneath, getting them wet and cold. She began to worry until the others started to bail out the water with pots.

Once, when she was huddled under the tent covering, Joshua lifted up the cover.

"Sarah," he asked, "are you afraid?"

"A little," she answered.

"Don't be. I will look after you. You will be safe. We will reach shore after many hours and you will warm up and eat. You must be brave."

"I am." Sarah managed a weak smile. The man's warm smile made her feel good and not afraid. She fell asleep and slept soundly for many hours. She woke up once as her mother brought milk with honey and an avocado.

The waves remained high but the boat continued on without tipping over. Finally they landed on an isolated beach just before dawn on the second night. They emptied the water that had come into the bottom of the boat and dried off the tents and their clothes. After a bowl of wheat and honey and milk and grapes, and a little bit of dried meat, Sarah felt safe and warm and watched as the men set up the tents inland from the beach. They all slept during the day, and when dusk arrived, they set out sailing along the coast.

"Where are we and where are we going?" Sarah asked Joseph.

"I'm worried about being too far out to sea after the high waves we encountered," he explained. "To be safe, we will sail north along the coast past some islands and then stay in close to shore where we will stop at a place called Tacapae. Then we will follow the shoreline until we reach an island off the coast near a city called Taparura. We will try to fish as we sail. Before we leave Taparura we will make sure we have enough water for the remaining trip."

"The remaining trip?" Sarah asked. "To where?"

"To Site Punique," Joseph continued, "where we will rest and prepare for the trip across the big sea. We still have the option of stopping at a couple of ancient cities called Ruspina and Hadrumetum if needed but I am anxious to prepare for the long voyage."

This seemed to satisfy Sarah. The light from the stars was very bright as they sailed to Tacapae and continued on the next night to Taparura. Sarah loved the rhythm of the sea as the boat sailed along rolling gently from side to side and up and over waves. She often peeked out at the stars and felt the mist from the spray on her face. It was cool and she liked the slightly salty taste. She watched the men catch and haul in some reddish fish. She liked their taste when they were cooked and ate them with milk and figs and some of the flat bread her mother and Martha had made before they sailed.

They stayed an extra day and night at Taparura. It became very hot during the day and Sarah longed for the coolness of the nights. She woke up once in the heat and looked around her tent. She was drowsy from sleep. Suddenly she noticed a huge spider above her. It was six inches long with a big eye and sharp pincers. Sarah was terrified and let out a scream. Joshua rushed to her, opened the tent, and Sarah pointed to it. He reached in and took the spider gently with his bare hand. He came back in a moment and spoke softly to her.

"It is called a camel spider and it will not hurt you. I carried it away from here. Do not be afraid. I said I would look after you and make sure you come to no harm."

"Did you kill it? It looked terrible," Sarah asked anxiously.

"No, Sarah, I did not. I took it away but it meant no harm. It will catch beetles and even lizards and snakes."

The next night they followed the coastline past Ruspina and Hadrumetum and reached Site Punique just as dawn was arriving.

"This is one place I wish we could visit," Joseph said, "because it has many ruins from the Punic town of Kerkouane, including a famous necropolis where many soldiers are buried. The three wars fought here a few hundred years ago between the Romans and the Carthaginians determined the fate of the two civilizations. I have a special fondness for this ancient land. The Carthaginians have the same origins, the same ancestors as we do. They came here centuries ago from Judea. Sadly, however, their civilization was destroyed forever by the Romans and this town has the most surviving remains of that great civilization."

"Then why don't you want to stop here?" Sarah inquired.

"I am anxious to continue on." Joseph responded. "We will rest up for a day and a night and eat well before we leave. We won't bother to go to Hippo Diarrhytus but will sail directly from Site Punique across to Ichnusa."

"How long will it take?" Sarah asked.

"With favorable winds, we might make it in one night."

Sarah and the others slept soundly during the warm day and sailed out into the sea at dusk. She smiled at Joshua and he smiled back through his full reddish brown beard.

"Sarah, you need not worry about this trip. You will be all right. I will make sure of that."

"I am not worried. I just want to know everything that is going on. I want to know about the birds and the fish and I want to watch the wind and the waves. I have never been on the sea in a boat before but I feel very special. I know everyone is looking after me and I don't want to be a problem."

"Sarah," Joshua said very softly, "you could never be a problem. It is we that are privileged to travel with you. You are very brave and curious and should never stop asking questions." Sarah felt very happy and warm at those words.

CHAPTER SEVENTEEN

Massacre At Stenay

Western Francia
Late Spring, 751 AD

The next morning Clotaire, Jeb and Magda, and the group accompanying them, set out carrying as much food as they could manage. They each carried a little water, some dried meat and bread, a piece of cheese, and a few vegetables. The course that Clotaire set took them east along the River Loire. The trees and bushes along the river had white and pink and yellow blossoms and even some purple ones and the low ground cover created a thick carpet. Magda thought *the smell of the flowers is lovely*. She asked Jeb what he thought of the smells and sights at this time of year and he replied he liked the leaves and flowers on trees and bushes not just for the fragrance but for the cover they provided. They still were able to avoid mountains but the rivers continued to pose challenges.

They traveled for some distance and then, when the river turned south, they crossed it. This time they were lucky. They found a makeshift raft on their side of the river. They were entering much more populated areas and finding this raft saved them a day of hard labor. It was built strong enough for this wide river.

But there was a disadvantage to being in a populated area as well: the chance of encountering other travelers was high. They could no longer risk being seen in broad daylight; they had to begin traveling at night. They could ill afford to come across another group of armed men like the one they had hidden from earlier. The next time they might not be so lucky.

Magda was becoming a veteran traveler and had earned the respect of the men as well. She was only a little thing but carried her own sack now and moved as quietly as the others through the forests. Even at night they stayed away from open clearings and small groups of huts that they knew were inhabited. It was tough going but they made steady progress. Jeb soon learned that he had amazing night vision and could see well even in the darkest of nights. Once he stopped Clotaire and told him he saw a small village in the distance and all five of the buildings had been burned. Clotaire approached cautiously and discovered a few bodies, the fire still smoldering. It appeared to be a recent attack.

"Jeb," Clotaire said, "thank you for stopping us. There could still have been some attackers present. We must proceed very carefully from now on."

After crossing the Loire they had little trouble getting across a couple of other rivers. Jeb joined the men in building the small rafts. He cut the vines for lashing the logs together and Magda even helped by dragging the vines to the men.

"We're fortunate in one way," Clotaire told Jeb, "we don't have the high mountains to cross. Within another week of steady hiking we'll soon encounter the Seine and head east, following its southern banks for a few days."

When the Seine turned south as the Loire had done, Clotaire found a place to cross that seemed just right. The current was not too strong and they were able to use the portable boat and ropes, and to pole across much of the way in the dead of night. Jeb was amazed at how quiet they had learned to be. He felt at home with these men as they crossed rivers and marched through the darkness.

They reached the opposite shore and waited and listened as usual. This time they heard noises in front of them on the trail so Clotaire sent a scout ahead to locate the source of the activity. If it was a group of men the scout would determine their numbers and where they were camped. He came back quickly and reported a large group of armed men blocking their way.

Clotaire led them north and along the river until they could safely resume their easterly direction. They found that traveling at night not only had the advantage of being on the paths when others were not, but also the cold damp night air helped sound to carry far. It made it easier to hear encampments of men but it also meant they had to be even quieter as they traveled.

It also had the disadvantage of having to find a place to rest during the day. The days were still short but they were getting longer and this meant shorter nights and shorter times for night travel.

They managed to find dense woodland to camp in but they could no longer risk building fires. The woodland consisted of oak trees, ash, and yew and was thick with snowberry, elderberry, and nettle tree brambles as well. When they found an open spot of ground it was usually covered with damp oak leaves and they would put down the sailcloth. They once found a hut that showed no sign of recent use. A fine rain had begun so the hut was welcomed, but they still had to post a guard and take turns listening for any men on the move. They also heard many small animals such as squirrels scurrying about but fortunately encountered no bears, wolves, or snakes.

They were traveling very quickly and soon encountered the River Marne. This proved to be much more of an obstacle than Jeb had imagined. There were two parallel rivers to cross.

Clotaire explained, "It's better to cross two smaller rivers than to hike downstream and attempt to cross where they merge."

They were becoming adept at building rafts. The key, Jeb learned, was selecting the right wood. They picked the more buoyant and softer woods and learned to build smaller, lighter rafts very quickly. One of the men had found a large cloth in a hut. They used it to cover the floor of the raft to keep water from seeping through the logs.

"It's a lot like the sailcloth we already have," Clotaire pointed out to Jeb, "that we've used for sailing on the huge sea at the southernmost end of our land."

After crossing this double river at night they found a secluded place to camp. Clotaire told Jeb they were within a few days of Stenay. However, they would first stop a day out and not approach the River Meuse just yet. They would stop along the banks of the River Aire instead.

"We have some other kinsmen," he explained, "that can provide a safe haven just in case enemies are looking for us. These people are not kinsmen of your father but of one of our men, and I trust them completely."

They approached the Aire in two days and crossed as usual just before dawn. The man carefully approached the hut of his kinsmen. When he was sure Clotaire's group would be safe, he returned for them. They crept to the hut under cover of darkness. While the men went inside for the hoped for mugs of beer, Jeb and Magda asked if they could bathe in the river before dawn broke. They had not been able to for many days. Clotaire told them it would be all right but still set a guard nearby. The water was getting warmer but still very cold. It was a special treat for Magda to splash and swim but they promised to be very quiet.

Magda was watching Jeb very closely as they played in the water. "You seem more quiet than usual. What's wrong?"

"I've been thinking about Clotaire. The closer we get to Stenay the more nervous he becomes. He told me he was worried because we had taken over four months to get here."

"What was wrong with that?"

"I asked him what he was worried about."

"And what did he say?"

"He said 'If anything happened at Rhédae in the last couple of months and someone came looking for us at Stenay, they would get there before us and ambush us.'"

"How could they do that?" she asked.

"'They could get there in a month by the direct route we took going south' Clotaire told me. 'The group of men that Childeric left there are not enough to defend Stenay against a large force. They could be overwhelmed or besieged and could not hold out for long. If we could get there before any of the enemy approaches we could join them and prepare for attack. At any rate, Stenay might not be the safest place for us.' He told me that several days ago. He's been acting nervously ever since."

"Then maybe we shouldn't go there after all," Magda said. It seemed logical to her.

As they were getting out of the water Clotaire came rushing up.

"Get dressed quickly." He was distraught. Jeb had never seen him like that before.

"Our kin told us that a messenger came many weeks ago. He said that your father had been usurped and taken prisoner. All the men with him have also been captured. This messenger was not with Childeric's entourage at the time so he was not captured. He was a kinsman of the people here so he rode swiftly for several days to report this. But that was long ago. After giving his sad news to Tulca and Romille, the messenger left for Stenay to report the news since they probably had not received it yet. He planned to join the garrison quartered there to help just in case they were attacked."

Clotaire had a stricken look on his face as he gave this report. He indicated they should come to eat while he gave some thought to this sudden predicament.

They dressed and came to dinner in the hut. Dinner was really breakfast time. Jeb watched Clotaire and he could see the worried look on his face that never seemed to go away. They ate another warm wonderful meal that included mutton, cabbage, carrots, turnips, and onions. It had been three weeks since they had left the hut of Clotaire's kinsman Clothilde and the cooking of his wife Sarah. Romille was the name of the woman in this hut and she was just as kind and generous as Sarah had been. Even though it was just beginning to be daylight Jeb and Magda were ready to sleep. Clotaire and Romille's husband Tulca found a secluded place in the barn for them. They curled up in the hay and fell fast asleep. Clotaire slept close by with his axe and bow and arrow by his side.

Jeb had another dream about rafts. He and Magda were alone floating on a huge sea when the wind died. They were too weak to row and they fell asleep. By some miracle when they awoke they were sailing swiftly toward land. Suddenly in the dream he fell overboard and he woke up and realized he had rolled off the piled hay. He laughed and went right back to sleep.

Later in the day when Magda and Jeb awoke, Clotaire gathered everyone together and explained what he had planned. Clotaire would keep Magda and Jeb with him at all times and stay secluded while all the rest of the men would go to Stenay under the direction of his trusted second-in-command, Guillaume. They were to approach stealthily just in case they were too late and Stenay had already been attacked. If all was safe Guillaume would return for them. But under no circumstances should Jeb and Magda be discovered by the attackers.

The men took all their weapons and enough provisions for two days in case they would need to return. Clotaire gave a big bear hug to each of the men and they departed.

"We will head north a short distance to the fork where two rivers come together," he then told Jeb and Magda. "It's a safe place to stay hidden while we await the return of Guillaume. I am taking no chances. I don't want to be found at the hut."

After traveling north just over half a mile, he found the cave he knew about. It was uninhabited just as he hoped. It was a good thing. The rain had begun in earnest but they would be safe and dry there.

Clotaire left them after two days and told them not to venture out while he was gone.

"I will just go to the hut to see if anyone returned."

He came back within an hour and told them to follow him. No one had yet returned from the short two day round trip to Stenay. They went back to the hut and found Tulca and Romille.

"Will you look after the children while I'm gone?" he asked them. "I never should have let the men go without me. They should have returned by now."

He turned to Jeb and Magda. "It would be better if I had left you safely here while I went with them. I fear the worst. I don't want you to worry about me. I'll be all right but I want you to stay hidden in the barn. You can go out at night. I trust you both to stay very quiet."

He turned back to Tulca, "If men wanting to harm the children haven't come by now they probably won't, but if someone does come looking, play innocent. Then let them force it out of you that Jeb and Magda left a couple of days ago and headed north. That's all you know." Tulca nodded his head.

Clotaire left quickly with only his axe, long sharp knife, and bow and arrow, plus a small amount of dry food and water. Jeb and Magda went immediately to the barn and fashioned a hiding place along one wall by creating a space in the loose hay, then using bundles of hay to close the "door" behind them. They then made a breathing hole in the back against the wall. When they went out at night they did so briefly and quickly hurried back.

Magda thought this was exciting. Jeb was worried. He began to think about what he would do if Clotaire didn't return. Jeb would have to take Magda somewhere away from there to a place where it was safe. He thought perhaps he could take them back to the farm of Sarah and Clothilde.

Clotaire returned in less than a day and a half. His face was ashen. He brought Jeb and Magda in to the hut with Romille and Tulca and told them the sad news.

"They have all been massacred." Clotaire broke down and wept. Jeb had never seen him like this. He and Magda went to his side and put an arm around him and he in turn put his arms around them and continued to weep.

CHAPTER EIGHTEEN

Flight to the Coast

Stenay, Northern France
Early Summer, 751 AD

When Clotaire finally stopped weeping he told the four of them what he had seen.

"It looked as if the palace had been attacked some time before and all the men, women, and children inside had either been captured, or killed and dumped in a common grave. When Guillaume and the other men arrived at the palace a couple of days ago they must have been ambushed and slaughtered. Their bodies were scattered all around. I did what I could to bury them. I looked around very carefully for survivors who might be hiding before I went into the castle and saw this horror. If the assassins had left anyone alive they took them as captives, perhaps as hostages."

"What makes you think they've gone?" asked Magda.

"From the heavy tracks heading south. The tracks are recent and show the men were in a hurry. They didn't find what they came for."

"What's that?" Jeb wanted to know.

"The two of you." There was silence after that. Clotaire turned to Tulca and Romille. "We have to leave here immediately. If we stay you will be in danger too. And we must not tell you any of our plans for the same reason. If you are threatened you can tell them what they want to hear. Make something up."

"We will say nothing if they come here," Tulca assured him.

"But I doubt they will come. I think I know where they've gone. Thank you so much for your generosity and help. I'm very sorry about your kinsman. He was one of my best friends. We had done many things together. I only wish I had gone with him. Perhaps I could have saved them or at least fought with them."

"You did what you thought was best. These children are alive. Look after them." Tulca spoke with downcast eyes.

"Tulca," Clotaire leaned close to him and spoke softly. "I have a favor to ask. May I borrow an adze? Just for a few months. I'll return it next time I go by here."

"Certainly," Tulca replied. "No explanation needed."

"We will leave our portable boat with you if you don't mind. With just the children and me we can no longer carry the parts."

"Of course, Clotaire." Tulca answered. "We will hide it in the barn."

"Come," said Romille, "we will give you food for the journey. We don't want to know where you are going. You are right about that." She gave them bread and meat and cheese and they each carried a deerskin of water.

Clotaire and Jeb packed up the food with their gear and tools. When Clotaire sent the men off to search the castle he'd kept the waterproof sailcloth since it wasn't needed. Now he carefully packed it up for the crossings to come. They said their goodbyes to Tulca and Romille, gave them big hugs, and off they went. They headed south along the river in case they were being watched by Tulca and Romille or someone less friendly. When it was dark, Clotaire turned back northwest, bypassed Tulca's farm, and continued on.

"What are you doing?" challenged Jeb. "Why are we going this way?"

"We aren't going to do what anyone expects. We can't stay anywhere around here and we can't go south. They'll continue to look for you for as long as they have any hope of finding you." Clotaire paused. "You are going to get your wish, I'm afraid."

"What do you mean?" Jeb responded.

"We're going to build a boat. It'll be much bigger than those rafts and have a real sail. You'll sail on the sea." Jeb was silent and Magda was gleeful.

"Oh Jeb, smile," Magda challenged him, "this will be so much fun."

Clotaire described the plan. It would take a couple of weeks at least to reach the coast. They had two major rivers to cross on the way and, since there were only three of them, it would take longer to build the rafts. He smiled at Magda when he said all this. He wanted her to know she was a full-fledged partner in this effort. He said he would take a slightly southern route to avoid areas where he thought there might be groups of dangerous armed men. He also reminded them they would not have to deal with high mountains that way. They would reach a bay below the point of land closest to the land across the sea. There they would build the boat.

"How long will it take to build?" Magda wanted to know.

"I'm afraid it will take about a year, maybe longer. We will need to hunt for meat and other things to eat. I'll try to pick a secluded place with running water near us and perhaps a cave to stay dry in. We'll have to get through the winter somehow and that won't be easy, but we have no choice. We no longer have a safe haven in this land. I need to get you to a place where you can grow up in peace and become educated."

They continued as before, traveling by night and resting by day. They managed to avoid several rivers and crossed a couple of small ones. Within three days they came to their first good sized river. It took most of one night for them to build a sturdy raft which they hid during the day. They no longer had the men to build a raft, but it only needed to be big enough to carry three of them. Still, Magda laughed at its small size.

"Clotaire, are you sure it will carry us across?"

He smiled. "You'll see. We'll get across."

Magda laughed and giggled as they crossed early the next night. They made it without trouble and made good time after that.

Then they stopped briefly while Clotaire did some hunting. They chanced building a small fire at night just long enough to cook the deer meat. They ate a hearty meal, packed up what they could carry, and left the rest. Wild dogs and wolves would find it eventually. They traveled during the remaining hours of darkness and reached two more major obstacles, a wide river followed in short order by another river.

In both cases they spent most of one night building a small raft just big enough for three of them and covered the bottom with the waterproof cloth before starting across. The children were adept at riding the raft and helping Clotaire to guide it. They crossed the first river without incident. Magda was so excited she screamed until Clotaire told her she had to stay quiet no matter what.

In the middle of the second crossing they had a scary moment where the river was very deep and the current was swift with rapids. They hung on to the raft and bounced down the river half a mile until Clotaire managed to steer them toward the opposite shore. They had learned early on to construct rudimentary paddles to help when the water was too deep to use the long poles, but they had not yet become proficient at handling the raft in strong currents. Jeb realized how much they had relied on the other men, but they were learning fast from watching Clotaire.

After drying out from the second crossing and having a good meal, they started walking at a brisk pace and made excellent time several nights in a row. It helped that they didn't encounter any more wide rivers. Also, Magda was becoming a very strong walker and they no longer had to wait for her.

After another week of hard travel they approached the bay Clotaire had described. It had taken them just over two weeks since they left Stenay. Before the light of dawn, Clotaire found the cave he was looking for. It was close to the shore of the River Canches where it entered the inlet. The inlet was slightly salty but the river was fresh. The entire area was very secluded and surrounded by thick forests of oak, ash, yew and pine, and underbrush of juniper, snowberry, honeysuckle, and rosemary thickets.

"Could I go in the water?" Magda asked. "I haven't had a decent bath for this entire trip and I would like to bathe."

"Wait until I check all of the area surrounding our cave," Clotaire replied, "to make sure there's no sign of other people. We'll most likely stay here for many months and it's very important that we never attract any attention. We need to remain alone and secluded for the entire time it takes to build the boat."

"We understand," Jeb and Magda said in unison.

Clotaire returned in just over an hour and gave them the go ahead. He warned them that they must not make any noise this time until he had a chance to check both shores of the deep inlet, the river upstream for some distance, and the forest for miles around. He said they could not risk any chance of discovery.

This did not seem to dampen Magda's enthusiasm. She said she would play in the water quietly and stay very close to shore in the shallows. It was still dark. Clotaire went off to make camp in the cave and prepare dinner of dried meat, bread, and the last of the turnips they managed to hoard on the trip. Magda slipped into the water first and Jeb followed. The water was warmer than the last time they bathed but still caused goose pimples. While they were playing and swimming Magda came up to Jeb and touched his chest. She whispered in his ear.

"You have the birthmark too, the cross on your chest. I noticed it when we first went swimming." He touched her thin chest with his hand and she grabbed it and held it.

"All of us that are Merovingians of royal blood have the cross on our chest," Jeb said. "When you said you were a royal princess I knew you would have it too." Jeb took his hand away.

"It means we are descended from ancient royal kings, right?' Magda inquired.

"My father once told me my great, great, grandfather was Clovis II and my great grandfather was Childeric II. I am named after Merovée who was the first Merovingian King but you must never tell anyone. I use the name Jeb even though several people have figured out my father is Childeric III. We are all descended from the great King Clovis who conquered the Visigoth King Alaric and also from Childeric I before him and Merovée before him."

"Then we are cousins, distant cousins. My mother told me my great, great, grandfather was Sigisbert III and my great grandfather was another famous King, Dagobert II."

"Then your grandfather, Sigisbert IV is still alive somewhere in the south," Jeb stated.

"No," Magda corrected him, "he's not my grandfather. My grandmother was his sister. Her name was Magdalene. I am named after her. My mother's name is Giselle and she says we are all descendants of The Magdalene, the one they named the church after in Rhédae. You know, Sainte Marie-Madeleine." This was becoming too confusing for Jeb.

"You've lost me." Jeb shook his head. "I wonder where Clotaire is."

They had stopped swimming during this conversation and now were shaking from the cold. Just as they were drying off, Clotaire came to get them. He said it would be daylight soon and they must eat and sleep. They had to start work the next night building the boat.

They began work the next evening as soon as it was dark. It was Magda's job to look for certain trees that were of light soft wood such as pine. They were to be only two or three inches thick and just over sixteen feet long. Magda could not see in the dark quite as well as Clotaire and Jeb, but she could see quite well, even without the moonlight. Clotaire said he wanted just enough length so that when he trimmed the ends and fitted everything together the boat would be exactly sixteen feet long bow point to stern. He showed her the type he was looking for and how to mark it with an axe. He also asked her to look for spruce along the shore.

It was Jeb's job to collect the vines that would be used to bind the logs together after Clotaire had prepared them. He also showed Jeb how to peel bark from the cedar tree. He said this was to be used to cover the outside of the boat once it was assembled. They would use pitch or pine tar to fill the cracks and to stick the cedar bark to the smooth exterior of the assembled hull.

When Clotaire was ready to fell the trees he made a circuit around the area to make sure no one would be within hearing distance when he cut them down. Then he posted Jeb up river and Magda along the shore. They were to run back and warn him if they heard any suspicious sounds. Clotaire worked quickly with his axe, which he had sharpened on hard stone. He felled each tree with a few short sharp strokes then stopped and listened. He worked only a short time before stopping for the night. He then dragged or carried the trees to a dense part of the forest a short distance from the cave but close to the water's edge. He then covered them with branches so they were invisible.

The next night he did the same and soon he had all he needed for the basic construction of the boat. On the following three nights he then trimmed all the logs using Tulca's adze. He made all of them uniform in thickness and flat on one side. This took a couple of weeks since he had to work very quietly for only a few hours each night, always with lookouts. The nights were getting shorter as they approached midsummer.

When Jeb and Magda were not helping by finding logs and vines and cedar bark, they searched for edible roots including wild onions and turnips, chestnuts and beechnuts, as well as apples and berries. Clotaire told them to remember three things: stay within a couple of hundred feet of the cave, make no noise, and return quickly and silently if they heard any noise. They learned rapidly to move around the forest without stepping on twigs and leaves.

After trimming all the logs, Clotaire then set them aside in the dense thickets where he thought they would get the most wind blowing through. He piled them high and arranged them to allow air circulation so they would dry quickly. He stacked them with rocks between the centers so they would warp and curve slightly as they dried to give shape to the boat. He explained that this type of soft wood would dry faster than oak or other hard woods and was easier to work with. It also would float much better than the hard woods.

"You know, we don't need the boat to last forever," he laughed. "It only has to get across the channel once."

"I hope you're right," Jeb spoke softly. He thought to himself that he wasn't so sure.

CHAPTER NINETEEN

Boatbuilding

North Coast, Francia
Fall, 751 AD

Clotaire said that they needed to let the wood dry for a long time. He explained that he still had many things to build for the boat but now was a good time to stock up on food. They needed lots of it for the months ahead. He pointed out they were slowly running out of dried meat.

"Before I start to hunt," he said, "I need to figure out how to cook the meat without creating visible smoke that can be seen for many miles. That would bring lots of trouble. Any ideas?"

"Why don't you build a stove?" Magda offered. "I mean an oven to cook the meat. Maybe an oven wouldn't have as much smoke as a fire."

Jeb and Clotaire laughed. Magda's feelings were hurt.

Then Clotaire said slowly, "You know, maybe you have a great idea. If I build an oven and put it inside the opening of the cave the smoke will escape slowly and spread out into the forest. If I use the stove only for a short time at night the smoke will all be gone by dawn and there will be no smell left in the trees."

He started work on it the next night. He began by carving pieces of wood that fit together in a curved shape and tied them together on the outside with bands of reeds and vines. He assembled the lid of their oven and tied it together tightly. Then he soaked the entire thing by weighting it down under water for a day and a night. The wood expanded and the binding grew tight.

Meanwhile he built a base of rocks for the inner oven which would hold the planks that held the meat for cooking. He built another outer wall to support the oven lid which would keep the smoke inside except for a few small holes to let it out slowly.

"Most of the smoke," he explained, "will stay inside to cook and smoke the meat. The escaping smoke will go to the roof of the cave and slowly disperse into the outside forest and be absorbed. I think very little smoke, if any, will rise above the trees, and besides, it will be night when we do the cooking. I hope it will work."

When the lid was soaked and tight he assembled the stove. The last piece of the puzzle was a flat thin piece of hard wood he carved carefully with his knife. He also soaked it for several hours.

When it was dusk he spoke to Jeb and Magda. "Go out into the forest and keep an ear open for sounds. I'll call you back in a while."

Just inside the cave entrance he set up the inner set of rocks that formed a square fire box with an opening to feed the fire. He built a fire with a small flame and very little smoke, quickly put the soaked plank on top, put a few green twigs and needles to substitute for meat, and covered the whole thing with the outer lid.

After a few minutes went by, the amount of time he thought it would take to cook the meat, he quickly removed the plank, covered the entire oven with the cloth which was soaked in water, and waited. The smoke stopped. He called Jeb and Magda after several minutes.

"When are you going to start the cooking test?" These were the first words from Jeb.

Clotaire showed them the burned plank and they sniffed.

"I didn't smell anything at first but now I do," Magda spoke up, "just a little."

Now Clotaire knew the oven would be a success. He prepared several planks to hold the meat he hoped to catch during the next night's hunting. Meanwhile he worked on carving the small curved pieces from the yew tree for the inside of the boat. Last of all, he began work on the mast he would install in the bow section of the boat for the sailcloth to fly.

"As long as we have these clear skies and moonlight," Clotaire stated, "let's get as much done as we can." The light filtered through the tree branches and, when overhead, the moon shined brightly on their cave entrance.

The next night, as soon as it was dark, Clotaire went hunting with his bow and arrows and came back with a huge stag. He spent the rest of the night cutting the stag into thin strips of meat with his long knife. Jeb and Magda became adept at putting the pieces on the plank just long enough to cook them. They would take turns as lookouts, listening for noises while the other cooked. As soon as the meat on one soaked plank was cooked, they switched it for another as fast as they could to keep the smoke inside the oven. The meat cooked swiftly. Clotaire cut up about half the stag that night and salted the rest of it. They also salted the cooked meat to preserve it as well.

They tested the air while it was still dark outside. There was no smell several hundred feet from their cave and the rest of the smoke in and around the cave disappeared rapidly. At dawn they had their dinner. It was a splendid feast with lots of meat and edible roots Jeb and Magda had found. They also used the oven to cook a pot of parsnips, wild onions, turnips, and dried peas they had brought with them. They finished up with apples, nuts, and berries they'd collected.

"What a wonderful meal," Magda exclaimed, "we are so lucky."

"I never imagined," Jeb added, "we could eat so well out here in the wilderness."

"And I thought the time would go by so slowly while we built this boat," Magda replied, "but we are so busy inventing things and testing things and cooking food that the time seems to go by quickly."

"What about you, Clotaire?" Jeb asked, "This is an adventure for us but is it wearing you down? Are you tired of all this and wish you were back with the remaining men? Where do you think they are?"

"The ones in the south that survived went into hiding and I'm sure there are many scattered across the land. I admit I would like to search for them but this is an adventure for me too. I have been learning quite a lot about surviving and building, much to my surprise. But remember, my first priority is to get the two of you to a safe place and it has taken much longer than I had hoped. To answer your question though, I am also busy and having fun as well, although I am constantly worried about danger."

A few nights later Clotaire repeated the process by cooking the meat that had already been salted.

"Which do you like better: the meat that was cooked raw and then salted or the meat that was salted and then cooked a few nights later?"

"I liked the meat cooked raw and then salted," Jeb decided.

"I liked the second," Magda said, "but I think I would prefer the meat just cooked raw without salt."

Clotaire tried to explain that the salt was needed to help dry and preserve the meat and that she needed salt as well but she would not be swayed in her opinion. Now that they had a good supply of meat and a proven method of cooking, they turned their attention back to the building of the boat. Summer was almost over and the nights were getting longer so they could make better progress.

Clotaire tested one of the logs by lifting it and then by trying to float it but it did not float that well.

"It needs much more time to finish drying," he said, "but I will start laying out the boat anyway."

As the weeks went by Jeb and Magda had grown accustomed to being alone. They still did not use an open fire but they did take their swim at least once a week. They both looked forward to it since the water was now quite warm in comparison to the cold runoff in the spring and early summer. They stayed close to shore on the river's edge or sometimes ventured out into the calm waters along the inlet. They were very good about not making noise.

On one occasion they had a huge scare. It was just dark and they were playing when they saw a boat in the distance crossing the mouth of the inlet. They froze like deer. They did not want to make any move to attract attention. As they watched, the boat paused as if to enter the inlet then continued on its way. They quickly climbed out of the water and dressed and ran to Clotaire.

When they told him what they had seen he looked very serious and took them back to the cave and made sure there were no signs of life in the area. He checked to see that the boat sections were covered very well and brought Jeb and Magda inside.

He told them to stay there while he checked to see if any people had come ashore. He returned after an hour and said he thought whoever was in the boat had continued on. He decided to forego any work on the boat that night. He stayed in the cave and listened all night long for any sound. They had a quiet meal before dawn and slept lightly during the day.

The next night Clotaire continued on the design of the boat but Jeb could tell he was distracted and disturbed by the incident. They all realized that, at any time, a group of armed men could stumble upon them by accident and they needed to stay on guard constantly. For the next few nights he sent them both out as sentries while he worked on the boat, but he cut back on the time he worked to lessen the noise.

Clotaire designed the boat first by drawing it on the ground. He showed Jeb and Magda how he would construct it. The logs with the greatest curves would form the sides, tapering in and up to form a high pointed bow. The straighter logs would form the bottom along with several shorter, slightly curved ones along the side. There would be special logs forming the keel in the middle.

Clotaire wanted to have a squared off stern with a rudder aft. The inside of the shell would be supported by the yew rods spanning the width of the boat. The reeds and vines would tighten the outside. After completing the construction they would put the boat in the water to expand the wood again. Finally, he would cover the outside of the boat with pitch and then cover it completely with bark.

"Well, I hope it works," he said. "Let's give it a try."

With Jeb and Magda watching and sometimes fetching tools, Clotaire laid out the bottom logs first and tied them together with the vines. He supported the ends on temporary cross pieces so the keel could take shape as he fitted the logs together. The outside of each log was the flat side while the inside still had a rounded surface. The bottom of the boat curved outward and then inward to form a surface that would slice easily through the water. He assembled the stern section before he added the sides. He often stopped to taper the front sections to fit together snugly, forming the high bow.

Clotaire only worked a short time each night to minimize being heard. He sent his two sentries out to listen. When he had a full moon he took a chance, worked longer hours and when the new moon came he ceased altogether for a couple of days. With only one man working on the boat the process took an inordinately long time. Sometimes he would have to call Jeb in to help lift a log and hold it in place while he tied it in or fixed a temporary support.

The nights were getting longer but they were also getting colder. He had to take breaks when food was getting short so he could hunt for enough game to last a few days or a week. When he had a successful hunt, they would assemble their oven to cook the meat. This process of working, then hunting, then working again, went on into late fall. Finally the boat structure was in place.

"We are lucky again," said Magda, "that we have heard no men or boats passing or dangerous animals." She felt perhaps she had spoken too soon when, that night, a large brown bear lumbered into the area where Clotaire was working. Magda warned him of its approach and he chased it with his spear.

As the boat grew in size, hiding it each night became a greater problem since it sat near the water. They gradually built up a surrounding wall of sticks and branches and vines and any material they could use to make it look as if a heavily overgrown thicket was there. They took no chances on anyone accidentally coming by.

The nights grew much colder and finally they received what they feared most: a huge snowstorm. As it grew colder, they switched to wearing warm clothing and their boots. Clotaire had been worried about the children staying warm enough during the winter and had saved all the deerskins to make warm sacks for sleeping. He stopped work for a few days while he completed them. Each of them had a thick dry bed of leaves, a deerskin mat, their sleeping sack, and their fur covering them. Magda thought it was nice and snug and warm and slept very well.

Clotaire told them, at this rate, it would take until spring to complete the boat and make it waterproof. The water in the river and inlet grew much colder, and when Jeb and Magda found time for bathing, they did not stay in very long. But they still went swimming at least once a week. Before they went in they had the oven going so they could warm up after their swim. To Magda this was her happiest moment. She braved the cold water no matter what the temperature.

As fall turned into winter they found themselves running short of salt so Clotaire developed a method of evaporating the water from the inlet using the oven. This was essential since they needed the salt to preserve the meat. Clotaire had completed the entire structure, including the supports to hold the mast, and was starting the process of adding the "skin" to the outside of the boat when two major milestones occurred. Jeb turned twelve and Magda eleven before the end of the year.

Jeb announced that since he was now twelve years old, he was a Merovingian King.

"And what is your wish, Your Majesty?" Magda gave a sweeping bow. "Perhaps His Majesty would like a special treat tonight," she said, thinking of the wild boar Clotaire had shot earlier while hunting in the thick woods.

They stopped work for one night and celebrated with a special meal. Clotaire celebrated their turning eleven and twelve by preparing a wonderful dinner including both pork and venison. Magda announced she preferred the pork to the deer meat. Jeb agreed.

"Not only am I now a King," announced Jeb, "but I am now a man as well."

"Well," Clotaire responded, "you certainly are getting taller and stronger."

"And I'm now a woman." Magda's narrowed eyes showed she would not let Jeb outdo her.

"You have grown quite a bit too since we left Rhédae," Clotaire declared diplomatically. "Perhaps you're both right. This deserves a toast."

Clotaire heated some cider he had made from apples and special spices from barks he'd found in the forest. He had also taken a break from carving on the boat and had carved three cups from soft wood. He drank a toast to them upon reaching these milestones and their coming of age. Then he continued.

"Since you are both growing I need to find time to make new shoes and boots for both of you and even some clothes. I can tell you are outgrowing them." They agreed and thanked him. Shortly after that the year ended and they celebrated the New Year with yet another special meal. Clotaire had shot a pheasant and this delicate game was a pleasant surprise and a treat. They were feeling good about their progress on the boat and the prospects ahead.

And then the blizzard struck.

CHAPTER TWENTY

Tracks in the Snow

North Shore, Francia
Winter, 752 AD

The blizzard lasted several days and the snow piled up in huge drifts. Jeb was glad they had stored enough dried meat to last for a couple of weeks. Clotaire told them that this snowstorm would slow the completion of the boat but that was not the biggest problem now. They could not venture very far because they would leave tracks. If a party of men passed near them and discovered their tracks and decided to investigate, they would have no chance. They had to stay hidden for the time being. They stayed in or close to the cave for several days and nights. Clotaire used this time to carve seats and oars and oarlocks out of hard oak wood. And then he began work on the rudder which he would install last.

They stayed on the routine they had established: doing what work they could manage at night and sleeping during the day. This suited Clotaire since he had more time now to work. The nights were much longer and things were progressing rapidly. Then one day while they were sleeping, Clotaire was awakened by a noise. He listened, woke Jeb and Magda, and told them to listen as well. They heard male voices not very far away from their cave. Clotaire dressed quickly and stood silently, holding his axe with one hand and his bow and arrow in the other, ready to fight.

They listened to the men coming closer. Suddenly the men stopped moving and started to laugh. Then their chattering resumed and they moved on. Jeb started to relax but his relief was short-lived. He heard the voices of two men coming even closer than before. They were approaching the location of their cave and then they stopped moving. There was silence for a moment. Clotaire, Jeb, and Magda were frozen.

Finally, the two men began to talk again and move away. Then they heard them moving swiftly away to catch up to the others. The group seemed to be coming from upriver, following what appeared to be a trail that was some distance from the shore. The voices disappeared in the distance as if they were heading along the coastline going south.

Clotaire followed them, telling Jeb and Magda to wait until he returned. He came back smiling. "We are in luck," he said. "We can use their tracks to move around a bit. That is, until it snows again. The tracks of the two men came very close to us. For some reason the two of them decided to leave the trail to relieve themselves, perhaps out of habit. I connected easily to their tracks through the heavy thickets next to them. If someone else comes along they will notice just what I noticed and follow the heavy tracks. And now I am going back to work tonight."

"What are you going to do?" inquired Magda.

"Try to finish covering the boat before it snows again."

"Can we help?" Jeb asked eagerly.

"You certainly can! We need to heat the hardened pitch I collected just a bit to soften it and apply the bark."

Over the next week Magda would start a small fire and soften the pitch so Clotaire could coat the smooth sides of the logs, especially in between them to provide a sealed exterior. All three of them worked rapidly and covered the pitch with the sheets of bark that Jeb had collected. Clotaire made rapid progress and had almost completed the siding when Clotaire announced that he would stop for a few days. He said he thought it would snow soon and he needed to hunt again. He was gone all night and came back carrying a buck.

"I used the trail the men made," he explained, "so as not to leave new tracks, and when I saw deer tracks crossing the trail I knew I had found a path the deer used regularly. I waited for several hours and sure enough the stag came by. I killed it with one arrow and covered the area where it fell with snow and carried it back. I didn't want to drag it and leave evidence."

"I think I made the right decision to stop work and hunt," Clotaire spoke as he cut up the stag. "We can't risk being caught in a fresh snowstorm with little food since hunting will be almost impossible without creating a huge danger for us. I hope I'm right about the snow now. It will cover all the tracks."

His wisdom was rewarded the next day. While the snow came down for two more days and covered all the tracks from the passing group and the hunt, they followed their normal routine of cutting up the deer, preparing the oven, and then cooking and salting the meat. Those days of snow were well spent.

"I know the snow makes it difficult to move around and hunt," Magda said, "but it is so beautiful with all the trees and bushes covered in white. It is so quiet now in the forest you can hear the woodpeckers during the day and the owls at night. I love it when it snows." There was no reply. Clotaire just nodded agreement.

After the skies cleared and the cooking was complete, Clotaire continued with his work of carving the rudder. Then he began work on the mast. The weather warmed a bit and he put the finishing touches on the skin of the boat. All that was left, he said, after he finished the mast, was to install the seats and oarlocks and to test the boat before he put the mast in.

While he continued work for several days, Jeb and Magda were allowed to play quietly in the woods. They helped occasionally when Clotaire needed some lifting or to hold some part of the boat but generally they amused themselves nearby. Once in a while he would ask their opinion about some aspect of the boat just to keep them involved. With all their free time Jeb and Magda had a plan to build a fort near the cave but they felt they should check with Clotaire. He thought it was an excellent idea and suggested a safe place in the brush to build it.

The days and nights grew warmer over the next couple of weeks and the snow gradually disappeared. They began work on their fort during the warm nights. Clotaire continued working on the boat, putting the finishing touches on it, while Jeb and Magda continued with their plans.

"And how is your fort coming along?" Clotaire asked one day. "I've been so busy I've haven't had a chance to look at it. And I must say I haven't heard any noise from you while you work."

They led him through the brush and proudly showed him their "fort". They had collected logs of different lengths and thicknesses, with thicker ones at the bottom and longer ones forming the front and back. They had stacked them six feet high on all four sides, and created an entrance four feet high and three wide.

"How do you keep all the logs together?" Clotaire had a quizzical look on his face. "It looks quite solid. I'm surprised." Jeb and Magda looked at each other and then Magda explained.

"We used the mortise and tenon technique you told us about."

"So that's why I've seen you working in the cave now and then so you won't make noise. You do this just using your axes?" Clotaire asked.

"Yes, plus our knives. And we have the roof almost done as well," Jeb answered.

Magda added, "It will slope a little and we are using the same technique to build it."

"And we are covering it with pitch and bark just like you did for the boat," Jeb continued.

"You two are amazing. There is no end to your surprises. And of course you must keep it covered so no one can discover it."

"Oh yes, of course." Jeb replied. Magda thought Clotaire was impressed and she felt he was proud of them.

The end of winter was fast approaching and Clotaire was ready for a test. At dusk on a moonlit night they dragged the boat to the water. He fitted the oars to the oarlocks and rowed out a short way into the inlet. He stopped, shipped the oars, and lay down in the hold out of sight. The boat floated! He soon returned silently and beached it. Then they hauled it into hiding and covered it completely with branches in the same artful way they had learned over time. Clotaire did not utter a word until they returned to the cave.

"Well?" inquired Jeb finally. "How is it? You haven't said a word."

"It's pretty shipshape. I just need to patch a few places. I think it will hold up pretty well for the crossing. But I was just thinking."

"What about?" asked Magda.

"I need to build a storage area. We need one that is watertight to hold meat and other things to keep them dry. I was just trying to figure how to do that and place the rudder aft."

"Did you figure it out? Perhaps the rudder would be safer anyway if it were under the stern and not sticking out behind," Jeb offered.

Clotaire smiled. "That's just what I was thinking. The rudder will go down and backwards to allow a wide arc for steering. It will sit just under the storage area."

Clotaire worked for three straight nights to install the storage area, and then Jeb and Magda helped him to raise the boat on blocks so he could install the rudder.

"It fits perfectly." Clotaire smiled. "What a great idea we both had!"

"What if we hit really rough weather crossing the sea?" commented Magda. "Is the boat going to leak?"

"It's not quite finished yet," explained Clotaire. "I need to make it all watertight."

"How do you do that?" asked Jeb.

"The final step to completing the boat," replied Clotaire, "is to seal the storage area with pitch and to create a tight fitting hatch on top of it."

This took him only one more night of work and then he announced the boat was ready.

"Pretty soon you won't need to worry about being discovered, or bothered by any bad weather. All I need to do now is to hunt for deer and maybe a wild boar or two to stock up on enough food for the first couple of weeks. Jeb, now is a good time for you to learn more about hunting," Clotaire offered. "Will you join me?"

Jeb was delighted to learn.

"I don't like to kill things but I'll get the oven ready." Magda said, with pride and joy. "After all, it's my idea."

The next night Jeb and Clotaire set off as soon as it was dark. Three hours later they returned. Jeb was ecstatic. He'd shot his first deer. They had hidden beside the trail downwind and when the first buck ambled into sight Jeb had stood up and shot quickly with deadly accuracy.

"Well done," Clotaire had congratulated him.

As Clotaire started to pick up the deer he heard a rustle in the bushes. When a wild boar appeared Clotaire shot him with one arrow. Jeb carried the boar back and Clotaire the deer.

"Let me show you how to carve up a carcass," Clotaire said and Jeb followed his moves. Together they cut up the two animals and Jeb found it to be lots of fun developing this new skill. For three nights they ate like kings and smoked the meat carefully as always without leaving traces of smoke.

Clotaire showed Magda and Jeb how to find aromatic leaves with which to wrap the salted meat. Then he announced they were ready for a test sail. They would all go out to sea the next night.

It was very dark with just a little bit of moonlight. They dragged the boat to the water's edge in the dim light. Clotaire inserted the rudder in the hole with a tight ring of springy vines to allow it to move from side to side and sealed it off with pitch. He installed the mast in the support structure with six vines that were tied down tightly to the top edge of the boat. They would hold the mast no matter how much the boat bobbed and swayed or how strong the wind became. At least he hoped they would be strong enough.

He then rigged the sail on the mast with holes where he would install the sheets. Then he produced his first surprise. He had found a plant that appeared to be a type of cannabis from which he made hemp. He had used a length of it to create the sheets which allowed for jibing and tacking of the boat. He attached them to the clew of the sail. The oarlocks doubled as cleats.

All three of them climbed in and pushed off. When they were far enough out, he gave them a sailing lesson. Jeb saw how very proud Clotaire was of his handiwork in designing and building the boat. He taught Jeb how to handle the rudder and the sail. The wind was slight and Clotaire did not want to stay out in the open very long anyway so they soon returned to shore. He announced that Jeb only needed a few more lessons before he'd be a good sailor.

Jeb began to be suspicious. *Why am I suddenly learning how to hunt and how to sail?* Then Clotaire made his big announcement.

"The boat is ready and you are ready. Now I can safely return and leave you on your own. I'd love to go with you but I must look for any survivors of our people. I will tell you where to go and how to travel. You'll be all right, I am now confident."

Jeb and Magda were stunned. They'd had no idea Clotaire would leave them and send them off alone. They both were silent as they ate another wonderful meal of wild boar to celebrate completion of the boat. Then Clotaire explained his plan for them.

After they'd had another couple of sailing lessons and another night of hunting, they would prepare for the journey which he believed would take several weeks. They would smoke enough meat to fill the storage area along with their gear and tools and would set sail when the moon was new and the wind was sufficient. It was spring and he expected good breezes.

"I want you to hug the coast north until you reach Cap Gris-Nez," he said.

"Why Cap Gris-Nez?" asked Magda.

"You'll find a small inlet to hide in during the day. You need to remove the mast, pull the boat ashore, and cover it with branches and vines during the day," Clotaire added.

"I think I understand all that," responded Jeb.

"The next night after that," Clotaire continued, "The two of you will rig the boat again and set sail across the channel. You should sail almost dead west until you reach a point of land projecting out into the sea. You then go west along the coast to a bay where a river flows into it. It will be dark and you'll have to use the stars to navigate."

Clotaire went on to say he'd give them his last lessons in navigation and show them how to find the Big Bear and the Little Bear and the North Star, and point out the other constellations and how to navigate using these stars.

"That will be part of your lessons. You'll be a great sailor one day. I'll tell you about the rest of your journey over the next couple of nights. Now you must get some sleep."

CHAPTER TWENTY ONE

Across to Ichnusa

Site Punique
Late Spring, 36 AD

As dusk approached, Sarah and her seven companions launched their boat provisioned with water, goat meat, bread, honey, milk, grapes, dates, and figs. They set sail north of Site Punique. Joseph thought it would take them all night to cross the treacherous sea to Ichnusa and beyond. Sarah heard the sound of a bird calling in the sky off shore: "*kew-kew-kew-kew*".

"What is that bird? I hear him but can't see him."

"That is the alarm call of an osprey, Sarah," Lazarus answered. "Something may be too near its nest."

They sailed across the open water for a while, and as they cleared the tip of land north of them, Sarah again wanted to know where they were.

"Are we leaving land for good?" she asked Lazarus.

"That is the extreme north end of the country, Sarah," he replied. "It is called Hippo Diarrhytus. We are now sailing away from this land toward an island in the middle of the sea. That island is called Ichnusa."

Sarah heard another bird call. It sounded a bit like a gull and she asked again what the sound was.

"It is a black kite I think," replied Joseph. "There are many of them near shore but we won't hear them after we sail into the open sea."

The wind increased as they sailed straight north. The waves grew larger until the bow of their boat dipped down and rose up many feet. Lazarus struggled to keep the bow headed into the waves but the wind played tricks on them and tried to push them off course. Sarah and the four women huddled down under the tent covering while Lazarus, Joseph, and Joshua strived to stay on course. The waves towered above them and the wind created a mist that settled over the boat. They began to take on water and used tin pots to scoop it out as best they could, except for Lazarus, who stood his ground against the roaring wind. He ignored his cloak and tunic, whipping back and forth, sometimes even around his head. Joseph sometimes took a turn at directing the sail to keep the boat headed into the wind and waves but mainly directed the others when to bail the water. Joshua often helped Lazarus fight the huge waves rolling toward them.

Sarah huddled in the bottom of the boat under the tent covering and listened to the strong howling wind. The wind stirred the sea into a roiling tempest with huge waves rolling under them. She peeked out and saw a gigantic wave towering over the boat. She held her breath as the bow rose up and cleared the top. She prayed it would not break over the side and swamp them. She knew if it did, the boat would become filled with water and they would capsize and sink. Everyone, including Sarah, helped bail desperately. Lazarus struggled to hold course heading into the wind and waves. At one point, though, he was forced to come about with the sail and race ahead of the waves to prevent being swamped, but the boat still took on water and was perilously close to sinking.

Suddenly Joshua stood up in the stern and yelled in a loud voice. He uttered a strange word that sounded to Sarah something like "solnuyeh". It seemed to her that Joshua was calling to the waves themselves. His voice was loud and forceful and sounded much different to Sarah. As quickly as it had roared and howled, the wind slackened and the waves dropped from a huge height to rolling waves of a few feet. To Sarah it was amazing and miraculous that Joshua could calm the seas. He had saved their lives.

They all continued to bail out the water until it was nearly gone. Lazarus turned back on course and continued through the night. Daylight found the seas almost calm. Joshua said nothing more and continued helping Lazarus and Joseph with the sail to keep them on a northerly course. Sarah once looked at her mother who appeared serene and calm and not at all worried, as if she expected what had happened. They continued on for several more hours after dawn. Sarah saw a few gulls flying overhead and crying out. With her excellent eyes she was the first to spot land and Lazarus steered them toward an island to the west of the main island of Ichnusa.

They went past the first island on its west or sea side and continued to the west side of a second, smaller island. Lazarus pulled slowly into a small cove that appeared to be deserted. They all sat in the boat silently listening for the slightest noise.

"Look," Sarah pointed. "Isn't that a little red fox foraging along the beach?"

Lazarus replied, "Yes, indeed it is. What good eyes you have, Sarah."

They beached the boat and hid it in the brush. Joseph did not want to set up tents or build a fire before dusk which might attract attention but he did make sure they all ate some meat and dates since it had been a night and day since they had eaten. Sarah drank a lot of milk that they had stowed in the bow for her. It was late in the day and daylight was fading.

"Mama," Sarah asked her mother, "can we bathe in the water? It feels warm."

"We can if we are very careful," replied her mother, "but we must avoid the purple jellyfish. They will not kill us but they can sting us and cause painful sores."

Sarah and her mother went in very slowly and were joined this time by Martha who said she looked forward to the water since it had been a long time since she had a chance to bathe. Sarah saw a jellyfish nearby but avoided getting stung. She looked at the shoreline and noticed the oak trees and eucalyptus and a few acacia. The pines and the other trees created a lovely fragrance in the warm evening. Sarah washed her hair in the salty sea and even rinsed out her dusty clothes, except for her cloak which she covered herself with when she slept. Dusk turned to night and Sarah curled up on her rug and fell fast asleep with the sounds of the cicadas singing in the nearby trees. She woke in the middle of the night with the sound of the rain pelting her tent. She poked her head out and smelled the rosemary and fennel and lupin and blackberry blossoms.

Joseph and Lazarus and Joshua decided to spend the day hunting for wild boar to resupply them for the rest of the journey. They came back late in the day with four small boar they had caught with spears. As dusk was descending upon them, Joseph chanced a small fire to dry the meat. He used a flint and some fine dry wood and got the fire going. They cooked and dried the meat and stowed it in the stern of the boat. Darkness came quickly and they packed up and sailed slowly up the coast.

"I want to travel only at night," Joseph announced, "to avoid any Roman soldiers. I plan to stop one more time about halfway up the coast on a small island. It is some distance off of the main island, and I think it will be uninhabited. We will pass by the ancient city of Tharros, located on the southern shore of a huge peninsula which juts out into the sea."

"How ancient is the city?" Martha asked.

"It was founded by the Phoenicians over 800 years ago, then occupied by the Punics, and now by the Romans. Ptolemy mentions it as one of the most important places on Ichnusa and it has many structures including temples." Joseph paused. "It would be interesting to visit but we must steer clear of it now."

They sailed to the west of the city, and just before dawn, silently to the west side of the small island. He was correct in that it was not only uninhabited but also some distance from the main island. They set up tents just off shore in a dense stand of pine trees with honeysuckle vines draping the branches and acacia trees oozing sap which attracted black beetles and biting midges. Sarah stayed in her tent until strong sea breezes and cool rain cleared the air. Her mother coaxed her out to rinse off in the seawater. The water was shallow with ripples formed by strong currents, and the sea grass banks formed dark indigo patches in the shallow water, mottling the turquoise sand on the seafloor. A sudden thunderstorm drenched them with rain which delighted Sarah as she frolicked in the water. She dried off, ate meat and figs and flat bread, some grapes and blackberries, and drank lots of water, then curled up under her cloak and fell fast asleep.

She woke to the sounds of her family packing up, getting ready to take to the water as night fell. She helped by rolling up her sleeping rug and stowing it in the bow. They sailed quietly along the shore in the darkness with the sound of the water lapping on the sand and cicadas singing. Sarah thought it sounded like two combs rubbing together. She heard a crow caw and an owl hoot in the stillness of the night. They followed the undulations of the coastline, small coves, and inlets until they encountered a land mass projecting out into the sea. Joseph maneuvered to the west and around the peninsula and resumed his northern direction.

They made good time in the still night and, as dawn approached, they sailed along a peninsula jutting north across a small gap and to the west of an island running north and south. With early daylight Joseph could see the sea ahead of him and decided to find a secluded area along the shore. They hid their boat in thick bushes off the beach and set up tents inland in stands of oak and pine trees. Joshua brought Sarah boar meat and the beautiful goblet filled with milk and dates and figs, as well as a pomegranate and some grapes. She thanked him, and while she was eating, listened to the songs of the birds.

"What kind of birds are making that noise, Mama?"

"Those are crows cawing and jays squawking. You can hear the cries of hawks circling above, and even the chirping of little yellow birds. I don't know their names but they are lovely."

CHAPTER TWENTY TWO

Reaching Iles d'Hyeres

North Ichnusa
Late Spring, 36 AD

Sarah enjoyed the warm day listening to the birds and looking out over the gentle sea to the north. When daylight was waning, Joseph decided to head across the water to the island of Corsica. They sailed into warm breezes and low three foot waves and covered the short distance in a couple of hours. Joseph continued along the western coast of Corsica until dawn approached. He drifted past a deep bay in the twilight and then pulled into a second deep bay, landing along a shoreline covered with pine and fir and alder growing down to the water's edge. Tall cedar trees towered above. He did not want to risk being discovered in the daylight and hid the boat in thickets of nettle trees and honeysuckle bushes. They set up their tents in thick juniper stands and listened for sounds. They heard only gulls crying out as they circled above. Sarah looked up at the cliffs.

"The pink rocks are beautiful in the sunlight," she said to no one in particular.

She was allowed to bathe in the clear water and saw green lizards along the shore and a tiny brown frog she named Hoppy. On the edge of the thick forest she saw clouds of yellow butterflies with black and white spots. She saw colorful tropical fish under the water and again saw purple jellyfish and kept her distance. Her mother called quietly for her to come eat some meat, and drink. She stepped over dried sea grass that looked like ivory colored shredded papyrus. She was sitting in the sun when suddenly it became dark and clouds covered the sky. There was a sudden downpour and the wind grew stronger. Sarah crawled into her tent to stay dry and listened to the wind in the treetops. Darkness came early and the storm continued most of the night. Joseph decided to stay there rather than risk a storm at sea.

In the middle of the night Sarah's mother put her finger to her lips to tell Sarah to be absolutely silent. At first she heard nothing but soon heard the murmur of voices approaching. She peeked out and saw a group of men walking along the beach, talking and yelling. She realized they were soldiers and appeared to be searching for wood. Some carried axes and a few carried lances. Sarah held her breath and her heart beat faster. The soldiers did not notice the tents in the brush and carried on along the beach in the moonlight. She released her breath in a sigh of relief.

As soon as they were gone, Joseph spoke up.

"It is not safe to stay here. Quickly pack up."

They launched the boat and stayed far from shore so as not to be seen. They sailed past a large peninsula and then across the mouth of a deep bay. As the sun rose they could see daunting cliffs ahead. Joseph hugged the coast.

"It will be better close to shore so we cannot be seen from above on the high cliffs."

"Look! A cave." Sarah pointed.

Joseph sailed into the entrance of the cave, approaching slowly and silently until he was sure it was empty. Then Lazarus and Joseph beached the boat in the mouth of the cave and they walked thirty feet into it where the floor rose to a shelf. It was dry there so they pitched their tents on the high ground and stayed for the rest of the day. As night approached so did the rain. It came down in sheets.

"We can build a small fire at the entrance," Joseph stated. "We are so isolated it should be safe."

The three men climbed the hills above the cliffs and went into the forest to hunt. They returned with several rabbits and two small boar which they cooked and dried to eat during the remainder of their journey. The rain let up early in the night but Joseph decided to stay one more day since they were safe and dry where they were.

At the start of the second night they launched their boat, now filled with meat and water, and sailed swiftly to the northeast along the coast past another small bay. Joseph wanted to reach a long peninsula before daybreak. They saw fires on shore and what appeared to be large groups of men. He finally reached a thickly wooded area at the end of the island and pulled in before the sun came up. They remained hidden in the woods during the day. The biting insects began to bother Sarah and she stayed in her tent until nightfall. After eating as much meat and figs and honey and flatbread as they could, the group set sail and headed into the dark deep sea.

"How far do we have to go?" Sarah asked in the stillness of the night. The waves were low and the wind calm. The only sounds were the lapping of the waves against the side of the boat and a seagull crying overhead.

"It's about one hundred miles," Lazarus responded. "If all goes well it should take us all night and part of tomorrow before we reach the islands ahead, Les Iles d'Hyeres."

Sarah curled up under the tent covering and fell asleep. She awoke in the middle of the night with strong winds blowing and the waves beginning to increase in size. The rain began with a light drizzle but gradually increased to a steady downpour. Sarah helped bail the water out as the boat rocked from side to side in the waves which hit them at an angle. Lazarus struggled to keep the boat headed into the wind and slightly to port to keep on course toward the islands. They had some luck when the rain stopped, but the wind kept blowing strongly, the waves reaching ten to fifteen feet and slowing them down. Joseph took turns with Lazarus and Joshua holding the sail to keep the heading, but they were slowly pushed off course.

Joseph decided to turn directly into the waves. The boat rose up and crested before the wave broke, but this could be treacherous. If they could not crest the next wave, they would fall back and flounder and possibly sink.

"I think we should stick to the course we agreed on," Joshua suggested, "sailing to port at an angle."

This worked, and finally the wind dropped and the waves slowly decreased. Lazarus calculated how much he thought they had been blown off course and they decided to make adjustments when daylight arrived. They began to relax as they were able to keep to their heading, generally toward the islands. Sarah looked out of the tent cover and noticed the dawn was coming.

Then Sarah looked off the side of the boat and caught her breath. A gigantic twenty foot shark rose up out of the deep and settled alongside the boat. It was as long as the boat and twice as wide. Its cold lifeless black eye looked directly into Sarah's.

"Mama," she whispered, "what is that? It's monstrous and it's looking at me!"

"It is a Great White shark," said Joshua in a very soft voice. "It is just looking us over now but let us hope it is not hungry. It comes in to this area to reproduce and will probably leave us alone, but there is nothing much we can do if it attacks us."

The giant opened its mouth slightly and showed its large sharp teeth and Sarah held her breath again. It circled the boat and moved away briefly, then came back and nudged the boat. It was not a heavy hit but still Sarah heard a crack. Then the shark seemed to lose interest and disappeared. Sarah breathed a sigh of relief until she heard Lazarus yelling, "We have a leak!"

In the morning light Sarah could see land ahead and pointed it out to Joseph.

"Everyone. Keep bailing," Joseph said, "And Lazarus, head for shore before we sink."

They slowly took on water and, in spite of the frantic bailing, they were gradually sinking. They barely managed to reach the shallows of a small island, about four miles long and two miles wide. They landed on the extreme west end, almost missing it entirely, jumped out, removed the food and tents as quickly as they could, and dried out everything. During the day they moved off the beach into low lying bush. The men spent the day trying to find the right size tree to replace the cracked log and finally found what they were looking for. They trimmed the log and notched the tenon to match the one they were replacing. They had to dissemble part of the hull to replace it but finally completed the repair and filled the cracks with grass and reeds and mud.

Joseph decided to stay another night and day before completing the trip to the mainland. He and Lazarus did some calculations, and based on the size of the island they landed on, determined they were at the extreme west end of the string of islands in the Iles d'Hyeres.

"Perhaps we are very lucky after all," Lazarus said, "since we know we want to go to the west when we reach the mainland. We must be very close to the peninsula that juts way out into the sea."

When night came, they launched their boat with the new log in place and silently sailed almost directly north. Sarah was the first to spot land. They shifted to a north by northwest tack and reached the tip of the peninsula, sailing slowly to the west side and continuing on directly west across the open sea. The water was calm with a slight wind to starboard and they made good time. They approached a landmass just before dawn. Joseph sailed around it to an island west of the mainland and slowly drifted to the west side, landing on a sandy beach in the dark. They listened as usual for sounds and heard only the breeze in the treetops and a small owl hooting. They hid the boat in low rosemary and wild jasmine bushes off the beach and set up tents. Joseph decided not to build a fire; they would take no chances on discovery in the daylight. They ate cold meat and dates and flatbread with honey.

"We are getting short on meat and water," Lazarus noted. "We must do some hunting or fishing soon." From others that had travelled here before, he had heard about a small river along the coast not far from where they were. "We will head toward it and fish as we go."

They set sail at dark, drifting slowly and fishing at the same time. They caught a large number of fish with shimmering silver skin and tender white flesh and also some reddish fish. When they found the small river and sailed part way into it, they hid the boat and tents in brush alongside the river bank and started a small fire before dawn hoping it would not be seen or smelled. They cooked all the fish, ate some, and dried the rest. They found both kinds of fish to be delicious with a rich succulent meaty flavor.

"We will sleep for a few hours," Joseph said, "but we will get an early start and try to reach a protected island I know about some distance away."

They sailed out away from land for the rest of the day and into the night with a brisk wind behind them and low four foot rolling waves and made good time. In the dim light of early dawn, Sarah was the first to spy a group of islands in the distance. They sailed slowly on the portside of the islands until they cleared them. Then they sailed directly north until they reached a long narrow island well off the coast. As the sun began to rise, Joseph approached carefully on the west side and they saw no signs of human activity. They drifted slowly in and beached the boat. The men checked out the surrounding area and found no signs of habitation. To be safe they hid the boat again in thickets of snowberry, honeysuckle, and rosemary and set tents up in a secluded pine grove. They ate some of the dried fish, dried boar meat, bread, and dates. Sarah slept fitfully at first. She wondered where they were and where they would go next. She vowed to ask her mother and Joseph as soon as she could. Finally, she fell fast asleep and slept soundly the rest of the night.

CHAPTER TWENTY THREE

Marya

Southern New England
Summer, 1949

Jes turned twelve that winter. It was now summer and a very warm one at that. Now twelve and a half, he was growing stronger and taller. He was beginning to have a light brown beard that matched his brown hair and he felt more grown up. He also somehow felt much wiser. He couldn't really explain it but he seemed to be more aware and to notice more things. He'd not seen the black bearded man that tried to grab him since the day Grandfather ran to save him but ever since he'd turned twelve he had the odd feeling the stranger was secretly watching him again. It was perhaps only a couple of times he'd had that feeling but that was enough to keep Jes on the alert. He never really felt safe in the field so he stayed up near the corn house or played out in the apple orchard. He felt the most nervous when he went to collect the chicken eggs. He was so convinced he was being watched he contrived ways to try to catch a glimpse of the stranger but so far he'd been unsuccessful.

Jes turned his thoughts to one of the more exciting events of the past year. Marya and her mother had moved into a little house at the end of the dirt road. Jes had met her when he was younger, living in the city. She was only seven at the time and visited her grandparents a few houses up from where Jes lived. Her grandparents' house was much bigger than his and she had lots of toys. Jes went there often to play.

They were both delighted when she became a neighbor. She was now eleven and a half years old. She had light reddish brown hair and hazel eyes that seemed to look deeply into his. The house Marya lived in with her mother was very secluded and surrounded by lots of trees. It was a nice house and Jes went there sometimes, but Marya was lonely living at the end of the road and much preferred to visit Jes and his family. They had the old barn and out buildings with lots of land and an orchard with many fruit trees. It was a very exciting place to play since there were so many places to hide. Marya and Jes found a secret place in the old barn. There they would talk and play.

Marya became part of the family. She was there often, had dinner with them now and then, and stayed overnight as well. Marya spent most of her free time, especially in summer, playing with Jes and the other children in the neighborhood when they were at Jes's. These were wonderful times and they became close friends.

Then Marya's mother became very ill. When she had to go to the hospital she asked Jes's father and mother if Marya could stay with them until she was well enough to return home. His parents said of course. Jes was delighted when this happened. He felt he now had the sister he always wanted. Since there was a spare bedroom upstairs, Marya had her own room.

Jes would sometimes go to the hospital with his mother and Marya. Then one day his father took him aside and said he had very terrible and sad news. Jes couldn't understand what could be so sad.

"Jes," his father said, "Marya's mother is not going to leave the hospital. She has passed away from the disease. Marya will live with us from now on. Please help us look after her."

Marya stayed in her room and cried almost continuously for two days and nights. Jes wanted so much to help her but didn't know how. One day before he went to bed she came into his room and sat next to him. He could see she was trying to fight back the tears. He didn't know what to do so he put his arm around her. She clung to him and began sobbing. He held her until she stopped. Finally she went back to bed and fell asleep.

The next day she began to eat again. She was ravenous. But the death of her mother seemed to change her. It was as if she grew up overnight. She still laughed and played with Jes and they continued to have fun together and share secrets with each other but there seemed a stronger, deeper bond between them. It was as if he was all she had left.

Then one day the thing Jes feared the most happened: he saw the stranger again. Jes had come out of their secret hiding place in the old barn followed closely by Marya. He saw the black bearded face with a black hat peer out from behind the maple tree. He was looking toward the house away from Jes and the barn.

"Look out, Marya!" Jes quickly ducked back into the barn pushing her ahead of him into their hiding place. He was pretty sure the stranger had not seen them. Jes held his finger to his lips to be quiet.

"What is it?" Marya asked anxiously.

"It's him again. The one I told you about," Jes explained softly. "I had a feeling about being watched. Now I'm sure I have been."

"What are we going to do?"

"Nothing. Just hope he goes away. He mustn't see us."

After several minutes Jes ventured out and told Marya to wait. He came back quickly and motioned her to come.

"No sign of him. He's gone. Let's get to the house quickly."

They ran to the house and Jes held Marya's hand to make sure she kept up with him. They entered the safety of the house and, with a mutual understanding, decided not to mention the incident. They both realized it might make his parents worry about them. Jes knew his parents had enough to deal with in keeping their farm going. Besides, it might lead to giving away their secret hiding place.

Jes's grandfather had recovered completely from his illness and was now strong and robust. He'd spent most of his time away from them in Europe doing research for several books he was working on. When he returned to live with them he resumed his story telling. He would sit in his old Boston rocker, rocking back and forth, and tell Jes and Marya stories on a broad range of subjects for hours on end. Jes realized Grandfather was very worldly and knew many things but Jes's favorite subject was Nova Scotia. He was fascinated by the stories Grandfather told about all the islands and coves. It seemed romantic, somehow, to have all the adventures Grandfather described and to live by your wits.

Grandfather always found time to talk to them and answer their questions, invariably about being a boy in Nova Scotia. Sometimes he would ramble a bit and the stories would jump around but Jes always loved to listen and would gently put him back on track by asking more questions. One day Grandfather left on another long trip to visit several friends, many of whom were ill. Jes missed him more than he had expected. He felt very close to Grandfather and could not explain the reason.

After he left, Jes kept asking his father about Mahone Bay but his father could not answer his questions. One day he sat Jes down and asked him if he would like to take a trip to Halifax Bay and Mahone Bay to see where his grandfather had grown up.

"Oh yes," Jes answered quickly, "I've dreamed of going there."

"When you come back," his father added, "your grandfather will have returned and you will have even more questions to ask him. I'm sure he will be delighted. Many of our ancestors settled there and grew up there. It would be interesting to learn more about them and where they lived. Your Uncle Pete also wants to go, so we can share the driving. It's a long drive."

"Could Marya go, too?"

"She can if she wants to. After all," he said, "she's like a sister to you. Let's just make sure she knows it's a long trip, that she doesn't mind being in a car for long stretches. Make sure you pack some games and a book or two."

"I'll ask her to go with us. Then I'll have someone to talk to," Jes said.

It was summer so they were not in school. When Jes asked Marya she jumped up and down with glee. *She is a lot like me,* Jes thought. He realized she was not really his sister but sometimes he wished she was. At other times he liked it just the way it was. Whether she was or not did not make too much difference. They were best friends.

Before she died Marya's mom had made Jes's parents Marya's guardians. Marya inherited the house they had lived in but nothing was done with it for the time being. She would decide that when she came of age.

Jes asked his father when they would leave and he said in two days. When the day came, Jes was already packed up and set to go. His father was still getting ready. Marya packed a small suitcase for the trip and they both waited outside for Uncle Pete to drive up. While Jes was carrying their suitcases to the driveway near the corn house Marya was in the field picking a small bouquet of flowers. Jes thought they might be for his mother who was staying home.

As Jes watched her, the black bearded stranger dashed out, straight at Marya. She saw him and started running but he caught her with one hand. She screamed and wriggled as hard as she could but could not escape. Without hesitating Jes raced toward them and threw himself at the man's legs, knocking him down. Marya wriggled free but the man leaped up and grabbed Jes in his arms and started dragging him away. Marya ran back and bit him on the hand. He cursed and swung wildly at her. He missed but still held Jes in his grip.

As the man continued to drag Jes, Uncle Pete drove up in his big station wagon. He leaped out. The man dropped Jes and ran swiftly around the tree and down into the woods. Jes's father had heard the screaming and came running out just as the man disappeared. Jes and Marya got their breath back and then told them what had happened. His father and uncle looked at each other silently. Each nodded.

"It's a good thing we're taking this trip now. I thought we'd seen the last of that man when your grandfather drove him away a couple of years ago. Get in and I'll tell you what I know about him as we drive."

"You know that man?" asked Marya.

"Not exactly," Uncle Pete responded. "We've heard about him before, but we don't know what he's after."

"Well, he seems to want me and Marya. Why?" Jes asked.

"Why me," Marya spoke up, "what does he want with me?"

"We think he's after something," replied his father, "and probably wants to kidnap you for ransom, or for something he's looking for and thinks we have. Let's get going. We'll talk about this later."

CHAPTER TWENTY FOUR

Pursuit to Nova Scotia

Southern New England
Summer, 1949

Jes and Marya quickly piled into the back of the station wagon with their luggage and his uncle drove along the main road that went through town continuing east and northeast for several miles. Jes couldn't remember the route numbers. He thought the one they'd been on for a while was Route Six and then maybe Route Forty-four, but wasn't sure. He did notice the roads almost never went in a straight line but seemed to wind through very scenic land with lots of farms and woods, and along rivers. The road would cross a river several times over old arched stone bridges and meander through the countryside. It was as if the road builders avoided going over hills and mountains and meandered through the countryside. He did remember that eventually they would reach Route One which went all along the coast. His dad took over driving while Uncle Pete rested.

"Dad," Jes asked, "why do they have so many wandering roads along rivers and through valleys?"

"These roads were built where old pathways existed before there were cars. It was almost always better to follow rivers and valleys in those days of foot travel. It remained true when people eventually travelled on horses and sometimes with carts. The roads always got bigger as the traffic required it. Following old roads was usually easier than creating new ones."

"Why don't they just build bigger roads that go in a straight line, even over mountains and hills if they have to?" asked Jes.

"I'm sure they will one day. They already are building some roads like that in parts of the country. But they do take a lot of money. I like these roads even though they're slower. I think you would miss some beautiful things on big fast roads."

Marya added a question to the conversation. "Why are there so many stone walls all along the road?"

"This land is and was full of stones." Uncle Pete woke up. "So most of the earlier settlers made these walls to mark the boundaries from the stones they dug up to clear their land."

"Of course," added Jes's father, "they also used the stones to build bridges and wells and stone foundations and all sorts of things."

When they were within a few miles of Route One, Jes asked if they would stay on this road along the coast for a while.

His uncle answered, "Yes, this road goes north all the way to the border."

Marya piped up, "I hope so because I like going along the ocean coastline. I love the sea. I wish we could take some of the trip on a ship and not all of it in the car."

"We will, we will," Uncle Pete responded, "just you wait and see."

Jes was looking out the back window when he saw the black car behind them.

"Don't look back, Dad, but I think I see that black bearded man following us."

"I'll look in the rear view mirror," Jes's dad said. "Don't anyone look back."

After a moment his uncle and his dad had a conversation between themselves.

"It's him all right. There are two of them," his dad acknowledged. "You're the better driver, Pete. Take over."

"Then don't go north up ahead," Uncle Pete directed. "Take the southern exit and pull over first chance you get. Then I'll drive."

Jes and Marya held their breath as the plan unfolded. Just as directed, his father went south, then stopped in a small pullout. The black car went by slowly. After his father and uncle changed places, Uncle Pete told them what he was going to do.

"There's a construction zone ahead. I was here a couple of weeks ago. This is where I'll try to lose them."

They passed the black car which had pulled into a gas station and was trying to hide behind the pumps. Then it pulled out and continued to follow them. When they entered the construction zone, Uncle Pete waited until just before the end where the road was dirt. He spun his wheels and zigzagged back and forth to create a cloud of dust behind him. Then he accelerated out of the construction zone and took the first exit west. He drove quickly for several miles, took a road north for several more miles, then a road east back onto Route One north.

"I think we lost him," Jes's dad finally said. "Good job."

Jes wasn't completely convinced. He kept looking back for many miles as they sped north.

"Dad," he spoke up at one point, "why is it that that man doesn't seem to come around often but then comes by and tries to kidnap one of us? If he really wanted to catch me I think he would come by every day."

"It's hard to explain, Jes, and I am only guessing, but I think he is uncertain about what he is doing and is seeking instructions from his organization. He might really want to capture you or Marya or both of you, but I think he is looking for something else that his organization thinks is even more important."

"If he really wants to kidnap us, why doesn't he come with more people?" Marya interjected.

Jes's father and uncle both laughed. "He might just do that," his father responded. Then his dad and uncle had stopped laughing and took it all more seriously. There was silence after that. Jes thought *Marya seems to ask direct practical questions. That's nice.* He smiled.

They drove all day and all through the night, his dad and uncle taking turns at the wheel. Jes asked his dad why they had to drive nonstop and he said they could make better time at night and would stop tomorrow in the day time.

"I think my dad and uncle just like to drive," Jes told Marya quietly. "Besides, they won't have to spend money on a place to stay." Then he added almost in a whisper, "I don't think they have that much money so maybe that's the real reason."

"Maybe," Marya said, "but I think they aren't sure they've lost the black car and don't want to take chances."

At any rate he and Marya became drowsy and used blankets and jackets to make a cozy place in the back of the station wagon. They slept soundly all night.

When they woke up in the morning, Jes poked his head up.

"Where are we now?" he asked in a groggy voice.

"You haven't missed a thing. We just went through a detour with lots of dust and bumpy driving," Uncle Pete explained. "I'm surprised you didn't wake up with all those bumps. Go back to sleep and we'll wake you for some breakfast."

"How far do we have to go?" Marya piped up.

"A few more hours and we'll cross the border. Then a few more hours after that we'll reach the ferry."

That seemed to satisfy both of them for a short while and they dozed off. Soon they woke up because of hunger. After a short breakfast stop at a diner where they had juice, ham and eggs with potato fries, and coffee for the grownups, and a short walk to stretch their legs, they climbed back into the station wagon and continued on.

"Wouldn't it be a great idea," Jes remarked, "if someone came up with a plan for a drive-in place where you could pick up a quick breakfast like the one we had or even a little hamburger without leaving your car and eat it while you drove? That kind of fast food would save so much time."

"You can bet," replied Uncle Pete, "that if it will pay off, some company will do it one day."

To pass the time Jes and Marya played games. The first one was the alphabet game. Each took a different side of the road and called out letters in order from A to Z as they spotted them on signs or buildings. Jes got stuck on the letter Q but Marya saw a Dairy Queen sign. Jes was peeved when Marya moved far ahead of him and trounced him. Then they played a game looking for as many different state license plates as they could and soon counted fifteen before it got harder and harder to find new ones. They became bored and stopped after nineteen states.

But playing games did pass some time and before they knew it, they had crossed the border and were headed to the Saint John's ferry in New Brunswick. It would take them across the Bay of Fundy to the southwest corner of Nova Scotia. Now they played checkers and this time Jes was a much better player which annoyed Marya. Then Jes tried to teach Marya how to play chess but she wasn't interested. Instead they played WAR and double solitaire, both of which Marya won, but then she fell asleep so Jes just played single solitaire.

And then Uncle Pete spoke up. "There it is!"

Marya awakened quickly. They looked up and saw the line to the ferry. His dad drove in, bought a ticket, and parked the car in the line. They found out they had only a short wait before the ferry was to be loaded. They took a moment to get a hamburger and to walk around a bit, but the line of vehicles started to move so they jumped back in their car and drove onto the deck. Jes and Marya ran up to the bow and watched the crew cast off. Then the ferry headed out across the Bay as a light rain began to fall.

"I love the smell of the sea, don't you Marya?" Jes reveled in the sting of the salty sea spray against his cheeks and lips. "It's hard to describe. It's like a fish market but with seaweed and other smells."

"Yes," she answered, "I like the sound of the birds calling, the seagulls as they circle, the boats honking and their sails flapping in the wind. It's so full of life."

Jes thought *I'm finally in Nova Scotia, just like in one of Grandfather's stories.*

Uncle Pete caught up to them and explained that the Bay of Fundy had the highest tides in the world.

"The tide rises and falls more than forty feet in many places," he told them. "But Burntcoat Head, a nearby cliff in Minas Basin, has recorded the highest tidal range of anywhere. The tide gauge there has shown an average tide of about fifty six feet with a high just over seventy. The Head is now virtually an island."

"Wow!" Jes burst out. "Where is this place, Uncle Pete?"

"It's three or four hours from where we get off the ferry but it's almost straight north of Mahone Bay, just a few miles out of town."

"Could we see those tides some day?" Marya asked.

"We'll see if we have time, but now you should eat something else to keep from getting seasick. It will take about three hours to cross the Bay," he said. "When we get in sight of land the ferry will go through a gap into a protected inlet to reach the ferry dock on the southwest side of Nova

Scotia. Then we'll get off the ferry and drive northeast a little way and then follow a road up and over mountainous land. We'll go past a National Park and past lots of beautiful lakes. I haven't seen this land since I was a boy but I don't think it has changed too much since then."

He explained, "This will take several hours of driving before we reach the other shore of Nova Scotia. Then we still have to take another road along the south shore coast, which will take a few hours more."

Knowing they still had a long way to go, Jes and Marya walked around all the decks. Meanwhile, his uncle and father took advantage of this time to stretch out and sleep since they had had very little of it during the night.

"When we get close to the dock come back here," Jes heard his father say as they skipped off to explore.

"You might need to wake us up," yelled Uncle Pete.

They looked out at the various sailboats passing by.

"I'd love to do that when I get older," Marya said wistfully.

"We will." That was all Jes had to say.

After a short sleep they docked and drove off the ferry following the route just as Uncle Pete had described.

Marya whispered to Jes, "Wouldn't it be nice to come back here some day and stop at some of these places."

They looked at all the many lakes along the way and wished that they could stop and play and maybe even swim, but they knew Jes's father and uncle had planned to drive without stopping. They'd been warned this was the plan. Finally they reached the east shore of Nova Scotia and turned north. After a few hours they passed a big harbor. Uncle Pete said it was called Lunenburg and soon they'd be in Mahone Harbor.

GREAT AUNT'S HOUSE

125

CHAPTER TWENTY FIVE

Exploring Mahone Bay

Mahone Bay, Nova Scotia
Summer, 1949

They reached the home of Jes's great aunt just before dark. Marya noticed it had a screened porch off the end of the house with a balcony above. The house was white with a blue gray roof. She walked up the hundred feet of stone pathway through the large bushes on the edge of the large lawn, and when she reached the small porch with the four columns she turned and glanced at the water and the islands in the Bay. As she followed Jes inside, she turned.

"Jes, what are those sweet fragrances permeating the house?"

"I smell cooked onion and something I can't identify. It reminds me of snow and Christmastime."

His great aunt had kept dinner warm for them knowing how hungry they'd be. They were! Very hungry. Dinner was meat loaf, mashed potatoes, and peas. When they had dessert the smell he'd noticed before was explained: baked apples with brown sugar and cinnamon.

"These are delicious." Jes said and his aunt smiled. "My mom makes apple pie and I think she uses Baldwin apples from our orchard. We eat the McIntosh and she uses greenings for apple sauce. What kind of apples are these?"

"These are also Baldwin apples but sometimes I use Pippins in baked apples as well as for apple sauce. It is so nice that you take such an interest in food. At your age most boys gobble things down and don't even notice or appreciate what they are eating."

Uncle Pete had warned them about how important manners were to his aunt. They must be on their best behavior. Jes sat up straight and used his napkin and tried to keep his fork in his left hand and his knife in his right and take small bites. Marya was wonderful. She was the best of any of them. She kept up a conversation with his great aunt while carefully eating in the most proper way. His great aunt was most impressed.

"How long have you lived here in Mahone Bay?" Marya asked her politely.

"All my life," answered his great aunt. "I was born here."

Marya later told Jes she was surprised at that but didn't say a word at the time.

"How long have you lived in this house?" she asked.

"All my life."

Marya did not show her surprise and continued on with questions which continued to delight his aunt.

"Do you have any children?" Marya asked finally. "Did they live here?"

"I never married." The old lady was not as delighted with that question.

"Do you ever swim in the bay?" asked Marya innocently. His aunt laughed.

"No one does. It's very cold."

Jes spoke up. "We will. Won't we, dad?" His dad and uncle both nodded.

He learned later that they had never been swimming in the water here. They all agreed they would try it the next day, except for Marya who didn't say a word. Great Aunt's house overlooked the harbor on the southwest side. She smiled as she told them that if they really wanted to swim they should go either to Mader's Cove which was along the shore or go past it to Westhaver Beach. Jes wondered why she was smiling since she had not been smiling before. Perhaps she thought it was great sport that they would try swimming. He didn't think about it much after that.

Jes finished his dinner and thought it was wonderful. After that he began to feel very tired. Great Aunt's house consisted of a living room, dining room, huge kitchen, a bedroom and bathroom downstairs, and four bedrooms and a large bathroom upstairs. The front bedrooms facing the water had double dormers.

Each of them had a separate bedroom with a big comforter. Jes fell asleep in a few minutes. He was awakened in the middle of the night by Marya, who said she couldn't sleep. He let her in bed and she promptly fell asleep, as did Jes. Marya woke up early in the morning and tiptoed quietly back to her room before anyone else was awake.

The next morning Jes had so many requests for his father that he didn't know where to start. He wanted to see where the barn was that his grandfather told him about where they played a Halloween joke. He and his friends had showed their skills by putting a wagon on top of the barn. His father asked his aunt where the barn was and she gave him directions. Jes explained to Marya that the group of boys had taken apart a neighbor's hay wagon during the night and put it back together on top of the man's barn. In the morning everyone in town laughed and wondered how the wagon had "flown" up there. The man was not very pleased and set about to find out who had played the practical joke. When he eventually found out, the boys had to take it down the same way they had put it up there.

Then Jes wanted to know where the islands and coves were that Grandfather had told him about. He said he told him there were many islands and coves named after the family. Great Aunt took him to the window and pointed toward the mouth of the harbor.

"See that little island right in the middle of the entrance to the harbor?" she said. "That is named after our family, the ancestor that settled here a couple of hundred years ago. Below it is Westhaver Island where our ancestors were the lighthouse keepers. I told you about Mader's Cove, which you will pass by on the way to Westhaver Beach. Both of them are named after our ancestors. On your way here you went past Lunenburg Harbor. Ritceys Cove there in the Harbor is named after my mother's family. North of here just off of Indian Point is a big island named Zwicker. It's also named after another one of our ancestors. Did your grandfather tell you about them?"

"He told me a little about them and how he loved to go fishing there."

"What about Oak Island? Did he mention that?"

"Yes, he said there might be buried treasure but strange things were going on there. What did he mean?" Jes queried.

"There have been strange activities on that island for many years. Did he tell you about Mason Island and the cove on the ocean side of it?" she asked.

"He mentioned it but didn't tell me about it," Jes responded. "Is that named after another ancestor?"

"It certainly was." Great Aunt looked surprised when he said he hadn't heard about it. "I'm surprised he didn't mention it. It has a very interesting history. So does Oak Island."

She said she would tell him more about it that night but now they should enjoy the day and get out into the town and the Bay. She said these and many other places around the area had been named after their family. Most of Jes's ancestors had settled here several centuries before. Jes asked about the little island that had just been pointed out to them and wondered if they could go out there to see it. His father thought it was a fine idea.

His uncle rented a small motor boat which was just big enough for the four of them and out they went. Jed noticed Uncle Pete had bought a map of the Bay and had studied it before they left shore.

"Why did you buy a map?" Jes queried him.

"Jes, I don't know these waters as well as your grandfather and I know there are many hidden shoals and ledges and even small islands just below the surface. Even a small boat like ours can run aground at low tide. If we sink we could drown. This water is very cold."

Uncle Pete said that first they would go to the little island sitting right in the middle of the mouth of the harbor. Jes imagined it was the sentry or watchdog for the town of Mahone Bay.

As they slowly approached the shore of the rocky island, Marya stepped closer to Jes. The northeast wind whipped her hair around her face. She whispered to Jes, "Do you think it has any caves?"

"It doesn't look like it," Jes whispered back.

Uncle Pete said that after they stopped here then they would go to Mason Island and, after that, Zwicker Island. Then they would see how much time they had left.

Jes knew his uncle had been in the navy. He seemed to know a lot about sailing as well as carpentry. He thought about what his grandfather had said about inheriting skills or abilities. Uncle Pete certainly had inherited skills from someone. Perhaps he had inherited the carpentry skills from his father, and the sailing and navigating skills from Jes's great grandfather and great, great grandfather who were skilled ship captains in this area. Perhaps they had all inherited these abilities from someone long ago.

As the boat hit the shoreline and ground to a halt, Jes lurched forward and was brought quickly back to the present. The sharp wind that had been rushing past his ears had stopped. They had landed. He walked around the rocky island with Marya and thought it was about a thousand feet wide and maybe fifteen hundred feet long, bigger than it looked from shore, she said.

"If a small cannon were installed on the point of the island, it would stop any ship from coming in to the harbor. Wouldn't that be a great idea?" Jes said to Marya.

"Wouldn't it be nice to build a hut out here?" Marya replied. "We could sleep inside the hut and build a fire and listen to the waves and the birds."

"And go fishing," said Jes.

They didn't stay long before his father called to them. They headed out slowly into the middle of Mahone Bay. Jes and Marya were told by Uncle Pete to watch very carefully for shoals ahead or any land lying just under the water.

"The left side of the boat is called the port side and the right the starboard side."

Uncle Pete set a course in the direction of Mason Island that passed next to a couple of ledges. Jes and Marya each took a side of the boat and called out the shoals as they went by them. Jes's father handled the tiller and his uncle was the navigator. His father commented once that they made quite a good team together. Marya said this was lots of fun.

"What are the buoys out there for?" Jes asked.

"The one on our starboard side is called a port hand buoy because it tells incoming ships to keep it on their port side," explained Uncle Pete. "The one coming up is a different color and is called a starboard hand buoy for the same reason: telling us to keep to port. That will be the southwest ledge ahead."

Sure enough, Jes thought. He had port side watch and called out the ledge as they approached.

"What if you were out at night?" Marya piped up. "You wouldn't be able to see the buoys to tell you how to avoid the shoals and ledges."

"That's right," Uncle Pete responded, "and you would probably crash."

"And sink and drown," Jes put in.

"That's not funny, Jes." Marya said. Jes decided not to say anymore.

They cleared the ledge and his uncle said to go straight north to Mason Island. His dad took them to the south end of Mason and his uncle told him to keep the point on his port side. They sailed right up the east side and went into a cove about half a mile from the south end and pulled on to shore.

Mason Island was much bigger than the other island. It was over a mile long and very narrow in the middle. At its narrowest place it seemed to Jes to be only a few hundred feet across. Jes and Marya walked around and noticed the many rocks and crevices and even what looked like small caves or holes that went down between big rocks.

"Wouldn't this be a nice place to hide a treasure?" said Marya.

"Let's look for one," Jes replied. "Look in every crevice or hole that might be a cave."

"If I were going to hide it, I'd pick this island."

"What about Oak Island? There may already be some there."

"Maybe you're right. Your aunt didn't answer your question about buried treasure. Let's go there."

It seemed to them as if they had just started their exploration when Uncle Pete said they were going to visit one more island before returning the boat. Then they'd have a nice lunch. They piled in, headed north around the end of Mason Island, then directly west.

"It's only one or two miles," explained Uncle Pete. "We'll come into Zwicker Cove in twenty minutes or so."

"That's where Grandfather said he used to fish when he was a boy," said Jes.

"What kind of fish did he catch?" Marya asked. Jes's dad looked at Uncle Pete.

Uncle Pete spoke up. "Probably salmon or cod, I would think."

"The truth is, Marya," said his father, "I don't think we know. But we'll find out."

They coasted into the cove and jumped out. Jes asked if he and Marya could walk to the other side of the island and look across at Indian Point.

His uncle pointed.

"That's the way to Eel Cove. You can see Indian Point from there across the water."

"Don't be gone too long," his dad added, "we'll have to go pretty soon."

Jes and Marya walked straight across the island but saw nothing on the way that looked like a cave or anything as exciting as the places on Mason

Island. They looked at Indian Point from Eel Cove just as his uncle suggested and headed back to Zwicker Cove.

"Could we visit Oak Island?" Marya asked quietly.

"If we have time we'll visit it later," answered Uncle Pete.

His father added. "It could be pretty dangerous to go there from what I know."

"Why is it dangerous?" Marya persisted.

"Grandfather said Oak Island has buried treasure there. Does it?" Jes added.

"From what I know from your grandfather and great aunt, lots of people over the years have thought there was. Some kids uncovered a deep well at the east end of the island, around 1795 I believe. They found a wooden platform after digging ten feet. Since then many people have found platform after platform by digging down more than one hundred feet. So far they've found very little: some gold coins, gold chain links, and some other strange objects. Your grandfather can tell you more about it when we return home. Two people have died so far, including one that fell down the well. The people excavating there now are still convinced of a vast treasure below and don't want us poking around."

Jes and Marya seem to be satisfied for the time being and asked no more questions.

Back in port, the weather was still warm so they bought bread and cheese and meat and fruit in Mahone Bay and had a nice picnic on the dock.

As the men talked, Jes whispered to Marya. "I wish we'd had more time to explore."

"Me too. Wouldn't it be special if we found something buried in a cave?" Marya said. "It would be our secret."

"I hope we go to Oak Island. That might be where the real treasure is." She nodded.

CHAPTER TWENTY SIX

Family History

Nova Scotia
Summer, 1949

In the afternoon Jes, his dad, Marya, and Uncle Pete put bathing suits on and went down to the beach below Great Aunt's house to look for the best place to swim. First they stopped at Mader's Cove and saw a small beach with very little sand.

"Let's go to Westhaver Beach," Jes's dad said, "it must be the place to swim."

They went on to Westhaver and decided it was the best place. It had a lot more sand but Jes wondered why there was no sign of any other swimmer in the water anywhere.

Marya had put on a swimsuit and then a large baggy sweater over it. She didn't look as if she wanted to go into the water and stood back and watched. The first one to try was Uncle Pete who took a running dive into the water and went under. He immediately jumped high in the air and screamed and dashed out of the water and shook all over.

"It's damn cold," was all he could say.

"That's what Great Aunt said," responded Jes.

"All right, Jes, shall we go together?" asked his father. Jes nodded and stood next to his dad. They took a deep breath and ran in together. It felt to Jes as if he had jumped into an icy pond. His breath almost froze in his chest. He leaped in the air and yelled and then ran back to the beach. He thought it was the coldest water he had ever felt. His teeth chattered and he ran up to get a towel where Marya was standing. She stared at him. He quickly put on a shirt but he still shivered.

And then the most surprising thing happened. Marya took off her big baggy sweater, dropped it to the ground and walked into the water. She took a few strokes and, without uttering a word, walked back out and put her sweater on. Then and only then did she start to shiver uncontrollably. Jes walked over and put his arm around her to warm her up and stop her chattering teeth and shaking body. He realized how much courage it must have taken not to be left out. He was amazed because she had remained so calm, and unlike everyone else, had not yelled or screamed. The other thing that amazed Jes was that he had not realized that she had developed a figure and didn't look like a girl anymore. He looked at her in a different way. But he was conflicted. He hoped they would still be friends and play together as they always did. But he also began to feel a little differently now looking at her. He felt a desire he had not had before. He could not explain it. He wanted to hold her in his arms and was afraid for a moment of his feelings. But then she pushed him away and grinned.

"That wasn't too cold, was it?"

He tried to swat her on the shoulder but she ducked. His feeling of desire had passed.

They returned to his aunt's big house and had a shower and another warm dinner. This time they had pot roast, boiled potatoes, and beans. Jes was getting drowsy from the air and exercise and dinner but he wanted to ask his aunt the questions on his mind. When the time seemed right and they were sitting around a fire, he leaned forward to be closer to her.

"Grandfather said our ancestors settled here hundreds of years ago. And you told us about the islands and bays and coves named after them." Jes started with the first thing on his mind. "When did they first come here? Why did they come at all?"

"Well you've already been to the island in Mahone Harbor named after our family. It was named by Jacob who settled here in the 1700s." She spoke slowly. Jeb realized she was not answering his questions and he felt she was being a little evasive, or maybe she couldn't answer. But she went on. "Earlier ancestors Frederique Mason and his son Peter came here from Montbeliard, Doubs, France. They named Mason's Island after their family. Why are you so interested in our ancestors, Jes?" She peered at him.

He hesitated, "It's not just Grandfather's stories. I guess I've been interested for as long as I can remember in our family names and who and where we came from."

She offered a seemingly bit of trivia. "If you go back a few hundred years your ancestors were members of the Freemasons."

"What are they?"

"Your father will tell you." She looked at Jes's father and he nodded. "And also Magdalene seems to be a family name. My mother's name was Magdalene and my middle name is also Magdalene and so is your aunt's. Did your father or grandfather tell you that?"

"No," Jes answered quietly.

"But that might not be so unusual," she went on. "Lots of people have ancestors that came here hundreds of years ago. Some of ours came to Plymouth in the early 1600s as well as the many others that came to Nova Scotia at that time. It's possible they came here earlier than that." She seemed to hesitate briefly. "I'm glad you're interested in genealogy Jes." It seemed time to change the subject. "Have you seen the ruins of the old castle up on the hill? You go straight up and across from Mahone Bay to get there. Ross Hill."

"No. I didn't know about it." Jes looked at his dad.

"Perhaps we can go there tomorrow Jes," his father interjected. "Time for bed now."

Jes was ready for sleep. It had been a long day. He was just dozing off when he felt Marya slide into bed with him again. He felt a little shy which he hadn't felt before.

"Do you know what I was staring at when you came out of the water?" she whispered in his ear. She didn't wait for an answer. "I saw your birthmark, the cross on your chest, that's why." She waited for a response.

"I forgot. Don't talk about it with anyone, all right?"

She nodded agreement. "I have one too. It's in the same place as yours. I'll show it to you if you like."

"You do? My dad says this birthmark is rare and is inherited from very ancient ancestors, and not to show it to strangers or discuss it with anyone."

"He's right, but I'll show you." She was wearing a long tee shirt and took it off. She pointed to the Merovingian Cross between her breasts and then put her tee shirt back on. Then she moved her hand slowly across his chest to the spot where his birthmark was. He shivered at her touch and felt a strange excitement. "It comes from the Merovingians. My mother told me about it. Now we have another secret to share."

She kept her hand briefly on his chest then abruptly got out of bed and went to her own room. Jes had trouble going back to sleep but eventually did and dreamt he was being chased by a man who was trying to kill him. He ran and ran and hid in a deep cavern until the man went away. He woke up in a sweat and finally dropped into a deep sleep.

In the morning they went to see the castle ruins on Ross Hill. These ruins were reported to be from about the year fourteen hundred. Jes thought *I wonder what it was like to live in that time. There would have been many natives living here then and surviving must have been very difficult. What did they eat and what shelter did they have? Did they live in tents or stone huts or wooden buildings?* He was not sure he would have liked it but he found it fascinating to imagine what it was like then.

The next morning it was time to say goodbye and begin their return trip. They were introduced to a very nice neighbor. She was just a little younger than his great aunt and a good friend of hers. Great Aunt presented Jes with a very old sextant that belonged to her grandfather. Both her grandfather and father had been great sea captains who sailed out of Nova Scotia. She said it was in his blood and perhaps when he grew up he too would become a sea captain. He said he might. They said their goodbyes, gave her a hug, and climbed into the station wagon. Jes and Marya made the back into a cozy nest.

The return trip didn't involve any boats. They drove north and saw many covered bridges. Just as at home they were where the roads meandered along rivers and streams below rolling hills. Here in Nova Scotia, there were so many of them and they were all so different. They also crossed a couple of stone arch bridges which Marya said she thought were beautiful. They saw an occasional fox hiding in the forests of pine and oak and beech. They passed groups of birch trees and scattered groups of elm and alder. Marya pointed out a couple of deer jumping over a stone wall. Jes thought it would be a perfect place to build wooden huts sitting on top of stone foundations. Robins and jays and woodpeckers flew in and out of branches and Marya thought she saw an eagle above the treetops. Jes pointed out a flock of crows sitting on top of a bridge.

"Why do they have all these covered bridges?" asked Marya.

"They were built so that the horses would not spook as they crossed the rivers," Jes spoke authoritatively. "Isn't that so?" he said to his father.

"I think that's true," replied Uncle Pete.

"Some of them have a separate walkway on the outside of the bridge. Why is that?"

There was a silence while Jes looked at his uncle who smiled. Finally Jes answered. "Marya, would you like to walk in the dark through there after the horses just went through?" There was a long pause.

"And why are the stone bridges so narrow?" Marya continued, "There's only room for one car."

"Because," replied Jes's father, "when they were built they didn't have cars. A horse or horse and carriage could go across easily. But I'm glad they are still here even if they are usually one lane."

The return trip went quickly. After a day and a night they arrived home. Jes and Marya vowed to each other they would return and explore some of the islands and ruins again.

When they drove up the gravel driveway and pulled to a stop next to the corn house, Jes ran down the path into the kitchen to tell his mother about the trip. The others followed behind. As Jes stepped inside he stopped in shock, stunned. The house was a complete mess. Everything was turned upside down and scattered and broken. It looked as if the house had been ransacked.

"Mom! Mom! Where are you?" Jes yelled. "What happened? Mom? Mom?" There was no answer. He hesitated, "Grandfather? Grandfather?"

There was no answer.

His father came in behind him and stared. "Dad? Dad? Are you here?" There was no answer. "He might still be on his trip." They quickly checked all the rooms.

"What happened, Dad?" Jes asked.

"It looks as if someone was looking for something while we were gone."

"Where's Mom?" Jes asked.

"She said she would visit Mabel while we were gone. I'll call her to make sure she's all right."

"What were they looking for?" asked Marya.

"Something very important. But I don't think they found it."

"They'll be back one day," Uncle Pete said, shaking his head. "Let's clean this up."

CHAPTER TWENTY SEVEN

Cathars and Templars

Southern Greenland
Early Summer, 1398

Henry and Jed and Martha spent several days on shore at the southern colony waiting for good weather. The time passed quickly for the children, but not for Henry. He was anxious to continue his journey to New Scotland. Now that they had good weather he wanted to make up time. They were already several weeks behind the ships that had gone to the West and he wanted to reach them as soon as possible since none of the crews of those ships had been to these lands before.

Henry made sure his crew took on board enough hay for the sheep and enough dried beef for the men in case the advance group of ships had trouble hunting. They also took enough wheat and maize to make it through to the harvesting of the first crops.

Henry planned to leave a few men behind that had initially come with him on the ships. They were needed by the colony to help with the harvesting and to produce enough wheat and onions and turnips and other food to make it through the next winter. Henry hoped several of the ships going to the West would return before then so that the men left behind would not have to stay too long and overburden the colony. The hope was that the colony itself would be able to plant more hay and corn and wheat, and the lambs and sheep would grow so by the end of summer it would be on good footing again.

Henry decided to leave immediately for the West before any other storms came in. He hoped to avoid running into icebergs. They selected the sheep he'd take and stored wheat for the men to make bread. He planned a trip of one to two weeks. They bid farewell and sailed out into a sea still rolling with small waves from the storm.

The rough seas lasted a couple of days but that didn't stop Jed and Martha from romping around the deck. They found it to be most exciting when it was rolling from side to side and the waves were splashing over the bow and sides. They now had their sea legs and seemed to be at one with the movement of the ship and reveled in the feel of the salt spray flying over their heads. They were given small chores such as coiling up ropes or stowing gear, but most of the time they roamed the deck and crept down below to peek into every space and through every door. One door was always locked but one day they found it unlocked and slipped inside.

When they became accustomed to the darkness they were stunned by what they saw. In the small room was a treasure of gold and silver objects including chalices, goblets with ornate gold and silver and rubies, as well as swords and daggers and religious objects, especially ancient crosses covered with precious stones and gold and silver. Among the goblets and chalices was one beautiful silver goblet wrapped up in a fine linen cloth. Martha looked at it, then wrapped it up again. She opened one of the many beautiful chests and found it filled with thousands of gold coins. Jed started to open one of the other chests and just as they noticed old manuscripts inside, they each felt a big strong hand on their shoulders.

"Not a sound, you two. Come with me." It was Henry and he had a worried look on his face. He didn't seem angry as they expected. They followed him out of the room and he locked the door behind them and put another large lock on the outside. "I only left it for a moment. I should know better with you two poking around."

"We didn't mean any harm," Martha blurted out. "We saw it was open and wanted to investigate."

"You are not to tell a soul about what you saw. I'm the only one that goes in there."

"We understand. We won't go in there again." Jed was contrite.

"You are right about that. It will stay locked for the rest of the journey. But I think it's about time I told you more of the history of the Templars."

"Oh, sir, would you?" Martha was excited.

"Come to my quarters in a few minutes. I need to give some directions to the crew and then I'll tell you the whole story."

Jed and Martha took another look over the bow and waited until they saw Henry return. Then they followed him into his quarters and sat down in a comfortable high backed chair around a small circular table. Jed looked around at the small portholes and a couple of pictures of ancestors on the wall. Henry settled in to his massive chair with ornate carvings and began.

"After the Cathars were hideously persecuted and burned at the stake and massacred in some of their strongholds, many of the Templars became very worried that they would be next. They had amassed a great deal of wealth just as the Cathars had but were even more powerful and a great threat to the Pope and King Philip of France."

"Why were the Cathars such a threat to the Church?" asked Jed.

"They were a threat to the Catholic Church because of their pure religious views," Henry went on. "They disdained the extensive corruption that permeated the Church and felt it had deviated from the ideals espoused by Christ. The Templars were not only a threat to the Church because of their enormous power and land and wealth and religious views, but they were also a problem for Philip. He owed them more money than he could ever repay."

"The Templars controlled all commerce as well with their huge fleet of ships," Henry continued. "This proved in the end to be their salvation. From 1244 to the end of the century they developed a plan just in case their fears were justified. They had a large fleet of eighteen sturdy ships based in the port of La Roshelle on the west coast of France."

"Were our ancestors Templars?" asked Jed.

"Your great great-grandfather, Sir Henry Sinclair, was with the Templars at the beginning of this century when they feared they would soon be attacked by the Church and the King. He was descended from Norman knights, and many other members of the Sinclair family were also associated with the Templars." Henry paused and smiled. "Get comfortable. It's a long story."

CHAPTER TWENTY EIGHT

Treasure Of The Knights Templar

Rennes-le-Château, Southern France
October 13, 1307

Sir Henry Sinclair and the other Templars had been searching Rennes-le-Château for years, hoping to find any of Dagobert's vast treasure horde and ancient artifacts and scrolls, some from Egypt and the beginning of the millennium. They had begun in earnest in 1303 after Philip the Fair, King of France, had secretly arranged for the kidnapping of Pope Boniface III. The Pope died soon thereafter, a defeated and disgraced man. Sir Henry and the Templars saw for the first time how false charges for the practice of magical sorcery along with the usual political and criminal charges could be used against innocent and defenseless people.

Seeing these used against the Pope was a warning of what might happen to the Templars who were seen by the King of France as becoming much too strong, both financially and politically. When Pope Clement V became Pope in 1304 he supported the tactics of the French King.

"I'm sure," Sir Henry told a gathering of Knights Templar, "it's only a matter of time before Philip turns his attention and his vicious court toward us. We must take action before they do." Not only did the Templars have vast wealth and power and influence but they controlled the seas and the commerce on it with their huge fleet of ships. Many of these ships were in the fortified harbor of La Roshelle.

From 1303 to 1307 the Templars not only moved their own treasures to La Roshelle, but accelerated their search for other treasure. Besides searching Rennes-le-Château, they also searched for the huge Cathar treasure left in the fortified cave nearby, and found it with the help of one of the surviving descendants of the Cathar parfaits. This included ancient religious objects such as ornate crosses covered with jewels as well as simple crosses of gold and silver. It also included goblets but, most importantly, it included documents dating back hundreds of years, carefully scribed and protected from damage.

"You must make the long journey," Sir Henry directed a team of Templars, "to take this treasure quietly across land to one of our ships in the harbor of La Roshelle."

Whereas it was less than a day to get from Montségur to Rennes-le-Château, it took several weeks to go from Rennes-le-Château to La Roshelle. Several wagons filled with the Cathar treasure were pulled by horses as the Templar band rode alongside to guard it. They crossed the Garonne where it was not much more than a stream, floating the wagons on barrels. Crossing the Dordogne was much more difficult. The Templars cut logs to keep the wagons afloat and from tipping over. They lashed the cargo to the wagons and would first pull a hemp rope across with the horses and then pull the logs and wagons across. In some cases where they had to cross a river the Templars were fortunate in finding an old overgrown stone arch bridge built by the Romans. This saved much valuable time.

The Templars were a formidable force and seldom had trouble with those that might attempt to stop them. The one exception to this was the even more formidable armed forces of Philip, King of France. The process of moving the treasure was done at night and with advance guards. They always had to be on alert for the King's men, even at night.

When the Templars began moving their treasures from various strongholds before 1307, there were over two thousand Templar Knights as well as the rest of the Templar organization and many of them were engaged in collecting and moving their vast wealth to La Roshelle. Their wealth had begun with the First Crusade and had grown as they became the de facto bank of the church, kings, and nobles. This included numerous chests containing gold and silver coins dating from their own era back to the turn of the previous millennium as well as jewelry, and swords and daggers and knives often covered with gold and silver and sometimes adorned with diamonds or rubies or emeralds. These chests also contained many religious objects including crosses of all sizes and beautiful chalices and goblets.

After these treasures were secured at La Roshelle, the concentrated search for other treasures began. Some of the Templars searched the undercroft of the church in Rennes-le-Château and found, still hidden in the hollow structure, Dagobert's diversionary treasure. They decided to leave it there and continued to search until eventually they found the scrolls hidden behind the brick with the mark of the cross. Henry examined them and realized they were copies of the original scrolls. He copied them but decided to leave them there behind the brick. It was the originals he sought.

At the same time, other Templars searched the caverns around Rennes-le-Château and finally turned up the huge treasure that Dagobert had buried under a pile of rocks in the back of a cavern. He had acquired not only ancient coins, religious objects, and jewelry, but more importantly, the artifacts, cups, and a scroll from Egypt. Again a team of Templars loaded up the treasure and hauled it to La Roshelle on several wagons and hid it on one of the ships in their fortified harbor. As part of their plan they disassembled the wagons and loaded them on board, too.

Philip the Fair and his court certainly knew about the fleet of ships the Templars had in La Roshelle and other ports in the Mediterranean but they were not completely aware of the amount and kind of wealth the Templars had or its location. They were also largely unaware that the Templars were searching for other treasures and moving them to a safe location out of the reach of Philip's men.

The Templars' searches also recovered the documents and manuscripts hidden by the four parfaits who escaped from Montségur in one of the caverns now under their control. Some of these were from ancient times but many documented the corruption, excess, and moral bankruptcy of the Church that drove the Cathars to separate from it.

"We'll take all these documents," Sir Henry decided, "and leave no evidence, but this small treasure trove under the church will stay. There's no harm in leaving that for others to find. In fact it might be a good idea if they find something for their efforts."

Their last discovery was stunning. A group of Templars digging in the deepest recesses of an old section of the church of Sainte Marie-Madeleine found a burial site. It was the mummified corpse of a woman. From the objects found with her that were of Judean and Egyptian origins, and the fact she was mummified in Egyptian fashion, Sir Henry and the others believed they had found the church's namesake. They felt it was improper to take this sacred corpse and felt she deserved a better burial, a proper Templar burial, so they prepared a site and reburied the body. No one was ever to speak of their discovery.

Finally, the day the Templars had all dreaded arrived. It was Friday the thirteenth of October in 1307. The King's armed men flooded the countryside and began rounding up as many Templars in as many locations as they could find. The plan was coordinated well. They made an effort to arrest Templars in all known locations simultaneously. It was easy to arrest the Grand Master, Jacques de Molay, since he was negotiating with the Pope and King. Other officials were also arrested. The Templars were told by their organization not to resist arrest. The raids and arrests appeared to be extremely successful. There was only one major problem. The raids didn't find and arrest most of the Knights Templar.

There were only fourteen Knights in the group of one hundred thirty eight initially heard by the Grand Inquisitor. As the inquisition continued over many years and more Templars came out of hiding or were discovered, very few of them were Knights Templar. All told, less than one hundred of the more than two thousand arrested in the inquisition were Knights.

The reason for this was simple: almost all of the Knights had ridden to La Roshelle prior to the night of the 13th. An informer in the court of Philip had been able to warn the Knights in advance of this terrible night and the word spread.

Two thousand of the Knights Templar had arrived at La Roshelle. Along with Sir Henry, they had embarked on the eighteen ships before the arrival of Philip's armed men. The Knights had arrived from all sections of France, particularly from the south, over the course of several weeks. The word had spread quickly across the land and the Templar Knights had ridden swiftly to the waiting fleet. When Philip's armed men arrived at La Roshelle, all of the eighteen ships had disappeared.

On board, Sir Henry spoke to a group of Templars. "I feel a great sadness for the Knights Templar who cannot be with us. They are being arrested along with many other Templars. I know their fate will be horrible. The King and Pope will make sure they are all tortured, and if they don't die from that, they'll be burned at the stake."

La Roshelle was strategically placed along the coast of France. It was protected from the sea by a huge harbor nearly surrounded by land. It was accessed from the mainland via a single narrow point, and provided very quick access to the open sea. The fleet sailed directly west. Once out to sea they sailed far enough from land to avoid encountering a possible stray ship for they would have been forced to destroy it. The fleet then sailed swiftly northwest along the coast of France after making sure they were not observed.

Sir Henry reviewed the plan on board his flag ship with other leading Templars. They had carefully distributed the treasure so as to accomplish three plans. The Knights were distributed according to the size of the ship and most ships had over one hundred Knights on board along with a proportional amount of the combined treasure.

There was one exception. One small ship named the Flamingo carried none of the treasure. The Knights on board had a special mission: to recover a treasure in southern England and bring it back on board. It would then follow the fourteen other ships that would have already sailed past the white cliffs and the southeast tip of England and headed north for the northeast shore of Scotland.

When they reached the treacherous northwest tip of France where many ships had long been lost, they would split up. Three ships laden with some of the Cathar treasure, which dated to ancient times, would sail directly west into the Atlantic Ocean on a perilous journey to unknown lands. Sir Henry made sure these ships did not take significant historical evidence. He kept that to himself. The remaining ships would sail into the channel between France and England and around the coast, with the exception being the Flamingo which would stop in southern England.

They encountered good weather, and in a few days, all ships in the fleet reached the islands off the coast of Pont-Croix uneventfully. Sir Henry and the other Templars on board the fifteen ships said their farewells to the courageous Knights on board the three ships heading west. They never saw these men again. The remaining ships sailed around the islands at the extreme northwest corner of France and, for the first time, began to encounter heavy seas and strong winds. The crews of all the ships had to tie down the treasure chests and ancient artifacts in the hold to prevent damage but finally they rounded the islands and headed on a course just north of the Island of Guernsey.

From there they sailed on a course that took them to the south coast of England. The Flamingo that contained no treasure sailed directly north from Guernsey to the east side of a narrow strip of land that projected into the sea. Sir Henry watched them go with trepidation knowing that, even though he expected to see them all safely in the spring with their mission accomplished, they still might encounter danger or have their ship discovered. Their plan was to anchor the ship in a location as secluded and protected as possible on the east shore of the peninsula.

Half the Knights would stay on board to protect the ship in the event of discovery and the other half would go ashore to march straight north to Glastonbury Abbey. They had reason to believe from ancient documents that a valuable treasure was hidden there. Their biggest concern was the weather. Winter was beginning to arrive and would be in full force before they returned. Sir Henry did not expect to see the ship until spring simply because he felt the men would have to winter over at some point before returning to their ship.

Sir Henry and the fleet of ships continued on their own journey to reach Roslin, where Henry believed they would be safe from the forces of King Philip. They sailed along the coast of England past the white cliffs and around the southeast point. They wanted to reach the Firth of Forth as soon as possible before winter storms hit them. They were fortunate until just before they reached the coast off Tynemouth. It was mid-November.

A ferocious storm blew in from the north. The winds and high seas rocked the fleet and scattered them into the North Sea where some of the ships encountered forty foot waves and gale force winds. Sails were ripped and some ships sustained damage to rigging. One ship began to founder. Several others had to come to its rescue. They decided the ship would not survive the storm and, in the most perilous conditions, they transferred the precious cargo to two other ships and then transferred the men. No one was lost and soon thereafter they watched the ship founder and sink.

All the remaining ships reached the Firth and anchored on the south side of it, somewhat protected from the gale. Winter snows began to fall and the Knights waited for slightly better weather before completing their journey.

After the storm passed they ferried the wagon parts ashore, assembled them, loaded them with the treasure, and set out immediately for Roslin

Castle, Sir Henry's home. They arrived within two days and settled in as the winter storms descended upon them.

CHAPTER TWENTY NINE

Reaching New Scotland

Newfoundland
Early Summer, 1398

Henry stopped as if he had finished his story. The ship rolled from a wave hitting the starboard bow and Jes could see the spray through the portholes in Henry's cabin. He hung on to the table with both hands and shivered.

"What happened to the treasure after the Templars got to Roslin?" Martha asked Henry.

"They buried it under the ruins of the old castle that had fallen into decay. Later on, after Sir Henry built his new Roslin Castle in the 1330s, he had the treasure buried underneath in the crypt."

"What happened to the Templars that went to Glastonbury?" asked Jed.

"Those Templars came back empty handed. They found nothing. But Sir Henry figured out that it wasn't a treasure trove buried there but something even more valuable, and he returned later when the opportunity arose. I told you before that many members of the Sinclair family have been associated with the Templars. At the trial of 1309, some members of the family took a position denouncing the Templars which deflected attention away from the family as a whole, even though they were harboring many Templars that had fled with Sir Henry to Scotland. Then, after 1314 when Bruce defeated the British at Bannockburn with Sir Henry as one of his leaders, Henry secretly returned to Glastonbury and found what he knew was there. We have it on board and I'll tell you about it later after we land."

"What happened to the Templars after that?" asked Jed.

"Look around you. Many of these people on this ship and on the other ships are descendants of the Templars. I am a descendant and therefore you are too. Martha's ancestors come directly from Merovingians who fled southern France and settled just south of Roslin several hundred years ago. Why do you think we are all taking this voyage? The possibility of persecution still exists, by the same forces. I thought you had figured that out."

There was a silence. Then Martha spoke up.

"I guess maybe I had an idea of that, sir, but I wasn't so sure."

"Father." Jed spoke quietly. His forehead was furrowed. "Why is it that I came on this voyage but my older brother Henry and my sisters stayed home? Aren't they in danger too?"

"That is a very good question Jed, and the answer is that they do not have the Merovingian birthmark, which is proof of your heritage and your bloodline. And don't forget that the Sinclair family denounced the Templars years ago. Your siblings may be in a little danger but our persecutors are after three things: the treasures, which are extremely valuable and contain some proof of this bloodline, the scrolls, and the Merovingian Cross. You are two of the few that have the Cross and that is why you are here."

"But why are all the others on this voyage if they don't have the birthmark?" asked Martha.

"The main reason is that the descendants of the Templars identified at the trials are still being sought. They want to avoid any possibility of persecution, and some want to seek a better life."

Henry said he needed to get back to the helm. He told them to eat well and sleep as much as possible since they would be near land in a day or so and he wasn't sure what to expect. Henry and the rest of the men had as near to a feast as they ever had. They had lamb, sweet potatoes, carrots, onions, parsnips, turnips, peas, and bread. Jed and Martha ate by themselves as they usually did.

"Did you hear what he said?" Martha asked Jed. "We are escaping from some kind of persecution."

"It sounded like that. Maybe we won't be able to go back home then."

"Besides our birthmarks, it has to do with the treasure we found in that room."

"It must. And I saw a lot of manuscripts in that chest. Didn't Henry say he brought on board what old Sir Henry found in Glastonbury?"

"Yes. I wonder if we have on board most of the treasure of the Cathars and the Templars. Henry said it all went to Roslin Castle. He must have brought it with him."

"It sounded so huge, I don't think it could all be in that storage room. He must have distributed it on several ships. But he has that important thing from Glastonbury, whatever it is."

"Maybe it's one of those manuscripts in the chest. They looked very old."

"Martha, I think the reason for this voyage is to bring all the treasures and manuscripts from the Cathars and Templars to New Scotland. What do you think?"

"What about bringing all the descendants of the Templars to New Scotland? And those of the Merovingians?"

"And the scrolls I have that he asked me to keep safe."

Martha didn't answer. They both knew they had discovered the real reason for their journey. They went to bed that night with many thoughts. Neither of them could sleep.

"Jed, I think you're right. We're not going home. This will be our new home."

They always cuddled together now but this night they curled up even closer than usual. As she had done before, she reached up to his chest and touched his birthmark. She left her hand there for a moment then gently took his hand and put it on her birthmark. She put her hand on top of his. A moment later she moved his hand from between her breasts to cover her right breast. They stayed that way until they fell asleep.

Early the next morning Jed and Martha went out to look over the bow. Jed loved the sound of the water as the bow cut through the four foot waves leaving a white wake on each side. Martha watched the Terns overhead and the occasional flying fish. They often did this in the morning after eating a little meat and cheese and bread for breakfast. They waved to their companion ship which sailed a slight distance behind and to port side of the flagship. The weather continued to warm as they sailed south. The days were getting longer.

Martha was the first to spot a ship five miles away as it suddenly appeared on the horizon. She called out, and Henry and the helmsman looked where she was pointing. They drew closer and Henry recognized it as one of the seven that had gone ahead. At noon, Henry's ship drew alongside.

The first mate swung over to their ship on a line. He appeared to be exhausted but with a smile of joy on his face. He reported to Henry what had happened.

"When our ships landed to hunt, we thought we were on a peninsula but it turned out to be a huge island inhabited by hostile natives," he explained. "We were driven off by an enormous group of them. They threw spears and attempted to board. We barely managed to escape. No one was killed, although some were injured."

Henry explained that the natives he knew were not from that island. The ships had stopped much too soon and too far north. They needed to go further south.

"Were you able to hunt at all these last few weeks?" Henry asked. "How is your food supply?"

"We haven't been able to hunt and we are running low on food. The other ships planned to sail southwest to find a suitable protected harbor. They hope, first of all, that the natives will be friendly, and secondly, they will be able to hunt for fresh meat. Our ship was assigned to intercept you. My captain expected you sooner. We were about to give up."

Henry thanked him and told him to ask his captain to follow him. All three ships then continued south. When Henry saw the open sea to the west and another body of land ahead, he remembered his previous trip and knew he was approaching New Scotland. He sailed down the coast on a southwest course looking for signs of the other ships.

He saw in the distance a deep bay and changed to a direct westerly course. As they approached, Martha, with her marvelous eagle eyes, spotted the group of six ships and waved and yelled. Henry and the other two ships sailed up to the convoy and found that most of the men had gone ashore to scout the terrain. The captain of one of the vessels lowered a boat and rowed over to Henry. Prince Henry greeted his old friend, Sir James Gunn, who summarized the events of the last several weeks.

"I really missed you," Sir Gunn said. "I thought I might never see you again."

He told Henry they had stopped briefly to hunt and were able to find lots of deer and elk and a large animal with huge horns that grazed in the wetlands and did not run away. It seemed to them to be quite docile.

"It was a shame to kill such a magnificent creature," he said, "but we needed the meat. We now have enough for a couple of months, but we need to find corn and wheat and hay and we need a place suitable for sheep. Shortly after stopping to hunt, a storm hit and rocked our boats fiercely. We sailed further south, spotted this deep bay, and felt we would be well protected from any storms."

Henry agreed but said they should go further in. He had been here before and remembered a narrow gap at the extreme west end of this bay.

Henry asked, "Did you encounter any natives?"

Gunn replied, "We did. They were not too hostile but not too friendly either."

Henry smiled. "Have you offered to smoke a pipe? Have you offered to trade with them? Have you given them gifts?"

Gunn hesitated. "After the encounter up north, we were nervous and kept our distance."

Henry said, "I'll fix that. Where have the others gone?"

Gunn replied they had been looking for a suitable site on the south shore. Henry told him he wanted to see all the ship captains on his flagship at dinner time. He would discuss the plan he had in mind now that they were all together again.

Jed and Martha had been listening to this conversation. They knew Henry was aware they were listening, but he did not seem to mind. They ran to the side of the flagship and watched Sir Gunn as he rowed back to his ship with the two crewmen who had come with him. They could see that there was a conversation going on but they could not hear it. Jed sought out his father and asked very timidly if he and 'Mark' could eat with Henry and all his captains, or eat nearby and listen to the conversation. Henry said that would not be appropriate, but that he had an idea. After they ate their dinner he would let them listen from a small cabin near the dining room where they could probably hear most of the meeting. It was not really a secret conversation but they were not to utter a sound. They both promised to keep quiet.

While waiting for dinner, they went out on deck to watch. Six dinghies made their way from shore, about fifty yards from the convoy. Each held about half a dozen men, in heavy dark clothes, carrying long bows. Nets hung in the center of each, filled with what looked like small dead foul, grasses, and plants. The boats split away from each other, making wakes, as they headed for their respective ships. At the same time, a boat went from Sir Gunn's ship to each of the others, one by one. The man in that boat seemed to have a brief discussion with the captain of each ship and then go on to the next.

"Jed," Martha said, "that must be the messenger from Sir Gunn about the dinner meeting."

"I think you're right," he replied.

Martha and Jed ate quickly in their cabin and went to the side room Henry had provided for them. It was off Henry's Captain's cabin and also on the other side of the dining room, so they could hear what went on. They did not want to miss a thing, so they got there before Henry's dinner began. They would have to stay there until the eight captains left late that evening.

"I want to thank all of you for your fine sailing," Henry began. "I'm sorry about your attack from the north island natives. We'll have to make sure that does not happen again." He paused. "I'd like to explain what I have in mind for the summer."

He told them the native name for this large bay was Chedabucto. He said they all should sail northwest to where the bay narrowed. They would be safer there. He would introduce them to the Chief of the tribe at that end of the island. He had met with him five years before and promised to return. He told the captains they should watch him and do everything he did. After the Chief and his key warriors met them and became comfortable with them, they would remain friends.

"It's my plan," Henry explained, "to split into two groups. One group of four ships will remain in this harbor and explore the area west and north. In particular they will go to a harbor on the north side the natives called Pictou, named after one of the tribes. The other four ships will join me and sail along the south shore to another harbor I visited on my earlier trip. After we meet here with Chief Kampalijek, we'll have another dinner together before parting and I'll explain the rest of my plan."

It was late in the evening but still daylight. It was the beginning of June. They departed for their ships in the glow of the setting sun, each in their own separate rowboat. Jed and Martha were told by Prince Henry they could leave now and return to their cabin. They thanked him for letting them listen in. They went to their little room and curled up together but couldn't sleep. They were so excited by what they had heard and what lay ahead, that they talked half the night about what they thought was going to happen next.

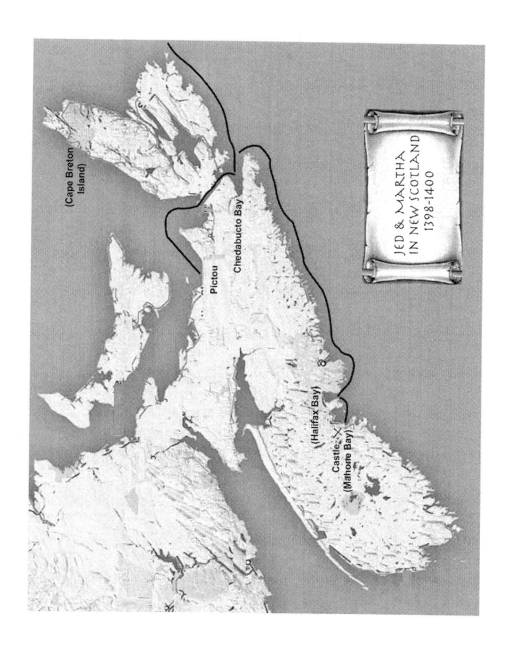

(Cape Breton Island)

Pictou

Chedabucto Bay

(Halifax Bay)

Castle — X
(Mahone Bay)

JED & MARTHA
IN NEW SCOTLAND
1398-1400

CHAPTER THIRTY

Sailing To Mahone Bay

Northern Nova Scotia
Summer, 1398

The next morning Henry's nine ships went through the opening of the long narrow strait. They anchored, and each ship sent a small party ashore consisting of the ship captain and a few of his officers. In each case it was the duty of the first mate to stay on board with the rest of the men.

Because they had been so quiet and responsible, Henry told Jed and "Mark" they could join the combined group and asked Sir Gunn to look after them. Prince Henry collected a variety of gifts to take with them along, with items to trade with the natives. These included metal containers, and salt and spices.

Once on shore, Henry was met by a chief of the Northern Mi'kmaqs. He was a strong burly man wearing an elaborate headdress over long hair pulled back and tied together. His loose deerskin shirt was sleeveless and came down to his knees. His bare legs were massive, like tree trunks, and his moccasins had straps that wrapped around his lower legs.

"I don't think he has anything on under the shirt, Jed," Martha whispered.

"Of course he does," retorted Jed, "he has a loincloth. Martha, your imagination runs away."

The Chief seemed very subdued but smiled. He called out in a low voice 'Glooscap'. He had with him a European who also greeted Henry. This person seemed to know Henry and served as a translator, although it appeared to Jed that Henry already knew certain words and could understand quite a bit of the Algonquin language.

It was the custom to smoke a peace pipe, so the Chief invited Henry forward to join him and other chiefs in the ceremony of peace. Henry invited only the ship captains and introduced them as such. The other members of Henry's party, including Jed and Martha, stood back from the circle and watched as they passed the pipe from man to man around, each taking a puff in turn.

After this ceremony, Henry presented the Chief with a special personal gift. It was very beautiful: a long knife with a carved wooden handle. The blade was over two feet long, very sharp and curved. It was designed to slash as well as stab and would be a formidable weapon in battle. Jed looked closely and recognized the cross carved on the handle. It was a very old Templar knife that had been passed on to Henry when his father died. Each of the ship captains had a gift they gave to one of the other chiefs in the circle. These were usually knives or axes that the natives greatly prized. In turn, Henry and the others also received gifts.

Henry received a beautiful headdress, and the others accepted similar headdresses. Then Jed watched as they discussed trading. Henry was particularly interested in obtaining various kinds of food such as corn and turnips and carrots and onions, as well as wheat and seeds. They also discussed Henry's plan to explore the area northwest of them. The Chief described where the areas were that were heavily occupied with natives but also other lands that they could freely explore since they were virtually uninhabited.

"There must be something wrong with those areas if they are uninhabited," Martha whispered, "There must be some danger he's not telling us about."

"Shhh," Jed whispered back.

The Chief also said he would send a guide with them to help explain their presence. After wrapping up the trading discussion, the circle concluded with another brief pipe ceremony. Henry and the rest of his party then returned to their ships.

When they were all back on board, Jed and Martha peppered Henry with questions.

"Who was the European?" asked Jed.

"Why is he here?" added Martha.

Henry explained, "He's one of the men that came on the previous voyage five years ago. He married a daughter of the Chief and very much wanted to stay behind. He has learned a great deal about the lives of the natives. But there is another man who came here many years ago on a perilous voyage and decided to stay. We'll meet him when we go further south. His story is similar in that he married in similar circumstances."

"Father," Jed asked, "we think that some of the treasure is on other ships, including the four about to go to the northwest. What will happen to that part of the treasure?"

"You are correct about the treasure but I don't want you ever to discuss it with anyone. A small part of the treasure is on those ships and I will instruct one of the ship captains as to its destiny. Now let us not discuss the treasure anymore." There was silence for a moment before Martha spoke up again.

"Sir," asked Martha, "you said you would tell us about what Sir Henry found in Glastonbury when he went there secretly. Would you now?"

"Oh, I thought you figured that out." He smiled. "Jed has them. Sir Henry found copies of the scrolls that he suspected were hidden there by the Merovingians."

"You say they're copies," queried Jed. "How do you know?"

"Look at the back of the Merovingian scroll," said Henry, smiling, "It doesn't have the mark of Dagobert. But then look at the other scroll you have. It is the original scroll with Dagobert's mark. That one also has updates of ancestors from the time of the Merovingians onward. From that we know that Martha's ancestor Magda had the scroll and passed it on from generation to generation until Martha's grandfather received it. At some point he decided to hide it in the castle for safekeeping from some approaching danger, and that's where I accidently found it one day. So now Jed has both the original and the copy left as a precaution in Glastonbury. Take good care of them."

"We will, sir." Martha replied. "Thank you for telling us."

"There is one other thing that Henry found. He took a little time to excavate under the current foundation of the Abbey and discovered some of the original structure from ancient times. There he noticed a tiny cavity and found inside an ancient goblet in perfect condition which we think goes back to the start of the millennium. I have it."

"You said scrolls but you only mentioned the Merovingian scroll." Jed questioned Henry, "What about the other scroll?"

"That other scroll appears to be from the Egyptian era. It is very old. Dagobert had it but there is no identification on it. From its appearance, it is authentic and shows the genealogy of Sarah. She apparently was the first person to have the Cross." There was a moment of silence.

"Father." Jed had a puzzled look. "You said my great great-grandfather was with the Templars. If I have the Merovingian Cross, we must be related to the Merovingians. Are we?"

"I'm glad you asked, Jed." Henry smiled. "We are descended from them. Not only was Sir Henry with the Templars, but if you go back many generations, we are descended from Clovis I, called Clovis the Great. Sir Henry's great great-grandfather was Eudes de Chaumont and there is a direct line from Eudes back to Clovis I. Not only was that the case, but the first Grandmaster of the Templars, Hugues de Payen, was a descendant of Eudes. So was the first Grandmaster of the Prieuré de Sion, Jean de Gisor. The second Grand Mistress of the Prieuré de Sion was Marie de Saint Clair. There is much more to tell you, but we will save it for a later time. We have a busy day ahead of us."

"What is the Prieuré de Sion, sir?" Martha asked in a very quiet voice.

"I shouldn't have mentioned it." Henry said ruefully. "Let's just say it is a secret group affiliated with the Knights Templar. It's best you just forget what I said for now."

Jed and Martha were speechless as Henry left them. After they returned to their cabin, Martha leaned over to Jed and whispered, "We must be related, Jed." He nodded and they fell asleep.

The next morning the ship captains went ashore to complete their trading with the Chief. They distributed the food in a manner that left less than half with the four ships that would stay behind, and the rest with Henry's flagship and the other four ships. Henry also left half the sheep with those that remained in order to establish a colony to the northwest.

Henry invited all of the ship captains to the dinner he had promised them where he would complete his discussion of the plans and say final farewells before sailing south the next day. After the captains finished dinner, Henry asked Jed and Martha to join them. Then Henry explained the overall plan and answered questions.

One of the captains wanted to know what specifically Henry thought they would do when they found the place they were looking for. "What are your expectations? How will we get the ships up and into the harbor once we explore and are satisfied with the location? How will we communicate with you?"

Henry patiently explained and answered all his questions.

"You should be able to continue sailing northwest through this narrow gap because it's at least half a mile wide at the narrowest point and quite deep. You don't need to sail northeast around the huge island and back down to Pictou harbor. Once you have decided where you will live and you have secured the area, you will grow hay and wheat and other crops. We have provided enough hay for the sheep for several weeks. You should be able to hunt wild turkeys and wild boar as well as deer. The fish are plentiful in the sea and you will find trout in the streams and rivers. The European and native guide will tell you where you should hunt. As for shelter, look around you. The landscape is the same there as it is here, with plenty of oak, maple, and elm, as well as birch and beech trees and even some ash. You will have thick forests as we do here and in the south. The center of the island may be a little hilly but not insurmountable."

Henry also explained that they would be on the opposite side of New Scotland from where he and the other four ships planned to anchor. If it was necessary to make contact, a sufficient force could march in a southwest direction up and over the middle of the island to reach them. He was not certain how friendly all the tribes were. He only knew about the Mi'kmaq here and further southeast where he was going. They should ask their guides about the natives living inland.

"For those of us that want to return to Scotland," asked one of the captains, "please tell us, sir, what your plan is."

"I plan to send one or more ships back before winter sets in," responded Henry, "and those that want to return will go with one of them. It's my hope they will return here with additional settlers in a year or so. In fact, I would like you captains to pick one of your ships to return to Scotland before winter. It should sail down to our harbor first and pick up any others that want to return. One ship might be sufficient." There was a pause.

"Any more questions?" There were none. "And now before we say farewell for the night I want to drink a toast to Jed and Mark. They both had birthdays recently. Jed is now twelve and Mark is eleven. They have both been very good about staying out of your way. To Jed and Mark." He raised his glass and there were a few hip hip hoorays in salute to Jed and "Mark". And then the evening was over.

The captains said farewells and left the ship except for Captain Arnold, Henry's most senior captain, who stayed behind for a private talk. Jed overheard part of their conversation, enough to realize it was about burying the treasure from the four boats going to Pictou. Again Jed and Martha were very excited listening to this and could not sleep. They went out on deck and looked at the land all around them and the sky. The nights were warm and daylight remained until well into the late evening. It was approaching the longest day of the year. They slept very little that night.

It was dawn in a few hours and they were up with the rest of the crew very early as they pulled up anchor and sailed slowly away. They waved to the men on the four ships that remained. Jed thought *I think there are about eighty men on those four ships*. They eased out into the large bay of Chedabucto, sailed east, and then maneuvered around the cape they had passed on the way in. Henry set a course of west by southwest along the coast of New Scotland. Jed came up to stand next to Henry on the quarter deck.

"Father," Jed asked, "I remember you said we started with about two hundred fifty men and a few turned back in the beginning because of the storm. Then we left two ships and a few other men at Greenland and now we are leaving about eighty here. Is that correct? How many men do you think are left now on the five ships?"

"Jed, I know what you are thinking," Henry responded with some gravity. "Do we have enough? We have about half the men left, perhaps one hundred twenty or so. I think that's enough for what I have in mind."

No more was said. Once they were well on their way, Jed and Martha had another chance to talk to Henry. Jed wanted to know how long it would take to get to their destination. Martha wanted to know what the harbor was like and the natives and where they would stay and for how long.

"You two are certainly full of questions, aren't you?" said Henry, smiling.

Then he tried his best to answer all of them. He said they would sail fairly slowly along the coast because he wanted to map it as best he could. Because the days were very long, they could sail at least sixteen hours a day without having to do any dangerous night sailing.

"If we average a very slow five knots," he calculated, "and wander in and out of a few inlets and harbors, we will arrive in about three sailing days. But I expect to spend a bit more time exploring several deeper bays and harbors I only glimpsed the last time I was here, so perhaps it will take four or five days."

"As for our destination," he continued, "it's a large bay with several smaller harbors and coves and inlets. It's very treacherous because there are many islands and shoals not visible at high tide that could wreck any ship. We will use plumb lines and move very slowly. I will anchor in the southernmost harbor. It's set pretty deeply within the bay and I liked its location the last time I was there. The natives are extremely friendly and I'm looking forward to seeing them again. I promised I'd return one day and I'm not going to disappoint them."

After establishing a base, he told them, they would march to a location inland where he planned to build a castle, using the large supply of stone there and the dense forest of oak, elm, and maple timber. The colony they would establish would grow wheat and hay and sheep and the many crops the natives had shown them.

"How long will we stay?" asked Martha.

"That is a very difficult question to answer. Some of those establishing the colonies there and on the north side of the island will undoubtedly stay several years or longer. At least one ship will return to Scotland, probably before the winter sets in. It is my hope they will return in another year or two with additional settlers. Finally, I have thought of taking another ship or two and exploring further south before I return."

"What about us?" Martha asked. She was very persistent, thought Jed. He had assumed they would stay with Henry wherever he went. But he began to see that might not necessarily be what his father had in mind. He knew that the reason they had come in the first place had to do with the danger in Scotland but he was not sure what his father planned in New Scotland.

Henry hesitated. Finally he answered Martha. "That's a good question. Tell me what you would like to do. You could stay in one of the colonies and help establish it. You could return on one of the ships returning to Scotland, but I am sure that you don't want to do that. Keep in mind that it is still very dangerous for you there. I would say even more dangerous for the two of you than for any of the Templars on this voyage." Henry paused. "Or…"

"Or what?" Jed narrowed his eyes. He thought he knew the answer and he thought he was pretty sure which choice he would make. He was not too sure about Martha.

"Or you could go with me, if and when I sail south. I don't know what we will find there. But we are getting ahead of ourselves. That is in the future. First things first."

Martha wouldn't wait. She knew her answer. "We'll go with you, sir, wherever you go. We're having so much fun." She paused and looked at Jed. "Aren't we?"

Jed didn't answer but thought to himself, *I guess you could say so, but you don't have the responsibility that I do!* Then he smiled. *If it weren't for Martha I probably wouldn't be having nearly as much fun.* Then he spoke quietly.

"'Mark' is right," he said quietly to his father. "We'll go with you."

No more was said on that subject.

CHAPTER THIRTY ONE

Meeting the Mi'kmaqs

Halifax Bay, Nova Scotia
Late Summer, 1398

Henry and the remaining group of colonists heading south with him sailed the rest of the day following the eastern shoreline. Henry's ship, the Guillemot, was in the lead followed by the other four ships in formation. Captain Smith in the Puffin sailed directly behind him, Captain Jones in the Arctic Tern was off the starboard stern, and Captain Sullivan in the Herring Gull sailed off the port stern. Sir Gunn's ship the Albatross took the rear position. Henry had devised a simple signaling system to communicate the directions they would take, when and where they would stop, and other operations. He would flag the three following ships. The middle ship would then signal to Gunn.

As they cruised slowly along the shore, Henry took time to point out to Jed and Martha the various types of trees: the oak trees and maples with their distinctive leaves, and the elms, all with full foliage. He pointed out the thick stands of pines and firs and showed them how to identify valleys and rivers before they saw them by the levels of the trees in the forest. When the height of the treetops dipped down and then up in a rolling manner it indicated a valley, and when they disappeared altogether creating a gap in the tree line it usually meant a river. Martha always saw the rivers entering the ocean or the bays and inlets before Jed.

When they discovered a deep bay, Henry decided to explore it. He signaled to the others to follow and they found several rivers entering the bay. All five ships took this opportunity to cast out lines and fish. Each ship caught more than a dozen large silver blue fish. When hooked, they fought ferociously.

Henry then sailed down the coast between several islands and into a very deep harbor with two arms reaching far into the interior. He signaled to set anchor.

While they were sailing this last stretch, which took a couple of hours, he had ordered each ship to clean and cook enough of the fish for a sumptuous feast that evening. The rest were to be smoked. After the feast Henry spoke quietly to Jed and Martha.

"Having a feast such as this is very important," he explained, "for a ship captain to maintain high morale."

"I understand," Jed replied, "and it was the most delicious meal I've had in a long time."

Martha added, "It was the best tasting fish I've ever had in my life."

Jed and Martha were having more fun than they'd had the whole trip. They still stayed in their little room, and Martha cuddled closer than ever to Jed, with her arm thrown over him.

"I'm so happy," she told him, "being with you here. In the beginning I wasn't sure I would like sharing this room with you but when we had so much fun together I changed my mind."

She still had to wear her 'Mark' outfit every day and never once let it slip she was really a girl and not a boy.

"Do you think I'll ever be able to look like a girl again?" she asked Jed that night.

"Of course you will. But we need to be very careful right now."

Henry had said that the ships would sail at dawn to cover more distance. They sailed in and out of bays and harbors, and around islands, and between islands and the main shore. At midday they encountered a large group of islands sitting off of a series of points and peninsulas. Then later they explored two bays, each of which sat at the mouth of a large river still flowing well late into June. Finally they encountered a large irregular peninsula projecting out into the ocean. At first Henry thought it was an island and tried to sail through on the northern side but had to turn back and go around it.

Then Henry observed a large deep harbor that went inland several miles before coming to an end where several rivers emptied into it. It was here Henry signaled all the ships to drop anchor for the short night. Each ship had another fine meal of fish and some of the game they had caught earlier. He invited all the other four ship captains to join him on his flagship after dinner.

While Jed and Martha listened, Henry explained that they would take another two days at a leisurely pace to arrive at the huge bay he had described. Before entering the bay, each captain would have a map and a separate set of directions from Henry about how to maneuver through the islands and shoals to avoid grounding and possibly sinking their vessels.

Henry explained that the harbor he would land in was very narrow and did not allow for more than one ship to anchor. It was the place he would land to greet the Grand Chief of the Mi'kmaqs.

Gunn and the other three ships would anchor off the northwest cove of the large curved island out in the bay. The ship captains would go ashore with Henry as they had done in the northern tribal area. They would rendezvous at the anchor point off the large island where he would explain more about these Mi'kmaqs and his previous visit.

Meanwhile, they had two more days sailing ahead of them. They would cover some distance on the morrow, he said, and be within a few hours of their destination on the final day of this journey. The other four captains departed as before and rowed back to their ships in daylight. They knew they would sail at dawn and cover many miles the next day. Henry, it was very clear, was anxious to reach this next bay. He had visited it five years before and hoped it would be as friendly now as it had been.

Jed and Martha were anxious to ask Henry if they could go ashore with the others. Henry had a very serious look on his face as if he had many things on his mind, but when they asked with such expectant and innocent faces, he had to smile. He hugged both of them and said they needed to get lots of sleep. Henry paused and then continued.

"You need to be well rested to go ashore with me to meet my friends, the Mi'kmaqs."

Jed and Martha quietly thanked him and disappeared to their room. Then they let out squeals of delight and hugged each other.

"Do you know," said Jed, "that my father almost never hugs me?"

Martha and Jed slept soundly for the several hours they had before dawn. They were awakened by the clanging of the morning bell, the shouts and calls of the crew, and the flapping of the sails being raised in the wind, as the crew made ready to set sail. They were underway at daylight. As soon as they had eaten breakfast, they were looking over the side of the flagship. It sailed out of the narrow channel, followed by the other four ships, and around the large headland projecting into the ocean.

It took almost an hour to clear this long peninsula. Jed and Martha marveled at the high cliffs and the birds soaring in the sky.

"Those look like the birds we saw after we left home. They are nesting high up on the cliffs." Martha sighed. "They are raising their young in such a precarious place. How difficult it must be."

"I bet they do it because it must be safer that way," responded Jed. Henry chanced to come by and overheard them.

"You are correct." They were startled and Henry smiled. "They are the same as the ones you saw in the Orkneys and Shetlands. The black bird with the white patch is the Black Guillemot and the bird with the massive bright bill is the Puffin. They nest there for safety as you thought. Their enemies are mainly gulls and skuas."

They sailed in and out of several small bays and harbors and around numerous islands along the coast. Henry took one major excursion in mid-morning into a long, very narrow harbor. He asked Gunn to explore the next one they would encounter in about an hour. He assigned each of the other ships one of three similar harbors to explore as they encountered them one after the other.

Each ship had a designated list of things to note about the land on either side and the birds and mammals they saw, and finally a description of any natives. Henry took another trip into the final narrow harbor they passed on this long day's journey. He instructed the other four captains to rendezvous there after they completed their explorations.

Jed and Martha helped by observing on both sides of the narrow harbor and identified the oak and maple trees. Jed pointed out the white and yellow birch, which Henry had told them about, and Martha spotted the Arctic Terns flying overhead and dolphins in the water. As they sailed deeper into the harbor, they saw several natives running along the south shore and pointed them out to Henry. He smiled. The natives tried to keep up with the ship as they sailed ever closer to the end of the bay. Jed and Martha stood on the port side and watched them running along. They were yelling in unison, "Glooscap. Glooscap." When the ship turned back, the natives kept running and yelling as if they knew where the ship was headed and they were spreading the word.

Henry was joined by the other ships as he approached the mouth of the harbor, and he signaled them to follow him. He took the convoy down the coastline for a few more hours until they encountered a large land mass ahead and a wide harbor that stretched inland for at least thirty or forty miles. It was getting well into the evening so Henry signaled that they would anchor at the mouth of this harbor.

Later that evening, Henry met in his quarters with the other four ship captains. He invited both Jed and 'Mark' to join them. Prior to the arrival of the captains, he reminded them not to say one word during the meeting. He looked pointedly at Martha and said that meant no questions. If they had questions they should ask him later, after the captains left. They nodded.

Henry explained the procedure to the captains. "It will be much the same as before. You will bring your senior officers with you and leave the rest of the men behind as we did when we met with the northern Mi'kmaq chiefs. There will be one difference this time, which is why I invited Jed and his friend Mark. The Grand Chief has a son named Mali about the same age as Jed. This age is a very important one for the sons of chiefs. Mali will soon be undergoing some rites of passage, some tests of manhood. I believe the Grand Chief will like it very much if his son meets Jed. Chief Kampalijek of the Northern Mi'kmaqs told me the Grand Chief's son has a friend, the son of a neighboring chief. This friend's father is a European named Charles. It is unusual for a European to be so respected as to become a chief."

Henry continued, "Jed and Mark will see what I mean when they meet. That is the reason I have invited them here tonight. They will follow whatever the Grand Chief's son does and learn a great deal about their culture in ways we never could. His friend, the son of the European, speaks our language, of course, and the Chief's son has learned some words as well. I explain this to all of you so you will understand when you see the boys together. So don't be concerned. We will have plenty of other things to be concerned with. Any questions?" There were none.

After the ship captains left for the night, Jed and Martha quietly approached Henry.

"You were very good tonight." Henry put an arm on each of their shoulders. "Both of you were. No questions from you, 'Mark'. I saw the two of you out of the corner of my eye. You were watching the captains. Was that to see their reactions?"

"No sir," replied Martha, "I was just wondering if they had sons or daughters and if they missed them. Perhaps the captains wish their children were here."

"Some of them do, but as far as I know the children are all quite young. I don't believe the captains are thinking what you might imagine."

"What do you mean, sir?" asked Jed.

"All of them know, as do many of the descendants of the Templars on board, that they have a choice. They are probably all wondering, as you are, what will be happening next. They will have a choice to stay here at the end of this summer or sail back to Scotland."

"I don't understand, sir," Martha frowned and narrowed her eyes in a squint.

"After we establish this colony and the other on the north side, we will need more people to populate it. Some of the men will return to Scotland with the news about this land, and I hope many others will then want to come here. Some of these men may want to come back and bring their families. You see, many of them are in a dangerous situation back there if they are identified as one of the key descendants of a Templar." Henry narrowed his eyes and stared at them. "I will also point out that there are still forces of the Church and the French King looking for the so-called missing treasures, and any association with the Templars or any treasure puts them and their families in danger." There was silence for a moment.

"I have a different question." Jed changed the subject. "What are these boys like?"

"The ones we will play with or explore with or whatever we'll do," Martha tossed in.

"That is what I want you to tell me." Henry ended the conversation. "Time for bed."

Jed and Martha curled up close together and whispered and asked questions of each other. Neither of them had any of the answers. What did these native boys do for fun? Could they shoot arrows? Did they have any horses? How well did they speak? Would they understand English? The questions went on until it was dark and they finally fell asleep.

The ship raised anchor and slowly sailed out and around the huge land mass. In just over four hours, they came to the entrance of a large bay. Its mouth was about five miles wide. Jed could see that it widened out inside the mouth, but he could not see the end of it. Henry said it went at least twenty miles in. He signaled that this was not the one they would enter. Shortly after they passed the entrance of the bay, they approached the end of a large peninsula.

Henry directed the helmsman to slow down, and he signaled the other ships to follow single file and not deviate from the line he took. He then took the helm and maneuvered his ship expertly through a narrow passage between two islands to port and shoals to starboard. Once clear of the shoals, he took a line to the south of a big curved island and north to a point off the northwest cove. Jed and Martha were fascinated with this expertise. Jed in particular was very intent on Henry's every move. They watched the men with plumb lines on both port and starboard and off the bow. They were expert at finding the depth and instantly calling it out.

All five ships dropped anchor at various points in the deep water around the cove. It was still only midday. It was imperative that Henry go ashore as soon as possible as a courtesy to Grand Chief Membertou now that they had arrived. He signaled to the captains to come aboard his flagship. They would sail on his ship into the narrow harbor to meet the Grand Chief and the other chiefs he would undoubtedly bring to the peace circle. The word must have spread rapidly from the time their boats had been seen in the neighboring harbor. The natives could easily have traveled to tell the Grand Chief that Henry and his ships had arrived during the time they anchored overnight. When Henry explained this to Jed, Jed wondered why the natives didn't know before.

"Couldn't the Chief from the northern tribe have sent a messenger to tell this Grand Chief?"

"It would take much too long to travel that distance overland compared to the time by ship."

Jed was mad at himself for asking such a dumb question. Jed and Martha went off to prepare for the meeting. They had an idea about presenting a gift to the Grand Chief's son when they met. While waiting for the ship captains to come aboard along with the mates they'd chosen to join them, Henry had decided to dig into his treasure trove for objects that would not be significant to keep for the Templar and Cathar legacies but would have major significance for the Grand Chief. He was sure his captains had done the same.

He gathered up his gifts and greeted the ship captains and their officers one by one. Each ship captain usually left his first mate in charge when he was not on board. Jed explained to Martha that if anything ever happened to the captain, the mate would become the new captain.

"I know that. Do you think I'm stupid?" she snapped.

Jed thought Martha was a little testy and nervous because of what they were about to do. She had already told him she was tired of being a boy all the time. She said she only felt like a girl when she curled up at night with Jed. Jed decided it was better just to be silent for the time being.

When all of the captains and officers were on board, Henry gave directions for the anchor to be raised and again took the helm himself. No one knew these waters better than he, Jed realized, and he didn't want any disasters now at this crucial point. Henry carefully took the ship southwest until he found the channel he sought. He headed west between a series of shoals and underwater ledges and small islands until he was approaching the shore dead west ahead. He then went north and west around a small island strategically placed at the mouth of this final harbor.

Suddenly, Jed heard shouts. Then he saw many braves and even women and children along both banks chanting Henry's name, "Glooscap. Glooscap. Glooscap."

Henry waved. All the men on board also waved, and the natives waved back.

Henry maneuvered the ship into the west end of the harbor as far as it was safe to go, dropped anchor, and lowered his boats into the water. He was the first ashore. He was joined by the four other ship captains in one boat and several of the other men in another. They rowed to the south shore of the harbor where the Chief and his braves were waiting. While the oarsmen returned for them, Jed and Martha watched the traditional formal greeting between Henry and the chiefs.

All this time, the natives stood on both shores and chanted his name. "Glooscap."

CHAPTER THIRTY TWO

Farewell to Clotaire

Northern Coast, Francia
Spring, 752 AD

Jeb looked out over the sea with Magda by his side. He delighted in the feeling of the wind in his face. His shoulder length blonde hair was blown behind him, while Magda's waist length black hair was tucked under her leather cap so it wouldn't blow around her face. They stowed the new boots and soft flat-soled walking shoes Clotaire had made for them in the storage area and enjoyed being barefoot while sailing.

"It's so beautiful out there now, isn't it Jeb?" Magda murmured, "With the sunset glow on the water?"

Jeb just nodded. He put his arm around her in the chilly air. The wind created low rolling waves lapping against the shore and the sun dipped behind the drifting clouds. Then the sun emerged briefly as it slowly descended to the horizon. They heard the raucous cries of the Black-Headed and Herring Gulls and saw them high overhead etched against the clouds.

Now that Jeb knew he and Magda would be continuing the journey without Clotaire, he was motivated more than ever to learn everything about sailing and navigation. He began his next two nights of training by sailing the boat himself with Clotaire urging him on and giving him advice. At the end of the lesson Clotaire was no longer saying anything but watching with admiration. He would say only now and then that Jeb was doing well. Jeb sailed part way out toward the mouth of the inlet, tacking back and forth, then came about and jibed on his return. He began to enjoy himself, feel confident, and thought that maybe this would not be too bad after all.

They spent some of their time hunting in order to stock up for the trip. Magda set up the oven to cook the meat they killed. They completed the preparation of the meat and began stowing it in the storage locker. Clotaire kept some of the meat for his own journey. At dawn they had a delicious meal of the fresh game they had just smoked and cooked. Magda had spent some of her time while the others were sailing to collect some birds' eggs she'd found on the ground. She was careful to leave one or two eggs in the nest. She also found some roots and berries. They all knew this was one of the last meals the three of them would share together. Jeb noticed how subdued they all were. They slept fitfully that day.

That night Jeb had his last sailing lesson. The wind was blowing from the north in much stronger gusts and the waves were a few feet high.

Clotaire was pleased to be able to teach Jeb how to handle the boat in stronger winds and seas. This time Magda came along as well. When the wind died down a little, both Jeb and Clotaire showed her how to handle the "sheet" to direct the sail. When Jeb gave directions she would move the hemp sheet from one side to the other and cleat it on the oarlocks. Magda also took a turn at the helm.

Clotaire explained, "Magda needs to know almost as much as you, Jeb, and in time, perhaps even more. You are growing taller and becoming stronger but there might be occasions when you will have to struggle with the sails and she might have to take the helm, perhaps in difficult conditions."

The wind picked up again and this time Clotaire stayed out of it altogether. Jeb handled the helm, giving directions to Magda when they needed to tack or come about. They began to have fun, even though the waves were high and the winds quite strong.

"You are ready to sail on your own," Clotaire said. "Drop me off and sail by yourself."

Jeb and Magda sailed out beyond the mouth of the inlet and back again in the dark. The only light was from the stars.

Clotaire told them what to do if the stars disappeared. "Once you know the direction you are going, if the stars disappear, you will use the wind direction and the waves to hold a course. We call this 'dead reckoning'."

Staying on course wasn't easy when a shifting wind required intense concentration and repeated tacking, even when the stars were out. But Jeb and Magda needed to know what to do if the skies became cloudy and stars could not be seen. It would be disastrous if they lost their sense of direction then.

Clotaire had done one last thing with respect to the boat. He cut a large amount of hemp to fashion a very long rope to which he attached an odd shaped rock on one end. The rock had crevices which allowed him to tie the hemp to it securely. This was to be their anchor.

He explained to both of them how and where to drop anchor and how to make sure they were in water shallow enough for the rock to touch bottom. But if the wind was too strong, the anchor would not hold. They would be forced to go ashore and pull the boat in and cover it. Clotaire also explained how to drag anchor when sailing against a very strong wind to keep their heading in the correct direction.

While they were practicing, Clotaire also cut enough cannabis to make hemp for a line to haul and tie up the boat. He also had some to use for safety lines when they were on the open water, especially in heavy seas, to prevent them from falling overboard. They could attach the lines to the oarlocks or seats. He also made enough extra hemp because he knew they would discover many other uses for it. He'd also been saving deerskin and boar hide and used this to make wineskins to hold extra water on their journey. He felt they should have no trouble finding water, but with the wineskins they wouldn't have to worry if they had to stay out to sea along the coast for a few days.

Jeb and Magda returned from sailing and the looks on their faces were magical. He'd never seen them so excited in all the time they had traveled together, except when they were swimming. They finished the smoking and cooking of the meat and stowed it in the watertight storage area except the meat for their last meal.

Then Clotaire revealed his plan to them.

He said, "I'll go first to the area around Stenay to see if there are survivors and then to the area around Rhédae. If I can find enough of my kin I will locate Childeric and attempt a rescue. If I can't, I will continue searching until I build up a strong force of skilled men."

Clotaire's last job was to explain to Jeb and Magda the remaining details of the journey they must take. They would sail only at night and with the utmost care. They could anchor only in narrow protected inlets or bays of small unoccupied islands away from the mainland. Even that would be dangerous in the daytime.

Clotaire insisted, "You should never be visible from land. It would be much better if you went ashore. You must always cover the boat completely while you eat and sleep. After you cross the channel to the south of the huge projection of land across the way, you will continue sailing along the coast in a westerly direction."

"Eventually you will come to a large island," he continued. "It's called the Isle of Wight and might take several days to reach. You will anchor on the southwest side of it. After that you will hug the coast north to a river and march north from there." He described the terrain going inland for the rest of their journey and then they all went to sleep. Jeb slept more soundly than he had ever done in all their traveling.

The next morning they completed the loading of the boat. Their bedding and gear went into the watertight storage area in the stern along with the tools and weapons, and the bread, nuts, roots, berries, mushrooms, and water. Clotaire and Jeb installed the mast and sail. Magda had one last request: she wanted to bring the oven lid. Clotaire thought a moment and decided he could stow it on the inside of the bow where it would be out of the way. Magda took a couple of the cooking planks as well.

Jeb teased. "Now, Magda, we don't need the oven rocks for ballast."

She looked at him with a little smile and said, "Perhaps I can find some rocks if I need to."

They slept soundly during the day and at dusk made ready to sail. The stars twinkled in the clear sky and the slight breeze caused the water to undulate ever so slightly. *It's a perfect night,* thought Magda.

Together they hugged Clotaire and clung to him. They would not let go, but finally Clotaire gave them one last hug, pushed them gently away, and turned toward the forest. They launched the boat and pushed off. Jeb looked back and thought he could see Clotaire wipe away a tear. Then he glanced at Magda and saw her wipe away tears. He felt a tear well up in his eyes as well and realized he might never see Clotaire again. Magda came back to the stern and sat next to Jeb on the storage box as he managed the tiller. She put her arm around him. Jeb shifted the tiller into one hand, grabbed Magda tightly with the other and put his head against hers. They looked back at the shore but Clotaire was gone. He had already disappeared into the woods. His mission had begun. So had theirs. They hugged each other for some time and listened to the soft lapping of the water against the side of the boat and the distant sound of gulls high in the sky.

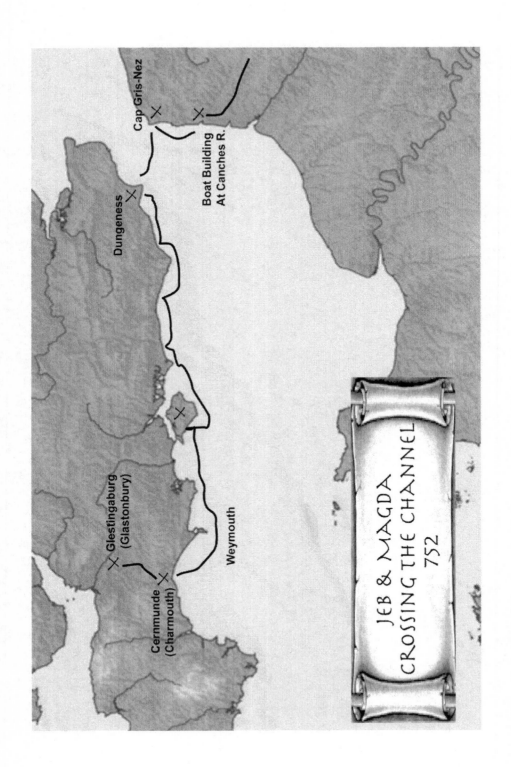

JEB & MAGDA
CROSSING THE CHANNEL
752

Cap Gris-Nez

Boat Building
At Canches R.

Dungeness

Weymouth

Glestingaburg
(Glastonbury)

Cernmunde
(Charmouth)

CHAPTER THIRTY THREE

Crossing the Channel

Northern Coast, Francia
Spring, 752 AD

Magda deftly managed the sail and Jeb the tiller as they sailed out into the channel, the wind increasing as they moved away from land. They set a course directly north along the coast. The moon was approaching its new phase so their light came mainly from the stars. Jeb thought *we will soon have a new moon.* He checked his direction with the North Star and the two Bears. He felt he was right on course. The wind that was coming into the channel was blowing in an east by northeast direction so Magda set a broad reach and they raced ahead of the wind. This time she didn't mind her long black hair blowing about her head or the spray kicking up as they raced along.

"Oh Jeb," she yelled above the sound of the water pounding and splashing against the sides of the boat. "This is so exciting. It's wonderful out here at night."

Jeb realized that Clotaire had designed a very fast boat. He was glad part of his early learning included mathematics. He and Magda developed a system to measure the speed of the boat. While she would count in a measured beat which they decided was a single second, he would mark a spot on the water such as a wave or ripple where the bow crossed and then count one boat length when the stern crossed the same point. When she said "Stop!" he would use the number of boat lengths he counted and the number of seconds she counted to calculate the speed of the boat.

Since the boat was sixteen feet long, at one boat length per second they would be traveling at about eleven and a half Roman miles per hour. But he didn't expect boat speed that high since it would be slightly beyond what Clotaire had estimated. Clotaire said two things about boat speed: Jeb should start to think in knots and told him how to calculate them. He also said he thought the maximum speed might be around eight knots, or less than ten miles per hour. On this first leg of their journey, Jeb thought they were skipping along at about eight miles per hour. He couldn't yet think in terms of knots.

Clotaire didn't know much about the coastline across the sea but he knew the distance to Cap Gris-Nez was less than fifty miles. He had also heard from kinsmen who had traveled across the channel that the distance from the Cap to the nearest point across the channel was between forty and fifty miles. Jeb felt with the good wind and fair weather they had, they would reach Cap Gris-Nez several hours before dawn. Getting across the channel in one night was a different matter. They would need just the right conditions. He would see what tomorrow would bring. But this was a beautiful first night on the undulating open seas.

Magda had set the sail just right and tied the sheet to the cleat. Jeb seldom had to move the tiller. In fact, it had just the right amount of tension which allowed him to take his hand off for extended periods. He would check the Bears now and then to make sure they were on course. The hours went by and Magda curled up much of the time in the bottom of the boat at his feet. Occasionally she would ask to take the helm for a little while. Jeb gladly gave her the tiller and stretched out in the boat. He would lie on his back and look at the stars and calculate the time. He knew that the stars moved from horizon to horizon in about twelve hours.

He could find the North Star and the Bears easily. When the North Star had traveled across about half the sky he knew they had covered about six hours, so he asked Magda to adjust the sail and he adjusted the tiller so as to move closer in toward the coast. As they approached they smelled the damp fog and felt it on their faces as it rolled slowly inland. Magda shivered from the cold and pulled her cap down and her collar up. They heard the distant screech of a gull.

Magda spotted the Cap projecting outward in the distance. They would be there in less than an hour. Jeb was now sailing along the shore. When they felt they were within a mile of the Cap, they searched in the dark for an indentation in the coast line and heavy growth along the shore. Magda spotted an overhanging set of trees and bushes and motioned Jeb to shore. They approached silently and listened. They heard nothing but the waves lapping. Then they heard the low, sighing 'oo-oo-oo' of an owl.

"Do you hear that, Jeb?" Magda held up her hand for quiet. They heard it again. "It sounds like something moaning. What is it?"

"I'm pretty sure it's a long-eared owl. It does sound like a moan, doesn't it?"

They listened silently as they came within one hundred feet of shore and slowly drifted closer. Then they took the mast down and used the oars for the last several feet, drifting under a huge overhanging tree that reached out over the water. They sat there quietly for a moment.

"Jeb, do you hear the sound of a small animal scratching in the undergrowth?"

He nodded, wishing Clotaire were with them. This was their first night and day on their own and he was still a little nervous. But then he realized no one could have seen them on the water. It was so thick along the shore there was no reason for anyone to be nearby. But Magda agreed it would be a good idea to eat their dinner in the boat. They sat quietly in the bottom of the hull and ate their first meal alone.

"Do you want to swim and bathe?" Jeb asked. "It will be dawn soon."

"I couldn't relax," she responded, "but perhaps when we cross the channel I will."

They listened quietly and heard nothing so they pulled the boat on shore, making sure it was not visible from the water. They got out their furs and gunny sack and Jeb brought his knife and axe. They settled down on shore a few feet from the boat and slept fitfully. They heard nothing the entire day.

As dusk approached, they stowed their gear and had a little meat and dry bread and an egg which Magda had brought along. As it got dark, they pushed out and hoisted the mast and installed the rigging. Jeb was anxious to leave, but Magda insisted they wait until it was completely dark. They could see nothing moving on the sea.

Jeb had gotten his wish about the weather. They were in luck. The wind had been to port and slightly astern on the way up and had now shifted, coming from the northeast. As they sailed almost west across the channel, it would be to starboard and slightly astern. The waves were only a foot or two high and lightly rolling. Magda pointed out a pair of dolphins following them for a short while until they suddenly disappeared. Seagulls cried overhead, but otherwise the only sound was that of the boat rhythmically hitting the waves as they raced along.

Magda set another broad reach and stayed with it for most of the time. They sped across the channel and Jeb calculated they were skimming the water at nearly seven miles an hour. He was used to miles per hour but did a quick calculation and decided they were doing about six knots. He felt the speed of this boat could be even faster when they became more comfortable with sailing. Magda looked back at Jeb and smiled a warm smile.

"We're really flying along. Do you think we'll get there before dawn?" she asked.

"At this speed I'm sure we will, but let's see if it stays this way."

They took turns at the tiller and holding the sail in place. Jeb checked the course the usual way. When he had a chance to stretch out he looked up at the Bears. They had covered about four hours according to his reckoning. Then it became overcast and the stars disappeared. He stayed calm and remembered his lessons. The light became very dim and he noted the angle of the bow against the waves and stayed on that course. The wind dropped and their speed slowed.

He could just make out the wave motion in the dim light and kept the tiller locked in the position to stay on this course. An hour later, fortune was with them again. Magda, with her eagle eyes, saw land off the starboard bow and Jeb steered closer to it. Dawn was not far off and the light increased just enough to see the coast. They skirted it for another hour until they could see the apparent mouth of a small river ahead. This must have been what Clotaire had talked about. His information was accurate.

They reached the mouth of the river and noticed the west side was covered with thickets of yew, alder trees, and elder and more of the overhanging willow trees. This time they felt much bolder but still drifted in closely and listened for any sounds in the dark before they dropped the mast and used the oars to draw in under the cover of the trees. They sat in the boat and waited. They didn't move. There were no sounds except those of the water lapping against the boat and the rippling waves on shore. There was a slight breeze rustling the leaves. After listening for several minutes they felt comfortable enough to put ashore.

Magda announced she was going to bathe and looked slyly at Jeb to see if he was game. It was not quite dawn. He sat and watched her dip into the cold water. She shivered but stayed in. Jeb finally felt comfortable enough to join her. They played silently and he wondered how she could splash him with water without making a sound. He realized she cupped the water and then lifted it over him. He was chasing her when suddenly she stopped and turned around, came up to him, and hugged him tightly.

"I'm so happy to be with you," she whispered in his ear and held him even tighter.

"I am too," Jeb softly answered. "We make a great team, don't we?"

"Yes." Magda spoke very softly and continued to hold him, "Clotaire was right. Do you know you've grown?"

"Yes." Jeb was so quiet Magda could hardly hear him. "So have you."

"You're bigger. All over."

"So are you. You're not so skinny anymore."

Magda held him just a little longer and then started to shiver. She finally pulled away and they dressed. They made sure the boat was covered and not visible from the water, then ate quietly and curled up close together next to the boat under their furs. Jeb made sure he had his knife and axe by his side. They slept very soundly that day.

CHAPTER THIRTY FOUR

Outracing Danger

South Coast, Britannia
Spring, 752 AD

Magda and Jeb woke in the afternoon, stowed their gear, and had breakfast. They ate the last of the bird's eggs and a little meat, cheese, and bread. Then they discussed what they remembered from Clotaire's directions. He'd told them it might take several nights of sailing to reach the big island down the coast of this new land Clotaire called Britannia. Then they might need another few days to reach a narrow peninsula projecting out into the channel.

They would sail to the center of the inner bay and leave the boat in a safe place. They would then head inland and march straight north. They would find the Abbey in Glestingaburg after a couple of weeks or so of night marching. They should plan on finding enough food for several weeks just in case. When Jeb asked 'just in case what' Clotaire had said in a low voice just in case they got lost or had to return.

"Magda," Jeb spoke slowly in a low voice, "Clotaire never told us about the people we might see along the coast."

"Don't worry, Jeb. We'll stay away from them as best we can."

"We may have to go ashore to hunt or gather nuts and berries. We can't stay out to sea all the time."

"Do we have enough meat and water for now?" Magda inquired. "Can we use the river water if we need to?"

"I don't think we should take a chance on the river. It's probably a little salty here. We need to find a spring soon. I think we have meat and water for a few days at least." Then Jeb smiled. "Perhaps you will have to use your oven lid after all."

She smiled with her head cocked to one side. Then she raised her eyebrows and rolled her eyes as if to say 'I told you.'

When it was dark enough they uncovered the boat and pushed it out. They installed the mast and set sail. Jeb thought they truly were a team. They worked together so well. They had a routine now that was becoming familiar to them. The stars were out to guide them. They did not talk for nearly an hour while Jeb set a straight southwest course. Magda reached down to pick out drifting seaweed from the water. She tasted the salt on her fingers and turned up her nose at the strong smell of the decaying seaweed. She listened to the familiar cry of seagulls and settled into her role as 'crew'.

When they left the shelter of the river, the wind was not strong but it was from the northeast, so they flew along with the wind behind them. Magda had the sail to port and almost perpendicular to the boat. They did their usual calculations and estimated they were flying along at eight knots. Jeb smiled and realized he had quickly become comfortable with nautical measurements and left behind his thinking in terms of land. In a couple of hours, the land receded back into a bay. As Jeb stayed the course, it gradually disappeared.

"This is magical," stated Magda. "I'm so very happy being with you, Jeb."

"I feel the same way, Magda," he responded. "I feel as if I am sitting on a cloud. Life is so good."

Magda set the sheet and curled up in front of Jeb. Then she rested her head on his knee and put her arms around his leg. They sailed for some time without saying a word. But then the wind picked up, bringing in thick clouds which covered the stars. This did not concern Jeb and Magda too much, but nevertheless Magda sat up and grabbed the sail, wanting to make sure they followed their direct course.

The waves increased but Jeb found he could ride the waves if he reached a certain speed and held it. Then the clouds cleared away and the stars came out again, and Magda jumped up.

"Jeb, look!"

Magda pointed to starboard and in the distance Jeb saw another boat, heading at an angle toward them.

It was a slim, narrow boat with a single mast close to the bow and the sail was used much like a spinnaker. It ran very fast downwind.

"He sees us," Jeb yelled. "He's trying to cut us off."

The boat appeared to be a little larger than their boat, perhaps twenty feet long or more, and the helmsman had set a course south by southwest to intercept them. He was taking an angle to the swells so that the boat rocked from side to side as it slowly crested a wave. However, the helmsman set a broad reach with the sail out over the water to benefit as much from the tail wind as he could. With a glimmer of starlight, Magda could see the boat clearly.

"It's coming closer to us, Jeb. What are we going to do?" screamed Magda.

"Let out the sail and hang on! We're not going to let them catch us if I can help it. We're going to fly."

Magda let it out and hung on. She used the cleat as a partial control so she could keep the sail as full as possible. Jeb steered slightly to port so the waves were at a very slight angle and allowed him to move away from the oncoming boat. They picked up speed and rode a wave and then dropped down into the trough and rapidly up the next wave and over. Jeb steered back to a course dead perpendicular to the waves and told Magda to let out the sail just a bit. He never imagined the boat could sail this fast. They ran before the wind for almost an hour, gradually gaining distance from the other boat.

"You're pulling ahead of him, but he's not giving up." Magda turned to look over the bow. "Jeb, look out. We're heading for those cliffs."

Looming out of the darkness dead ahead was an enormous cliff face dropping straight to the sea. Without even thinking, Jeb dropped off course and Magda pulled the sail tighter. They cut an angle to port of the waves and on a course that just cleared the cliffs. The other boat had to alter course sharply and was forced to take a line that was almost parallel to the waves, and with the sail so far foredeck it slowed down considerably. Jeb took their boat around the cliffs and back onto a direct course riding the crests. The other boat was forced to fall further and further behind.

"He's turning back," yelled Magda. "You beat him, Jeb!"

"You were wonderful, Magda! You handled that sail beautifully, gave us such speed, we must've been over ten knots."

"You were magnificent, my Captain. I'm so proud of you."

She threw her arms around him and kissed him on the cheek. When the other boat was completely out of sight, Jeb set a course to a more westerly direction and then to northwest by west which took the boat back along the coast. The wind dropped as they slipped around a headland jutting out into the sea. They sailed for another hour until the darkness of the sky showed signs of approaching dawn.

"We need to get off the water, Jeb." Magda spoke quietly.

Jeb pulled in closer to shore and they peered into the dim light. Magda pointed to an indentation and what appeared to be a river surging into the sea. Jeb went to the mouth and skirted the edge of the west shore.

"Magda," Jeb called softly, "isn't that a tiny cove?"

She nodded agreement.

They drifted slowly into the cove and listened. The only sound they heard was that of the gurgling river. The woods were thick with dense interwoven yew thickets and willow trees overhanging the water. This was a secluded place Jeb felt was perfect, so thickly covered they would be unlikely to encounter people. They would be invisible from the water.

Magda dropped the sail and got out the oars. She took the tiller while Jeb rowed. They approached the thickest of the growth. Jeb took down the mast and rowed carefully, squeezing between the trees until the boat was almost aground.

"Look Jeb." Magda pointed to an opening right in front of them. "It's a cave! And it's almost invisible."

They sat and listened again, but all was silent. It was dawn, and as the light began to filter through the willow trees, Jeb beached the boat without making a noise. He got out his axe and knife and went slowly into the cave, allowing his eyes to become accustomed to the darkness. Magda came up beside him. She also had a knife in her hand.

The cave had a low ceiling and was ten feet deep and six feet wide, but with an opening only three feet wide. The floor was flat eroded rock covered with sand. They turned the boat so the bow faced the water, in case they had to make a hasty exit, and sat together outside, listening as they watched the light increase and day arrive.

Finally, they felt safe enough and dragged the boat under the thickest brush they could find and covered it. Jeb got the gear out and the remaining food and water. They ate in silence for a while and then Magda started to talk quietly with a smile of joy as she recounted their near escape from the pirates or whatever they were.

"We need to find some water soon," Jeb remarked.

"I'll look for a spring. What about our meat supply?" Magda asked.

"I think now would be a good time to hunt. We have this cave and you have your 'oven'," Jeb teased. "We can stay here and cook whatever I catch just as we've done before."

They finished eating and set up their bedding. Jeb asked Magda if she was going to swim at all but she said she was too tired. They curled up and listened to the wind in the trees. It was high above them and still strong but down below it was calm. And then it started to rain. This was the first rain they'd had in many days and it poured. It was a deluge and the splattering of the pouring rain obscured all other sounds. Magda hugged Jeb as they lay together.

"We're pretty lucky after all, don't you think?" she asked Jeb.

"You mean escaping from that boat?"

"Yes, that too, but I mean finding this cave out of the rain. We're very lucky."

He nodded agreement and held her in his arms as they fell asleep. The rain continued all day and the wind whistled through the treetops. They slept soundly and woke to the patter of very light rain. The wind had stopped.

"When it's dark, let's go hunting. You look for water, and I'll look for meat."

"All right, Captain!" Magda smiled as they curled up under their furs, listening to the rain. "Anything you say."

They had their evening 'breakfast' of meat and a small amount of bread and a few berries. The darkness came quickly. Magda headed off to the east of the cave. She had fashioned a loop for her knife around her waist and carried all the empty skins to fill when she found a spring. Jeb followed her at first, carrying his knife in similar fashion and his bow and quiver. They listened in the night air for sounds as they moved almost silently through the forest. After walking slowly through the brush, Jeb put a hand on her arm.

"I hear it." She spoke in a very soft voice. "It's the sound of water running."

They moved toward the sound and found a small brook trickling from a spring. She motioned him to go. She imitated a bow and arrow and smiled. He smiled back and disappeared back toward the cave. Soon he came across a deer trail, checked the tracks, and found the most recent ones were heading west. He gambled that the deer would be returning in an easterly direction, so he looked for a hidden shelter facing the direction he believed they would come. He felt the slight breeze and decided it was blowing from the west so he would be downwind. He found a perfect hiding place behind two trees and waited.

Magda filled her skins with water and returned to the cave. She stowed the water in the boat and removed the oven lid from the bow. She pulled out the planks she had stowed in the storage area and soaked them under water held down with rocks. She then began to construct the oven as Clotaire had done.

She found a set of stones that approximately equaled each other in height and created the inner fire box just inside the cave entrance. She also decided to soak the oven lid just a bit and weighted it down in the water. She created the outer set of rocks to support the lid at just the right height above the inner firebox. She then waited and listened.

After two hours, Jeb was rewarded by the sight of two deer. He set his sights on the smaller of the two which was walking out in front. The deer came just in range. He aimed. Just as he released the arrow a small black bear lumbered out of the yew thickets and the deer jumped. Jeb missed and the deer ran off unhurt. Then the bear turned toward Jeb. Jeb tried to be as big as possible and held his bow and arrow at the ready. After what seemed like an eternity, the bear moved away.

Jeb sat down on a fallen tree, his head in his hands. *What a hunter,* he thought. *I can't even hit a deer at all.* Just as he was about to give up and head back empty-handed, he heard a rustle in the bushes. A small wild boar was rooting around. Jeb made ready with another arrow. When the boar was in sight, he let fly.

The rain continued to fall but Magda was prepared. She had saved some dry moss and leaves and kept them in the storage area to start a fire. She used these and found small dry twigs inside the entrance to the cave. She found more dry wood under the boat and had the fire in the oven ready to go for when Jeb returned.

Magda heard the sound of someone approaching. She hid in the cave and pulled her knife. She heard a voice.

CHAPTER THIRTY FIVE

Sailing The Britannia Coast

Southern Coast, Britannia
Late Spring, 752 AD

"No deer meat tonight." It was Jeb.

When Magda stepped out into the rain with a downcast look, he grinned and hoisted up the dead boar.

"You scared me." She came up to him, took the boar, struggling under its weight, and led him to the oven setup.

"You're sopping wet, Jeb. I'll get this going and you can warm up."

"You're pretty well soaked yourself. Let me help." He put more dry wood on and piled it up.

She started the fire with the knife and flint that Clotaire had made sure she took with her. The fire took off quickly and Jeb fed the crackling flames. He stayed out in the rain long enough to butcher the boar and cut the meat into strips. While he buried the remains, Magda set the strips on planks and cooked one or two at a time, covering them with the oven lid. The smoke rose to the roof of the cave and slowly dissipated into the alder and yew thickets. After cooking half the boar, she stopped and put out the fire. The smell of cooked boar permeated the cave.

"That's enough smoke," Magda announced. "Clotaire would want us to be careful. I'll finish the cooking and drying tomorrow night."

She said she loved the smell of cooked meat and it made her hungry. It was the middle of the night and the rain still came down. They dried their clothes around the fire, sat together around the warm oven, and listened to the sound. It came in sheets and splattered on the ground and made a pinging sound on the alder leaves.

After sitting in silence for many minutes, Magda looked at Jeb out of the corner of her eye. "Would you like to bathe with me?" she offered.

Jeb took her hand and took her into the water. They frolicked and swam quietly as the rain pelted their heads and arms. They came together and hugged, washed each other, and splashed each other with cupped hands, making almost no noise. Jeb washed Magda's long black hair and she washed his in turn. They swam under the water and chased each other and finally came out to dry in the cave. Then they ate some of the fresh meat that had just been cooked, leaving the rest to dry. It was becoming daylight, so they curled up and listened to the rain for a while before they fell asleep.

They awoke before dusk and had some of the fresh meat for breakfast. Then, when it was dark, they repeated the cooking and let most of the meat dry as much as possible before wrapping it and stowing it in the boat. This second night was to be their last in the cave, and they spent some of the night searching out nuts, berries, roots, mushrooms, and birds' eggs. But now it was early summer and the days were getting longer, the nights shorter, leaving them less time for hunting and gathering. They had another dinner of the freshly cooked meat and some roots and berries and slept very well.

They woke while it was still daylight. The rain had stopped. They had an early breakfast of meat and bread and discussed what they should do next. They remembered what Clotaire had said. It might be a week of sailing along the coast to reach the spit where they would stow the boat and head inland on foot. He had mentioned a big island halfway.

The wind was still coming from the northeast. It was brisk but not very strong and was partially blocked by the headland they had sailed around two nights before, so they were sheltered where they were. But surely the wind would be much stronger out in the channel.

"Why don't we take advantage of this while we can?" asked Magda, "We can go out where the wind is stronger and see how far we can get before dawn."

"Maybe you're right. It's blowing at least as hard as when we came here. Let's do it."

They loaded and stowed all the gear and food and Magda's precious oven lid and pushed out into the clear, away from the cave and covering willows and yew thickets. They hoisted the mast and sail and Jeb rowed out just far enough to catch the wind. They were off. Jeb set a course south by southwest to get to the stronger winds of the channel. They cleared the headland they had ducked behind and the winds picked up, now almost as strong as those they had encountered in the race from the strangers. Then Jeb altered course to west by southwest and sailed with a broad port reach. The wind was nearly behind them and slightly to starboard. Jeb's long blonde hair was tied at the back in a long tail and the wind whipped it around his neck. Magda's even longer black hair was blown all over her face until she put her cap on.

They raced along for several hours in the dark. The moonlight was growing brighter, but most of the light was from the stars. Jeb felt comfortable with the stars. He considered the constellations his stalwart never changing friends and missed them terribly when they were covered by clouds. Once they set the course, Magda settled down to rest in her usual place near Jeb. She spelled him now and then at the tiller. They spoke very little as they raced along rolling up and over the small waves. Jeb calculated they were doing nearly the same speed as their last time on the water. The hours of the night passed quickly.

"The nights are getting shorter and shorter," Magda said. "Shouldn't we begin to look for land? It will be dawn in a few hours."

"What if we stay out to sea and continue sailing during the day? We can take turns at the tiller and take short naps. We could make great time that way." Jeb was hopeful she would agree. "If we stay out away from the coast, I don't think we'll run into any ships."

Magda thought about it for a few minutes, "What if we get chased again? Where will we go this time?"

Jeb thought a minute. "I'll check before the sun rises. If I see anything out there I'll head to shore. But if it looks clear we'll stay on course. If we're spotted before nightfall we'll just outrun them and head for that island Clotaire told us about. I'm sure we'll find a place to hide. When it's dark we'll come out and put some distance between us and any boats we encounter." He paused. "I don't think anyone will see us if we stay out to sea."

"All right, Captain!" Magda continued to have fun calling Jeb captain.

Jeb stayed on his west by southwest course. As dawn approached, they scanned the seas and saw nothing. Jeb told Magda that they had the advantage over bigger boats because they could see a big boat before it saw them. Magda said she hoped so. Soon, the sun was overhead and Jeb cautioned that they needed to keep looking in all directions. They were both a little tired so they took turns handling the tiller while the other one slept.

"I forgot that you can see things in day as well as hear them," Magda uttered, looking up in the sky after having just awoken. "There are six seagulls way out in front of us. Their cries are so faint. And those are dolphins to starboard jumping together."

Jeb was on the helm in mid-afternoon when he scanned behind him and saw a large ship astern to port. He told Magda to handle the sheet. He tacked and changed course to port bow which took him on a heading dead west. The boat apparently did not see Jeb and Magda and kept on a west-southwest course in the middle of the channel which would take them out into the big sea. The ship was at least forty feet long with two masts. From what Magda could tell, it was very wide and moved slowly, even with the three sails it had. *Perhaps it is in no hurry,* she thought.

After his last tack, Jeb was now heading closer to shore. When he could no longer see the other boat, he corrected his course back to west-southwest and held it until night fell. Then, under the cover of darkness, Jeb and Magda decided after some discussion they should get closer to land, so Jeb took a northwest heading.

The clouds covered the stars and Jeb could no longer use them to navigate, so he switched to dead reckoning and monitored the waves and wind.

And then the wind changed direction and came into the channel from the west-southwest direction. They now were facing the wind and waves broadside which they had not had to deal with before. Jeb decided he would rather take a chance on missing the big island they were looking for than to capsize from the broadside waves. He came about slightly into the wind on a westerly course. Magda was magnificent handling the sails. They started making good speed again and took the slight waves well. At this point, Magda gave a yell and pointed off the port bow.

"Look, Jeb. It's land. Where are we?"

"This is perfect. We're very lucky, Magda. That must be the big island Clotaire was talking about. I can't see if it's really an island, but it must be the way it's sticking out into the channel. Let's go closer."

Magda let out the sail and Jeb shifted to a northwest course. They approached slowly.

"Watch out, Jeb," Magda whispered and pointed to several bonfires along the eastern shore. "Clotaire told us we should go to the western shore. Now we know why."

Jeb shifted back to a westerly course. They had been far enough out that with this tack and the wind slightly off the bow, they cleared the southern edge of the island in another hour. Magda said they should head to shore.

"It's only an hour or two to daylight, and I can't stay awake anymore. Can you?"

"No. Clotaire was right. It would've taken at least three nights of sailing, but by staying out to sea in the daylight, we sailed it in two. Look for a good thick spot with no fires."

They cruised along the shore and saw no fires and no other signs of people. The woods became thicker as they had hoped. Spruce and willows and low lying juniper and yew thickets covered the shore. They drifted slowly in and found a flat approach with slowly rising cliffs on both sides. They waited as usual for any sounds and drifted in within a hundred feet. The sky was still overcast and blocked the starlight and the growing moonlight. They dropped the mast and Jeb manned the oars. He went in backwards in case he had to take off quickly.

"Look, Jeb. A fox. A red fox," Magda murmured, pointing to the nearby shrubs. When it sensed her movement, the fox vanished.

They sat for a long time, hidden in the dark under the willow trees. Finally, satisfied there were no sounds or movements, they pulled the boat onto shore and under the juniper thickets. They had their knives out and Jeb his axe as they moved quietly along the edge of the brush in one direction and then the other. They heard only the sounds of the night and the forest. An owl hooted. And then there was silence.

They pulled out some of the meat and the water and a small amount of dry bread and ate quietly, listening to the sounds of night. They gradually

186

relaxed. The wind was still blowing but they were somewhat in from the open sea and slightly protected. They hadn't had any rain for a couple of nights.

"There's your fox again," Jeb whispered. "He smells the meat." He waved his hands and hissed quietly. "Scat. Go away." The fox ran along the shore to the west and disappeared.

"You scared him." Magda pouted.

"Do you want him leaning over you while you sleep?"

They were quiet for a few minutes, then Jeb asked as usual if she wanted to bathe but Magda shook her head and said she was too tired.

They set up their bedding away from their boat in the thick brush. They cuddled together and listened. Jeb slept lightly but Magda fell into a deep sleep. The days were long and they slept longer than usual. Magda woke up to sounds on the water. She nudged Jeb and put her fingers to her lips. They moved quietly toward the shore and peered through the branches.

It was dusk and getting dark quickly. They saw two boats several hundred feet off shore. There were two people in each boat rowing at a brisk pace, intent on getting somewhere before dark. They showed no interest in the shore where Jeb and Magda were and disappeared out of sight. Jeb exhaled. He had not realized he was holding his breath.

"I think this area has a lot of people. We'd better leave as soon as it's dark."

After a good day's sleep, Magda was her old self again and couldn't help teasing Jeb.

"Not going to ask me if I want to swim?"

He tried to ignore her teasing but betrayed a slight smile. They packed up their gear and hauled the boat into the water. They were getting very efficient. In no time at all, they had the mast up and rigged and were under sail. The wind was slight and from the west-southwest. Jeb headed straight out into the open on a port tack and set a southwest course. Once he was far enough out, he tacked to starboard and followed a westerly course.

As they cleared a peninsula, they could see in the distance a waterway to the north that went back around and to the northwest. Magda said it must have been an island after all. It was a beautiful clear starry night, and the wind did not shift as they sailed directly west for more than an hour on this tack.

Magda suddenly grabbed Jeb's arm and pointed directly over the bow. There was land dead ahead. Jeb quickly shifted to a port tack and headed southwest. They passed one headland and then another. The cliffs were daunting, towering fifty feet into the sky and dropping straight down into the water. There was no shore. It would have been impossible to land if they had to. And then they had another problem.

"It's getting light," Magda pointed out. "We have to stop soon. I don't want to stay out at sea all day, not when we're getting so close to the spit we have to find."

Jeb nodded. "Look for a place we can land."

They sailed close to a second set of cliffs. Just beyond, the land sloped down more gradually and dropped from a modest cliff to the shoreline. Between the cliff and the waterline, Magda spied a small beach below the hillside. They sailed even closer and saw that the thickets of yew and pear and juniper trees on the banks of the narrow beach were very thick. They dropped the mast and Jeb manned the oars. They approached in the dark as Magda squinted.

"Look!" she whispered. "There's a cave under the cliff. We're in luck again."

They became increasingly more confident about landing, but still approached with the utmost caution. They listened first for any unusual sounds and then drifted in very slowly. They felt they were learning to 'read' the shoreline. After removing the mast and rowing in, they searched the area very carefully and then beached the boat.

They turned it bow to water and covered it in the brush. Then with knives and axe at the ready, they first searched the cave and then a broad area around it. The cave had been occupied before: there was an old fire ring covered with dead leaves from months before. There were also signs that a bear might have spent the winter, but it was now summer and the bear had moved on.

They sat and listened while they ate their dinner. Their meal consisted of the usual meat, augmented with some of the nuts, roots, and berries they found, and a little bread. Knowing they were getting close to the place where they would stow the boat and travel inland, they calculated how much food they both could carry and what they would need to find along the way. The rest of it was fair game for dinners and breakfasts before they left the sea and started walking, so they planned to eat well these last couple of days.

Knowing that this might well be her last day and night on the sea, Magda announced she hadn't had a swim for some time, by way of inviting Jeb to join her. These moments were the most carefree and delightful ones for them both.

"Jeb," Magda said, "I know that soon I'll be back to hard walking, and this time I'll need to carry much more than before. I hope I can manage."

Magda had grown quite a bit since she first left the south of France. She was taller and stronger and had begun to mature. She was still petite but she was developing a womanly shape. But Jeb had grown even more. He was taller and developing strength in his arms and legs, and his voice was getting deeper. Both of them had grown stronger as well from all their physical activity, including the sailing, and yet both still had a lot of growing to do.

They played in the water as children, and yet both were very much aware of the fact they were becoming adults. Sometimes Magda would arch her back and stretch. She would splash Jeb one moment and hold him very closely the next, intertwining her legs with his and pressing her body against him.

Jeb was not sure what to do so simply responded when she came to him. More and more, he found himself aroused by Magda's touch. He would think of her as a child one moment and then as a woman the next. One thing he did know was that he wanted to be with her and to protect her and get her to safety. He hoped that the Abbey they would soon search for would be a safe place, a safe haven for both of them.

After they had had enough and were getting cold, they curled up under their furs and went to sleep.

CHAPTER THIRTY SIX

Massalia to Ra

Islands of Massalia
Early Summer, 36 AD

As dusk approached, Joseph discussed his plans with Lazarus, Mary, Martha, and Joshua: they needed to find more water and meat before they landed somewhere on the mainland, and they needed to decide where they would hide the boat and where they would go next. The two Marys listened but did not comment.

"I have contacts in Massalia," Lazarus said, "that will help us settle into this huge city. I will go find them."

"I agree," Mary said. "We should go into Massalia. Lazarus and I want to follow in the footsteps of Mark the Evangelist and do what he has done in Alexandria: preach our message and convert those in Massalia."

Joseph responded, "I am in favor of that but I myself have plans to travel to the north."

"Why north?" Martha asked.

"You may not have heard of him, but a famous citizen of Massalia named Pytheas, who was a mathematician and scientist, traveled to the north by sea a few hundred years ago. He was trying to establish a sea trading route for tin, but it turned out to be cheaper and simpler to use land routes. That is precisely what I intend to do: use the land routes built by the Romans to establish my tin business in the north."

Martha persisted. "You say the north? Where?"

"Across the sea." That seemed to satisfy Martha.

Sarah pulled her mother to the side and whispered quietly, "Why do the two women also named Mary almost never speak? They spoke to me once and were both very nice. They said I was very brave."

"Well, you are." Mary smiled. "They talk to me now and then but they do not want to draw attention to themselves."

"Do they have other names besides Mary? There seem to be many women named Mary."

This time Sarah's mother laughed. "It is a very popular name. But, to answer your question, they are called Mary Salome and Mary of Clopas, but you should not use those names for now."

"Why?" Sarah continued.

"They do not want to be identified, at least until we are in a very safe place." Mary paused. "And before you ask more questions, I am sometimes called Magdalene, but I also do not want to be identified." Sarah thought she understood and was silent for a time.

Joshua spoke up. "I will help find water and hunt for meat as you asked, Joseph."

They spent the night fishing and searching for water on the island. Then, at dawn, they sailed to an isolated spot on the coast north of Massalia, where they disassembled the boat and hid the parts in thick brush inland from the sea.

"What kind of bushes and trees are those?" Sarah asked Lazarus and pointed out the trees with the yellow berries.

"Those are loquat trees," he answered, "and there are also two different species of juniper. I think one is called prickly juniper."

"I can understand that," Sarah responded, "since the prickly bushes keep people from going into the hidden area where our boat is." She picked some of the yellow fruit from the loquat trees.

Joseph felt more comfortable traveling at night, so they rested until the day ended. Before dusk came, Sarah asked her mother if she could bathe in the sea before they started their long trek.

"Yes, Sarah," her mother said, "and I will go with you. It will feel so good."

Martha joined them.

After they dried off, they rejoined the group. They all rested briefly, but as soon as it was dark, they began walking toward Massalia. Each of them carried food such as wheat or maize, nuts, mushrooms, figs or dates, roots and berries, and of course, dried meat, bread, and water and other essential items. Sarah had a small pack with a little water and a spare linen garment. With Lazarus leading, they walked all night until they approached the outskirts of Massalia. The land was flat and dry and they were able to set a good pace. While the others rested at daybreak, Lazarus went ahead to locate his Massalia contacts, returning just before dusk.

"My friends are expecting us. They have found a place we can stay and rest. But be warned that Massalia is unlike any place you've known before, including Alexandria. It is a very Roman city but more lawless, with many people migrating here from parts far and wide." There was silence.

The rest of the group followed Lazarus then into the outskirts of the city to a warm barn filled with cows and chickens and goats, and the most important thing for Sarah: hay to sleep on. Sarah drank some goat's milk from a mug, with a small amount of the bread and meat they still had left, a few nuts and some berries, then curled up in the hay and fell asleep.

While she was sleeping, Joseph, Lazarus, and Joshua left, but soon returned with water and dried goat meat and dates. They also had a special treat for Sarah: avocados. The group stayed in the barn for a few weeks but within a month they found a hut to live in that was big enough for six of them. Lazarus, Joseph, and Joshua shared a room in cramped conditions. Mary, Martha, and Sarah shared another, while the two Marys occupied another.

Another month went by during which Lazarus and Mary explored the city searching for places in which to begin their goal of evangelizing the populace. Lazarus focused on open squares and Mary gravitated to the hills and caves. Accompanied by Joshua, Joseph spent some time purchasing and trading for food for the group. Martha took it upon herself to teach Sarah what she knew about history and mathematics. The two Marys explored the city for a time but found it to be a bit too dangerous so both decided to help Martha teach Sarah how to write.

After everyone seemed to be settled in to their new home, Joseph along with Joshua quietly left the group for the far north. Before he left, Joshua came quietly to Sarah and said with sadness that he was leaving and would miss her very much.

"I will return in a few years," he said with tears in his eyes. "You will be all right while I am gone."

"I will miss you too," Sarah replied. "I hope you come back soon."

While Joshua and Joseph were packing up to leave for the north, Sarah overheard them talking.

"We will take the Roman roads going north," Joseph said, "The Romans know me from my tin trade, and I will say I am on official business. I have identification papers for you that show you as an associate, but it is best that they don't even try to identify you. Wear your cloak and keep your face covered. Hopefully, they will accept you as a friend and associate of mine and will not have any suspicions."

"I understand. We will take Via Agrippa?" Joshua asked.

"Yes. We'll take the southern section to Lugdunum and connect to the north section that goes to the sea in the north."

"And then?"

"We will sail across to the coast of Britannia and thence to a place called Glestingaburg."

They left silently in the early dawn, attracting no attention as they went.

One day, Sarah asked her mother what had happened to the beautiful goblet she used to drink from and Mary replied that Joseph and Joshua had taken it with them.

"We thought it would be safer where Joseph is going than here with us." But that was all she would say about it.

While in Massalia, Lazarus and Mary slowly began their mission of preaching that they had embraced in Judea and continued in Alexandria. Mary found the catacombs above the harbor to be an excellent gathering place for those coming to hear her. Lazarus used open squares to gather people. He had a style that calmed people and brought them into the fold, whereas Mary was somewhat of a firebrand and often made enemies.

Lazarus talked in a gentle manner about kindness and generosity and treating one's fellow man with respect. Mary spoke with much more passion about unjust and unfair treatment of the poor and ordinary persons by the rich and powerful. Mary urged those listening to her to take action and speak out and not to accept this inequality.

They preached without incident for nearly four years, but gradually word leaked out from spies in the catacombs. Mary received more and more attention and concern from the Romans, and the authorities began to take note of her preaching and what they felt was dangerous: the stirring up of the populace and the incitement of anger toward their authority. Eventually, Mary angered the Roman authorities so much that they sought to silence her.

"Mary," Lazarus came to her one day, "I have heard from friends the Romans are coming tomorrow to arrest you. You must leave immediately."

Mary fled in the night with Sarah, who was then nine years old. With the help of friends of Lazarus, they made their way slowly inland to Aquae Sextiae, where she toned down her rhetoric for a few months. Lazarus joined her briefly, and together with Maximin, they sought to convert the local people. Mary and Maximin preached from a cave in the surrounding mountains. Lazarus returned to Massalia and became the Bishop there.

Soon Mary began to preach with the fiery passion that she was known for elsewhere, and she drew hundreds of followers to the mountains. But, within a year, word of her inflammatory rhetoric spread to the Roman authorities and she learned that they sought to silence her in Aquae Sextiae as they had done in Massalia. Knowing that she faced certain imprisonment, once more she awakened Sarah in the dark of night and told her to pack quickly.

"I'm sorry, Sarah," Mary said, "We must leave here."

"Why do we keep fleeing from place after place?"

"I know it's difficult to understand but my message and our presence cause fear in the minds of the authorities. But I must not stop my preaching."

Mary and Sarah returned in disguise to Massalia for a brief stay and then left with Martha, Mary Salome and Mary of Clopas, to retrieve the boat. At night with a full moon to aid them, they assembled it with some difficulty and finally made it watertight with reeds and brush and mud. They traveled west along the coast looking for the big river that came into the sea. Just before dawn, they landed on a long spit or low lying strip of sand and waited for dusk again.

While they were waiting, Sarah asked if she could bathe and Mary nodded agreement.

"Perhaps I will join you."

Sarah slid into the warm water and bathed quietly. Her mother and Martha, and Mary Salome, joined her. After bathing, Sarah ate dried meat, figs, grapes, nuts, and an avocado, with her water. She slept lightly, and then they continued on their journey again at nightfall.

They traveled up the big slow moving river at night and reached the outskirts of Arelate just before dawn. They found a hut to stay in, and Mary wasted no time before she began her preaching. She used the Roman theatre to gather crowds, which became larger and larger. By this time Mary was well known by the Romans, and she realized they were again about to seize her. She escaped from the theatre and stayed hidden for several days in an empty barn on the edge of the city, but she felt that the Romans were too numerous and, sooner or later, would find her. She was also concerned about Sarah, especially if she herself were caught. So, together with Mary Salome and Mary of Clopas, she decided to travel further west to a city named Ra which was on the sea. They all believed that they would be welcomed there from the reports they had heard about the inhabitants, who were considered to be very friendly.

"I don't think I will join you this time," Martha explained, "I have decided to travel north to Tarasco. It is located on the main road the Romans are building from east to west. I have heard that it has a large community from Judea and I believe I will be at home there."

Mary knew there was also a large Judean community that had settled at Ra. The three Marys felt it would be safer to travel by boat, but they realized they would save time if they ported the boat from the big river to the inland étang, a large lake or lagoon separated from the huge sea. It was four miles across to the shallow lake, but the going was very slow with only three of them and Sarah to move the boat and carry all the supplies. Sarah was now ten and able to carry a pack with some food and water while the three women concentrated on carrying the parts of the boat. However, they did not want to leave everything behind, including the food and some of the clothes, so they first carried the boat parts overland, left Sarah with the boat, and returned for the remaining items.

While waiting, Sarah had a chance to observe the birds of the étang. There were beautiful flamingos with long pink legs and black bills, and cranes and egrets and herons. Sarah loved sitting and watching these lovely birds forage for small crustaceans in the shallow water. After moving the boat and food and supplies overland in one night the adults were exhausted and so they rested on the shore of the étang during the day.

They ate most of the food they had been carrying and drank the water, and that night, sailed across the étang and through the low lying marshlands until they approached Ra just before daybreak. They thought it would be more dramatic if they arrived from the sea, so they ported across a narrow strip of sand and sailed a short distance out to sea. Then they turned and sailed ashore into the port of Ra.

"Isn't this deceptive," Sarah asked her mother and the two Marys, "Pretending we came from the sea when we didn't?" They all shrugged and didn't answer Sarah. The group was welcomed in awe, as if the gods themselves had aided their journey. The fact that they were hungry and thirsty added to the impression that they had somehow miraculously arrived from across the sea. Sarah and Mary and the others were stunned by the reception they received.

Sarah in particular was revered and treated in the most special way. She looked like the inhabitants of Ra with her long dark hair and dark eyes and dark complexion so she was considered to be a special gift from the heavens and was worshiped. Her mother Mary and the other two Marys were also treated as miracles that arrived by sea and were adored almost as much as Sarah. With her gentle manner Sarah gradually became so revered that many started referring to her as Saint Sarah. She was worshiped and idolized wherever she went. Sarah was surprised at first by this attention, but soon learned to accept it and responded in a kind and generous manner to her admirers. She learned quickly how to act and to earn her adulation. By the time she was twelve and was a slender young woman with hair down to her waist, she was even more revered.

Sarah and the three Marys stayed in Ra for two years and thrived there as respected and loved women. The population had begun to refer to the three women named Mary as Saints as well because of their miraculous appearance from the sea. But, in spite of the respect and adulation bestowed on her, Sarah's mother Mary became restless and felt she needed to continue to the west to find her final home.

Mary spent several days preparing to leave, gathering food and water, and repairing clothes. Mary Salome and Mary of Clopas helped her assemble the boat and make it seaworthy. Mary and Sarah loaded up all their supplies. Then one spring evening at dusk, with warm winds blowing from the land, they prepared to launch the boat and sail away in the dark. The two other women named Mary planned to stay behind and explain to the populace that Mary and Sarah had been called back to the sea. They felt no one would question this, but would accept it as if it was inevitable.

And then a wonderful thing happened.

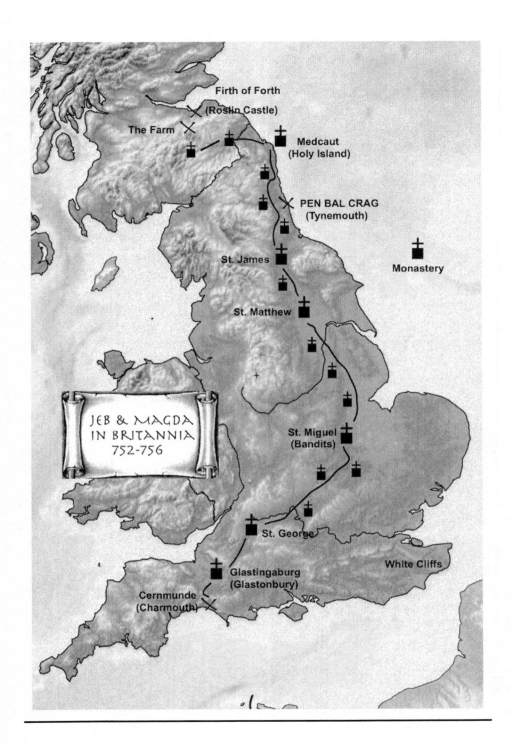

Firth of Forth
(Roslin Castle)

The Farm

Medcaut
(Holy Island)

PEN BAL CRAG
(Tynemouth)

St. James

Monastery

St. Matthew

JEB & MAGDA
IN BRITANNIA
752-756

St. Miguel
(Bandits)

St. George

White Cliffs

Glastingaburg
(Glastonbury)

Cernmunde
(Charmouth)

CHAPTER THIRTY SEVEN

The Killing

Southern Coast, Britannia
Early Summer, 752 AD

Jeb and Magda were up early, well before dusk, and had their breakfast of meat with a little cheese and bread. They stowed their gear and sat quietly waiting for darkness, then slipped their boat out into the water and hoisted the mast. Jeb set a course west by southwest. In less than three hours of sailing in a light southwest wind, they saw land ahead as they had hoped. They could tell it was the long spit reaching out into the wide channel. Jeb changed course to south by southwest and kept a distance from the end of the spit.

The boat had a very shallow draft but Jeb didn't want to take even the slightest chance of running aground. They rounded the spit and Jeb set a course of northwest, keeping the beach about a thousand feet off his starboard. The stars that had become their companions twinkled in the clear sky and the wind barely ruffled their hair. They were close enough to shore for Magda to hear the echo of a large owl hooting from a tree on shore. Jeb said he thought it might be the large owl with the long ears.

"We need to land at a spot just before where the shore turns and starts south again," Magda said, "Look for a small river that comes into a cove."

There they would seek the thickest woods they could find, uninhabited woods especially. After another couple of hours of sailing along the open shore, they noticed the forest was again filled with oak and birch and chestnut trees and thickets of wild roses, hawthorn and firethorn, pears and crab apples, and other low lying shrubs forming almost impenetrable thick brush. Then they saw the river. This time Jeb sailed into the mouth and dropped the mast. He stayed close to the west side of the cove and rowed a quarter of a mile up river. Then he found what he was looking for: thick impenetrable brambles with hearty thorns and dense growth of dark green clumps of oval leaves.

Magda and Jeb pulled the boat into the thicket until it was hidden. Then they sat quietly, out of sight but close to the water.

"Jeb, this boat has gotten us out of trouble several times. It's very special and I hate to leave it. Will it be all right here?"

"Magda, it will be fine. If we need it again it will still be here."

They sat silently for an hour and then had a little meat and water. Then they began to fill their packs with their gear and with the rest of the dried meat and the little bread they still had. Jeb carried his knife and axe and bow and quiver, and Magda her knife. Compared to the days where everything was stowed on the boat, they felt really weighted down.

"I know," Jeb said, "our travel pace will be much slower than when we traveled with Clotaire. We're both much stronger now, but I'm not sure we can carry everything we need for three weeks. I hope a straight northerly direction will get us there in two."

The nights were getting longer but were still quite short, and they would not be able to travel for very long. Then he smiled to himself and realized, that with such a heavy load they each had, they wouldn't be able to travel very long each night no matter how long the night was.

"I'm not too sure of the distance to the Abbey," Jeb continued, "but from a comment Clotaire made, I think it might only be a little over forty miles. If that's so and we average just four miles a night, we might get there in less than two weeks. All we have to do is hold to that pace."

Jeb and Magda said goodbye to their boat and started along the river's edge. He noticed tears in her eyes, and gently and briefly put his arm on her shoulders. They moved slowly, looking for any trail that would take them away from the visibility of the river.

"Jeb," Magda said, "I think we have a couple of hours left before dawn."

Within minutes they crossed a deer trail perpendicular to the river. They followed it to a worn pathway going north and stayed on it for an hour in spite of the danger in doing it for so long. Jeb decided to take a small trail that went toward the river, which turned out to be none too soon. They heard the voices of a group of men heading south on the main trail, so they quickly hid in the brush. Magda caught a glimpse through the bushes of the savage looking men. They had long unkempt hair and beards and were clothed in ragged dirty sackcloth and animal skins. They carried spears or pikes and some had swords. When the men were out of sight and sound, Jeb and Magda continued on until they turned off onto a small, little used but safer path going north parallel to the river. They walked until the daylight began to peek through the trees.

"I calculate," Jeb said, "we've only gone a mile north, but that's enough for a start. I think it's time to stop for the night."

"I'm very tired," Magda replied, "so as far as I'm concerned, it isn't soon enough to suit me."

They stepped carefully off the trail so as not to leave tracks or broken branches or any other sign that would point to them and camped in a thicket of roses and wild and spiny pears and blackberries. After eating some meat and drinking lots of water, they set up their bedding. Then they lay awake looking at the stars for a while before falling into a sound sleep.

When they awoke in the late afternoon, it was quiet and peaceful. Magda heard the faint drumming of a small woodpecker.

"I'm pretty sure," Jeb said, "the meat will last at least two and perhaps three weeks, but we'll need to find water every two or three days since we're not carrying much. Let's walk only several hours this night and not overdo it. I don't want to wear either of us out. And then before dawn we'll search for fruit and water."

They hoisted their packs and Jeb followed a narrow trail that went almost directly north. He thought it was mainly used by deer staying close to the river. *Perhaps*, he mused, *deer needed to find water every two or three days as well.* Magda was doing much better but they still continued at a very slow pace. The packs were very heavy, the thick shrubs made it impossible to see very far in the dark, so Jeb and Magda often stood still to listen for any threatening sounds.

After a couple of hours, the narrow trail ended and merged onto a large trail that was heavily used. But they stayed on it, hoping no one else would be using it in the middle of the night. The trees were a mixture of ash, oak, rowan, yew, and various other short thin trees.

They soon headed east toward the river then picked up another narrow trail going north. After covering about four miles in four hours of travel, they decided to stop early. They rested a bit and searched for berries from the rowan shrubs. Jeb thought the bread would only last a few more days, so he suggested they have the bread only for breakfast at dusk. They curled up in the brush and listened to the day sounds of birds and the light wind rustling the trees until they fell into a long sleep, waking at dusk.

"Jeb, I think I can handle this journey," Magda said. "The more I eat, the lighter the load and the easier it is to walk." She smiled. "If we eat everything up soon, we'll get there more quickly."

Jeb smiled and felt this was a good sign. Magda's sense of play and humor always lifted his spirits. He was glad to see her like this.

They walked much harder this next night, and the trail carried them straight north most of the time, veering slightly to the west or east as it followed the course of the river. Then the river going north ran perpendicularly into a wide shallow river running east and west, and the trail going north stopped. Jeb had to make a choice.

"Magda, let's rest a bit. But then I think we have the best chance to cross by going east."

They followed a very small deer trail a few hundred feet from the river's edge and looked at the rushing river.

"This is the best place to cross." Jeb pointed out the spot to Magda. "The current is swift, but from the ripples in the water, it must be shallow enough for us to try."

The moon was still a sliver of light but just bright enough for them to see the rocks in the river bed. They took off their walking shoes, Jeb removed his pants to avoid getting them wet, and Magda hitched her dress up above her waist. In they went, with Jeb holding Magda's hand as they braced against the current and avoided submerged rocks. The water reached above their waists so they moved slowly, balancing against the rushing current and managing to get across without falling or being swept away. But in spite of their precautions, their clothes still got a little wet. They disappeared into the brush and dried off.

They found a deer trail going east and west and Jeb decided to stay with an easterly direction. Then they crossed a larger trail going north. It was the middle of the night, so they felt safe following it until they found a smaller one. They encountered no one and the trail soon split. They took the smaller path heading north by northeast. Within half a mile, they came to another small river flowing from the northwest. They followed a narrow trail along its edge, traveling in a north by northwest direction.

It was a couple of hours before dawn but Jeb decided to stop for the day.

"In spite of all the detours," Jeb said, "I think we've still covered another three miles north."

"Do you think it's all right to get water from the small river?" Magda asked.

"I think it'll be fine here."

While he made camp she headed down to the river's edge.

Several minutes later Jeb heard a scream. He raced in Magda's direction with his bow in his hand. He still had his knife in its place around his waist and his quiver on his shoulder. He saw her on the ground near the bank of the river. A burly man wearing a sleeveless leather vest and heavy leather pants stood over her. He was slapping her and tearing at her clothes. Without hesitation, Jeb grabbed an arrow and with deadly accuracy shot it into the middle of the man's back. The man roared, released Magda, turned toward Jeb and charged. Jeb grabbed his knife and stood his ground.

With the arrow in his back the man staggered but his momentum carried him into Jeb. He was much stronger and wrested the knife from Jeb's hand. Magda jumped up and grabbed her knife from its sheath and ran toward them. The man had Jeb down under him and just as he raised the knife to strike, Magda plunged her knife into the man's upper back. He pulled away and uttered a gurgling sound and fell to the ground.

"Magda!" Jeb cried out and then took her in his arms. "Are you hurt?"

She began to weep. He held her more tightly.

"I'm all right. Oh, Jeb, you came." Her tears streamed down her face. Her upper clothing was ripped away. She tried unsuccessfully to cover her breasts. They looked down at the man. He was not moving.

"He's dead. But he would have killed me if you hadn't stabbed him."

Her weeping stopped. "What are we going to do? We can't leave him there." She wiped away her tears.

"He has special tattoos on his arms. Clotaire told me about those. He must be a member of one of those tribes we hear marching on the wide trails. Where did he come from?"

Magda pointed across the stream. "He rushed over and grabbed me before I could run away. Look! He dropped his spear over there when he came after me."

Jeb crossed the river, grabbed the spear, and returned. "We've got to hide him," he said. "And we need to get away from here fast. He's probably not alone."

They dragged him into the nearest bushes. Then they tried their best to cover his tracks and their own by dusting behind them. Magda took the water she'd collected from the river and they moved quickly and quietly to their packs. They loaded up and walked swiftly away along the trail heading north. They still had an hour of darkness left. Their adrenalin kept them going at almost double their normal pace, but as dawn approached they had to stop. Magda was shaking, and Jeb could tell she was near exhaustion. But he felt sure they'd covered at least two miles since their near tragedy, so it was probably safe for them to stop.

He selected a particularly thick area of brush to hide in, and they made sure they had left no broken branches or footprints behind them after leaving the trail. They settled down under a tree and sat silently for an hour as the sun came up. Magda was still shaking and clung to Jeb. They covered themselves with their furs and sat up against the tree and listened. They were still so upset that they could not sleep and were not even interested in food. Jeb felt that Magda might be in shock. He held her until she stopped shaking.

Eventually she dozed off in his arms. He laid her down under the tree, covered her with her fur, and curled up beside her. He vowed never to let her out of his sight again.

CHAPTER THIRTY EIGHT

The March to the Abbey

Southern England
Summer, 752 AD

When they woke up, they were ravenous. While Magda ate, Jeb used his knife and a little hemp to repair her dress. He told her they should leave as soon as it became dark. He shuddered when he thought of how close they'd come to tragedy.

Magda suddenly interrupted her eating. "Won't someone miss that man and search for him?"

"I thought about that. If he was not alone, they'll miss him soon. But it will take them some time to find him. They will probably look along the river, and when they do find him and see the arrow mark and knife wound, maybe they'll think someone from another tribe killed him. They'll never think of looking for two little kids like us." Jeb paused. "I hope."

"We should get away from here as soon as possible," Magda said, standing up. "They could have found him by now."

They packed up hurriedly and were on the narrow trail by dusk. They moved quickly and almost silently. By dawn they had covered four miles, according to Jeb's calculations. Jeb felt he could not relax until they put another night's walk behind them. He dared not travel during the day, so they had to cover as much distance as possible during the shorter nights. He was concerned they were steadily moving west because of the north by northwest direction of the river and the trails that followed it. But he felt as long as they had the river and the trails going generally north, they should stay with it.

After a fitful day of sleep, they resumed their rapid pace and covered another four miles. Jeb thought they might be about half way to the Abbey if he had calculated correctly, but he knew they couldn't maintain this speed. Magda was exhausted and needed rest. He thought they were far enough away from any pursuit. So they would start later that night and cover less distance this time.

Now Jeb decided they were traveling too far to the west, so they needed to go in a more northerly direction as soon as he could find a suitable trail.

After they ate he stood up. "We might not see a river for a while. Do you want to join me while I fetch water?"

Magda jumped up. "I'm going to stay with you wherever you go." They filled their water bags together.

After a much better day's sleep, they woke full of energy.

"As soon as it's dark," Jeb said, "we'll go slowly along the river and find a shallow place to cross. Then we'll look for a trail heading northeast to get back onto the northerly track we need."

When they crossed the river a short time later, they found a narrow trail along the river going northwest. Then Magda spotted an even smaller track cutting across their trail and going down to the river. They turned to the northeast and continued on for two hours until the trail led right to the edge of a lake. They circled around to the north side where the brush was very thick.

Magda spotted an inlet which was secluded and covered over with trees. Jeb knew what she had in mind since it had been several days since she bathed. It was just deep enough to swim. Jeb knew that having a swim every few nights was the one great pleasure she had on this grueling journey. He'd promised this was to be a short night of traveling, and she was not about to let him forget it. They checked the area as they always did. Then Jeb sat hidden, watching the lakeside. There was no sign of activity.

Finally Jeb signaled it was all right and he watched Magda slip into the water slowly and smile. She beckoned to him to come join her, mouthing, 'It's warm." Then she swam out several feet and stood up.

Jeb followed her in. This shallow lake was so much warmer than any water they had bathed in since they began this journey. The weather had been getting warmer for several days, and the sun had shone brightly while they slept. He finally began to relax, standing in the waist-deep water, feeling it lap gently against him.

But then Magda swam underwater and grabbed his legs as he stood there. Then she raised her hands slowly and playfully up his legs. He tried to grab her but she slithered away. He dove and chased her underwater. She let him catch her and put his arms around her. Then she broke away and swam under again. Jeb thought this was the most playful and most relaxed he'd seen Magda in all their traveling.

They finally came out of the water and dried in the still night air, with the dim light of the moon peeking through the clouds. They were very hungry and decided to look for berries and eggs and roots to go with the meat and the small amount of bread they allowed themselves. Jeb pulled up a few onions and parsnips. Magda almost stepped on a clutch of eight large eggs. She left four of them.

"What kind of eggs are these, Jeb?"

"They're huge. Probably from red or black grouse," he replied.

Magda liked to eat her eggs with bread and Jeb just swallowed them down. This was a very large meal for them, so they took their time eating, hidden in the thick brush surrounding the lake.

Jeb didn't want to say anything to Magda, but he felt they were not that far from the Abbey, if only he knew exactly how to get there. When dusk came again and they'd had a long and restful sleep, Jeb decided they should continue in the same northerly direction for another day.

In the dark, Jeb picked up a deer trail on the northeast side of the lake which they followed for a few hours in a more northerly direction but still northeast. Then they were faced with another dilemma: another small river, going west by northwest. They didn't want to go in that direction but they had to follow this river to the northwest until they found a shallow crossing and a trail that went northeast. They crossed the river and continued on this trail for another hour until they came to an open meadow.

"We shouldn't go out there," Magda said. "We should never be in the open, even at night."

Jeb agreed, so they skirted the edge of the meadow until they found thick brush covering the forest floor. They camped in the brush and away from any trails, eating very little and sleeping fitfully.

"I don't like being away from the water," Magda said, waking up in the middle of the day and peering up at the tall trees. "Everything's so close together here. And there's nowhere to swim."

At dusk they circled the meadow looking for a trail. Insects buzzed around them in the warm summer evening and crickets sang their grate-grate sawing harmony in the stillness. The sweet smell of trees and bushes and flowers in full bloom permeated the air. They found a trail heading almost directly north and slightly east and marched along this very narrow path for most of the night, determined to keep going until they reached some sort of landmark. They had to rest periodically but still made good time. Just as the dawn showed signs of arriving, they approached another river bank.

"Oh, Jeb, the river's perfect for bathing," shouted Magda, running down to the river's edge and wading in.

"You forgot to take off your shoes," Jeb noted.

"I don't care, I don't care, I don't care," Magda chanted and then threw herself into the water.

Jeb shook his head.

The river was flowing in the same northwest direction as the others in the watershed.

Jeb checked the area in both directions along the river and found no sign of life. So as soon as he could get Magda out of the river, they filled their water skins, then found a good place to camp safely during the day.

"All the bread is gone," Magda announced, "and all the roots and berries."

"That's all right. We only need a little meat and water," Jeb responded. "We must be getting near the Abbey. We'll find food there."

He'd calculated the approximate number of miles they'd traveled north. He also felt they hadn't strayed too far from the northerly direction they'd taken from the cove they'd left many days before. They must be close.

That night they resumed their march, this time going northwest along the river's edge. They continued marching all night, resting now and then, until the sun began to rise. They were looking for a thicket off their deer trail in which to camp when Jeb saw that it was about to intersect a wide track going northeast toward the river. Magda grabbed his arm. "Listen!" she murmured, quietly pulling him off the trail.

"Why?" Jeb mumbled as she dragged him into the thickets of yew.

"Shhh," she whispered urgently, pulling him down into a crouch as she pointed to the wide track.

He watched with wide eyes as two monks hurried past, walking in the dawn. *They must be going to the Abbey,* he thought. *Maybe they're late for morning prayers.*

But they could not follow the monks, not in the daylight. It was too dangerous. They would have to wait until dusk and follow the road, dangerous as it might be, until they found the Abbey. Then they would face their most dangerous challenge. They had to find the Abbé himself, or the Abbot as he was called here.

Clotaire had told them about the Abbot. If they did not find the exact man he described, then they must turn around and return to the boat. If enemy forces had removed the old Abbot, they would be in grave danger. If it was the old grey Abbot with the twinkle in his eyes and the mole near his right eye, then they would be safe. But they must never identify themselves. They could only say they had been traveling from far away and were told this Abbey was welcoming.

Jeb and Magda discussed their plan for the next night. They would wait until it was very dark to follow the wide path. When they reached the Abbey, they would hide and watch during the day to figure out where the Abbot was. Once it was night, they would wait until the Abbot was alone before they crept close enough to set eyes on him. When they were sure it was him, then and only then would they reveal themselves.

'What will we do if it's not him?' Magda asked, fidgeting nervously with the strap on her pack.

"Let's not worry about that just now," Jeb said, trying to sound reassuring, but his words were too shrill.

They settled down in the thick brush away from the trail to wait for dusk but the day seemed endless.

"Do you want some meat, Magda?" Jeb offered.

She looked at the strip of meat in his hand and shook her head. "I don't think I can swallow. I'm too nervous."

"I know what you mean," he said, regretfully putting the meat away. "We should get some sleep."

"I don't think I can do that, either," she said, looking at him. "I don't think I can do anything but wait."

When it was quite dark, they stepped out with their packs and walked along the edge of the wide path.

"I don't see anyone behind us right now," Magda said, looking over her shoulder. "But we'd better keep checking."

They soon came to a bridge running across the shallow river. It consisted of oak planks laid end to end, supported by crossed poles of ash, oak, and lime driven into the river bottom. Jeb and Magda looked in both directions as far as they could see but saw no one.

They scurried across the bridge, trying not to trip. When they reached the other side, they hustled off the trail and hid behind some bushes. The coast was still clear, so they hurried along the road in the dark. It was a rough rocky road, but the starlight revealed any rocks or wooden posts before they stubbed their toes on them. The sounds of small animals scurrying in the underbrush only added to their apprehension.

After walking nearly an hour, Magda pointed out the Abbey ahead.

"Look." She grabbed his arm. "It's huge. That must be the church."

Looming ahead in the dark was a massive stone building with high arches coming to a point. They could make out lower stone structures on both sides of the great church, also with arches at the top. They could barely discern wooden entry doors in each section.

"We have to figure out where the Abbot lives," Jeb whispered.

"Well, he doesn't live in the church," Magda muttered. "We know that."

"We don't know. Maybe he lives in the back."

Jeb knew they were getting into dangerous territory. They had to find a safe place to camp during the day where they could still take turns watching the Abbey and those who came and went. Magda pointed out a thick stand of yew trees and juniper bushes where they could keep an eye on the various entrances. They saw a small door off to the side. *Perhaps this was a private entrance*, Jeb thought. They decided it made more sense to try to sleep during the rest of the night. They ate the last piece of meat in the pack. If this didn't work and they didn't find the Abbot, Jeb realized, they would go hungry for some time.

They woke at daybreak. They were still tired but excited and nervous and filled with anxiety as they watched. Early in the morning, they saw some tradesmen who were definitely not monks go in a side entrance. Then they saw a couple of monks leave.

They waited for several hours and then saw a monk approach and veer off to a small entrance on the other side of the church. When he rang, they saw an old man come out. He was also clothed in a monk's habit.

"We can't see the mole from here but that must be the Abbot," Jeb whispered to Magda, tugging on her sleeve excitedly. "He's bent over a little, looks the right age with grey hair, and as tall as the old grey Abbot Clotaire described. But we need to get closer to make sure."

"Who else could it be?" Magda replied.

The two men talked for a few minutes and then parted. The old monk went back inside. The other monk went back the way he had come. Jeb and Magda were tingling with anticipation.

They waited until dark. They left their packs in the thicket, except for their weapons, and approached the side door stealthily but swiftly. They looked around to make sure they were not seen, and then Jeb rang the bell. They tried to hide in the dark against the stone wall beside the entrance and waited. Jeb rang again, this time more loudly.

They were both poised to run. Jeb stayed back out of sight as the door opened and an old monk with grey hair peered out. Magda looked for the mole but a hood covered the right side of the monk's face. Even so, Magda thought it must be the old Abbot they were seeking. His gaze was hidden from her but there was a smile flickering at the corner of his mouth. She stepped forward into the light to get a better look. And then before he said anything, Magda said in her smallest little voice.

"May I come in, please?"

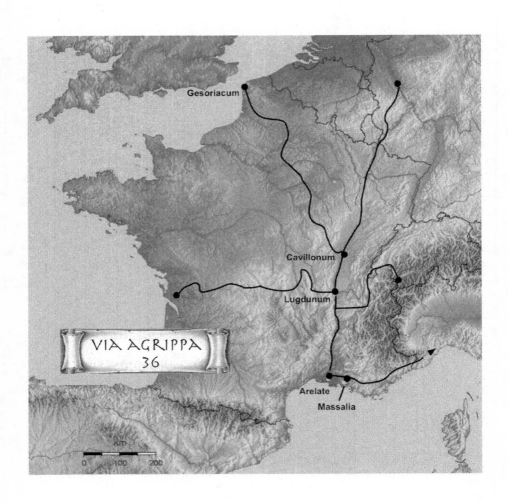

VIA AGRIPPA
36

208

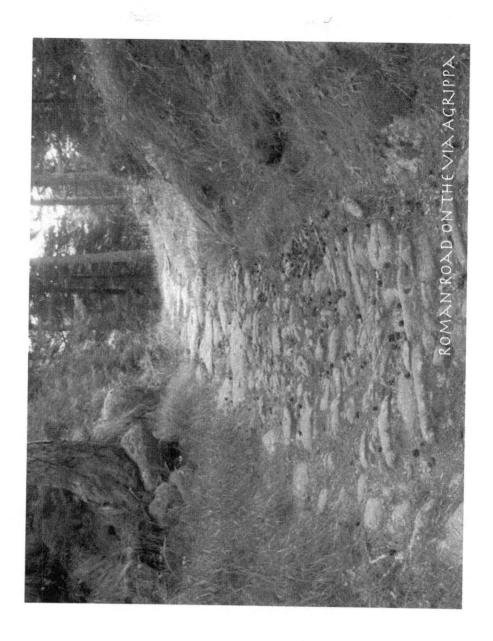

ROMAN ROAD ON THE VIA AGRIPPA

CHAPTER THIRTY NINE

Massalia to Glestingaburg

Francia and Britannia
Summer, 36 AD

Joseph acquired a pair of fresh horses at the Massalia way station on the Via Agrippa, and then at dusk traveled north with Joshua, heading first to Lugdunum. As Joseph had suggested, Joshua covered his head with his cloak whenever they came across other travelers or at the way stations.

"There are way stations every ten miles," Joseph explained to Joshua when they came to the first one and traded horses.

"Besides horses, what facilities are there?" Joshua asked.

"The mutationes are every ten miles or so and are for everyone who wants shelter. The mansiones are every twenty miles and are for officials. Since I am traveling officially on my tin business, we should be able to acquire fresh horses, and food and shelter at each station if need be. I prefer to travel at night when there is less traffic, and I expect to cover about sixty miles a day."

"It would be best if you carry the goblet rather than I," Joshua said at one of their stops. He gave Joseph the goblet wrapped in fine cloth. "You can always say it is one of your tin goblets if searched."

Joseph smiled and hid it securely.

They carried on throughout the night, usually exchanging horses every ten miles.

"Perhaps we should rest briefly on the trail rather than stopping at the mutationes," Joshua suggested, "to avoid arousing anyone's suspicion."

"I agree," Joseph replied.

They reached Arelate two nights later, where Joseph made sure they had sufficient dried meat, bread, cheese, and water.

"Do you think we could sneak into the Roman theatre here at Arelate without being seen?" Joshua asked.

"It's risky, but I understand why you'd like to see it. It is impressive. But aren't you afraid someone will stop us, question us?"

"I need not worry about being recognized, not at night, way up here. Besides, no sense worrying about something that might not be a problem."

Joshua followed Joseph with stealth into the center of Arelate. They saw only one centurion in the distance, who did not see them. When they reached the Roman theatre, Joshua stood on the edge of the stage, raised his arms to an imaginary audience, and appeared to Joseph as if he were about to preach. This was too much. He hurried Joshua away and onto the road.

"We can reach Lugdunum in less than a week if we continue at this pace," Joseph said as they rode straight north.

"I do not have money," Joshua said. "Will we be all right in that regard?"

"I have enough money for our journey north," Joseph responded, "and I also have several tin pots and cups to trade when I can." He paused. "And of course I have that special tin goblet you gave me." He looked slyly at Joshua and was rewarded with a broad smile.

"How long do you think it will be before we reach the sea?" Joshua asked.

"Not more than a month," Joseph answered.

At a way station two days north of Arelate, a soldier warned Joseph about danger ahead.

"We have guards stationed along the road, but even so we have had trouble with thieves north of here. Be careful and don't stop except at one of the mansiones."

Joseph nodded. He and Joshua each had a staff in a leather holder attached at their waists pointing down the horse's flank. It was not easily visible. Two nights later they began to cross a stone arch bridge spanning the river Rhone. Joshua noticed two men emerge from under the bridge in front of them, gripping pikes.

"Joseph," Joshua whispered calmly, grabbing Joseph's reins and stopping their horses. "We have a problem." Then he looked back and saw two men appear behind them wielding swords. They were caught in the middle of the bridge.

"Follow me!" Joshua yelled to Joseph as he spurred his horse forward. He rushed at the men in front as he grabbed his staff, knocking them aside.

"Quick thinking," Joseph said as they rode on. "I'm glad we only had to deal with two of them."

"We might run into more brigands and thieves on the road ahead," Joshua responded, "but as I've said before, no point in worrying about something that might not happen."

They rode on steadily for three more days and nights and reached Lugdunum without further incident. The mansione was one of the larger ones. The main center hut contained foodstuff, water, and various supplies. At one end were stables containing a dozen or more horses and off the center hut was a large room with bare mats to sleep on. Joseph exchanged their horses again, filled their goatskin bags, and stocked up on lots of dried meat, bread, nuts, figs, and grapes.

"Shall we risk your life again and visit the amphitheater?" Joseph asked with a glint in his eye and a smile. "Or perhaps the theatre on the hill of Fourviere in the center of the city?"

Joshua smiled back. "We can skip it this time. No one will come to see my performance anyway."

"I certainly hope not. Let's move on."

They stopped at other mansiones but did not stay long enough to rest. Joseph did not feel safe with prying eyes. He received only one question about his companion which he handled in a nonchalant manner, referring to his "assistant" who was learning his tin business. Joseph had brought a few tin utensils, and when he thought it wise, handed them out as gifts.

Joshua once asked with a grin, "You are not giving out those tin products as bribes, by any chance, to keep people from asking too many questions?"

"Of course not," Joseph retorted with a sly smile, "it is just good business sense."

It was a warm summer. They rode steadily each night and part of each day, resting in thickets far enough away from the road so the horses would not be heard. One day a large brown bear lumbered into the dense brush where they were camped and startled the horses. When Joshua confronted the bear it backed away but the shuffling and snorting from the frightened horses was loud and unnerved Joseph so they returned to the road. They carried on to the next mutatione and rested for the remainder of the day, trying to be as inconspicuous as possible.

There Joseph overheard a discussion about a large bandit group terrorizing the road far to the north. The soldiers were discussing the difficulty they had in catching the bandits. Joseph and Joshua left quietly and unnoticed. When they had traveled a short distance, Joseph stopped and asked Joshua what he thought about this danger.

"Should we take a detour to avoid confronting the bandits?" Joseph asked.

"We should not worry about a problem until we encounter it. We should carry on."

That was all that was said on the matter for several days. They covered hundreds of miles and seldom had trouble at the way stations. Joseph said he thought they would reach the northernmost point called Gesoriacum within a week at most.

Then in the middle of a dark night on a dark road, out of the surrounding forest, came a band of a dozen bandits armed with drawn swords. Eight blocked the road in front and four behind. With quiet dignity Joshua dismounted and handed the reins to Joseph. Joshua then stepped forward with his long staff in his hands. A bandit with a long black beard approached him with silent menace.

"Give me all your money," he growled as he raised his sword.

Joshua's voice was a loud thunderclap. "We have no money for you. Stand back or feel our wrath."

As the bearded bandit moved toward him with raised sword, Joshua lowered his staff and pointed it at him, freezing him in his tracks. The man turned into a block of stone. His companions stared, horrified. The other eleven bandits shrank back and retreated into the brush. Joseph and the two horses followed Joshua along the now open road. After they had passed through, Joshua turned and pointed his staff at the frozen man who immediately ran off into the woods.

As they continued riding at night along the Via Agrippa, Joseph said nothing about the encounter with the bandits as if it was not unusual. They rode silently most of the time, but now and then Joseph talked about the distance to Gesoriacum and how they were making good progress.

They passed two more mansiones, acquiring meat, bread, cheese, and water. They knew they were approaching the end of the Roman road when Joseph looked at a detailed map at the last of the mansiones and noted the way north. But then it began to rain. At first it was a light rain, but then the wind began to blow strongly and the rain became a downpour. They were soon drenched and soaked to the skin.

"We have to find shelter soon. I don't know about you but I am cold and wet," Joseph shouted above the splatter of the rain hitting the cobblestones. The horses splashed through the puddles, and finally Joseph and Joshua reached a small mutatione where they dried off and rested.

They traded in the horses for fresh ones and acquired tools as well as more food. Then they continued on for several hours bypassing the main part of Gesoriacum. Joseph looked along the docks until he discovered an obscure port with old small ships where he bought a boat about twenty feet long. It had been damaged, but it had a solid hull with both bow and stern curving high up to a point. He determined it was seaworthy enough to get across the sea.

He then found a large storage shed where they could camp and begin work on the boat. Joshua used his carpenter skills to fashion a mast, a rudder, and a secure dry storage area in the stern. Joseph found a sailcloth for him to cut and sew into a sail. In less than two weeks, they had a seaworthy boat.

"All we need now is food and water and with a bit of luck we can cross the sea," Joseph stated.

"I don't think we can buy luck," Joshua responded, "but some dried meat, bread, nuts, olives, and fruit would be a nice start. Do you think you can manage that?"

"Consider it done," Joseph laughed. "I'll be back soon."

When he returned loaded with food and the goatskins filled with water, they ate heartily, and then stowed the remaining food, the tools, and spare dry clothes in the dry storage area of the boat. Then they set the mast and sail and pushed off into the sea.

They headed north along the coast where Joseph knew they could sail the shortest distance across to Britannia. Once there, they waited until dark to avoid any Roman ships on the water. The warm summer night, clear skies, and two foot waves made the crossing pleasant, and they covered the distance in one night.

Joshua looked up at the hunter's belt. "Joseph, I can't help thinking of Sarah when I see the hunter up there. I miss her and Mary."

"You will see them again one day."

They made their way southwest along the coast for several nights until they passed a large island. Sailing northwest along its coast for a couple of hours, they passed the south entrance of a solent, a twenty mile long channel, separating the island from the mainland.

They encountered no other ships and sailed west a few more hours until they encountered the daunting cliffs of a headland. Joseph sailed just north of it to the mouth of a river, and they beached the boat.

"Why are we stopping here?" Joshua challenged.

"We could sail two or three nights more around a couple of heads and a long peninsula to save a day or two of marching. But I prefer traveling northwest from here on foot. It is safer and will only add one day to our trip."

Joshua nodded. They hid the boat in thickets of nettle trees and juniper shrubs, loaded up the remaining food and water, and marched inland for three nights and part of each day.

One night, with a clear sky and a full moon, Joseph pointed out the muffled drawn out *ooh-ooh-ooh* of an owl.

"Joshua, listen! I believe that's the call of a long-eared owl."

Suddenly the owl swooped silently in front of them, framed in the light of the moon, and dropped to the ground. They heard a squeak, and then the owl settled up on the branch of a pine tree.

"And that," Joshua replied, "was the distress call of a short-eared mouse."

Joseph said nothing after that but Joshua hoped he was grinning.

As they traveled on, they saw deer grazing along the trail, seemingly unafraid although a bit wary. A pair of foxes crossed their paths. They reached Glestingaburg at dawn of the third night.

Joshua noted the sheds and barns made of hazel and willow wood, and covered with reeds. He was delighted that Joseph seemed to be known to the people that lived there and was treated as if he were a returning king. They were given a spacious hut as shelter and were fed a sumptuous meal of boar and venison, together with turnips, onions, parsnips, nuts, and apples. After being there for some weeks, Joseph slowly began to preach to the inhabitants, which numbered only one hundred when he arrived.

Over the course of several years, the word spread of his teachings and many others came. Joshua asked him what his intentions were.

"We will build a place of worship right here," Joseph responded.

"What about the tin business that you were going to establish here?"

"I've found a better calling." That was all Joseph said.

He made good on his word when one day he called the people together, thrust his staff into the ground, and spoke.

"It is here that we will build a holy place of worship," he said. "Our dwelling will be of such beauty and grace that many will come to this town to see it and pray with us."

Not long after, a hawthorn tree grew where he had set his staff.

"Joseph," Joshua told him one day, "I believe you have found the most wonderful and perfect calling."

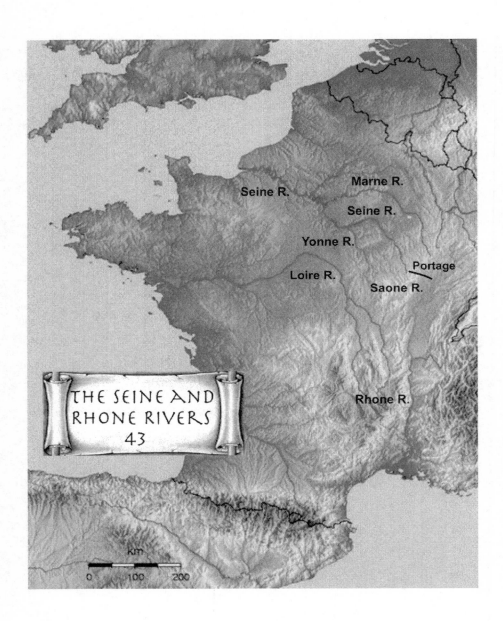

Seine R.

Marne R.

Seine R.

Yonne R.

Portage

Loire R.

Saone R.

Rhone R.

THE SEINE AND
RHONE RIVERS
43

km

0   100   200

CHAPTER FORTY

Glestingaburg to Ra

Spring, 43 AD

Over the next several years, that which Joseph spoke of did indeed happen. The people joined together under his direction and a small modest abbey of stone and wood rose up next to the hawthorn tree. Joshua was amazed by how much Joseph accomplished, and he gave what help he could with his own carpentry skills. One day he came to Joseph.

"I have heard that the land will soon be invaded by the Romans, and the people here will be in danger. My presence will only add to their peril." Joshua said. "It is time for me to return to the place whence I came and to the people I left and the cause that is theirs. I pray that those here will withstand the invasion and will prosper."

"How do you know this about the Romans?" Joseph asked with furrowed brow.

"I cannot explain, but I know. The people must prepare."

"I will see to that," Joseph replied. "I have already prepared a crevice in the foundation of the Abbey for the goblet you gave me. I will hide it immediately."

Joshua smiled. "A good idea. It should not be found, at least for many years. Mary insisted."

"I understand. When do you leave?"

"Tomorrow."

Joshua prepared a pack that included his tools and spare clothes and filled it with dried boar and deer meat, bread, some nuts and berries, a few turnips and onions, and apples, and carried his goatskin filled with water. He left quietly at night and traveled swiftly southeast to the shore where he and Joseph had hidden their boat. He arrived two nights later and spent the next day preparing the boat, which was still in good condition. At dusk he launched it and sailed east toward the solent and the large island.

But soon, he heard the splashing of hundreds of oars and the voices of countless soldiers. In the dim light he saw large barges filled with thousands of Roman soldiers headed into the solent. He observed that the barges appeared to be traveling along the shore of the island. With a pounding heart, he quickly sailed directly south so as not to be seen in the moonlight, then decided it was much safer to continue sailing south to Francia until he reached a huge peninsula Joseph had described to him. The seas were rough with four foot waves but he covered the distance in two nights and a day. On the second night the clear skies became cloudy, the northeast wind increased, and rain started to fall. He was drenched when he finally reached shore near the mouth of a small river. He replenished his water, found a small shed above the east bank, dried his clothes, and rested for a day.

He then sailed east at dusk, following the coast in a southerly then easterly direction, and reached the mouth of the river Joseph had told him about. It had taken less than a week of sailing. Joseph said it was a slow moving meandering river called the Seine but it would take him far inland. Joshua stopped in a secluded area on the north bank and spent a day searching for mushrooms, nuts, berries, and wild roots. He caught a pheasant and took a chance building a small fire at night to cook it. While he was tending the fire, he heard the long call of an owl 'HOOOOOH, a long delay, and then ho hooh-oohooHOOoo-oo-oo'. He recognized the courtship call of the tawny owl and looked up. It was perched on a branch, its silhouette etched against the clear night sky.

Joshua sat motionless next to the crackling fire and watched a red fox creep close, drawn to the smell of the cooking pheasant. When the fox came too close, Joshua chased it into the woods, and came across a chestnut tree, and a nearby apple tree. He added the chestnuts to the embers of the dying fire, then ate some of the pheasant with the chestnuts and apples, wrapped what remained in leaves, filled his goatskin water bag, and sailed slowly up the river. The current against him was slow, so he made good time, even traveling only at night. After three nights, he entered a tributary river which was only big enough for a small boat like his.

Joshua continued up the tributary for another three nights and reached its source. He now faced a daunting challenge. He could not carry the boat, nor did he want to travel on Roman roads to return to the south. So he filled his pack with what food he could carry, filled his goatskin, and traveled overland for four nights to try to find a tributary of the mighty river called the Rhone. He was out of food, almost out of water, exhausted and discouraged, when he noticed a twinkling star above, moving rapidly through the sky in a southeast direction.

He was convinced it was guiding him and followed it throughout the fifth night. At dawn he came to the bank of a small river, whereupon he fell face down and drank his fill. He gave thanks to the heavens, filled his goatskin, and searched for nuts and berries. He hoped this river would lead to the Saone and then the Rhone. His next challenge was to find a boat of some sort. He walked south along the shore of the river for one night, and just before dawn, came across a small barge on the bank that was in need of repair and seemingly abandoned. It was about thirty feet long and eight feet wide, with a ten foot mast in the bow. The rudder was broken, along with a couple of cross support pieces, and the sail was dirty and torn, but the hull appeared to be undamaged. He tested it to make sure it would not take on water, and then he repaired the damaged rudder, cross pieces, and the sail, and in two days had the barge in shape to float down the river.

He set out at dusk, stayed close to shore, and drifted. The winter rains had swollen the river and the current was moving rapidly. He stopped every dawn to rest and eat, and to hide from the river traffic. He would look for thick overhanging willows or thickets of yew or nettle trees to hide in.

Joseph had given him a little money and he used this to acquire some rugged clothes at a shop on a dock he passed. These included a thick ragged woolen shirt. He also created a small "load" of logs on his barge. He tried to look as if he were a rough river man bringing wood to the south. He never knew when he would pass curious prying eyes or encounter Roman authorities. The logs also served as ballast and weight to speed the boat downstream. He was such an insignificant river man on an insignificant barge that he attracted very little attention.

Nevertheless, one day he was forced to test his disguise. When a heavy spring rain drenched him and began to fill the barge, he stopped at a small dock next to a boat shed. Another longer barge filled with stones had stopped at the same place. A large heavyset man came up to him, and shook his hand.

"Where are you headed?" he asked.

Joshua replied. "To Arelate."

The man stared at him.

"You have that load of logs too far back. How long have you been on this river?"

Joshua sensed the man was suspicious. "Only a year."

"I felt your hands. They aren't those of a real river man. Who are you anyway?"

Joshua decided the best answer was to confess. "I'm not a river man. I'm a carpenter, and I'm bringing these from far up north to build a house."

That seemed to satisfy the man somewhat.

"Where are you headed?" Joshua asked, deciding it was best to engage in conversation.

"I'm taking this load from the quarry upstream down to Arelate. If you like, we can travel together and I can show you some places along the river to stop."

"Thanks. I appreciate the offer, but I plan to travel without stopping if possible."

As soon as the rain let up, Joshua left quietly and efficiently, trying to act as if he knew what he was doing. From then on, stopping every now and then to search for food was the only delay as he swiftly floated down the Rhone.

Joshua was not sure where he would find Mary and the others, so when he reached the south part of the river he began to stop along its bank and wander in disguise throughout towns listening for gossip or rumors. One evening he stopped at the Roman town of Avennio and overheard two men discussing the miracles of a Saint Martha in Tarasco. That clue was all he needed. He returned to the barge, drifted a short distance south to Tarasco, and wandered throughout the town until he located her. She was sitting quietly in a courtyard facing the street.

"Hello, Martha," he spoke very softly.

"It's you," Martha exclaimed. "You've returned." She was dressed in a white toga.

"How do you know who I am?" Joshua was still disguised as a rough river man.

She smiled. "I know your voice."

They went inside her dwelling and sat in a corner of the room where they would not be heard or observed. They exchanged stories of their travels during the past seven years. Martha said she had heard from the large Judean community about the three saints in Ra that had miraculously arrived from the sea, and she thought that would be the best place to start looking for Sarah and the three Marys. After Joshua explained his travels to the north and back, she told him how she became a saint.

"There was a beast called the Tarasque terrorizing the people. It was somewhat like a dragon. It is hard really to describe. I confronted it with a cross and tamed it. I became a living saint because of this miracle." Martha paused. "I learned some things from you, I guess."

Joshua gave her a broad smile. "You seem to have managed quite well on your own here."

"How did you manage to avoid the four legions of twenty thousand Roman soldiers?" Martha asked. "They were under Claudius and invaded the land in the north across the sea. We heard they marched along the Via Agrippa to Gesoriacum and sailed across the sea."

"I was fortunate," Joshua said, and that was all he said.

Martha nodded. Then they parted, and Joshua once again traveled down the Rhone and took its small western branch. He drifted to the mouth of this branch and then sailed along the coast a short distance to Ra.

It was dusk on the night when Sarah and her mother were about to leave Ra. Sarah was twelve years old and had not seen Joshua for seven years. She was just waking up when a man appeared in front of her. He looked like a rough river man but she recognized his penetrating brown eyes. It was Joshua, the gentle and mysterious man with the reddish brown beard.

"You've come back," Sarah exclaimed. "I was beginning to think you never would."

"I said I would," he answered, "and here I am."

"Is Joseph with you?" Sarah asked.

"No. He decided he was needed in Glestingaburg. I returned alone."

Sarah's mother Mary entered. They did not speak but immediately embraced. It seemed to Sarah that they held each other for a very long time.

Mary explained to Joshua that they were about to sail west, and looked at him expectantly.

"I'll come with you." he said.

She nodded in agreement, and then told him about their four years in Massalia, the year in Aquae Sextiae, and the two in Ra, and how they were now considered saints. Then they said goodbye to Mary Salome and Mary of Clopas, who stayed and continued to be treated as living saints.

SAM'S WIKUOM

CHAPTER FORTY ONE

Mali and Sam

Mahone Bay, New Scotland
Fall, 1398

Jed and Martha watched from the deck of the flag ship as Henry was greeted warmly by Grand Chief Membertou and invited to smoke the peace pipe. Henry and his men sat in a circle with the Chief and the chiefs of the neighboring tribes.

Martha could see the entire village from Henry's ship. "Jed, what are all those round things? Is that where they sleep?" They seemed to be of different sizes and styles. The dwellings were circular, some dome shaped and some conical, and from ten to twenty feet in diameter. One appeared to be even larger. She counted several dozen and then lost track.

"My father told me those are called wikuoms in their language. The biggest one is the Grand Chief's."

Martha noticed that the wikuoms were on the edge of the densely packed pine trees but not in the forest itself.

"I wonder why they are so close to the water."

"Let's ask them when we get there, but I'll bet it has to do with fishing. See all the canoes on the shore? My father told me they eat a lot of cod and shellfish and even eels."

Martha made a noise like 'yuk' and grimaced.

Jed added, "Of course, they also hunt animals like deer and boar and moose."

After the pipe completed the circle, Henry produced a gift for the Grand Chief that was of extraordinary beauty and caused all to stare. It was a long knife with a curved blade that glittered in the light, but it was the carved handle with many embedded jewels that amazed the onlookers. The other ship captains recognized the knife as one from their treasure chests. Henry must have felt it was one without historical significance that could be spared.

The Grand Chief, not to be outdone, produced a gift for Henry that was of equal beauty. The huge headdress contained a wide range of feathers from many birds, as well as porcupine quills. The result was stunning, equaled only by the headdress of the Grand Chief himself. The gift exchanges continued for some time between the other chiefs and the ship captains, who knew how much the natives valued weapons and tools and other goods that they could not make themselves. The gift exchange concluded with another round of smoking the pipe.

Jed and Martha were being rowed ashore as they watched the ceremony. As they approached, the smoking of the pipe concluded. The Grand Chief stood up and motioned to his son and his son's friend to step forward. Henry greeted Jed and Martha and brought them forward as well. Jed's red hair was in stark contrast with the dark hair of the Grand Chief and the other natives. Jed was not sure what to expect, but the son indicated that Jed and Martha should follow him. The Grand Chief beckoned Jed to do so too, and Henry did the same. Then Henry and the Grand Chief returned to the conclusion of the peace pipe ceremony.

Jed and Martha followed the son and his friend to a small clearing where they sat in a circle. The son introduced himself as Malikiaq and produced a small headdress for Jed. Jed introduced himself, glad he was prepared to give a gift in return. He pulled out a small ornate dagger for Malikiaq.

"You can call him Mali," the friend explained, "and my name is Sam."

"My name is Mark," Martha offered as she and Sam exchanged similar gifts.

Martha noticed Mali and most of the braves were bare-chested and wore a loincloth, while some of the braves as well as Sam wore a deerskin shirt with an animal design embroidered in beads. Sam had deer and bears on his shirt.

Mali was tall and lean with long black hair below his shoulders and deep dark penetrating eyes. He stood stiffly and was not smiling.

Sam was short with even longer brown hair tied with a beaded thong to form a long tail, and sparkling brown eyes. He was beaming.

"Normally we would be joining the other braves for "war game" activities," Sam explained in very good English, "but since we are hosting the two of you we are temporarily exempt." He looked around the circle, his grin getting broader all the while. He could hardly contain himself.

Mali managed a small smile at Sam's excitement. "It is true," he said haltingly in English. "You are our guests."

"Besides," Sam added, "Mali is the best at everything. He can shoot better with the bow and arrow, run faster and jump further, and track better than any of the other braves his age. In fact," he continued proudly, "Mali already killed his first moose, which none of the others have done yet. It is one of the requirements for passage to manhood which they all must do soon."

Then Sam stood up and led them into a somewhat isolated spot where they had their own wikuom. It was conical and about ten feet across at the bottom. Mali motioned for them to sit outside in a version of the pipe ceremony without the pipe smoking. Now Mali produced more gifts for Jed: a beautiful leather native shirt with decorations adorning it and a pair of beautiful native moccasins. Sam did the same for Martha, and in turn

Jed and Martha gave them short knives with carved handles and short axes, also with carved handles. Jed put on the shirt and moccasins. Martha turned her back and quickly exchanged her "Mark" shirt for the native shirt, then put on the moccasins. They both began to look like native boys.

"Is this your own wikuom?" Martha asked Sam.

"Oh, you know the name in our language." Sam smiled, pleased. "Yes. We built it ourselves. Mali cut the spruce saplings and tied them together at the top and then around the middle, and I put on the birch bark and covered it with the grass and brush for extra camouflage. It's big enough for many people, so it will be fine for four of us."

Martha asked if she could look inside so Sam took her in. She soon came out smiling.

"It's so much bigger inside than you would think from the outside," she told Jed. "And it looks nice and comfortable." Then she turned to Sam. "Why is it open at the top?"

"When it's cold we build a fire. That's to let out the smoke."

"Of course. I should have thought of that." There was a pause. Martha continued. "Your father is chief of a tribe some distance from here?"

"Yes," Sam hesitated, "but he was killed in a war with another tribe. So I came to live with Mali and his father. Can I tell you the rest of the story later?" He turned to Mali. "Can we go to the waterfall pools?"

"Yes," Mali said and then turned to Jed and Martha. "We always take bows and arrows."

"It's mandatory," added Sam, "as you will learn." Following Mali's lead, Sam slung his quiver full of arrows on his back and his bow over his shoulder.

Mali began to lead them into the thick woods nearby, then stopped after a short distance, and began to show them how to move through the forest without leaving a trace.

"Never step on twigs or branches," Mali said. "They leave a trace or make noise. Move like a deer does, silently and swiftly. Very hard to track."

Then he demonstrated by moving rapidly through the trees without making a sound and soon disappeared. He was only a short distance away and virtually invisible. There did not appear to be a trail of any sort. In order to find him, Jed and Martha had to follow Sam, who was almost as adept as Mali.

Mali explained that these same skills could help track animals or people. Then he bent down and pointed to several broken twigs and crushed leaves, and further on, more crushed leaves and broken branches.

"Moose," he said simply.

Then Mali asked Sam to lead. He wanted to follow Jed and Martha to see how they were doing. After following them through the forest for a few minutes, he stopped them. "Good. You learn quickly," he said. "But get down," he added, crouching low. "Like a fox. Don't hit branches. No noise."

Then Mali took the lead and they moved swiftly on invisible paths that he seemed to know well. They soon arrived at a river several miles away from their camp where Mali stopped them, stood still, and listened. Martha was amazed at how acute Mali's hearing was. Somehow he was able to hear things despite the rush of water, for he pointed out a deer moving slowly nearby. They followed him as he walked in the water along the edge of the river. Then Mali stopped briefly to tell them about a woodpecker he heard far away.

"It's one half mile away. A big woodpecker. Probably a pileated."

They soon arrived at a pool below a waterfall. Sam barely contained his excitement. He looked at Mali for his approval and then led them to a secluded spot where the sound of the river did not drown out their voices.

"I said I would tell you the rest of my story. Now is a good time, and Mali says it's all right." Sam settled down on the ground and continued. "Everyone is told the main reason I am here with Mali's tribe is to teach Mali English. That is true, but there is another big reason."

"I have always looked like a boy," Sam explained, "but I am really a girl. When my father died several months ago, that meant I would soon be given in marriage to a brave chosen by our new chief. But my mother and I wanted to avoid that, so I was dressed as a boy and hidden away. When Grand Chief Membertou visited us soon after my father's death, he agreed to take me with him back to his camp. I could be a companion to Mali, teach him English, and remain disguised as a boy. When the Grand Chief left soon thereafter, I also left quietly and unobserved, and returned with him. Only my mother and the Grand Chief know of this arrangement, and of course Mali. I am from a distant tribe so no one would know me here. Mali says I can trust you two to know my secret," Sam smiled, "and besides, I'd like you to know who I really am."

"Since you have been so trusting with us, I will do the same," Martha interjected. "I am also in disguise as a boy and for a similar reason. Our men have been told I am a friend of Jed and it would not be good if our men knew I was a girl. But I am so longing to be a girl now and then. I hope you understand."

"I understand completely, and we can fix that. Is it all right to swim, Mali?" Sam asked.

"It's all right. I will stand guard at the waterfall. We are far from our village. I don't want to take chances. Soon we will go downstream to a pool. It is silent there and I can hear while we swim."

Sam dropped her clothes and Martha did the same. They ran under the waterfall while Jed thought it advisable to stay with Mali and keep him company. At the top of the waterfall, a large rock perched on the edge split the water into two streams. The near waterfall fell into a shallow pool where Sam and Martha frolicked while the far waterfall fell into a deep pool. The sounds of their splashing would be covered by the noise of the waterfall, but they understood they were not to talk at all since those sounds would carry.

Mali explained to Jed how to listen and tell which sounds were made by animals or falling branches or wind. If anyone heard any noise that was not normal, they would all be on the alert. While they waited for the girls to finish, Jed noticed the woods thick with spruce and birch and oak stands, and the underbrush of yew and juniper thickets was so dense it made it difficult to see anything moving through the forest. The shallow pool rippled over the downstream rocks and flickered in the filtered sunlight but the deep pool was silent and dark and seemed not to move at all.

After a few minutes the girls came out, and they all hiked a short distance downstream to another pool that was deep and almost motionless. The sound of water gurgling over the rocks as it entered this pool mingled with those of water streaming in from the side where the overflow from the pool below the waterfall created two small rivulets. The water in the lower pool then flowed out again over a low waterfall.

All four of them hid their clothes nearby and slid into the pool. Jed noticed that Mali and Sam always kept their bows and arrows within arm's reach. Suddenly Mali motioned to all of them to move out of sight or under the water and to remain motionless. He quickly grabbed his bow and arrow and stood as still as a statue. Jed could hear nothing at first, but then he heard the noise which had caused Mali to freeze. It was different than all other forest sounds, gradually growing louder. It was the heavy sound of something large being dragged.

Once Mali realized it was the sound of a large moose moving slowly through the underbrush, he relaxed and told the others to do the same.

"How is it, Mali," Jed asked, "that you have such acute, sensitive hearing? It's remarkable."

"It's not just my hearing," Mali explained, "I've learned differences in forest sounds."

"Mali knows all the sounds of the forest," Sam said proudly. "All of them."

"We should not stay here," Mali said. "The water hides sounds even for me. We should leave this spot and work our way back slowly." When all of them were dressed, he took a different route through the forest on a trail that was again invisible to the others.

After they returned to camp, Sam and Mali spent more time with Martha and Jed teaching them how to move through the forest even more silently, leaving no marks that could be tracked.

"You both learn very quickly," Mali said. "You are ready for my test. Each of you will quietly make your own trail, leaving no evidence of your presence," Mali explained. "I will try to track you."

"That will be quite a challenge," Jed said with a smile, "but we'll try."

"Is Sam going to track me?" Martha said hopefully. Mali just smiled.

Later that day Martha and Jed met with Henry, who explained that in a couple of days he wanted them to travel with him to the top of a nearby hill where he would begin building a castle.

"You should enjoy these days with Mali and Sam while you can," Henry added.

That evening Jed and Martha spent time talking with Mali and Sam about exploring the islands in the bay by canoe.

CHAPTER FORTY TWO

Exploring Mahone Bay

Mahone Bay, New Scotland
Fall, 1398

"Mali knows these islands better than anyone," Sam declared, "We have some favorite places to show you."

"We will go out early in the morning." Mali smiled and Jed and Martha nodded.

The next morning they took two canoes, Sam and Martha in one, and Mali and Jed in the other. They left the narrow harbor with Mali in the lead. There was no wind and the water was still and reflected light almost like glass. After paddling more than a mile he took them past an island right at the mouth of the harbor which was not very hilly. They continued for several more miles past a series of shoals and then a small island next to a very large one and out into open water.

Mali explained, "There are shoals all along this route that are cause for concern to a ship like Henry's but are no problem for our canoes. I want to take you to a favorite island of mine well out in the open part of the Bay."

They continued through shoals and ledges to reach his island. It was long, and narrow at one end with a cove Mali liked. They reached the south tip and turned north. As they coasted up the east side Jed noticed the hilly nature of the larger lower end. He glanced at Martha to see if she might be thinking what he was. She looked back at him and then up at the hilly terrain. He was sure she was thinking the same: that hills meant possible caves and caves meant possible hiding places. Jed knew he still had to find very safe places to hide a scroll and possibly some of Henry's treasures.

They continued on to the cove and beached the canoes. Jed and Martha wanted to explore a bit. First Mali hid the canoes in a large crevice and covered them with branches and leaves. It was unlikely anyone would have followed them to the cove but Mali was always cautious. Jed realized that Mali never took any chances about being discovered and he thought it must be something learned at a very early age. Then they walked north along the narrow end of the island and came to a lake. Sam didn't hesitate and dashed into the water at the very narrow end where they would be concealed. Martha followed soon thereafter and then Jed. Mali, always with his bow and arrow nearby, went in where he was nearly invisible. The two girls played quietly because they knew Mali's rule of no talking and no noise. For Martha these chances to swim were special after she had spent all that time on the boat carefully dressed as a boy. Here she could be a girl again.

Mali finally indicated it was time to go and they walked back to their canoes. He made sure they were undetected as they pushed off into the cove. Jed wished he'd had time to explore the lower hilly section of the island but didn't want to arouse suspicion about his search for caves. Mali took them around the north end and directly to several large islands, clustered off a point of land.

"That," Mali pointed, "is where we look out over the islands and Bay to keep watch for anyone approaching by sea."

They followed the shoreline back to the inner harbor and to their camp. Jed and Martha had a chance to talk to Henry that evening about the building of the Castle on the hill.

Henry explained, "I've already negotiated with Grand Chief Membertou about farming up in the higher lands close to the top of the hill. I gave the Chief gifts in appreciation for this like metal objects, pots and pans, tools, and weapons. We also provided spices and sugar and food items that are not available to the natives. The Chief was very thankful and provided some grains and meats that had been cured. He also agreed to the establishment of a farming colony many miles up the hill away from the camp. A group of men have already gone up the hill and are constructing some buildings from the wood in the forests."

Henry continued, "We've also herded the remaining sheep to the farmland area. There is just enough hay to feed them. I also promised the Chief some wool when we do the shearing later on. We'll show the women how to clean and card and spin the raw wool into yarn to make it useable for them to weave. They are quite adept at using other types of hair from animals so this should be easy to do."

Henry's men also quickly planted the corn and wheat and root crops, onions and turnips, they would need for the winter ahead. When they had completed the buildings and the fences for the sheep and the planting of all the crops, they would start on the castle. There were many large boulders close to the site where he would build the foundation and a large supply of timber as well. He hoped to have the base done before the onset of winter.

Henry told Jed and Martha he wanted them to hike with him to where they were establishing the colony and had invited Mali and Sam to join them. Chief Membertou had given his consent. Mali and Sam eagerly agreed to join them on this trek along the river and through the woods and up the hill to the farming colony.

The four of them spent the next two days preparing for the trip, which would be four days long. They also found time to visit their secluded waterfall and pools and to explore the woods and practice crouching and creeping silently. Mali said they were getting quite good and, with a bit more instruction and practice, they would be superb and he would not worry as much as he had been, though he still corrected them on minor errors.

Then it was time to accompany Henry to the colony. They followed the meandering river for three miles, skirting pools and a pair of low waterfalls. Mali pointed out six salmon swimming upstream to spawn and how they were trying to leap up the waterfalls to an upper pool. When Henry reached the pool above the last waterfall, he turned perpendicular to the river and they marched two miles steadily through the forest of oak and maple trees up a gradual slope. Then they climbed straight up a grassland hill for a mile until they came to a clearing. They had covered more than six miles. They saw sheep browsing on fresh grass and realized the colony had found an excellent spot for farming and grazing. The soil was rich and the plantings grew rapidly. Jed noticed buildings had already been constructed for the men and one for the sheep. They also had fencing around the fields where the sheep grazed during the day. When it became dark they would be herded back into their building.

Before it was nightfall Jed and Mali and Sam and Martha quickly made their own wikuom. Mali showed Jed how to select and cut the saplings and tie them up while Sam showed Martha how to cut the birch bark and select the brush. The four of them constructed the wikuom together near the buildings and then joined the men for a wonderful meal of corn and beans and wild game: pheasant and hare. Then they turned in to their wikuom as darkness descended. Mali slept with his bow and arrow by his side and Sam did the same.

All was silent, but in the middle of the night Mali put his hand on Jed to keep him quiet. He made the sign of the bear claw and Jed understood. They heard the sheep moving around in the barn in fear. Mali slid outside with his bow and arrow in hand. It was very quiet and then Jed heard the bear try to rip the door off the sheep barn. Then there was a squeal as Mali's arrow struck home. Sam and Martha awoke and Jed signaled they should be quiet. No one else in the buildings heard any of the noise. Mali came back soon with a smile on his face and settled down to sleep.

In the morning the men were amazed that they'd heard nothing. They cut up the bear to be cured and saved the magnificent claws for Mali, as well as the teeth. The claws would be made into a necklace and presented to him by the Chief as part of a bear claw ceremony. The teeth also would be prized. His father would be proud of him, he knew. That morning Henry walked them over to the castle site. The many rocks and boulders in the vicinity made it relatively easy to construct the base on top of which the wooden structure would be built. Henry would supervise the construction so as to leave a crypt at the bottom, where he intended to hide some of the Templar treasure.

He asked Jed and Martha to observe the building of the castle base since they might do it themselves elsewhere. He showed them how they dug down ten feet and created a solid foundation of rocks and a second inner wall also of rocks with several compartments between the two walls. They created a floor of heavy timber at ground level and then the foundation was built up another ten feet. They used smaller rocks for this level. In both cases they used mud made of fine dirt dried into a kind of mortar to keep the rocks together. He then asked the four of them to scout the timber in the nearby forest to locate the best places for the men to harvest wood for the castle. This would save much needed time.

Fall turned into winter and Jed and Martha were about to get their warm breeches and vests from the ship.

"No need to do that," Sam said.

Mali and Sam presented a warm parka to each of them. It was made of heavy buckskin lined with fine hair, and a huge hood trimmed with fur. As it grew colder, snow began to fall. At first it was a small snowfall and Martha and Jed and Mali and Sam delighted in the opportunity to try the very difficult challenge of moving through the forest without leaving a trace. Mali showed them how to follow paths with little snow or to use animal tracks. He looked for heavily traveled deer paths at the edge of the snow areas where they would not be detected. When the snow was very heavy they needed to find deer prints or tracks made by hunters. When all else failed he even walked backward on his toes to make one think he was moving forward. It snowed lightly for one day but then began to come down heavily. Mali said from the nature of the snow falling it looked as if they were in for a big storm. He was right. The storm turned into a blizzard and the snow piled up into large mounds and covered the branches of the trees.

"It is so beautiful," Martha remarked one day, "so quiet and peaceful and serene."

The blizzard finally stopped and the weather became warmer. Soon an early spring turned the forest floor, still blanketed with snow, into a lovely carpet of spring wildflowers including jack-in-the-pulpits, crocuses, skunk cabbage, jonquils, nasturtiums, and wild orchids. The snow melted, the low ground covering vines and wild rose bushes bloomed into white and red and yellow and blue flowers, and the shrubs and cherry and apple trees began to bud.

As time went on, the four of them became very strong friends and Mali and Sam continued to teach Jed and Martha about traveling in the forest.

Because of his skill, Mali was invited to join the men's hunting parties on occasion and increased his reputation with his accuracy and his sense of the location of game. He shot several deer and a wild boar during his short forays. Chief Membertou and Henry were increasingly impressed with Mali but his father did not want him to become a permanent member of the hunting party. He was, after all, the son of the Grand Chief and had already shown his skill and leadership. He was to stay with Henry and Jed.

Once spring and then summer arrived, the building of the castle progressed rapidly. They had gathered sufficient wood for the next several floors with the help Mali, Jed, Sam, and Martha had provided in locating it. Carpenters erected walls and floors for two more levels. After this, Henry spent less time there and took the four of them on a special project to one of the islands in the bay. That summer Jed turned thirteen and Martha twelve, as did Mali and Sam.

Henry and Chief Membertou arranged to have a special ceremony celebrating these milestones. Mali was given the tusk of a giant wild boar to honor his expertise as a hunter. Jed was given an ornate headdress to honor him as a young chief and as a warrior. Martha was given a golden arrow indicating "his" expertise with bow and arrow. These gifts were presented by Chief Membertou. Henry then stepped forward to present the final gift to Sam. He presented a silver cup to Sam and spoke of "his" all around skills as a warrior and Sam's acknowledged generosity in helping and praising others. This final gift was much admired and coveted by all the warriors. Generosity and kindness as well as skill were considered admirable qualities by the entire tribe. Sam beamed as she held the cup on high.

CHAPTER FORTY THREE

Flight to Mahone Bay

Southern New England
Fall, 1949

Jes and his father and Uncle Pete, with help from Marya, spent a day cleaning up the terrible mess in Jes's home. Jes and Marya were covered with dust, their clothes dirty and streaked, their hair disheveled, his brown hair caked with mud, and her lovely light reddish brown hair had turned to dull orange. They both said they looked forward to a shower. Jes's father called his mother at Mabel's, who knew nothing about the mess or who could have done it or why. While they were still putting the house in order, a neighbor stopped by to see what had happened. She told them she had seen two men in a black sedan go into the house without knocking. She was surprised, she said, because she knew no one was home. They stayed an hour and then left.

Two days later, Jes's grandfather returned from his trip. They told him what had happened and what the neighbor had said. He was not shocked as the others were.

"I'm not surprised at this," he explained. "They are desperate."

"What do you mean?" asked Jes. "Who are they?"

"They belong to a large, well established group that has roots going back many years." Grandfather went to a brick in the wall between the Dutch oven and the large fireplace in the kitchen. The fireplace had been used for cooking and heat for many years but was seldom used now. He pried the brick out. It was just loose enough to remove. He reached in and removed an ancient scroll plus a set of scrolls wrapped in parchment.

"These are what the man with the black beard was looking for and didn't find," he explained to Jes. "These are why he tried to kidnap you for ransom and why he ransacked the house. You and Marya are in danger and must leave here. I will take you. We must tell no one we are going or where, not even your mother and father. Sooner or later the man with the black beard and his friends will return to seek what they believe they overlooked. They will also discover you are gone but won't know where or with whom. We must leave immediately. Pack your things."

"Are you sure you can do this, Dad?" Jes's father asked.

"I know what I'm doing," Grandfather said, "where to go, how to get there without being detected, and what to do when we get to our destination. Now, don't ask me any more questions. The less you all know, the better."

Grandfather left for an hour while they were packing and came back in an old yellow sedan with Texas plates. It looked awful but the engine sounded great.

"Where on earth did you get that?" asked Uncle Pete.

"Never you mind," Grandfather replied.

Jes hugged his father and mother.

"Don't worry, Mom. We'll be all right."

Jes and Marya piled in with their belongings and off they went. Grandfather took a route that was generally straight north, mainly on Route Seven, taking his time and driving during the day.

"I plan to take a route that doesn't give away our destination," he told Jes and Marya, "just in case we are followed. So I'll be keeping an eye out behind us."

"Can we help?" Marya asked.

"No. Just enjoy the trip. I don't think we need worry."

They were not aware that they narrowly missed danger. The day after they left, the black bearded man and two others came to the neighborhood. One was short with blond hair and the other was very tall with red hair. The blond haired man came to the door of the house while the other two stayed a distance away. He had an envelope and pretended to be delivering it only to Jes. Jes's father answered the door and simply said Jes was not there. The blond haired man and the two others, observed by the neighbor, watched the house from the dirt road for the rest of the day. Finally, at dusk, they began yelling at each other, piled into their black sedan, and sped off.

Grandfather had arranged to call Uncle Pete that evening, and when he found out that the black bearded man knew Jes and Marya were gone, he changed his plans. They had reached the middle of Vermont when he called. Rather than stopping, he decided it was time to drive only at night and continued on. Careful that no one was around, he drove quickly to the intersection of Route Two and headed east. His destination was eventually Nova Scotia but now he wanted to take a more circuitous route.

While they were travelling, Jes and Marya asked about the scrolls and what was so important about them.

"The scrolls," Grandfather told them, "contain evidence tracing the bloodline back to the Merovingians and earlier."

"What's the bloodline?" they asked, "what is it?"

"The two of you have the Merovingian Cross on your chests and this is evidence of the bloodline in modern days. The existence of the Cross is rare in the world and the black bearded man and others like him are charged with eliminating that evidence if possible. The gene causing the bloodline birthmark often skips many generations before surfacing again."

"I also have the Merovingian Cross although no one today knows it. Like you Jes, I was taught from the earliest age to conceal it. Your grandmother also had it but it skipped your father's generation. Unfortunately it became known that you had it and the black bearded man was given his assignment."

"And they also found out I have it?" asked Marya.

"Unfortunately, yes. It was not concealed very well. It was not an accident that you were brought to live with Jes and his family."

"Do they plan to kill us if they catch us? Eliminate us from this bloodline?" asked Jes.

"Quite possibly, sad to say. We don't know. But I told you once, Jes, I would never let anyone hurt you, and I won't. And that also goes for Marya. I will make sure you're both safe. Now go to sleep. We have a long drive ahead, a roundabout route to make sure we are not followed."

Grandfather did indeed take them on a roundabout route to avoid any chance of detection. He travelled mainly at night and usually found a secluded place off the road to rest briefly. He did stop now and then for food but generally did everything in a way to avoid suspicion. Jes and Marya stayed out of sight, hunched down in their seats, with blankets and pillows piled up against the windows. He took them east on Route Two almost to the coast, then north for a long distance, then Route Two east again until he crossed over into the north end of Nova Scotia. In this way he approached Mahone Bay from the north instead of the usual way across the Bay of Fundy.

He did not take any chances and continued to drive at night. Jes and Marya got used to this routine. They arrived in Mahone Bay in darkness and went straight to the home of Jes's great aunt, who knew they were coming. Grandfather had called her the day before and she was prepared for them. He hid the car after unloading them and their belongings and finally relaxed a bit, hoping the organization of the black bearded man did not know about or suspect where they were.

Grandfather expressed his concern to his sister, "I don't think we should stay here very long. We should find another place to stay out of sight."

"Why are you so worried?" she responded. "The children were just here not long ago. They'd been tracked for a while by that black car, but Jes's father was not worried. The kids went all over the place while they were here."

"Perhaps they should have been more careful," responded Grandfather. "They aren't as old and wise as I am," he added with a twinkle in his eye.

"Relax and let them enjoy it here," she said. "They're just children."

He grudgingly agreed but still resisted.

"Do you know of another place we can stay?"

She pondered his question. "I'll think about it."

Meanwhile Jes and Marya were delighted to see his great aunt again and to talk to her and his grandfather about Nova Scotia and its history. Jes wanted to know more about the islands that they both had talked about. Marya asked if they knew much about the history of Mason Island and the ancestor Mason from long ago.

"It always has had a mystery about it. There is a legend passed down that says Prince Henry of Scotland landed here around 1400 AD and Mason was a favorite island of his," she answered. "But I really don't know much about the islands."

"What about Oak Island?" Marya asked. Jes noticed that Marya put on her little innocent look and he knew she was up to something. "Do you think Prince Henry went there? Is treasure buried there?"

"As I said, I don't know much about the islands. Your grandfather can tell you more than I can."

Jes and Marya looked at each other with a knowing look and nodded. This was noticed by Grandfather. Jes changed the subject and reminded his grandfather that he had promised to take him fishing on the islands as he did when he was a boy. Grandfather said they would go fishing in the next few days. Meanwhile he warned Jes and Marya not to be seen leaving or entering the house. They should go out the back door and make sure they were not seen around the house.

"This is just for the time being," he added, "as a precaution."

They nodded.

"We won't stay in this house for very long," he said. "For safety reasons, it would be better not to be seen here just in case we've been tracked to Nova Scotia."

Great Aunt scoffed. "It's not likely. You shouldn't worry."

In the next few weeks Grandfather took Jes and Marya on a number of trips. He took them fishing as he had promised. They fished off Mader's Cove, which was close by. He'd said it was the best fishing spot when he was a boy, and sure enough, they caught several fish each and cooked them later for dinner.

"What kind of fish are these, Grandfather?" asked Marya.

"The silver blue ones are salmon and the bigger ones are cod. You're lucky we're catching the smaller ones. You could not hold them if they were over fifty pounds."

He took them to Indian Point and Zwicker Island to fish, and finally, to Mason's Island. Not only did they fish off the shore but they all explored the island from north to south.

"You told me that you went to Oak Island when you were a boy," Jes said as they were leaving. "Did you ever fish there?"

"I don't think so." Grandfather answered tersely. Jes thought Grandfather was abrupt and annoyed.

But Marya persisted. "Could we go to that island?"

"I'll take you one day but only at night." He offered no more explanation.

Jes waited a minute and then continued. "Grandfather, my father told us about Oak Island when we came up here in the summer. He told us about the discovery of the hole and the platforms and how someone found gold coins and chain links and someone fell in to the deep well. He said you would tell us more about the history of it."

There was a long pause while Grandfather thought about this.

"I see. He did, did he? All right, I'll tell you what I know. Around 1804, a group called Onslow Company dug down through several more of those oak platforms and at ninety feet found a stone tablet. Someone translated it from old English as FORTY FEET BELOW, TWO MILLION POUNDS ARE BURIED. This group and many other groups after them kept digging and went down well over one hundred feet. As far as I know, no one has ever found a buried treasure, but that hasn't stopped them from coming up with many theories."

"Could you tell us more about the island and the theories?" Marya quietly asked.

"We'd better get back to Westhaver. I'll tell you more as we go." As they motored back, he continued. "Some have tied it to a pirate, Captain Kidd, but one major theory is that this is connected to the Knights Templar and that their treasure was buried here. They haven't found the treasure but they have found several peculiar stones that look like crosses, and one with the letter H. Frankly, I'm skeptical about this. I think someone that was very clever and sophisticated with engineering created this mystery from a natural sinkhole just to toy with those that came later."

Marya looked at Jes and he nodded but said nothing. They landed back home and no more was said that night about Oak Island.

Grandfather had notified Jes's father and mother that they were all just fine but they should not ask any questions for their own safety. He said they would be gone at least until the following year. Jes's father said there had been no other sign of the black bearded man and his friends since the day after Grandfather and the children left.

Jes's great aunt told Grandfather that she had a very good friend named Gertrude who would be gone for a year. She'd left her house in her care, and they could stay there. Jes and Marya and Grandfather promptly moved. It was not far away. In fact, it was close to Westhaver Beach where Jes and Marya had gone swimming. The house was a simple single level cottage nestled in a stand of pines. The steep dull greenish blue roof with a chimney at one end, and the light brown color of the house blended in with the pine forest. The shutters were similar in color to the roof. It had three small bedrooms, kitchen, living/dining room with a fireplace, and bathroom.

They stayed there throughout the winter, and when weather permitted, they explored Ross Hill. And one night, as Grandfather had promised, they snuck onto Oak Island and saw the activity around the so-called Money Pit. This satisfied Jes and Marya and they turned their attention to other islands and explored closer to Westhaver. They were always careful to keep their whereabouts and comings and goings secret and unobserved as much as possible.

Winter arrived with a fury. There were strong winds and snow almost daily, it was very cold most of the time, and they had snow on the ground all winter. Jes and Marya spent those days in the house Great Aunt had provided but went outside frequently. They liked the cold weather because it kept others inside. It was uneventful in that no strangers appeared and Grandfather had begun to relax. Jes and Marya stopped asking questions and simply enjoyed Mahone Bay: the islands, coves, snow, and exploring. They turned thirteen and twelve, early in 1950, and both were growing into adults. Their birthdays were close together, and they celebrated them in quiet fashion. Grandfather had bought each of them warm clothes since it was quite cold and they had been outgrowing their other ones.

Spring arrived and with it the death of Jes's great aunt, quietly one night in her bed. The reason was not clear but Grandfather simply said it was old age. It was a big surprise to Jes when he discovered, that in her will, she had left the house and everything in it to him. Jes asked Grandfather if it was all right to move back since it now belonged to him and was more comfortable and a "family" house.

"I guess it will be all right," Grandfather replied, "since there does not appear to be any sign of the black bearded man or his friends. But we should still be cautious and keep our eyes open for strangers."

However, Grandfather informed Jes's father of the death of his aunt and thus broke his vow of keeping their whereabouts unknown. Jes's father said he'd come to the funeral. Then he also said the black bearded man had come again to their house.

CHAPTER FORTY FOUR

Ra to Rhédae

Ra
Spring, 43 AD

Mary had filled the boat with bags of water, dried meat, dates and figs, grapes, nuts, mushrooms, avocados, olives, and berries. She, Joshua, and Sarah set sail one spring night and glided quietly along the marshlands and strips of sand separating the sea from the inland lakes and waterways. At dawn they reached a remote strip of sand where they stopped for the day. Sarah loved the warm water and stayed in it for an hour. The flamingos were not too far away. And all the herons and cranes and egrets were also eating small crustaceans at the bottom of the shallow sea. They ate some of the food they had brought but Sarah was not very hungry. She put her rug on the sand and slept outside the tent and looked at the clouds drifting by. She was as happy as she had ever been. She was with the two people she loved the most: her mother and Joshua.

At nightfall they continued on and bypassed the ancient town of Agathe Tyche and sailed southwest along the shore with a slight breeze blowing behind them. Just before dawn they came to the mouth of the Aude and sailed up river a few miles to replenish their supply of fresh water. They returned to the sea and stopped on an isolated beach on the sea side of a small étang, or inland lagoon.

"Why do we travel always by sea?" Sarah asked as they were eating in the morning. They had a variety of different foods including nuts and dates and olives and grapes and avocados they had gathered before they left Ra. "Why don't we travel on the road the Romans travel on?"

"That is exactly the reason," answered her mother. "The Romans do not like to travel by sea. They prefer traveling on roads they build for that reason: to travel in large groups along those routes. They even have a series of *mansiones* along them that are about a day's journey from one to the next. At these they can find shelter and provender and even fresh horses. They fear the sea."

"And we fear the Romans?" Sarah asked.

"Yes." Her mother spoke in a low voice.

Sarah thought for a moment. "Why do we fear them? What have we done?"

Mary took some time before answering. "Perhaps you are old enough to understand now. We fear them because they fear us. We have spoken up about the way they have treated the people under their control, especially those from Judea. We fled from Judea to Aegyptus years ago.

Even though there is a large protective Judean community there and Mark the Evangelist has been allowed to preach, we were sought because of our religious and political views and the fact that we have been outspoken against Roman rule." Sarah took this in and then continued.

"And that is why we fled Alexandria when I was five years old?"

"That is the main reason," Sarah's mother replied. "And also we wanted to journey to the Roman cities across the sea. We wanted to follow in the footsteps of Mark the Evangelist."

"And why we left Massalia, and then Aquae Sextiae and then Arelate?"

"Yes, Sarah." Mary spoke in a very low voice. There was no more to say after that.

"I want to swim," Sarah announced.

As she had done before, Sarah went bathing in the warm water with her mother while Joshua kept watch. After a short time when he was sure they were safe he also dropped his cloak and clothes and joined them. It was a warm day and they all dried off in the soft breeze and then ate some of their meat, nuts, and figs. Sarah slept on her rug in the open air. As the day progressed, the slight breeze became stronger and the dark clouds came over their heads and blocked the sun. The rain began lightly and then the storm came through and the winds increased in intensity. Sarah and her mother and Joshua set up their tent and crawled in. It became very dark outside and the rain came in torrents. The storm lasted several hours and let up gradually just as dusk approached. They emptied the boat and set off southwest along the coast.

"I'm glad we weren't sailing in the boat," Sarah stated, "when the storm came."

"We would have been forced ashore no matter where we were," Sarah's mother exclaimed. "We were lucky."

At the end of the night they stopped again by going through a gap in a long strip of sand into a huge étang and camped there. The lovely pink flamingos were set against the light of the rising sun. Sarah told her mother it was one of the most beautiful sights she had ever seen. They set up their tent and all of them slept fitfully after the experience of the storm the day before. Before nightfall they ate most of the remaining dried meat and dates. They still had nuts, figs, olives, and avocados, and sufficient water for a couple of days. As the light disappeared at dusk they returned through the gap to the sea under the cover of darkness and continued southwest. Sarah could hear the cries of gulls high in the sky.

They were able to make good time sailing in front of a brisk wind and reached the mouth of the Têt river in the city of Ruscino before daybreak.

"There is a beautiful basilica in Ruscino," Joshua mentioned as they were sailing upstream. They journeyed for a couple of miles until daylight forced them to find a secluded place. "Joseph told me about it. It would be wonderful if Sarah could see it."

"Shall we take her there before we go further upstream?" Mary suggested.

"I should stay out of sight here with the boat but why don't you take her there dressed in disguise. She should have a chance to see such a sight."

Joshua stopped in thick stands of prickly juniper under a canopy of stone pine and some tall cedars, while Mary escorted Sarah into Ruscino to visit the basilica. He hid the boat in a thicket of nettle trees, and set up their tent in the dense undergrowth of snowberry, rosemary, wild jasmine bushes, and honeysuckle vines. Mary returned in a couple of hours.

"It was beautiful," Sarah said. "It is so nice to know there are beautiful things made by men as well as by nature."

"Made by God," Mary added.

During the day they could hear groups of soldiers several miles to the east marching on a road under construction.

Joshua prepared to leave. "I want to find out the direction of the roadbed and if soldiers are moving toward us." He started walking toward the sound. "I'll be back in an hour or two."

While he was gone Sarah quietly spoke to her mother. "Mama," she asked. "When we were bathing the other day I noticed I was beginning to look like a woman. I don't look like you yet. Will I someday?"

"Sarah,' her mother responded. "You look lovely. As you get older you will change a little. I am not sure if you will look like me but that's not important. What is important is that you look like you and you are a lovely young girl growing up."

"Mama," Sarah continued. "I have not seen a man before. Do all boys and men look like Joshua?"

Her mother laughed. "You are full of questions, aren't you, but I understand. Just as women all look similar, so do men. He is a very wonderful man and I am so happy he came back and is traveling with us."

"I feel the same way," Sarah paused. "Mama, I wish he were my father."

"Why don't you ask him?" Mary replied, "Perhaps he will be."

Sarah still had one more question.

"Mama," she asked. "You still carry that scroll with you. Do you have it all the time?"

"Yes."

"What are you going to do with it?" Sarah persisted.

"I'm going to give it to you one day," Mary spoke softly. "To have and to hold and to update and to protect."

Sarah asked no more questions that day. Joshua came back an hour later and said the Roman troops were constructing the road from east to west and were now leaving for the day and heading east.

When darkness arrived they loaded up their gear and set sail upstream until the Têt began to narrow. They traveled fifty miles in six hours against a strong current. When Joshua realized they were not going west anymore but heading southwest, he stopped following the river. He decided it was time to leave the boat and march directly north.

"I think it's about forty miles," Joshua said. "It will take several days to reach Rhédae since we'll have to get around some small mountains and at least one small river."

They hid the boat without disassembling it, and loaded up the remaining food and a little water and created packs for each of them. Joshua carried the tent in case they encountered stormy weather. They left at dusk on a warm night with very little wind. Sarah was much bigger and stronger than she was in the desert and carried her rug, some food and water, and her few extra clothes.

They made good time the first two nights and camped in thickets of nettle trees. Sarah felt tired since she had never walked as far before but she was very hungry and slept soundly during the two days. They continued on at a slightly slower pace and circled around the base of a mountain. After another two days they came to a small river and replenished their water supply. The water was not too warm but Sarah decided to bathe anyway. It felt so good she stayed in for half an hour until her mother called her out.

As they sat in the early dawn eating a light meal, Joshua announced, "This river will go almost to our destination: the ancient town of Rhédae. We have already covered thirty of our forty mile journey."

And then it began to rain. It rained for two days and came down in sheets. They became very cold and huddled in cloaks inside the tent most of the time. The sky finally cleared and they could see the stars again as night arrived. Sarah felt happy when she saw her favorite stars and the belt of Sah, the Hunter. They packed up and marched along the banks of the river, which meandered a bit but generally went in a northern direction. They encountered a sizeable town and decided to stop early and camp during the day and wait again for darkness. They managed to work their way around the quiet town during the night and returned to the shores of the river. This path took them very close to Rhédae, which was inland a short distance. They filled their water bags before leaving the river.

They found refuge in a cave in the hills on the outskirts of the town. The cave was set in the side of a steep incline and was higher than Sarah's head. It was thirty feet deep and dry inside. It had a view of the valley below with the spring flowers and the blossoming trees spread across the horizon. Sarah and her mother rested and ate some of the remaining figs and Sarah ate the last of the avocados. Joshua left them for a couple of hours while he searched the town for food and a better place to reside. He came back with some dates and grapes and avocados and bread but said that he could not find a better place to stay than the dry cave they were in.

They stayed for another day before Mary felt it was her turn to try. She wrapped up in her cloak so that she would be anonymous and hoped no one would ask questions. While Mary was searching the town, Sarah walked with Joshua to the river to bathe and collect more fresh water.

While they were bathing, Sarah got up her courage.

"Mama said I should ask you," she paused, "I don't have a father. Would you be my father?"

Joshua smiled, "Is that what you really would like?"

"Yes, more than anything."

"All right. Then, I am your father." Joshua gave Sarah the biggest hug. "Forever." Sarah was filled with warmth and the greatest joy.

Mary found a small community that had settled there from Judea over the course of ten years and recognized a woman that she felt she could trust. The woman kept Mary's identity secret and helped her find a small hut to occupy. Sarah and Joshua returned just before Mary did and the three of them walked into town at dusk with their meager belongings and their small amount of food. They found the hut and settled in.

The hut had some pots and bowls and a sound roof. While Mary fetched water from a well, Joshua collected dry wood and built a small fire. It was nighttime and he ventured outside to search for grain. He returned soon thereafter with a bucket of wheat. Sarah did not ask where he found it. By now, she had learned it was better not to ask questions like that. Her mother saved some of the wheat to make bread and cooked the rest of it and gave Sarah a bowl of it mixed with the small amount of honey she had. Then she heated water in the largest pot she could find and washed the sand and dirt from their clothes. Sarah even had a chance to wash herself with warm water, and finally she and her mother washed and rinsed their long hair. While they were doing this Sarah asked her mother about the beautiful goblet.

"Is the cup I used to drink out of gone forever? Does Joseph have it?"

"Yes, I believe so. Nothing is gone forever but I'm sure it's in a safe place, safe from people that want it."

"Why do people want it, Mama?"

"It came from Judea with us. It was used on a very important occasion."

During the night rain began to fall. Joshua kept the fire going for a few hours but then let it burn out as the rain became a downpour. The three of them ate some of the figs, dates, nuts, and avocados, and Sarah curled up on her rug near the glowing embers of the fire and fell asleep. She woke up briefly and heard her mother talking quietly about how lucky they were to be there. Then her mother asked Joshua what he thought they should do next.

There was a long silence. Finally he spoke in a low voice.

"When you are in a place where you can stay, you should stay in that place. I am not known here. I will work with my hands as a carpenter. Sarah needs to be educated and this is a place where she can be. She needs new clothes and we need food. We should stay here in this town as long as we can. We will hope that woman you recognized keeps her own counsel."

And so it came to pass that which Joshua had stated. He remained anonymous and found a livelihood as a fine carpenter. Mary worked as a seamstress and, together with Joshua, helped to educate Sarah. She also made Sarah and herself new clothes. The woman Mary knew kept her own counsel. They prospered and were at peace for a year.

One day at the end of summer Sarah was at the well filling a pail of water. A shy boy with long blonde hair and blue eyes stood waiting his turn. Sarah was struggling to lift the pail from the well so he helped her. She smiled and thanked him. She asked him his name and he answered Alaric. She found out he was just half a year older than she was. Sarah noticed Alaric was as fair as she was dark. She liked that.

Two days later she was walking through town on an errand for her mother and saw him again. Over the next couple of months they managed to speak to each other often and gradually became friends. She discovered his father was the local blacksmith. Mary and Sarah became friends with Alaric and his mother and the blacksmith traded services with Joshua, who was soon known as the town's best carpenter.

One day in the fall Sarah asked Alaric if he would like to go with her to swim in the river. He followed her and they swam and bathed together in an inlet where the water was not flowing as rapidly as in the river. They became very good friends and often studied together with Mary or his mother, who was also a very knowledgeable and worldly woman.

Before the end of the year Sarah turned thirteen years old and just before that Alaric became thirteen and a half. It was a cold winter with lots of rain until snow filled the air. By then Mary had provided Sarah with warm clothes and a heavy cloak. The weather was severe, drifts of snow covered everything and eventually sheets of ice covered the ground.

Shortly after the start of the New Year, another event occurred that surprised and shocked Sarah and her mother: Lazarus arrived one night in a cold wind. He had traveled from Massalia mostly on foot and was near starvation. He was exhausted and disheveled from the journey and looked almost like a ghost. In fact, Lazarus looked as if he was risen from the dead. Mary gave him some warm soup and bread and found a place for him to sleep. When he awoke, Mary gave him new clothes to replace the rags he had been wearing. When he had had more soup and bread he explained that he had become the victim of lies and rumors and had grown out of favor with the Romans. He realized he might soon become a martyr and he was not ready for that, so fled at night while he still could. He only had the clothes he was wearing and a cloak which was soon in tatters. Mary nursed Lazarus back to health by springtime and he once again began to think of evangelizing the people of the town. But Mary talked him out of it for the time being. She said the time was not ripe for this yet.

The weather became warmer, the trees were in bloom and Sarah was happy. She had a good friend in Alaric and she was learning rapidly. She could read and write. She studied science and history and mathematics. But then her peace was shattered by that which Sarah's mother had dreaded. The woman that Mary had recognized from Massalia who had helped her, no longer kept her counsel and began to spread rumors about Mary and her history of firebrand evangelization. This seemed to be triggered by the presence of Lazarus. The woman also remembered him from Massalia and began to spread vicious lies about him as well.

The wonderful times for Sarah seemed to end just when she was so happy. Lazarus was not strong and seemed to decline rapidly when the woman spread rumors about him. This reflected on Mary and Sarah, as well. Sarah's mother seemed to become dejected and worried and depressed and Sarah was at a loss as to what to do to help. She went first to Joshua and asked what she could do.

"Will we have to leave here because of this awful woman?" Sarah asked him with downcast eyes.

"No, Sarah," he replied. "People will believe what they want to believe and we cannot change that. We can only have strength and act as the honest and caring people we are and do what we must do to show our true nature. If people choose to believe what others say, even if we know they are lies, and if some people are full of deception, we cannot change that. We can only hope that most people see the truth and recognize the lies."

Sarah was not happy with that answer and wanted to take some sort of strong action but was at a loss as to what to do. She confided in Alaric and he said he would do whatever she wanted done and would stay with her as a friend no matter what. Sarah asked Alaric to come with her to the river to swim even though the water was cold. While they were bathing he came up to her and hugged her and told her not to worry and that he would be by her side no matter what.

"Alaric," she said softly. "Let's run away."

He hesitated and then replied, "All right. Where should we go?"

CHAPTER FORTY FIVE

Fleeing the Abbey

Southern Britannia
Fall, 752 AD

As Magda stepped inside, the monk's hood flipped off and she realized too late he had no mole. She hesitated and stepped back to leave but he grabbed her arm and dragged her inside. Jeb stayed back out of sight.

"I've been looking for you for some days," the man said. "Come join your friend, the Abbot. He is locked up in a cell and I am sure there is room for two. Where is your companion that you were traveling with? You haven't been alone, I understand."

The door was left slightly ajar and Jeb stepped inside. He pulled his knife.

"Oh, there you are." The monk turned to Jeb.

"Leave her alone," Jeb ordered.

The monk let her go and charged. Jeb was surprised by his speed but stepped aside just as the monk reached him and avoided the full force of his attack. Jeb did not have a chance to use his knife and was knocked to the ground by an arm of the bigger man. His knife was knocked from his grasp and flew several feet away. Jeb jumped up quickly as the monk came after him in rage. He circled back toward Magda. As the man charged again, Jeb threw himself at his feet and they both fell to the ground. Jeb jumped up and tried to reach his knife.

"Look out, Jeb," Magda yelled as the monk leaped up and charged recklessly before Jeb could grab the knife. He ran full speed toward Jeb who was up against the stone wall of the Abbey. As the monk lowered his head to ram into him, Jeb ducked and spun away and the man struck his head against the wall of rocks and toppled to the ground motionless.

"Well done, Jeb!" Magda yelled. "You beat him. He's knocked himself out cold. He's not moving."

Jeb looked down at him. "I don't want to take a chance. Help me tie him up with the cord from his habit."

They tied him securely, then Jeb grabbed Magda's hand. "Let's get out of here and find the Abbot. He must be down that hall."

Jeb took the monk's keys and they left the entryway and ran down a long hall with a ceiling eighty feet high past what they thought was the Abbot's kitchen and store room and then past the library. They ran past several other rooms and passageways, calling out for any sign of him. Suddenly they heard a weak voice calling from behind a wine cellar door.

"I'm here."

Magda opened the door and saw a man lying on a cot and immediately saw the distinguishing mole.

"Father, are you all right?" asked Magda, as she stepped into the cellar.

"I'm weak but otherwise all right," he replied, then hesitated. "Where is the monk?"

"Follow us," answered Jeb.

They took the Abbot back to the room where the monk lay.

"He's unconscious," stated Magda.

"He's dead," answered the Abbot as he checked his pulse. "We'll have to hide him."

The Abbot did not ask them who they were but told them about a friend named Clotaire, who was a warrior. He described him perfectly. "He would know what to do."

"Clotaire sent us here. We know who you are, sir," Magda said.

"It must be the mole," smiled the Abbot with a twinkle in his eye. Magda nodded. He seemed to be gaining his strength back. He asked if they had packs with them. Jeb nodded yes.

"Get them while it is still dark. We must leave quickly. I will take care of this scoundrel. Be very careful that no one sees you."

Jeb and Magda snuck outside and made sure no one was afoot, then brought their packs inside. The Abbot had moved the body of the dead monk to the wine cellar and made it look as if he had hit his head, with a shattered pot on the floor near him.

When Magda complained that they were hungry, the Abbot smiled, took them into the kitchen and showed them the well-stocked store room. He told them to eat and fill their packs with as much as they could. The Abbot did the same with his pack.

"While you do that, I need to get some documents from the library. Make sure you take lots of bread and other food items we might not find along the way," he stated. "We're going on a long journey, but I don't think we'll be followed."

"I'll go with you, sir." Magda followed him out.

After Jeb collected bread for his pack, he leaned against the wall next to the oven for warmth. His shoulder shifted against the bricks, and he heard the grating of masonry against stone. He ran his hands over the wall; a single brick jiggled under his touch. He dug his fingers into the spaces around the brick and pulled. It came loose, sifting dust, and fell out into Jeb's hands. A cavity lay exposed in the space where the brick had been. He had been looking for a safe place to hide the copies of the scrolls from Dagobert and Egypt and realized he had finally found one. He placed the scrolls inside, wedged the brick back securely, and followed after the others.

The Abbot took them down a long series of tunnels. They emerged when it was still dark and moved swiftly away from the Abbey. After an hour of hard walking in silence they stopped briefly to rest. The Abbot explained as they recovered their strength that they would eventually get to an Abbey perched high on a rock. It was on an island called Medcaut and they would be safe once they got there.

"It is a very old monastery," he explained, "it is very holy to all the monks. It will take many days and even months of travel to get there, but I know several small monasteries along the way."

"How far is it, sir?" queried Magda quietly as they sat.

He told them he thought it was about four hundred miles to the Holy Island.

"In fact," he said, "it might be even longer since we might not travel in a straight line. We will have to cross some rivers and avoid main paths and search for the monasteries along the way so we will be travelling very slowly. We won't get there before winter sets in so it will take even longer, perhaps as much as a year altogether."

"Sir," Magda asked, "Will we be able to stay at these monasteries along the way?"

"And what is our plan for food?" added Jeb.

"These monasteries are spaced every twenty five miles or so and most of the monks know me. We can rest there, and if they are occupied as I believe they are, the monks will help feed us, but we will still have to hunt and gather food as we travel from one monastery to another."

"How long will that take?" Again Magda pressed the Abbot for details.

"I don't want to sound too pessimistic but we will have to travel at night to avoid detection and will be going through thick woodland and crossing rivers much of the time. We will need to take time to hunt and gather food, to build rafts to cross rivers, to rest and recover, and to avoid tribes of men on the march. Under these conditions, travelling at night, it might take eight to ten days to travel between monasteries. But, if we need to find shelter because the weather is bad, it may take longer. We must be prepared for the worst."

"What about bathing now and then in a river?' Magda asked.

The Abbot smiled. "We certainly will find time for that."

"And if we can't find these monasteries, or if we do, what if there is no one there?" asked Jeb.

"At least we'll have shelter. If we miss one we'll keep going," answered the Abbot. "We have no choice," he continued, and with a twinkle in his eye, added, "and I know you two have traveled in this way for some time. I know we can do it. We must. Let's move on."

They moved swiftly and silently away from the Abbey in the dark. The Abbot wanted to be sure they were far away before the collaborator of the dead monk realized he was missing and discovered his body.

"How will we know these monks are not like that bad one back there?" Jeb asked.

"I have my ways just like you did," the Abbot said with a twinkle in his eye again. He stopped talking and moved with a strong pace through the night. They were all very tired but Magda thought the old Abbot was amazing after being so weak from being locked up.

And so began the long journey of Jeb and Magda to a safe haven.

The three of them traveled day and night for three days to make sure anyone following them was left far behind. After that they travelled only at night.

"He had only one companion, I think," said the Abbot on one of their brief stops to eat, speaking about the dead monk, "that knew anything about you or me. But one is one too many. Somehow the word spread about your possible arrival at the Abbey, so our enemies cannot be underestimated. But I don't think he will do anything. Thankfully, he won't know of your arrival and will wonder only about my disappearance."

After three nights they were all exhausted and found an abandoned shack to take refuge in and sleep. The shack was dilapidated but Magda thought *it is better than sleeping outside as I've had to do*. It was in the midst of thick stands of beech and oak and quite secluded so Magda felt safe with the old Abbot leading them. The route he took was a good one since they encountered no one. They knew they would see someone sooner or later so they stayed with the plan of traveling only at night. They augmented their meager supply of food with fruits and berries and nuts, and a few mushrooms Magda found. But they also needed meat, so after resting Jeb went hunting and returned with a deer. The shack had a fireplace so Magda showed her skill by building a fire to cook and cure the meat. They had managed well enough so far.

The Abbot was able to follow a route that skirted many rivers but they could not avoid all of them. In some cases they were fortunate in finding old stone arched Roman bridges covered over with wild thyme and mint but still visible. If they did not find a bridge or if they could not wade across, Jeb came up with the idea of building a small raft using their mortise and tenon technique. The raft was generally only about ten feet long, made usually of beech or spruce. It was barely big enough for the three of them but it held together long enough to cross the river. The Abbot would take the stern and steer using a pole or paddle depending upon the depth of the river. Jeb would take the bow and Magda would hold their packs in the middle. It took time to build the raft and they would get wet crossing the river and take more time to dry off but they still managed to stick to the overall plan.

After resting for a day and eating well, they all felt much stronger and continued on at a good pace. On the third night they encountered a group of four travelers but heard them coming and hid. Jeb and Magda were well seasoned at travelling unheard and unseen at night, but the Abbot surprised the two of them with his skill. He also could travel unseen and unheard and detected others long before they approached. Magda learned from him that he had a long history of escaping danger and travelling from monastery to monastery without detection. She thought *his only fault is that he is not that good at hunting, but Jeb makes up for that. We are a very compatible group.*

They had averaged three miles per night, and with the rest day, had covered twenty miles in seven days. They stopped one more time to rest and gather food and then pressed on for three more nights before approaching the small monastery the Abbot knew about. They had covered thirty miles in ten nights.

"This is a good pace but we definitely will have to winter over before we reach Medcaut," commented the Abbot. "I will try to reach a certain monastery that I know very well since I spent some time there. It is several monasteries before Medcaut and we can spend the winter there. It is somewhat south of the wall but still many weeks and months from here. It is larger than most monasteries and it would be a good place to stay. I hope we can reach it, but the weather is unpredictable. Winter may arrive early."

They approached the monastery carefully through the oak and elm trees and noticed it was dark and seemingly unoccupied. It was a single building and looked like any ordinary place made of stone except that it was a little larger and had a small cross discreetly placed near the door. Below it was a small sign that said Monastery Saint George. It had two sets of windows on either side. The upper part of the monastery was wood with a thatched roof. The Abbot realized there was no one inside and was disappointed. They entered and saw that there was a good supply of food and some clothing on a shelf at one end but otherwise the furnishings were sparse. A wooden table surrounded by several chairs had a couple of cups and plates left on it. There was a door to a back section in which there were a couple of rooms where travelers such as themselves could stay for a brief time.

"Where is the monk?" asked Magda.

"Actually there are two monks in this monastery. It is strange that neither is here now."

They settled down to rest and eat and after a few hours dawn came. In the faint light they heard the noise of someone approaching. They hid in a small pantry next to the main room and heard the person enter. The Abbot peered out and then stepped into the room.

"Hello, Brother John." The monk was startled at first but recognized the Abbot immediately.

"Oh, it's you," spoke the monk in relief, "what brings you here, Sir?"

"We are on a journey. It's best that I don't tell you much for your own safety. Where is Brother James and where have you been? I was worried when no one was here."

"Brother James is on a long trip to visit the monastery Sainte Michelle twenty miles west of here. He should return tomorrow or the next day. I was visiting a family that just lost a son," replied the monk, "will you stay for a day or two? You are most welcome."

"That is very kind of you. We will stay for one day. We only travel at night. And if you have any spare bread, we would be most appreciative."

"I will do better than that. I have fresh meat from a farmer, vegetables from the summer, spices for flavor, and bread of course. While you rest I will make a delicious hot stew. When you wake you can partake of my good cooking." The monk seemed happy to have visitors and showed them the rooms he had for them. They rested for a while in their rooms and then they all had large portions of the monk's hot stew.

"It has been a long time since we had a really good hot meal such as this," praised Jeb, "It was indeed delicious, tasty, and hot. We thank you."

They spent that night hunting and gathering food and rested again the following day. As they prepared to leave for the next part of their journey, the monk made sure they took lots of bread and then gave them a warning. He did not ask of their destination but guessed it was generally north.

"We have heard reports that several monasteries from here, in a northerly direction, perhaps one hundred miles or more, the monastery Saint Miguel has been attacked a couple of times by bandits. So far the monks have repelled their attackers but I give you warning: if you go there, be very careful."

The Abbot thanked the monk and the three of them headed into the dark.

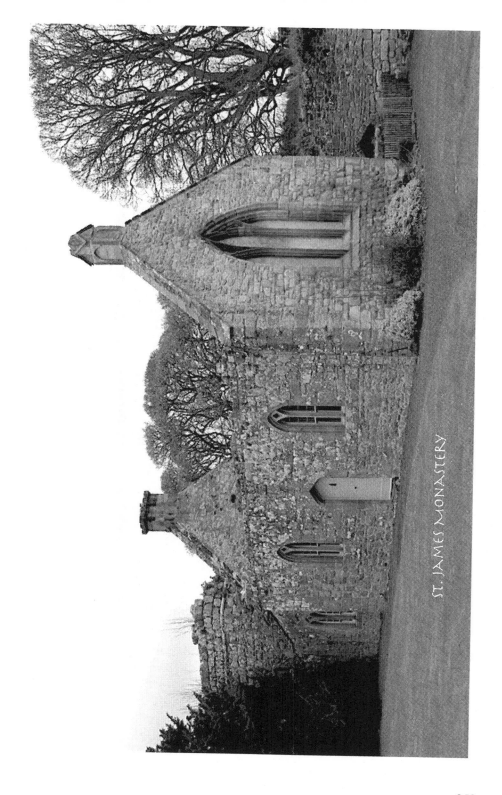

St. James Monastery

253

CHAPTER FORTY SIX

The Bandits

Northern Britannia
Winter, 752 AD

After staying at Saint George and recovering their strength, Jeb, Magda, and the Abbot pressed on with renewed energy. The Abbot had traveled much of this route before and knew enough to stay to the east of a large river that ran almost north and south.

"This will allow us to avoid having to cross the many rivers west of our pathway," he told Jeb.

Their course was increasingly more to the northeast. There was still a long way to go but the Abbot traveled quickly and showed no signs of faltering. Magda worked hard to keep up. At one of their rest stops she could no longer hide her curiosity about why the old Abbot was so fit.

"Sir, you are not at all what I expected when we set out on this journey. What I mean is that you seem so fit, as a young man. You set a fierce pace."

The Abbot laughed, "I suppose you thought of me as that old Abbot. Will he be able to stand the rigors of this hard journey? Lots of people have thought of me that way. It's simple. I was in a couple of situations where I had to travel far and fast, and another requiring much physical effort in the forest. I have maintained my fitness ever since."

They travelled night after night as they had done before on the first part of their journey with rest stops every three or four days to hunt and gather apples and pears and crab apples, blueberries and blackberries, roots, nuts, mushrooms, and any other food they could find. After six days travelling, Jeb shot a wild boar, which they enjoyed eating. Magda did her usual magic with a concealed fire, cooking some of the meat, and smoking the rest after they gorged themselves.

They needed to cross two rivers to reach the next hut. This required stopping for a night each time to build a small raft. Including the time for hunting and gathering, and for building rafts, they took ten days to cover the twenty five miles to reach this monastery. Following the same pattern, with one river to cross, they took ten days to cover thirty miles to reach the following one. They encountered no dangers in reaching these first two, and in each case they arrived at dawn. The Abbot knew the two monks at each, and the three of them received a warm welcome. They were given warm breakfasts of porridge, as well as fruit and cheese, and dinners of meat, onions, turnips, mushrooms, and bread. They rested during the day, leaving at dusk.

As they approached the next monastery, the Abbot sensed some danger. They crept in cautiously and found three frightened monks hiding inside. The Abbot did not know them, but once they knew who he was, they relaxed and welcomed the three of them.

"We didn't know who you were," Brother Isiah spoke up, "we were worried about being attacked by the same bandits that had been attacking the monastery twenty miles from here. We have not heard from any of the three monks living at Saint Miguel for some time but a traveler coming through told us of the relentless attacks there and we feared the worst."

The Abbot was not deterred, and after resting and eating for a day, decided to press on. He told Jeb and Magda that they must move quickly, and perhaps, if they arrived in time, they could help the beleaguered monks.

"You are fearless," praised Magda, "aren't you afraid there will be too many bandits to fight, or that we will walk into a trap?"

"It's my duty to help if I can," answered the Abbot, "I am not worried about a trap. We will approach with stealth at night. And," he added with his usual twinkle, "I am not going there alone. I have with me two fierce warriors."

The Abbot thanked the three monks and told them to be brave, and to prepare in case the bandits did come their way. They left at twilight and covered the distance rapidly in six nights with one rest night. As they approached the monastery they could see something was wrong because there were horses outside and there was laughter inside. This was not the usual situation they would expect. It was still dark as they crept silently to the one little window. There was no sign of the three monks but the Abbot saw five men inside drinking ale and eating the food the monks had in store. The men wore heavy coarse woolen shirts and pants and bandannas around their heads. They had put their long knives on the table. The Abbot had no doubt they were the bandits and realized they were too late to help the monks defend against them but he was not to be put off easily. He retreated to a safe distance and whispered his plan.

"They will go to sleep soon. We will wait until they do. There is a back door as well as the main entrance. We will test them to make sure they are open, but I am pretty sure they will be. We will attack simultaneously. Magda and I will enter through the front entrance and Jeb will enter through the back."

The plan worked quite well but did not go as smoothly as the Abbot had hoped. The bandits did indeed go to sleep within an hour and the doors were unlocked since the bandits felt they had nothing to fear. The three of them burst in and confronted the five drowsy bandits as they awoke. Two turned toward Jeb and he shot them with his bow and arrows, the Abbot leaped forward and knocked out two with a club, but Magda held back as one stumbled toward her. She was cornered and had no choice but to strike hard with her knife into his midsection. He was able to knock her to the floor before he staggered and collapsed.

Jeb rushed to her and lifted her up. She was trembling and her face was white. "Magda, are you hurt?"

"No," she whispered, "I just don't want to kill anyone but I had to."

The Abbot surveyed the scene. Three were dead and two were unconscious. He bound those two, then they looked in the other rooms and found one monk bound and gagged. He was disheveled and showed signs of having been in a scuffle. There was a cut on his face but he was otherwise unhurt.

"The bandits attacked three days ago," he told them. "We tried to fight them but were outnumbered and could not defend ourselves. I am Brother William. I'm sure Brother Samuel is dead but I don't know the whereabouts of Brother Arthur. I myself have had no food or water for three days and I'm very weak."

The Abbot roused one of the bandits and was told that the other monk, Brother Arthur, was in another room, weak and injured, and bound and gagged as well. They found him quickly, and with the help of the weak but unhurt Brother William, tended to his wounds. Both monks drank water and ate with gusto. The Abbot put the two bound bandits in a secure room and let the monks decide what to do with them.

The Abbot and Jeb cleaned up the mess in the hut, and the three of them stayed two days until the monks had recovered from the ordeal. They enlisted the help of the nearby farmers who had also been terrorized, and the farmers locked the two bandits in a makeshift jail. There was talk of hanging them but the Abbot stayed out of the discussion and prepared to move on with his two companions. The three of them left on the third night for the next monastery to the north.

"We have a good chance," the Abbot said, "of reaching the large monastery south of the wall before winter sets in. Even with the unexpected delays and extra rest stops, I think we've made good time so far."

"How do you always seem to know which direction to go to reach the next monastery?" Magda was curious.

The Abbot laughed. "You may not have noticed but I check the stars now and then to stay on the course I remember. If there are too many clouds I just keep going in the same direction as best I can. You can call it experience, I guess."

"We would call it 'dead reckoning', sir." Magda remarked. All three of them laughed.

The nights were getting longer and this allowed them to travel greater distances. However, it was inevitable that the journey would tire them a little, so their pace slowed a bit. They still had no trouble hunting for meat and gathering a variety of fruits, especially apples, as well as berries and nuts, and a few mushrooms. The days went by swiftly as they moved ever closer to colder weather. They found the monks in the next three monasteries to be friendly and hospitable and they had a hot meal at each. The first of the monasteries gave them soup and bread and the second provided a thick lamb stew, also with bread. The third monastery offered a delicious meal of mutton, carrots, turnips, onions, and beans. And of course, bread. The Abbot was given a mug of beer at each stop and Jeb and Magda each had a strong cider.

They covered the distances at a slightly slower pace, taking ten nights or more between monasteries, which averaged thirty miles between them. The Abbot took a northeast course following relatively flat terrain, avoiding the mountainous terrain on both sides but especially to the west. As they prepared to stop one morning, the rising sun in the east was bright in the cloudless sky and Magda could see hills in the distance to the west.

"What direction are we going, sir?" she asked. "I'm glad we don't have to climb over mountains."

"We've been marching slightly to the east just for that reason, to avoid them, but we will have some trouble crossing a couple of large rivers. It's better to try the rivers rather than the mountains."

"We know what to do." Jeb interjected. "We will build rafts as we did with Clotaire. They will be bigger than those we built earlier if the rivers are very wide. The ones we built before might tip over but these won't. We use crisscrossed logs and vines." Magda agreed this would be better.

When they encountered the first of the large rivers the Abbot stood back and watched Jeb and Magda as they laid out the boat, then he pitched in.

"You children amaze me with your determination and resourcefulness."

It was hard work and took most of one night in the dim starlight to build the first raft, and then the next night they launched it slightly upstream, floating and paddling across. They landed downstream but easily returned to their course. After that, with the Abbot helping with enthusiasm, they became adept at building just the right raft in a short time to cross a river. As usual Magda giggled and they all got wet below the waist and had to dry out but they became a close knit group tackling each such challenge.

Travelling at night, they encountered few other people and the several they did see they avoided by hiding briefly. As always, the Abbot was excellent at sensing any travelers before they could be spotted. They passed many farms and small towns in the night without incident. However, as they approached the next monastery, Monastery Saint Matthew, they encountered a different enemy. The cold rain came down for hours and when they reached the monastery they were soaked to the skin. They dried out in front of the roaring fire built by the two monks.

"We are indeed fortunate," the Abbot said to the monks, "that we were close enough to reach you, wet as we were. Further away from here we would have had to find shelter in a barn or abandoned shack for all this time. I would never take a chance asking the local farmers for shelter. I could not be sure they were friendly and besides, they might ask too many questions. We know you will be discreet as well as hospitable. We can never repay you."

"You need not worry. As you know, it is our mission to help others," answered Brother George, "in this case it is a fellow Brother and two friends, and we do not want to know where you are going. It is not our business."

The Abbot was very grateful for these words.

"But it is our business to share a warm meal with you," added Brother Harold. "Come dine with us."

They enjoyed the first of several wonderful meals with lamb or venison or boar and onions, turnips, parsnips, and carrots. And of course they also had bread and beer, and warm cider for Jeb and Magda.

The rain lasted for three days and they stayed warm and well-fed in the monastery for that time.

"We are very thankful," Magda said, "for the wonderful warm meals you have given us and also for the warmth and generosity you have shown us."

Finally the rain stopped and they resumed their journey. The Abbot thought they would encounter one more monastery before reaching Saint James, where he wanted to winter over. They travelled ten nights with two rest stops and covered over thirty miles. The Abbot thought they had less than a night's travel before reaching this next monastery.

Winter came early. The snow began to fall as they trudged onward. They picked up their pace as best they could with the snow falling silently all around them in the forest and fields. They were fortunate to reach the monastery just as daybreak came.

The Abbot noticed there was no activity or sign of life in the monastery. As they crept closer they realized it was unoccupied and had been for some time. They came in out of the snow. The Abbot did not want to build a fire since he thought it would draw attention to them and he did not know the situation around the monastery. There was very little food in the store but he did find some bread and a few vegetables. They still had some dried meat to make a meal. They slept fitfully during the shorter days, always on guard, and wrapped warmly in their furs.

"Are you all right, Magda?" Jeb asked in the middle of the day, "it's been a long journey for you."

"I'm fine, Jeb," she responded, "as long as I am with you."

The Abbot waited until the following night to build a small fire to cook some vegetables, so they did have a warm meal of sorts. The snow fell silently for three days as they decided to wait for some sign of better weather.

When the snow stopped, the Abbot decided to take a chance on reaching the monastery, which he thought would be thirty miles away. They set out at night, and Jeb and Magda used the skills they learned from Clotaire. With snow on the ground, they sought a well-travelled path near the vacant monastery and covered their tracks to get to it. It was the Abbot's turn to be impressed at their skills in the snow. During the first three nights the snow remained on the ground. They heard approaching travelers only two times during their travels, and cleverly left the trail at a point where they would not be noticed, and then resumed their journey. The snow disappeared after three more nights making travelling much easier and they covered nearly fifteen miles during the following three nights. For three or four hours during the daytime, they slept in thickets wearing their warm clothes curled up in their sleep sacks, then ate some meat, bread, and cheese, and carried on before dusk.

"I think," the Abbot guessed, "we only have one or at most two nights of travel to reach the big monastery."

And then winter really arrived. The snowfall began again but this time it was much heavier. The wind blew in strong gusts and it was bitter cold. The Abbot insisted they must press on as long as they could. If they sought shelter now they would be trapped for the winter and surely would perish, so it was essential that they try to reach the monastery.

As the snow continued to fall the drifts grew bigger. They pushed on through the night, encountering no other travelers, but the snow showed no signs of letting up.

"We should keep going during the day," the Abbot urged, "and take a chance on being seen. I'm sure we're only a short distance away. We've been lucky that we haven't encountered any people so far in this heavy snowfall but we're also making very little progress."

They pushed on through the drifting snow and the swirling winds for three more hours. Visibility was almost zero. The Abbot led Jeb, and Magda followed behind. At one point Magda tripped and rolled down an embankment.

"Jeb," she yelled, "I'm down here." Jeb and the Abbot tumbled down and pulled her from the deep snow.

"I'm holding your arm from now on, Magda." Jeb held onto the Abbot's coat and grasped Magda as they plunged slowly through the drifts. The snow filled the air and obscured everything around them. They were all cold and wet, but somehow managed to struggle onward.

The snow let up for just a few minutes and the Abbot saw Monastery Saint James in the distance, and with sheer will, they covered the last several hundred feet to the entrance. Magda could see the clerestory windows through the swirling snow and the entrance on the side. They were exhausted but were welcomed by a couple of monks at the door and brought into the side of the chapel. They would be safe for the remainder of the long winter.

HOLY ISLAND/MEDCAUT

261

CHAPTER FORTY SEVEN

The Road to Medcaut, the Holy Island

Northern Britannia
Winter, 752 AD

Magda, Jeb, and the Abbot were welcomed and brought back into the rooms of the monastery behind the chapel. They were given warm dry clothes to replace their cold wet ones, bowls of warm stew, warm cider for Jeb and Magda, and a mug of ale for the Abbot. The monks recognized the three of them were exhausted and took them to rooms in the back of the monastery to rest. After they recovered the Abbot told the monks about their journey, the bandits, and all the challenges they had faced. Magda loved the chapel and often went there just to look at the beautiful stained glass windows high above. The rooms adjoining the chapel consisted of many bedrooms, the kitchen, the store room, dining room, and a large room they used for prayer, music, and other activities.

It was just before the end of the year. Jeb turned thirteen and Magda turned twelve. The Abbot and the six monks celebrated Christmas with a simple meal and then the Abbot toasted Jeb and Magda on achieving their birthday milestones with a mug of spiced cider. He spoke of their skills and strengths and especially of their remarkable abilities in handling the many difficult situations they had encountered. He thanked them for saving him from capture and for teaching him the many skills they had learned while on this challenging journey. The New Year arrived and the snow continued to fall.

It was a very harsh winter. The severe winter conditions continued for four solid months. The snow piled high and the wind blew most of the time, creating large drifts higher than Magda's head. These conditions continued day and night with scarcely a break. When the snow did stop for periods of time, the temperature dropped to all-time lows. It was a time to stay inside but Jeb wanted to go out in spite of the conditions and Magda joined him. They tracked and shot two deer that wandered close to the monastery. This meat was appreciated because the supply was in danger of running out.

When the weather conditions were too severe to venture outside, two of the monks would play musical instruments and sing, and Jeb and Magda even learned some basic dances.

Jeb and Magda had been used to curling up together when they slept and one day the Abbot spoke to them.

"I have noticed that the two of you seem intimate and sleep together, you both seem mature, and you have undertaken enormous responsibility.

With your permission, I would like the honor of blessing your union in the presence of the monks."

"We would be delighted if you did." Jeb responded.

"And indeed we would be the ones honored, sir." Magda added.

In a very simple ceremony in the chapel with the six monks present, the Abbot gave his blessing and wished them a long, happy, and prosperous life together. He hugged each of them, and the monks joined in and blessed them with mugs of ale raised on high. Even Magda had a small mug of ale. The wind howled around the monastery and the snow piled up and the owls crouched in the trees to stay warm, but Jeb and Magda were warm and dry and happy and curled up safe from the storm.

The monks in the monastery were used to cold winters but they said this was the worst they had ever seen. They had a good supply of grain and other food so, aside from meat, they believed they would weather the long cold winter.

"Are you ever worried about being attacked here?" Magda asked one day, thinking of the recent experience with the bandits.

"We are very well fortified in this monastery," responded Brother Matthew, "and, in spite of being monks, the six of us are well trained in martial arts. One has to be in these remote places."

The Abbot discussed with another monk the distance to Medcaut. In this case he was not worried about disclosing their destination. The monk estimated it was about one hundred miles and there were four monasteries in between. The Abbot told Jeb and Magda they would leave in the spring as soon as conditions permitted and it would probably take a month or more of travel to reach Medcaut.

The winter seemed to Jeb to go on forever. Magda tried to get him to forget the long delay and enjoy the snow outside. They made the best of the situation and went out as often as possible. Only the strongest of winds kept them inside. Finally the weather warmed up a little and the early crocuses bloomed. The nights were getting shorter and, one day in April, the Abbot announced that they would leave the next night. They packed up a good supply of dried deer meat, onions, carrots, turnips, parsnips, beets, nuts and berries, as well as lots of bread. They thanked the six monks who wished them a safe journey and headed out into the night.

Their journey was uneventful and went according to the Abbot's plan. The journeys between the monasteries averaged ten nights of travel, including a couple of rest days. They found the monks at the four monasteries before Medcaut to be very hospitable and they were able to provide a little bread for their continuing journey. There were either two or three monks at each monastery. They stayed over one or two nights depending upon how the Abbot felt about the weather. Now that Medcaut was within reach the Abbot seemed to be less concerned with setting a fast pace each night. They did not tell the monks where they were going but Jeb guessed the religious men had a good idea. The Abbot seemed to feel safer the further north they travelled, out of reach of possible enemies.

As they were about to leave the last monastery before Medcaut, Magda took Jeb aside. In a soft voice, she told him she was expecting a baby. Jeb jumped with joy, hugged and kissed her. They agreed not to tell the Abbot until they reached Medcaut. On the journey north Magda showed signs of early pregnancy. To the Abbot she appeared to be sick with some disorder so they slackened their pace just a little and reached the Holy Island in twelve nights of travel.

They crossed the sand and mud flats at low tide and climbed slowly up the rough stairs to the entrance high on the rock. As she climbed higher Magda looked up, her mouth open in awe, and saw clouds drifting by the tall towers and a flock of geese flying overhead. She realized that they were still below the tops of the highest towers.

"Jeb, look!" Magda called to Jeb climbing ahead of her. "It's spectacular! The walls are amazing, high above the giant rock, and the towers way above them. What is that tall one at the end?"

"The Keep!" the Abbot answered. "I'll show you when we get there."

"Look at the small windows!" Jeb yelled. "And what are those slits in the tower?"

"Those are for defending the monastery from attack. Let's keep climbing. We still have a long way to climb."

They trudged steadily up the pathway, climbing ever higher until they reached the solid oak door. As the Abbot expected, they were welcomed with open arms by the many monks and all the people who were there seeking refuge.

"At last," Magda told Jeb, "we have reached a safe haven." Thus began a new chapter in their long journey to safety. And now they had an added responsibility. They looked forward to the birth of their first child, and it was in a very safe place.

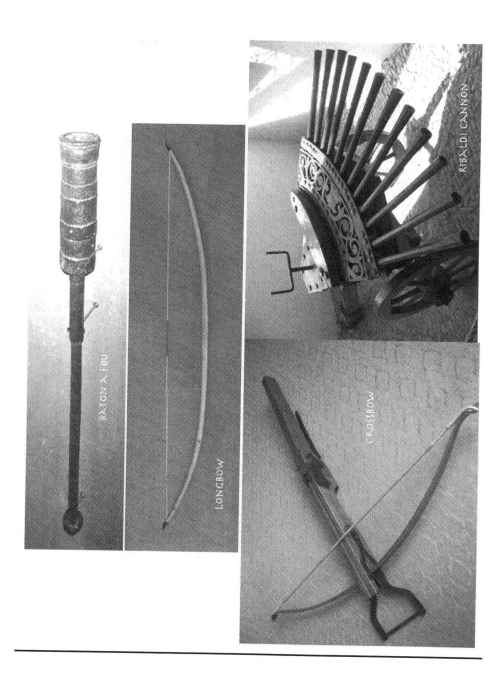

BATON À FEU

LONGBOW

RIBALDI CANNON

CROSSBOW

CHAPTER FORTY EIGHT

Hiding Treasure

Mahone Bay
Summer, 1399

One morning in early June, when the sun had warmed New Scotland and the grass on the islands was the color of ocean swells, Henry took Jed and Martha and Mali and Sam in a large canoe to an island that was special to him. They traveled north along the coast, passing the point Jed remembered from their own trip. They kept going and passed another headland projecting into the bay. Finally, they came to a large island nearly attached to the mainland. Jed could see the island was covered with many large oak trees. They beached the canoe in a cove on the south side and concealed it, then followed Henry to the east a few hundred feet. To the west just over half a mile from where they landed was the overlook to the mainland. There he showed them a deep well. Jed noticed that the well was not only close to where they landed on the south side but even closer to the bay water on the east side of the island.

"My men have determined," Henry said, "that the sea water comes into the bottom so it is not a freshwater well. It is most unusually deep and I believe it was formed naturally as a sinkhole."

"How deep do you think it really is, sir?" Martha inquired.

"We are only about sixty five or seventy feet above sea level as you can see, but we dropped a plumb line and my men determined that the bottom is well over one hundred feet down. Of course, you hit sea water before that."

"Is it this wide all the way down?" Jed continued.

"No. It's about thirteen feet wide here but it quickly narrows to seven feet."

"Sir, do you know where the sea water comes from?" Martha asked. "We are very close to the sea."

"That's an excellent question. We have been very curious about that, too." Henry started to walk away as if the conversation was ended. Mali and Sam watched silently during this exchange.

Henry quietly told Jed that he planned to do a test by dropping in some colored liquid and watching to see where it came out. He would explain later what he had in mind, but now wanted all of them to see the well. Henry then took them back to the canoe and down the shoreline until they veered far out into the bay to the island Mali had taken them to earlier. This time they explored the larger southern part of the island and Jed confirmed what he had suspected, that it was very hilly. He noticed several rock formations on hills that could contain caves. He would have to come back at night with Martha to look for them. At night, the location of bats' roosts, where they flew in and out of the hills, would be the key to finding one.

After looking around the island a bit, Henry took them back to camp in time for dinner. Jed wondered if Henry had the same thing in mind as he did. The islands would be a good place to hide some of the treasure. After dinner Henry took Jed and Martha aside and explained his elaborate plan for the deep well.

"I plan on constructing a series of platforms," Henry began, "using oak planks, extending from the bottom of the well up to the top. I won't hide any treasure at the bottom but it would look as if someone did. I am having fun imagining what will happen in the future."

Martha asked, "Sir, why are you going to all this trouble if you don't plan to hide treasure here?"

Henry smiled but did not reply.

From this point on, Henry spent most of his time overseeing the construction of the castle tower. The men added two more levels in wood using the sturdy oak from the forest. The round tower was capped by a slanted roof overhanging the top level. Each level had narrow slits for firing protected guns or arrows at attackers. These were placed all around the tower. The men had several types of weapons: crossbows, longbows, and a hand cannon called bâton à feu, developed by the French. The men preferred the crossbow and longbow but Henry wanted them to become adept at hand cannons.

Mali took this opportunity to add to Jed's arsenal of skills. He had told Jed and Martha that he had watched the two of them take to his teachings about moving undetected through the forest and he could no longer see the difference between them and all the other young braves. Now it was time for them to learn the art of the bow and arrow. Mali taught them the basic skills, and then Sam worked with Martha and Mali with Jed.

First they practiced on a stationary target and Mali gradually moved it further away. When they were both expert enough to hit the bull's eye nearly every time, Mali created a moving target and they gradually were able to hit even that. These lessons were spread over several weeks as summer was turning into fall. Mali noticed that Martha was slightly more proficient and accurate although Jed was almost as good. She was ambidextrous, but what really surprised Mali was that Martha was just as accurate shooting either way. Mali thought it was time to give them a true test. He taught them how to camouflage themselves when hunting in the forest and where to strike the animal for a clean kill.

They all moved silently into the trees and took a concealed position in the brush beside a deer trail. They waited for some time until a buck came walking slowly along the path. Mali motioned to Martha that he would give her the first shot. She aimed left-handed but something caused the buck to lift its head just as she fired. She missed the shot and the buck galloped silently into the brush. Martha was heartbroken at missing her first attempt.

"You just learned a valuable lesson," Mali told her, "you must line up your shot and fire quickly. You both must work on speed. It's not enough to be an accurate shot, you must shoot with the utmost speed and it's not only in hunting that this is very important," he explained. "As a warrior in battle, speed could be the difference between shooting the enemy or the enemy shooting you first. I'll also teach you how to shoot while moving. You will not always be able to stand still as you do when hunting."

The lessons continued until one day, as fall approached winter, Henry came to them and said he was very concerned about overstaying his visit. There were signs of danger. He did not want to explain but as soon as the castle was completed they would move away from the Grand Chief's hospitality. He would soon describe his plan but now they must learn everything they could.

Mali felt it was time for the next lesson in the forest so he took them to a different place, which he called a deer run. The deer were moving from one area to another and generally came through without stopping. Jed was once again amazed at how Mali knew so much about the forest and everything in it. They found a place along the trail hidden from view and with wind in their direction. Then they waited.

"Get ready," Mali told them, "because I hear distant hoof beats."

The small group of deer, including several bucks, came into view. Mali had told them to aim for the bucks and to spare the does. They came through faster than Jed expected but he and Martha each stood up and took aim at a passing buck. Martha's first shot fired right-handed was dead on target but Jed's shot missed. He ran after the fleeing buck and with his second shot, at full speed, hit him and brought him down. Martha was thrilled at Jed's success but Jed was crestfallen at missing his first attempt.

Mali showed he was proud of Jed and ignored the first miss. Jed had recovered and showed he had developed the skill of shooting while running. But he would have to work on his accuracy so there would be no need for a second shot. Together, they dragged the carcasses back to camp.

"The two deer," he explained, "will be welcome this time but we must not overdo it in providing fresh meat for the camp. If it is not eaten tonight it will need to be cured and the women that do that will not appreciate the extra work."

As it happened, that night they had a feast. The men from the farming colony returned briefly to celebrate the completion of the castle. They also had a visit from the ship that would sail to Scotland. It had sailed down from the northern colony as planned with a few men that chose to return. Several of the men from the farming colony indicated they would join them when the ship sailed for Scotland. Henry convinced the men on the ship to overwinter since it was a dangerous time to be sailing the north seas. There was still much to be done at the castle site and all the men offered to help and continue working on the site until they sailed in the spring.

Henry took Jed and Martha aside while the feast was going on.

He explained, "The men still have to move into the castle and prepare the defenses in case they are needed. The fences and buildings will be used to provide an enclosure and barricades. There is room at the lower level for the sheep. A small group of men can defend from the castle if attacked. The farmland is the only thing that is vulnerable, but the men can hold out in the castle for many weeks or months with the existing food stock." He added, "I don't expect they will be bothered but I want them to be prepared just in case."

Then Henry explained in a very quiet voice, "I plan to go with Sir Gunn and bury some of the treasure in the crypt at the bottom of the castle and seal it up. I also want you to know I will disappear for some days with a few of my skilled and trusted men. We will all go to the deep well I showed you. They will build the various layers of planks from the bottom up. We did the test I told Jed about and know where the sea water comes from. It was a lot of work to dam up the places around the edge of the island but that won't last long. We determined that it all comes in at a certain spot down below, so first of all my men will seal off the sea water temporarily and create a kind of plug they can remove from above. Then they will drain the water and build platform after platform with the oak planks. This will take some time, so I'm not sure how long I'll be gone." He smiled, "Jed, this will be one of the most enjoyable efforts I've done. I'll bring with me my most skilled engineers and carpenters. I only wish I were here many years from now to watch and smile when people try to solve this mystery."

He continued, "You must think seriously about where to hide a copy of the updated scroll since it must stand the test of time, of weather, of animal predators, and most importantly, of human predators. I am planning to hide a map on one of the islands showing where I've hidden parts of the treasure. I confess I really hope someone finds the treasure one day. Finding the map will lead to that."

The feast ended after Mali and Sam and their skilled students were praised for their successful hunt. Henry left soon after that and Martha came to Jed and spoke quietly.

"Jed, why would your father go to all that trouble with that deep well if he doesn't plan to put some of the treasure down there? I think he does plan to bury some of it there."

"You heard what he said. I think he is just having fun with anyone in the future who might find the well and the platforms. Knowing him and all this about the map, I wouldn't be surprised if he puts clues down there to keep them searching for treasure that doesn't exist. Besides, if he were really going to hide some of the treasure down there, why wouldn't he just drop it down in the water below?"

"I can't believe he would go to all that trouble and time, and do all that work just to play a joke."

"Then maybe it's a diversionary tactic to draw attention from the tower. Or maybe he was planning to bury something but changed his mind for some reason."

Martha persisted. "Jed, do you remember when I asked him why he was going to all that trouble? He just smiled. I still think he plans to bury some of it down there. Didn't he say Sir Gunn will go with him to bury treasure in the castle crypt? I'll bet Sir Gunn will also go with him to bury some of the treasure down that deep well. It would be easy to drop that chest of gold coins down there, wouldn't it?"

Jed thought *'She is really stubborn when she has her mind made up. But maybe she's right.* They talked no more on the subject and went to see Mali.

Mali felt that Jed and Martha had learned all of their lessons well. They could move through the forest silently, they could shoot with speed and accuracy, and had learned to shoot while evading an enemy's shot or chasing game. He still had to teach them how to shoot while on horseback. He hoped they would never use this as he would, in battle against another tribe. He said fall was coming to an end and asked if they would like to celebrate their success with a last trip to the pools.

"Oh yes, oh yes," yelled Sam and Martha together.

They followed Mali silently on yet another invisible trail. Sam and Martha were in the water in no time at a lower pool where the sounds of water were not too strong. Mali reminded them it was essential that they always keep their bow and arrow within arm's reach. He was emphatic and very serious. Jed and Mali eventually went in and all four were near shore where bushes could hide them if necessary. They knew they could not speak and must not make any noise.

Mali was about to motion them out of the water when he heard something that was alien to the normal forest sounds. He motioned to them to hide and to grab their bows and arrows. But they were too late. The noise was from a group of five young men from a distant tribe. They saw Martha and Sam in the bushes reaching for their bows and arrows and all five drew their bows. Jed and Mali stepped out to join Sam and Martha in the shallows and they fired quickly and then rolled into the water. Mali came up immediately and fired another shot at the remaining brave and dispatched him. Their first four shots hit with deadly accuracy, as did the second one from Mali. The fifth enemy did manage to get off a shot but it sailed into the water where Sam had been only seconds before.

Mali congratulated them. They had learned their lessons well. But now they had a very serious problem. They did not know where these braves came from but they would be missed. They dragged them into the brush and covered them very thoroughly. Mali noted the markings on their faces and their clothes and hair so he could describe them to his father. They went straight back to the camp and Mali told the story to his father and described the young men. At first the Chief had a very serious look on his face but then realized his son and friends could have been killed by these strangers and congratulated Mali on his skill and training of the others. He asked again about the intruders into his land. He thought they were from a distant tribe sent on a long foray as a test of manhood and may have gotten lost and wandered in the wrong direction. Nevertheless, they would be missed and their tribe would search for them. Hopefully, they would not connect their disappearance with his tribe. He sent two men with Mali to identify them and bury them as best they could.

While they waited for Henry to return, Jed and Martha borrowed a canoe one night and quietly paddled out to the hilly island they had first visited. When they had returned with Henry, Jed had seen the perfect cave to bury copies of the scrolls. He had learned to be silent in every move he made. There was no moon and virtually no wind so they could hear everything and not be seen. Jed had wrapped the copy of the Merovingian scroll and a copy of the Egyptian scroll in an oilskin as an extra precaution but the main thing that would protect the scrolls for a very long time was the location. Deep in the cave, the soil was very dry and they could dig down several feet. Martha and Jed dug a deep hole, buried the scrolls, and covered the place with large rocks. Then they covered their tracks as they had learned from Mali. They returned silently and felt satisfied they had done the job well. Jed knew that they would leave as soon as Henry returned. He and Martha would cherish each day with Sam and Mali until then.

But winter came early and it snowed very heavily. Henry returned within a few days of the first storm. When Jed told his father about shooting the young men, Henry had a very worried look on his face and said he was afraid of something like this. He did not at first realize how close to death Jed and Martha had come and how skilled they were. He explained that there was a war between some distant tribes and he thought it might soon spread to the Chief's tribe. He had hoped to complete all of the work on the tower, split the men into two groups, and leave the area before winter. But now the early winter would delay his departure.

However, even with the snow coming down, he planned to mount the Ribaldi cannons on the top of the castle in the special openings in the turrets he had constructed. The men that would remain on the farm would stay in the castle for the winter with the other weapons and provisions. The possibility of a tribal war made it essential that they complete the fortifications rapidly. Meanwhile Henry would prepare to leave as soon as winter allowed.

The Grand Chief came to Henry and said his departure would be none too soon. The young men were indeed from a distant enemy tribe. He did not know why they were so far from their own land but it did not matter. Not because of the missing men, but for other territorial reasons, two distant tribes were at war and, because of alliances, the war would likely spread and they would be involved no later than early spring.

Henry told the Chief that he was planning just that, to leave as early as possible.

CHAPTER FORTY NINE

Danger from the South

Mahone Bay
Spring, 1950

On a weekend in February, Jes and Marya turned thirteen and twelve. When Jes's great aunt died, Grandfather became the last survivor of that generation. Jes hoped he would stay healthy for many years. He had grown very fond of his grey beard, the twinkle in his eye, his smile and his humor, his worldliness, and his kindness and gentleness. In fact the death of his great aunt drew him even closer to his grandfather. Jes and Marya had not been asking many questions in recent months but the death of his great aunt caused Jes to want to know much more about the history connecting the bloodline and the scrolls and anything having to do with the Merovingian Cross.

"Grandfather," requested Jes, "I want to know everything there is to know."

"There is much more to tell you. Let me start with the Templars and Cathars and their treasures."

He told them about the Cathars and how they split from the Catholic Church because they felt the Church was morally, spiritually, and politically corrupt and no longer pure in its actions. Aside from that, he said, the Cathars had amassed a treasure which was thought to be tied to the Merovingian bloodline back to the Magdalene, and provided proof of this connection. Over a period of time ending in 1244, they were massacred by the Church for religious reasons but also for the treasure and evidence of the bloodline connection.

"The Templars," he continued, "were a much more powerful organization, originally created by the Church, but in 1307 the Church and the King tried to destroy them because they had become too wealthy and too powerful. They were created initially to seek the Holy Grail but ended up protecting the bloodline and amassing a fortune. It was said this treasure included proof of the bloodline. Most of the Knights Templar escaped the massacre on October 13th 1307, ordered by the King of France and supported by the Pope, and took the treasure and the proof with them. In fact some of the Knights apparently had the Merovingian Cross."

"What happened to the treasure?" asked Marya.

"It's a long story. I'll continue it later but right now I'm worried about the black bearded man and his friends. He won't give up. I hope your father is careful about being followed when he comes to the funeral."

The next day Jes's father arrived with Uncle Pete. Also arriving home was Gertrude, the friend of his great aunt. The funeral was held the following day. Before the funeral, Grandfather explained to Jes and Marya that it was important for their sake that he not be connected to them and would keep his distance. He also told them he was glad they'd moved back to the family home before Gertrude returned. It would have been hard to explain, he said, why they were at her home and not at Great Aunt's home.

After the funeral, Jes and Marya were alone with Grandfather. Jes asked him what they would do if the man with the cold black eyes did find out somehow that they were here in Mahone Bay at this house.

"Yes," Marya jumped in, "what would we do? Hide? Go somewhere else?"

"We will stay right here for now. We don't know if they have tracked us here. I doubt it and your father and uncle are pretty good at eluding anyone who might try to follow them. I think we are safe here for some time to come."

Jes's father and uncle stayed for a few days and then returned to Connecticut. Marya reminded Grandfather that he said he would tell them more about the treasure of the Templars. He told them how the Knights escaped aboard their fifteen ships from the west coast of France, along with the treasures of the Cathars and their own accumulated wealth.

"Legend has it," he continued, "that they carried the treasure to Scotland, to the castle of Prince Henry. Some years later, around 1398 AD, the descendants of the original Templars continued to be persecuted and were still being hunted that far north by agents of the Church. It was thought by Henry and the Templars that the Church sought to exterminate them altogether and capture the scrolls and the treasure."

"Why are they after these scrolls? I'm confused. What do the scrolls say?" said Marya.

Grandfather went on at length, "The original scroll of the Merovingians, together with the Egyptian scroll, show the progression of the bloodline from Jesus and Mary and their daughter Sarah to the Merovingians and beyond. The Merovingian Cross, the birthmark you both have, originated with Sarah, and when she married into the earliest ancestors of the Merovingians, it was perpetuated from then on. It has been claimed that a people called the Marvingians were ancestors of the Merovingians. Others say the name came from the earliest Merovingian King named Merovée."

"At any rate," he continued, "the gene carrying the bloodline via the visible Merovingian Cross birthmark shows definitively who the descendants are. The scroll and the copy of it simply document the ancestral path that the bloodline gene took. The scroll, copied from the original, lay undiscovered for centuries. When it was discovered the descendants were added and this traced the bloodline from the time of the scroll to the time when it was discovered. In other words, the scroll was progressively updated by successive descendants of the original Merovingians to modern times. This is a remarkable documentation of generations of those that had the Merovingian Cross and thus were descendants. The older scroll, including the original one from the end of the Merovingian era, apparently contained revealing information as well."

"What about the original scroll from the time of the Merovingians? Where is that?"

"That's a very good question, Jes. I don't think anyone today knows where it is. One thing I can say is that it's quite valuable. In fact, it's priceless and many would like to find it."

"How would you know, sir," asked Marya, "whether you had the original scroll and not a copy?"

"Because," responded Grandfather, "the original scroll has the mark of Dagobert on the back."

"Why are they after this scroll and those of us born with the Merovingian Cross?" persisted Marya.

"Its existence poses a threat to the legitimacy of the Church which is not based on or descended from this legitimate origin," he replied. "In other words, the real reason for the existence of these organizations is to destroy the bloodline along with the record of it, that is to say the scroll. In fact, the original scroll is the most significant evidence of the bloodline. The copy, if accurate and updated with successive generations, would be substantiated by the original scroll and would show the progression of the bloodline."

"You haven't mentioned the treasure of the Templars," interjected Jes.

"I was wondering when you would get back to that," smiled Grandfather. "Seeking the treasure came well after the creation of the Templars in Jerusalem by the Church and then much later when the Church thought there was evidence in the Templars' wealth of the continuation of the bloodline. And of course, the treasure itself has great value. That's where Henry comes into the story. I mentioned Scotland before and the belief that the Templars and the treasure went to Scotland for safety. They also had in their possession the scrolls as well. By 1398 persecution and pursuit caught up with them. The same enemies that tried to eliminate the Templars now tried again but Henry was too quick and sailed west with the treasure and the Templar descendants, and those with the Merovingian Cross. It seems Henry and his ships sailed to Nova Scotia and Mahone Bay, where he was known and revered by the natives there."

There was a long silence while Jes and Marya tried to digest this story. They appeared to be overwhelmed. Marya broke the silence.

"So this treasure must be here somewhere," Marya spoke quietly.

"And perhaps elsewhere," added Jes. "Don't forget the scrolls that Grandfather got from behind the brick." He turned to Grandfather. "Where did they come from?"

"They were probably hidden by someone named Magdalene or her descendant hundreds of years ago in a secret crypt in the foundation of a stone dwelling according to a note on the updated document. Then they were found later by one of our ancestors some generations later and further updated," he explained. "They were passed from generation to generation. That house that you and your parents live in was built a couple of hundred years ago and the scrolls were hidden there by yet another one of our ancestors. I found them by accident some years ago when I visited Jes's parents and noticed the loose brick. I knew what they were because our ancestors' names are added on a separate scroll." He paused and went on, "but I agree with Marya. I think most of the treasure is around here, although perhaps not all in one spot."

Jes and Marya were silent taking it all in. Finally Jes spoke up.

"So I am descended from this Magdalene, but who was she descended from?"

"Another older scroll shows her ancestors going back to a Magda and Jeb from the end of the Merovingian era."

There was another long pause. It suddenly dawned on Jes that there was still an unanswered question.

"Marya has the Merovingian Cross, Grandfather. Do we know who her ancestors were?"

"I thought you would get around to that one day so I did some research. It seems that Marya's ancestors go back to France and the House of Chaumont a thousand years ago. They were descended from the Merovingians as well."

Now that Marya knew how important all this was to those searching for her and Jes, she became very concerned about being discovered. Grandfather convinced her not to be worried. He was sure the black bearded man and his organization had not followed them and didn't know where they were.

"They might figure it out one day but we are safe here for now," he said. "But we should continue to be careful leaving and returning to the house or being seen too much. We must continue to be low key so people won't pay too much attention when we are exploring. And remember, I don't believe the black bearded man ever saw me and only knows about you. So that is why I am very careful about not being seen with you and Jes and why I do the shopping and other errands by myself."

"But you will keep showing us the islands, won't you?" asked Jes, "and also I want to go to Ross Hill again one day."

"Absolutely!" replied Grandfather, "Nothing will keep me from showing you my favorite places and exploring with you. Not even the black bearded man."

The months went by as they explored together. Marya was better about taking precautions and not being seen. She would often grab Jes as he was about to leave through the front door by mistake and direct him to the back exit which was concealed from view. Grandfather had acquired a boat which he kept hidden near Westhaver Beach. They often met there and quietly went out to the many islands.

Often they would fish at Grandfather's favorite spots. Sometimes they would just fish from shore such as in Mader's Cove and other times they would go to an island and fish from its shoreline. Jes was surprised that Marya loved fishing as much as he did. She was not very good at fishing but tried hard nonetheless. More often than not they would go exploring on many of the islands that Grandfather took them to. Mason's Island was a favorite to explore. All three of them were intrigued and drawn to it more than any other.

"It seems to me," speculated Grandfather with a big smile on his face, "that you, Jes, are most interested in finding a hidden scroll and Marya is most interested in finding the treasure."

"I want to find a scroll too, Grandfather," Marya replied, "but I admit finding the treasure would be very exciting."

Jes also replied, "I know there is a scroll hidden somewhere and I want to find it."

They spent the summer and fall searching and exploring but found neither treasure nor scroll. They also took a couple of hikes up to Ross Hill. Jes was the one most interested in exploring that area and searching for any remains of a settlement since both Grandfather and Great Aunt had hinted that legend indicated the existence of a settlement and tower.

One day in late summer, when the water off Westhaver Beach was at its warmest, Jes and Marya tried to coax Grandfather into swimming there but he would have none of it. He said he'd had plenty of swims there when he was younger. Jes and Marya dashed eagerly into the water and yelled and screamed and ran out from the cold.

Winter came too quickly, Marya thought, but she enjoyed it as did Jes. Jes would lead them out the back into the snow and used a technique to conceal their footprints by going via a well-hidden path and connecting to the trails and paths already made by others. Grandfather and Marya both told him that he was very clever about concealing their footprints to and from the back of the house. Jes had the strangest feeling that he had inherited this cleverness from an ancestor and that it was in his genes, just as the Merovingian Cross was. He had an eerie feeling about his ancestry, but it soon passed.

They spent the winter uneventfully but continued to exercise caution. This did not prevent them from enjoying their time there though they were unsuccessful in discovering either a scroll or part of the treasure. With the arrival of spring, they were optimistic about their possibilities of finding something, but success continued to elude them.

And then their peace and tranquility and joy were shattered. They were warned of the imminent arrival of the black bearded man and his friends. Jes's father had notified Grandfather that the black bearded man and his organization had been asking many questions in town, especially of the loquacious postmistress. She told them she had seen mail from a relative in Mahone Bay, Nova Scotia. That was all they needed to know.

MALI'S VILLAGE

CHAPTER FIFTY

The Death of Prince Henry

Mahone Bay
Summer, 1400

Henry gathered the ship captains together and included Jed and Martha. He explained his plan for splitting the party. He felt that the encampment in the castle tower was now self-sufficient and that Sir Gunn and his group were adequately prepared. He wanted to increase the chances of growing the colony by spreading out and planting more roots in the new land..

"Rather than sailing south with Sir Gunn," he said, "I want to take an opportunity to develop another colony inland and I'll take some of the men with me to establish this settlement. I'll also go ahead with my plan to send at least one ship back to Scotland as I promised. The men on the ship have been very helpful in preparing the farming colony against attack and are now anxious to sail back to Scotland."

Sir Gunn and four ship captains would sail south along the coast. About half the men would go with the ships. Ten men indicated they would return to Scotland on the ship anchored in the harbor and about twenty would remain at the farming colony in the tower castle. Henry and about thirty men would march inland in a westerly direction. Half the men in the farming colony would have a bâton à feu, the French "hand cannon", and the others would have a choice of crossbow or longbow. Together with the Ribaldi guns, Henry was certain these would be a sufficient deterrent in case they were attacked. They had enough food and would grow more soon. The proximity of the tower to the Grand Chief was an asset both in terms of trading food and wool and other goods, but also they could possibly support each other in the event of war. Henry planned to do the same for his group of thirty: half would have a bâton à feu, the others would have a choice of crossbow or longbow. The remaining weapons would be taken by Sir Gunn and the men on the five ships. The ship returning to Scotland would sail the week after Henry marched inland.

After the meeting Henry took Jed aside and told him that there was still some of the treasure in the room aboard Henry's flagship. He gave Jed the key.

"I know it's a lot to ask of you but would you find a suitable place as you travel south to hide the remainder of the treasure? Sir Gunn knows the locations of all the treasure hidden so far." Jed indicated he would do that and gave his father a hug.

"Father," Jed spoke hesitantly, "I have never questioned your judgement before but would it not be better to stay with the castle colony for some time to make sure they are prepared for attack, rather than splitting them into two groups? I have learned the skill and art of the natives with bows and arrows and fear the men are no match with their crossbows and longbows."

"Don't worry, Jed," Henry said, "We have guns as well. I believe the attacking tribes will keep their distance."

Henry gave Jed a big bear hug and turned away with tears in his eyes.

Henry made ready to start his march. They carried basic foodstuff but would have to live off the land. They did not take native bows and arrows because they had not learned the skills nearly well enough from the natives to use them. They would rely on crossbows, longbows, or hand guns. The latter were very slow, firing a single shot and requiring considerable time to reload the next shot. These were the earliest developed in Europe and used by the English and French in their wars against each other. The crossbows also took much time to load and fire.

"I think this might be a big mistake," Jed said quietly to Gunn, "if my father's small group is indeed attacked."

They'd lost two ships and a few men at the beginning of the voyage, two more ships, their crews, and a few other men to help the colony in Greenland, and four ships and their crews had gone to Pictou in the north. They had less than half of what they started with and they were about to be split further into several more groups.

"My father's small party will not be fully trained or prepared to march inland," Jed said.

"Did you talk to him, try to talk him out of marching into the wilderness?" Sir Gunn asked.

"I tried but he is sure the guns will keep the attackers at bay."

Sir Gunn shrugged. He knew Henry's decision was final.

Henry told Grand Chief Membertou he planned to start a colony southwest of the Grand Chief. The Chief said he didn't know of any hostile tribes there but Henry should be very careful. He also said he did not have direct enemies but his alliances with northern tribes would draw him into a war that was already in full swing. The sooner Henry left, he said, the less likely he would run into the edges of the spreading conflict which would be in the north.

As Henry made final preparations for his southwest march, Sir Gunn and the other four ship captains made ready to sail down the coast.

Jed and Martha spent every moment they could with Mali and Sam. They had shared many adventures together and it was difficult to part. Mali and Jed would soon turn fourteen and Martha and Sam thirteen. What this meant was that Mali would undergo the traditional test of manhood. He was known to be an exceptional warrior already. What it meant to Sam was that she would soon be "promised" to Mali by Chief Membertou, who was her guardian and the only one that knew she was a girl. What it meant to Martha was that she would still be disguised as a boy for a little longer.

The four of them stood together away from the others at one end of the village and said their last goodbyes to each other. "Jed," Mali said, "we are going to war soon. I am sad the two of you will be leaving but glad at the same time you will not be involved in our war. I will miss you, my brother." He gave Jed a hug and Sam hugged Martha.

Martha looked along the shore where the wikuoms and canoes were spread out. She realized how much she would miss Mali's village, the friends she had made, and the fun and adventures they had together. She wiped away a tear.

They watched as Henry smoked the traditional peace pipe and gave gifts to the Chief from the coffers of his ship, which would now be in the hands of Sir Gunn. As Henry and his party marched off into the woods, the cries of "Glooscap Glooscap" began and got stronger and stronger. They continued for some time even after Henry was out of sight then gradually died down. Jed was reminded how revered Henry was, but wondered why Henry had split his original party into so many groups.

"It doesn't make sense." Jed said to Martha. "He selected a large group to found a colony on the north side and left ships and sheep with them. Then he created the farming colony around the fortified castle which I believe would have an excellent chance of success if they were trained in the use of the native bows and arrows. Now he marches into the wilderness with a band of men to found a colony in the southwest but they do not seem to be fully prepared to succeed. And our five ships are setting sail into parts unknown down the south coast. We have only about sixty men and each ship has a minimum crew. If my father would only listen to me." Jed ran his hands through his long red hair. His green eyes blazed their frustration. "I'm glad we are with Sir Gunn. And I'm glad I talked him into trading for canoes. I think they'll turn out to be useful."

As the five ships lead by Sir Gunn slowly sailed out of the harbor, they watched the beginnings of preparation for war in Chief Membertou's camp. Mali already had his war paint on and he and Sam walked along the shore for a short while waving goodbye to Jed and Martha who stood silently on the deck of the slow moving ship. Martha brushed away a tear as she realized they probably would not see their friends again.

Sir Gunn took the ships carefully out of the harbor, avoiding the islands and shoals, until they were in clear but unknown waters. They headed south along the coast which had numerous islands and headlands jutting into the sea. They calculated, based on discussions with the Chief, that it must be about two hundred miles to the end of the island. They had to sail slowly and carefully through these unknown waters and felt it would take many days before they would enter the wide open waters of the ocean. Sir

Gunn took every opportunity to anchor in harbors and inlets where they would be protected from the sea and where they could do as much hunting as possible.

Jed and Martha realized that the men relied mainly on the two of them for the hunting. They never missed and were able to get much closer to game than the relatively clumsy men. They brought down many deer and killed a wild boar once in a while. They let the men catch and kill a moose now and then. These creatures were so easy to catch that Jed and Martha felt sorry for them but knew they provided a lot of meat which was cured and saved for harder times. A wild boar was rare compared to the other game and the men loved the taste of the meat so they generally had a feast whenever one was killed.

Because of this disparity in hunting skills, they spent much of their sailing time teaching some of the men the art and skill of the native bow and arrow. The men did not like the bâton à feu and seldom used it. They were skilled in the use of the crossbow but found it to be difficult to use effectively in the dense forest. Only the longbow had some success.

Jed and Martha also taught the crew how to make arrows, one of the many skills Mali had taught the two of them. He said the main skill was selecting the proper wood. Creating the correct length and suppleness of the wood was also essential. Of course, Mali said with his dry humor, it helps if you never lose an arrow. What he meant was: never miss, and retrieve your arrows if you have time.

Not all of the men hunted. Some spent their time collecting nuts, mushrooms, berries, as well as apples, herbs, and whatever they could find in season. This included the delicacies of bird's eggs and shellfish along the shore. Perishables like these had to be consumed immediately so whenever they were found they had a fine feast that evening. The men had also learned from the natives to collect certain roots which were delicious when cooked. It was very important to use these opportunities to stock up on a variety of foods before they ventured into the unknown lands far to the south. Fishing off the boat whether sailing or anchored was an ongoing activity.

These days were very special to Martha. This was Henry's ship, now captained by Sir Gunn, and Martha was still a boy and Jed's friend so they had their old room back again. Martha loved to cuddle with Jed and now had an opportunity to do so. Time had gone by and both had matured somewhat but this did not seem to change things.

For ten days they stopped at the many coves and inlets along the south shore until finally coming to the end of the big island. They anchored in a protected inlet between the main island and a large island projecting out into the vast ocean before them. Sir Gunn invited the other captains aboard for dinner.

"It's time to discuss our plans," Sir Gunn said, "from this point on. I understand a couple of you want to head into the ocean. I advise against it but want to hear your views."

There was a difference of opinion about the course of action the group should take. Two of the ship captains intended to sail directly into the ocean on a straight course for a cape. This was based on some rudimentary maps they had of the ocean and shore. One of the captains was going to play it safe with Sir Gunn and head directly west to hit the coastline as soon as possible. The fifth ship captain was undecided until the last minute and went with the first two into the ocean. Since there was the possibility of a storm, Sir Gunn had the ocean going ships off load some of the food and some of the weapons. The ships would have enough food for the expected short journey and would not need the weapons until they hit land and met Sir Gunn, who might take longer but would probably get there without mishap. The remaining treasure had long since been moved to Sir Gunn's ship and concealed.

Just as they were about to sail their separate ways, they heard a brave from Mali's tribe yell from a nearby cliff and show the peace sign with his fingers raised high over his head. Jed took one of the canoes and paddled to shore as the brave ran down to the beach to meet him.

"You are the son of Glooscap?" asked the brave. Jed nodded. "And the best friend of Chief Malikiaq?" Jed nodded again. "Glooscap is dead," said the brave with the greatest sadness in his voice, "He was killed during an attack by a hostile tribe." Jed froze.

"I was afraid of something like that," Jed whispered, "I tried to talk him out of marching into the wilderness. They were not prepared for hostility."

"Oh no. Your father changed his mind about marching away. Instead he went to help that group in the tower on the hill. He was a hero. He died defending the colony from a surprise attack. They were outnumbered three to one but Glooscap drove them away and then was killed by an arrow just at the moment of victory."

"You mean he listened to me?" Jed was silent for a moment then spoke in a low voice. "Was he buried properly?"

"Some of the men carried Glooscap back to Chief Malikiaq and his father, who is quite ill. Our tribe wept when they learned the sad news and our Chief held a traditional burial ceremony. He was buried near the sea he loved so much. His body was covered with flowers and his headdress. Our people sent me to tell you. It took five days but it was not hard to find you. The tribe down here knew where you were."

"Thank you for finding us," Jed answered quietly. "And please let Mali and your tribe know I am thankful to you for looking after my father." He wiped away a tear.

"You are also much loved by our people, and we hope you will return one day."

He explained that once they left this island they would no longer be under the protection of Chief Membertou and his allies. The native tribes along the main coast were known to be very hostile.

While Jed returned to his ship, the brave returned to the cliff tops. As they sailed away, he yelled, "Please come back." He paused. "Glooscap." His voice echoed across the water as he continued to yell, "Glooscap. Glooscap. Please come back. Glooscap." His voice caused a shiver down Jed's back.

"How did they know where we were?" asked one of the men when Jed returned.

"They've known all the time where we were," responded Jed. "But they won't any more after we sail."

Jed explained that Chief Membertou's protection and that of his allies extended all the way to the southern end and eastern side of the island only, but not to the western side. This was the big mistake Henry almost made, but turned back to help defend the tower castle. When they heard of Henry's actions as a hero, defeating a surprise attack by a hostile tribe, only to die after his victory, the entire crews of all the ships were solemn.

From what the brave had told him, Jed explained, "Sailing west by northwest we will encounter the main body of land. The tribes understand that a storm from the big ocean is coming, so sailing for the near shore is the safe way to go south. The brave also pointed out the native tribes on shore will also be hostile."

Jed held his emotions in check while detailing this for the men and after he finished, Sir Gunn came up to Jed and put his arm around his shoulders.

"I'm sorry." He spoke softly then left Jed and Martha to themselves. They walked away together, and when no one else was around, Jed finally broke down in tears.

"I never knew he loved me so much until he hugged me that night," he explained. "And I did not know until now how much I loved him." She put her arms around him and hugged him tightly. He responded by hugging her, then put his head on her chest and sobbed for some minutes as she held him. They cuddled more closely than ever that night and no words were spoken. They had each other.

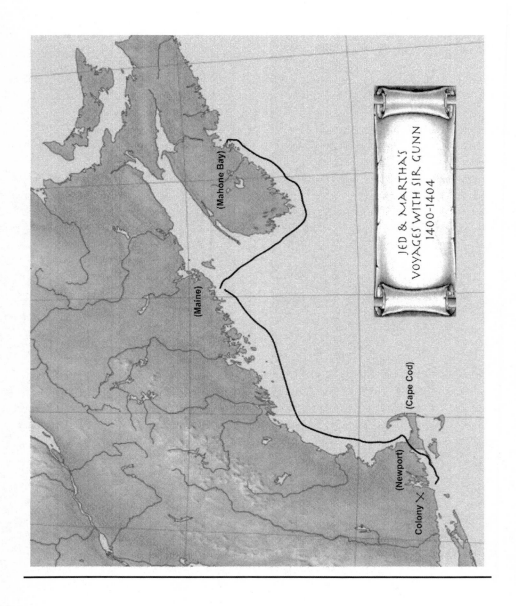

JED & MARTHA'S
VOYAGES WITH SIR GUNN
1400-1404

(Mahone Bay)

(Maine)

(Cape Cod)

(Newport)

Colony X

CHAPTER FIFTY ONE

Sailing into the Unknown

Mahone Bay
Summer, 1400

Sir Gunn had to deal with a major problem: how to proceed given the difference of opinion amongst the five captains. He understood from Chief Membertou and old rough maps that the safest route would be to follow the shore around the southern point of their land and head directly west. They would then cross open water for about the same distance they had covered since leaving Henry and the Chief. Once they reached land they would then follow the coastline in a southeast direction for many days. He held a brief discussion with the other captains.

"I calculate that if we sail day and night, which we must do," Sir Gunn said, "it will take four or five days, and then we can sail slowly south to stop for water and to hunt game. We'll search for roots, mushrooms, nuts, wild onions and garlic, apples, berries, herbs, and whatever we can find in season. Shellfish, bird's eggs, and fish are all on the menu. The difference is that we will be doing the hunting and gathering with the ever present danger of hostile native tribes."

They knew from reports that a large cape to the south would provide a safe haven. It was unusual in that it curled around almost in a complete circle and provided protection from the stormy ocean. This was their destination. Sailing southeast along the coast might take three or four times as long as sailing directly across the ocean but this was the choice of Sir Gunn and Captain Smith. With a menacing storm approaching, it was a safe route and they would have plenty of food available.

Captain MacDonald, who had taken command of Sir Gunn's ship, and Captain Sullivan, disagreed. Only Captain Jones wavered, but in the end decided on the open ocean. These captains were convinced it would take much less time and they would not have to deal with hostile tribes. Possible shortage of food and the menacing storm were risks they were willing to take.

In spite of the warnings from Sir Gunn and Jed, the three ship captains headed out in a south by southwest direction toward where they understood the cape to be. They were taking a deadly risk: If they encountered the approaching storm they could be blown off course and miss the cape entirely. They would sail for days and weeks into the unknown and would certainly perish from lack of food.

Sir Gunn and Captain Smith headed directly for shore, and as expected, hit land in four days. They continued south and encountered no trouble for the first few days, anchoring in coves and inlets and on islands. Led by Jed, who could detect signs of native tribes, their hunting at first was very brief and at night. During the next four days Jed became increasingly aware of the unusual movement of animals on shore and sensed the presence of natives. He warned that they were being watched and tracked. They should sail more rapidly, covering more miles, to outdistance possible attackers. After two days they anchored far offshore on the leeward side of the largest of a group of islands.

In the morning, much to their surprise, they saw a single ship approaching. It showed signs of damage to its sails but nonetheless was able to maneuver. It was Captain Jones. He came aboard and was in an agitated state as he reported to Sir Gunn.

"We lost two ships. There was a massive storm when we were a day out. It sank the two ships and nearly sank mine as well. We were able to save all the men and most of the weapons, as well as most of the food, but we lost clothes and everything else on board."

Sir Gunn asked Captain Jones to bring Captain Sullivan and Captain MacDonald aboard his ship and sent a man to bring Captain Smith aboard as well. While waiting for them to arrive, Sir Gunn talked quietly to Jed about the decision he and Henry had made about putting all the treasure on this ship. Jed was the only confidant Sir Gunn had and wanted Jed to know all he knew in case something happened to him.

When the Captains were aboard, Sir Gunn discussed the distribution of men, food, and arms, then dispersed men and supplies before they continued their journey. Captain Sullivan, who no longer had a ship, joined Captain Jones while Captain MacDonald joined Captain Smith. During the movement of men, Sir Gunn sent a small party to nearby islands to hunt and gather food. They encountered no natives and were able to kill three deer and gather fruit, nuts, and eggs to add to their limited supply.

When the distribution was completed, Sir Gunn sailed southwest followed by the other two ships. They stayed close to shore, and sailed day and night to recover lost time. They wanted to make sure the food supply lasted until they reached the cape, and stopped three times for water, and to hunt and gather food. Jed was able to see a group of braves peering through the trees and watching them as they sailed by.

"We will surely encounter hostile natives," Jed told Sir Gunn, "when we go ashore to hunt."

Fishing and gathering shellfish along the shore were safe activities but when they went inland to hunt they were in danger of attack so Sir Gunn sent a small group of armed men with the hunters and gatherers.

The first time they stopped they were observed from behind a group of boulders but not bothered.

"What are they waiting for?" asked one of the men, turning toward Jed.

"They are sizing us up," answered Jed, "They will attack if they see an opportunity to surprise us."

Jed knew this waiting game was making the men nervous and tried to keep them together.

On the second stop they had to go inland more than half a mile to find game and this time they were attacked by a small band of natives. Jed took charge while firing his arrows with deadly accuracy. Martha was by his side and the two held the braves at bay while Jed urged the hunters and gatherers to retreat, covered by the men armed with guns and crossbows. The guns proved to be useless because they were too slow to reload, and the crossbows were not much better. Jed and Mark shot down three attackers while the entire party retreated. Two of the armed men were killed. The native band realized there were some that could shoot with deadly accuracy so stopped following the foraging party after losing three of their own. This encounter was disturbing to Sir Gunn and he vowed to be more careful in the future.

The remainder of their journey sailing down the coast was uneventful and they reached the cape in three days and nights, encountering rain and a few squalls but no severe storms. They anchored well within the long projection of land circling around to the north which provided safety from the storms. After they rested and recovered, Sir Gunn sent hunting parties ashore with Jed a couple of times and they were successful in hunting deer and a single boar. Jed was extremely cautious in deploying the men and detecting the presence of possible attackers. Once, he sensed the approach of a band of natives, and quickly told the hunting party to retreat back to the ship. Martha joined him on every such endeavor.

The ships were anchored close to the mainland where the hunting would be best but still within the protection of the cape. The men stayed on the ships for several weeks while Sir Gunn pondered his decision as to where it was best to establish a permanent anchorage and go ashore to create a colony. He did not want to encounter more hostile tribes and was uncomfortable with their current location.

"Sir, Captain Smith and I are willing to explore the shoreline and seek a safer haven." Sir Gunn agreed.

The next day they sailed south with a few men on Captain Smith's ship and discovered a water gap between the mainland and the cape itself. Sailing very slowly through this waterway, they realized it continued on southwest into open water which extended westerly and marked the southern boundary of the mainland. Jed saw no signs of tribal activity, so they reported back to Sir Gunn and urged him to sail with all three ships west along this southern land boundary.

After another two days of hunting and gathering food, including fishing off shore and gathering shellfish, Sir Gunn thought they were well stocked enough to continue the exploration and the three ships sailed through the gap and west along the shore. They came to a large inlet leading north many miles and anchored at the mouth of this huge waterway.

Sir Gunn decided that here was the best place to found a settlement or colony, somewhat inland but still on the water. The ships remained anchored while he organized two parties to explore the land on both sides of the waterway. He himself led the group exploring the eastern shore and they went far inland to the east. His group included Captains Sullivan and MacDonald. Jed and Martha led the group that explored the land to the west. Captains Smith and Jones stayed on board two of the three ships.

Sir Gunn had travelled about six miles when his party was surprised and attacked by a large band of natives. One man, George, who was wounded in the initial assault and feigned death, was able to stumble back to the ship to tell of the attack.

"We were outnumbered two to one. Sir Gunn tried to get us into a protective circle but the men were cut down one at a time. Sir Gunn made a last ditch effort to kill our attackers but was overwhelmed. I saw him fall with five arrows in him. The natives left and I made my way over to him as he lay dying."

One of the men left on board for protection listened to his story.

"Did he say anything to you before he died?"

"He said to tell Jed it was now his job to look after the rest of us."

The man travelled quickly and at night to reach Jed and his group. They sent out a small party to locate Sir Gunn's body and brought it back to his ship. With the death of Sir Gunn and those with him they were down to twenty five men besides Martha and Jed.

The men asked Jed to assume command. As young as he was, he had become the unquestioned leader in numerous situations and had earned their admiration and respect for his skills and leadership qualities. Jed had Sir Gunn buried on shore close to the ship. He had a small round stone tower built over his grave as a monument. It took four days to build the tower. The men dug down eight feet in the soft soil, created a circular foundation of large stones, with columns rising above the level of the ground. The platform above the gravesite was supported by stone columns underneath, and Sir Gunn was buried underneath in the middle of the lower columns. As his father had done, Jed made sure there was a secret crypt under the tower next to Sir Gunn's body. At night, before the grave was covered over, and with Martha's help, he buried the remaining treasure as his father had asked. Only Sir Gunn knew about the treasure and now he was dead.

"Jed," Martha whispered as she picked up the goblet wrapped in fine linen. "Do you see this beautiful silver goblet? I remember it from the time we opened those chests on the ship. Could we keep it and bury all the rest?"

"All right," he answered, "but just that one. I promised my father to bury the remaining treasure."

Martha removed the goblet and wrapped it up again. After they sealed the crypt, Martha again whispered to Jed. "Did you notice that there are no longer any gold or silver coins in the treasure?"

He nodded.

"Do you remember when we looked in that chest on the ship? I wonder what happened to them."

Jed responded, "He must have buried them in one of the other places."

"Do you think he buried the chest in the deep well on that island? Remember what I told you."

Jed shrugged. "You may be right, Martha."

Jed and the remaining men completed the upper part of the tower over the next two days. Now that they were fewer in number, Jed's worry was to get the men to safer environs. They explored the land on the west side of the waterway, looking for a good water source, flat land that could be farmed, and natural defensive features. On one such foray they were attacked by a band of natives. Jed sensed their arrival and ordered the men into protected positions. This group contained some of the most skilled with native bows and arrow, and some used longbows. The prowess of the Europeans surprised the braves and halted their advance. Jed always wore his native clothing on all such outings to maintain camouflage in the forest. While the arrows continued to fly Jed moved unseen and unheard around to the back of the native band. He observed one with the headdress of a chief who was clearly the leader. Jed saw he was quite young, about his own age, and thought he was probably a chief's son. He came up behind him, put a knife to his throat and ordered him in the common native tongue to cease attacking and to have his warriors retire. The brave promptly did just that and the Europeans did the same on a signal from Martha. With Jed's knife to his throat, the brave asked him why he did not kill him as warriors always do.

"I don't see the point in killing someone if you don't have to," Jed answered. "If I spare your life, will you promise me on your honor that you and your tribe will live in peace and harmony with this small group of Europeans as long as they do the same?"

"Yes," answered the brave. "On my honor."

Jed removed the knife from his throat.

"How do you know I have the power to give such an order?" the brave said.

"From your headdress," replied Jed. "It is that of a Chief. You are either the Chief of the tribe, or more likely, the Chief's son since you are so young. And I know you have that power."

"You are right. I am the son of our Chief. How do you know so much about our ways, and how is it you and this other brave shoot so well?" he said, gesturing toward Martha. "You both are more skilled than any of us."

Jed explained that his best friend, Mali, belonged to a northern tribe and that he, Jed, had learned a great deal from him. As he spoke, Jed could see the young brave's eyes begin to lose their fear.

"Mali and I will be brothers forever. My name is Jed in our language," and he told him his native name. "What is yours?"

"I have a very long name in our language, but you can call me Joe."

Joe said Jed would be his brother for sparing his life and invited him to return to his camp to meet his father. He would leave three braves as hostage while they were gone. Jed agreed and brought Martha with him. Jed told his men to go back to the ship with the three hostages until he and Mark returned.

They travelled a short distance to the camp and met the Chief after a discussion between Joe and his father. They sat in a circle of greeting and smoked the traditional peace pipe with the Chief, Joe, and three other braves that Jed took to be senior warriors. Jed thought the taste of the pipe was a little bitter but was not as bad as he had imagined it to be. Martha sat off to the side and did not participate in the peace pipe ceremony. After that, Jed and Martha returned to their ship, and from that time on, Jed and Joe became brothers and friends.

Joe and his father helped Jed and his men find a suitable location nearby to settle and farm. Jed and Martha and Jed's men continued to live in peace and harmony with Joe and his tribe for two years.

CHAPTER FIFTY TWO

Saving the Enemy

Mahone Bay, Nova Scotia
Summer, 1951

Jes and Marya turned fourteen and a half and thirteen and a half early in the year and had enjoyed a peaceful existence for many months, safe and nearly anonymous. Great Aunt had been dead for nearly a year and a half, and Grandfather continued to care for and instruct the two children in Mahone Bay. But this peace was shattered when Jes's father told Grandfather about a conversation his neighbor overheard. The neighbor said she saw the black bearded man casing the family house again. She heard him say to one of the other men, that in all likelihood, the two kids were visiting the relative up north mentioned by the postmistress because that was where the father was headed when they had followed him.

"There was no mention of you, Dad," Jes's father told him. "They never connected you to the kids. They must not have seen you leave with them, but made the connection based on when they followed Pete and me, and what they found out at the post office."

This was enough for Grandfather to want to move out of the family house immediately. If the man with the black beard thought the children were now up north, they would easily find Great Aunt's house.

"The three of us have to move as soon as possible. This was bound to happen sooner or later and the time has now come."

"Where will we go?" Marya asked.

"I have an old friend from my earlier days that has an empty cottage. It's near the place where we hide the boat. It's secluded and big enough for us. We need to move there tonight so we won't be seen. Now you know the danger we are in. His organization apparently doesn't yet know of my existence and won't unless I make a mistake and we are seen together. I hope this is only for a short while before they give up and go away."

They packed up that night, removed evidence of living in the house, and moved to the cottage. It was even more secluded than Gertrude's house and smaller. They could not see the water but they were only a short walk away through the maple, oak, and pine trees.

"It's charming." Marya said. "Don't you think so, Jes?"

"Yes. I like the green shutters and the chimney. It must have a fireplace."

"And I like the screened in porch." Grandfather added. "Let's go inside."

There were two small bedrooms, small kitchen, bathroom, and a main room with fireplace at one end and dining area at the other. Though they missed the family house, Jes and Marya were glad they were only a short distance from the boat they used for fishing and exploring. It could be a useful way to escape the house if they needed to, but neither Grandfather nor his young charges said this out loud.

Grandfather told Gertrude they were moving out of his sister's house and did not want to tell her where for her own safety. "Hostile visitors," he explained, "might come by the house looking for Jes and Marya and they must not find them." He asked her to keep an eye on the house and he would check with her now and then to see if anyone came by.

Two days later when Grandfather called Gertrude, she told him she had just observed three men coming by the house, but left when they found it empty. He told Jes and Marya he was afraid that they would connect them to his sister and her house. He didn't know where the men would go now but didn't expect them to give up looking for the two of them.

"I'm afraid," Grandfather warned, "that from now on, we will only go out at night. The only exception will be when I need to go shopping and do other errands. If I am ever connected to you I won't be able to do that safely anymore and it will be time for us to leave this area."

"This won't stop us from fishing, will it?" Jes asked.

"No, but we'll wait a couple of days," he replied, "And we will just have to be careful where we fish. If we see anyone watching us we'll move slowly away from them. Anyway, the fishing is better at night and I can see quite well in the dark."

Jes added that he also had excellent night vision.

Marya told Jes she could also see well at night. "And we can still explore the islands for treasure?" asked Marya.

"And the hidden scrolls that I know are out there?" added Jes.

"You two are something else," laughed Grandfather. "After all I have said and the danger we are facing, you are both unfazed. The possibility of those three men capturing or killing you doesn't seem to bother you at all."

"Why would they capture us instead of just killing us?" Marya asked innocently.

"To find out what you know or what you have hidden, I would guess," he responded.

"Well, we don't know much and we haven't hidden anything. In fact we haven't even found anything so I don't see what we should worry about." There was silence for a moment.

Grandfather just shook his head at their youthful innocence.

Three days went by while Jes and Marya waited impatiently. There was no further report of a villager seeing the strangers in town. Finally Jes spoke up late on the third day.

"Can we go fishing now? It's getting dark."

"All right, but we'll fish further out for now."

Grandfather led them quietly to the boat and headed east, rowing between Loye Island and Herman's Island, to a cove on the west side of Coveys Island. They fished most of the night with good success. Jes was delighted but Marya was not. She said she liked to fish but was more excited about searching for treasure.

Grandfather said he understood, so the next night they ventured further out to explore a few islands. He rowed out past Loye Island and finally said he would take a chance and use the motor on the boat since it was much too far to row.

"I like it much better without the motor," Marya yelled above the roar of the engine, "I can hear the waves against the side of the boat, and the wind."

"I like the mist spraying over us when we race along." Jes countered.

Grandfather just smiled. He took the boat straight across the open water in a northwest direction between the shoals and then between Sheep Island and Goat Island, two small islands south of several larger ones. He continued on between Gifford Island and Rous Island and around Ernst Island until he reached Zwicker Cove on the east side of Zwicker Island.

"We'll go to Mason's tomorrow. It's much further away, so for now I'll let you search Zwicker for treasure or scrolls or whatever you can find," explained Grandfather. "I'd just as soon fish here as traipse across the island. I'll meet you in about three hours on the other side, at Eel Cove, and then we can check out Indian Point if we have time. I don't want to take a chance on being caught on the open water when the sun comes up."

"We understand," they replied and off they went. They walked slowly across Zwicker Island, which was about half a mile across. They were walking straight into a brisk wind. They used their flashlights sparingly, only while looking into caves. Jes looked in every crevice or spot where a scroll could be hidden without damage from weather. Marya looked in larger spaces for the treasure she was sure was there. They used every minute of their three hours but were unsuccessful in finding anything of value. They reached Eel Cove, with muddy shoes and shivering, just as Grandfather coasted in to a landing spot. They had just enough time to explore the shore along Indian Point and then Grandfather summoned them to leave. They cruised directly back to Westhaver Beach and hid the boat.

"I'm sorry your exploring was unsuccessful but I would think treasure and scrolls are not going to be easy to find," he said. "At least the trip was not altogether unsuccessful."

He held up several fish that he had kept in the water. Jes thought Grandfather was treating their failure lightly and without any show of sympathy but he let this thought pass. Marya said she was eager to go out the next night and was sure they would have success looking for treasure on Mason Island. Grandfather expressed concern about the trip, hoping the motor would not be heard from shore.

He called Gertrude that morning as Jes and Marya slept. Gertrude told him what he feared, that the black bearded man and his two companions had returned from wherever they had gone and were quietly asking questions of some of the villagers. Gertrude said they were asking if anyone had seen two children and described them. Even though Jes and Marya had not been seen for some time, one villager remembered seeing them at the funeral.

That was all the three men needed, Grandfather realized, for them to stick around and keep looking. They had guessed that the children were here somewhere but keeping out of sight. When Jes and Marya woke up he told them about the conversation and the fact that all of them had to be extremely careful. He was able to go out to shop and did not see the men.

"No one seems to pay any attention or ask questions about me. I think we will be safer a little longer as long as you two are not seen in the village. But I don't want to take any chances unless I am sure the men have left. So we will wait a few more days and hope we don't see any sign of them before we go out fishing again."

Jes and Marya were very disappointed but said they understood. Grandfather had not seen any sign of the men for several days so one night he finally honored his promise to take them far out to Mason's Island.

"From now on we must be extremely careful, but I believe we'll be safe going that far out," he said, "since it will be unlikely that anyone can hear the motor way out there."

"Maybe we can camp overnight on one of the islands," Jes said. "That way we know we will be safe."

"Just the thought I had," Grandfather replied. He showed them the sleeping bags and the tent he had acquired.

"Oh, this will be so much fun." Marya spoke with excitement in her voice.

Grandfather loaded up the boat with all the equipment and they headed out in the dark night. He rowed for some time until he was beyond Coveys Island. When he reached the shoals and ledges he motored through them to take a direct path to Mason Island and then went around the top of Mason to the cove. He hid the boat this time and went ashore with Jes and

Marya. Grandfather had checked with Gertrude around midday and she had not seen the black bearded man. While they were motoring to Mason he regretted not checking with her again before they left in the dark. If he had, she would have given him a dire warning that the men had returned late in the day and were asking more questions. One question they asked everyone was if they had heard anything unusual. One of the villagers answered she had heard some people out on the water in a motor boat, probably fishing at night.

Grandfather reached the shoals and started the motor. The three men, lurking near the harbor, heard the faint sound of an engine on the water.

"It's them," whispered the red haired man. At the boat rental shack, the shutters were closed. The black bearded man tried to rouse the owner but was unsuccessful, so he stole a large boat with an outboard engine and they headed out after the sound of the motor. They stopped often to listen. At one point the sound stopped so they had to shut off their engine and drift until they heard it again.

Jes and Marya, with Grandfather wandering behind, searched Mason Island from north to south and found nothing. Grandfather said it was time to leave so they could find a place to camp closer to home.

"I think Loye Island would be a nice play to camp tonight. It's not too far from Westhaver Beach."

They were south of the cove on Mason's and hurried back to the boat. He started the engine. A flock of gulls cried, flying up in the air. If anyone could see in the dark, Grandfather was sure this would pinpoint their exact position. He took the shortest route back through the shoals and ledges.

Then he heard the sound of a large motor boat. He was just about to clear Rous shoal when he saw it heading straight for them. The black bearded man stood in the bow. He had finally tracked them down.

"He's headed right for us, Grandfather! Do something!" yelled Jes.

Grandfather turned around and headed back into the shoals and ledges. It was dark and the tide was low so he thought he could maneuver better than the larger boat. *After all*, he thought, *who knows these waters better than I.*

He was right. They suddenly heard a sickening crash as the boat hit a shoal. They heard the yells of the men in the cold water. Jes knew they would not last very long in the frigid temperatures of Mahone Bay.

"We've got to go back," he yelled to Grandfather. "They'll drown in that cold water. We can't let them die."

Grandfather turned back and went slowly through the shoals in the dim light. It took them several minutes before they could see the wreckage of the large boat. The yelling had stopped and Jes could hear one voice calling out weakly.

"Help me. Help me. I'm getting numb. Please help me."

They came close to the sound of the voice. Jes could see the man in the darkness. It was the black bearded man. There was no sign of anyone else. As they came closer, he could see that the man could no longer stay afloat and was starting to go under. His dark head was visible for a moment then disappeared below the surface. With arms flailing, the man's head burst above the water, his mouth open, words choked by water he swallowed. As he began to sink again, Jes dove in and grabbed the man's arm. The ice cold water soaked Jes to the skin and he gritted his teeth. He pulled him toward their boat with all his strength. After Grandfather and Marya helped get him on board, the black bearded man lay prone for a few minutes, totally exhausted from his struggle. Finally he sat up and looked straight into Jes's eyes.

"You saved me from drowning. You saved my life. Why?" His voice was reedy, as though he could only summon the strength for these few words.

Jes hesitated a moment before he replied, "I couldn't let you die. I had to save you. It was the right thing, the Christian thing to do."

CHAPTER FIFTY THREE

Departures

Scotland
Winter, 756 AD

Magda and Jeb had a son they named Jeremiah. He soon became known as Jerry. Jerry was now two and a half years old and full of curiosity. His curly blonde hair was to his shoulders and his hazel eyes always seemed to be looking right through you. It was no surprise to Jeb and Magda that he also had the Merovingian birthmark in the same place as theirs. They made sure it was never visible to others. Jeb was now sixteen and Magda fifteen. They'd spent three years at Medcaut. Jeb reminded Magda of Clotaire's desire to see that they were not only in a safe location but also educated. And so, Magda made the most of her stay by studying with the monks. She learned to read and write and they both studied history and mathematics.

There were many other people living at Medcaut as refugees. Magda befriended a young girl not much older than herself who had a daughter named Madalene or Maddy for short. Maddy was just a little younger than Jerry and had red hair and blue eyes, and a dark complexion, and always seemed to be smiling and full of life. Maddy was a feisty young child and played often with Jerry.

One day her shirt pulled up and Magda noticed the birthmark, white as cream against her dark skin, just over the center of her ribcage. Maddy's mother Susannah quickly covered it and tried not to show her anxiety and fear, hoping Magda did not notice it. Magda put her at ease.

"Don't worry," she spoke softly, "I won't tell anyone. Jerry has one also." Maddy's mother looked relieved.

"Maddy's father was a descendant of the Merovingians," Susannah explained.

"Who was his ancestor?"

"His grandfather was Thierry IV."

"Then we are distant cousins."

From that day onward the two mothers became very good friends and worked together as best they could to conceal the telltale birthmarks. Maddy and Jerry became good friends and played together often and each learned to keep their birthmark covered without knowing why. Each knew the other one had the birthmark as well.

Jeb felt it was important to help with the welfare of the community so he used his skills to go hunting and often brought back deer or a rare boar. Magda learned to help with cooking and other inside activities. At first she rebelled against being cast differently than Jeb and did in fact go hunting with him now and then, but also realized that being a mother had its own responsibilities. Maddy's father had died in a skirmish before Susannah had reached Medcaut so Magda spent a bit of extra time and effort to help Susannah raise Maddy.

Life progressed slowly those three years until, one day, the Abbot came to them with a very serious expression on his gently weathered face. He took Jeb and Magda into the garden where they could not be heard.

"There are signs that an attack might come against Medcaut," he cautioned. "It might be years in the making but it is definitely coming. There have recently been raids on coastal settlements by attackers from the northeast lands. I urge you to consider moving inland to the west. It would be better for you to be in a less visible location. There is a small monastery located about fifty miles to the west of here."

"You should consider going there soon," he suggested. "The monks need not know much about you. After a short time you can find your own place such as a farm or other dwelling and make a living there. The monks will help you settle in peace and relative anonymity."

"What about Maddy and her mother Susannah?" responded Magda. "Shouldn't she go also since her situation is similar to mine?"

"I'm glad you brought that up yourself," smiled the Abbot. "I see that you have become good friends and your children as well. Indeed, it would be wise and wonderful if you went together."

Magda, Jeb, and Susannah prepared to depart with Jerry and Maddy within a few days. They received directions from the Abbot and chose a time when the others at Medcaut would be busy, not notice their departure, and if they did, would think nothing of it since settlers did come and go often. Jeb and Magda packed bread and meat and other foods for the journey and helped Susannah to do the same. Magda knew it would take much longer to cover fifty miles than she and Jeb had done in the past, now that they would be travelling with children.

Because of the possibility of encountering bandits, they decided to travel at night. Susannah was not used to this, and Jerry and Maddy, although they could walk, would require much more effort on the part of the three adults to get them to their destination. The Abbot told them about a small monastery about half way on their journey where they could rest. The monks would be hospitable and ask no questions.

Jeb, Magda, Susannah, and the two children left quietly the next night and the next day their absence was scarcely noticed. With frequent stops, they averaged only about two miles per night. The children walked as long as they could, and when they grew tired, were carried: Jeb carried Jerry, and Magda and Susannah took turns carrying Maddy. They stopped when they were exhausted. The adults managed to keep the children and

301

themselves well fed. With three rest nights it took sixteen nights to cover about twenty five miles to reach the first monastery. The two monks welcomed them and were very kind to the exhausted group, especially to the children. They entertained the children and played with them for the three days the group stayed to recover their strength.

Jeb did some hunting during this stay, and with the help of the monks, cured and dried deer meat to take with them. The monks supplied them with bread and some fruit and vegetables for the remainder of their journey, asked no questions, and sent them on their way. They followed a similar pattern for the remaining twenty five miles. As before, they travelled silently at night and avoided all other travelers. Jeb and Magda could always detect the presence of the few they did encounter and hid until the danger of discovery was gone. The children learned quickly the importance of travelling silently. The only problem they encountered was a day of rain when they had to take shelter in a small empty outbuilding on a farm until it stopped. It took them sixteen days as well to travel these last twenty five miles to the larger monastery.

The four monks living there welcomed them and looked after the exhausted and hungry children. They stayed at the monastery for three weeks under the kind eyes of the monks while Brother Samuel joined Magda in seeking a permanent refuge. Jeb helped the food supply by hunting every couple of days, and Susannah, Magda, and the children went in search of eggs, berries, fruit, nuts, wild onions, and any other edible plants. Magda explained to Susannah and the children about mushrooms and not to touch them until she or Jeb had made sure they were edible.

The monk and Magda found a small farm which was abandoned and available for them to occupy. They settled there peacefully and quietly and began farming.

However, as soon as they were all settled, Jeb announced his intention to leave.

"Magda," Jed began, "I've been thinking about it for some time. I plan to return to the boat and sail back to look for Clotaire."

"But why, Jeb?" she protested, "We need you here."

"I don't expect you to be happy about it, but I believe Clotaire can use my help. Magda, he was our protector, guide, teacher, our savior. He was our rock. I owe it to him."

"How will you find him? It will be very dangerous. You might be killed. Please think about it."

"I'll be very careful. I have thought about it a lot," he said quietly. "I must go."

Magda could see that Jeb was determined to leave.

"Jeb," she said, "You are right. I'm not happy at all about you leaving but I'll try to understand. Please come back soon."

Jeb spent time preparing to leave and quite a bit of time with Jerry. In a quiet moment, he came to Magda and told her that now it was her job to look after the scrolls he had been carrying all this time.

"These scrolls," he explained, "are the original Merovingian scroll and the original scroll from Egypt. I have been concerned for some time about something happening to both the originals and the copies. When we left the Abbey in the south, I saw the perfect hiding place to leave the copies as insurance. I hid them behind a loose brick."

He showed her the mark of Dagobert. He said updating the scroll should be done on a separate parchment and not on the original. He also pointed out the information on the Egyptian scroll showing the birth of Sarah and her Merovingian Cross and the history of her marrying into the first ancestors of the Merovingians.

"These documents are priceless," he explained. "They should be protected at all costs."

"I understand," she said. "I'll hide them in a special place."

Before Jeb left, he held Magda and lingered in her arms. Finally, she pushed him away, and turned to hide her tears. "Go if you must, but go." Jeb walked quietly into the night. Many years went by and Magda did not see the return of Jeb. She, Susannah, Jerry, and Maddy lived a quiet secluded life on the farm for many years.

CHAPTER FIFTY FOUR

Burying the Scrolls

Newport, Southern New England
Summer, 1402

Jed and Martha lived in peace and prosperity for two years. Jed turned sixteen and Martha fifteen. She no longer used the name Mark when she became Jed's wife. They had a son with jet black hair and dark brown eyes whom they named Jet. Jet also had the Merovingian Cross on his chest, which they concealed as best they could from the men in the colony.

Jed and Martha and the remaining men of the colony continued to live in peace and harmony near Joe and his tribe and Jed and Martha often spent time with Joe. But the peace was not to last. Joe's tribe was drawn into a war with a tribe from the north. Joe's father, the Chief, was killed during a surprise attack and the peace in the fledgling colony was broken when the invaders attacked them as well. Many of the men in the colony were killed along with many braves from the attacking tribe. The invaders retreated because of the skill of Jed and Martha and a few of the men in the colony who Jed had trained, but losing more men was the last straw for the colony, which was now reduced to only twenty. It was no longer tenable for them to survive in what they considered a hostile land. The remaining men in the colony, under the direction of Captains Smith and Jones, prepared to sail away to Scotland on two of the ships with a minimum crew on each. They planned to follow the route they had taken to reach New Scotland.

The situation was similar for Joe and his tribe. Joe now became the Chief of the tribe but the number of warriors left under his leadership had dwindled. After the battle Joe told Jed that he and his remaining braves and families were going west to join an allied tribe who would welcome them.

"They will also welcome you as a brother," Joe told Jed, "as well as your wife Martha and child. Why don't you come with us?"

Jed and Martha agreed since they could not survive by themselves and had become good friends with Joe and his tribe. Jed told the men in the colony of his decision to stay behind.

"I understand your desire to return to Scotland but we have found a new home here and will remain. If some of you change your mind one day and want to return here we will be here and will welcome you with open arms. I believe there are more colonists arriving to this land every year so you will not be alone."

Jed hugged each of the men and wished them all a safe journey. He wanted to keep Sir Gunn's ship safe and concealed just in case he had need to use it. Before the two ships sailed away, he asked the men to hide it as best they could before sailing.

"I know just the place," responded George, the survivor of Sir Gunn's party. "On our journey to the east we passed a very narrow inlet with huge overhanging branches. We will take it way up the inlet as far as we can and hide it under the tree branches. It will be safe there. Do you think you can find it?" Jed nodded. The crews said goodbye to Jed and Martha, wished them luck, and set sail.

The tribe allied with Joe and his tribe lived about twenty miles to the west. Jed and Martha were indeed welcomed by the Chief after Joe explained that he considered Jed a brother. They lived there several months, and when the time and weather were suitable, and there was a period of peace in the land, Jed and Martha offered to take Joe and a few of his warriors on a journey to sail north to meet Mali and his distant northern tribe. Joe eagerly accepted as did a few of his warriors. Joe was excited about the possibility of learning about another distant tribe and their culture, and perhaps even to develop a trading relationship.

"Mali and his tribe had hoped that I would return one day," Jed explained. "They will be delighted to see us again and I would very much like the two of you to meet."

Jed, Martha, and Jet travelled to the concealed ship accompanied by Joe and his small band of fifteen men and made sure it was still in good shape. They stowed sufficient water for a long trip as well as dried meat, onions, maize and wheat, nuts and berries, eggs and mushrooms, and other food for the journey. Joe and his men stowed gifts of fur skins and other clothing. Jed took a few days to train the braves on handling the ship and they set sail.

They sailed through the gap into the protection of the Cape and then on a direct course to the southern end of New Scotland. Jed and Joe both felt the spring weather should be favorable for sailing directly there. With Jed's and Martha's sea knowledge they completed the journey in the rapid time of just one week. Then they sailed up the eastern coast of New Scotland until they reached Mahone Bay. As Jed approached Mali's camp, the braves along the shore recognized the ship and yelled "Glooscap" repeatedly.

Jed sailed carefully to the same spot Henry had sailed to four years earlier and they dropped anchor. Mali and Sam had thought they would never see Jed and Martha again, and when the familiar sails of Henry's ship appeared, Sam gasped and covered her mouth with her hands. Mali threw his hands up in an exuberant greeting and waved. It was a marvelous reunion and the peace pipe ceremony was performed with great joy.

"You came at a good time," Mali told Jed. "Our war was over a few weeks ago and we have a truce with the other tribe."

Joe presented Mali with gifts as was the custom, and Joe and Mali talked about their tribes and customs and recent adventures. Mali introduced Joe to a couple of senior warriors, Kamji and Memtou, who took him in hand and showed him around the camp, introducing him to other warriors as they went.

Sam came forward toward Martha holding a small baby with brown hair and hazel eyes.

"I see you also have one," she spoke to Martha with a big smile. "We named our son Jedi after your husband. We are so happy you came back to visit us."

Martha told Sam her son was named Jet, and the two mothers went off to recount their lives.

"Will you take me to my father's grave?" Jed asked Mali.

"Of course. As you know we were very sad at the loss of Glooscap. It was a terrible tragedy." He led Jed to the gravesite and Jed placed an ornate sword on Henry's grave which he had found in the treasure hoard. It had the mark of the Templars. There were no words spoken.

During the first few days of the visit they had an opportunity to visit several islands, and even their favorite pools.

"The castle on the hill and the colony are still there," Mali mentioned to Jed. "I believe they are thriving as far as I know. We never see them."

"I should go up there and see how they are doing. My father would have wanted me to check on them."

"I understand." Mali spoke softly. "I'll go with you."

Joe joined them while Martha stayed with Sam. Following Mali, they reached the colony in a few hours. All the men were still there and thriving and they ran to greet Jed when he arrived. Mali and Joe stood to the side and talked.

"My father would be pleased to know you are doing well." Jed spoke to the gathering of Henry's men.

One of them, Archie, spoke for the others. "We are most sorry for the loss of your father. We owe our lives to him."

"The brave that found me said he was a hero but did not explain," Jed said. "What happened?"

"He changed his mind about marching into the wilderness and came up here with his men," Archie said. "He listened to your words and arranged for one of Mali's warriors to teach the art and skill of the native bow and arrow. We learned rapidly but one day we were surprised by an attack from a huge hostile tribe. Without the additional men we would have been slaughtered quickly. Even then we were outnumbered three to one and were under siege. Your father devised a clever plan to counterattack." The man stopped briefly trying to find the right words.

"Please take your time," Jed said gently, "I want to hear everything."

"He left a group of fifteen or twenty men in the tower with all the guns and the Ribaldis. Then he took the rest of the men, all armed with crossbows, and formed two groups, one on either side of the tower. Each group formed a compact line, and as the wave of attackers approached, he yelled, 'Fire!' The crossbows and guns could fire at a much greater distance and cut the attackers down before they could get in range. One group fired and then before the attackers realized it, the other group of crossbows fired a deadly barrage. Then the guns in the tower fired while the men reloaded the crossbows and fired another round from each side. The attacking group was decimated after three rounds and the few remaining retreated." It was silent for a moment.

Jed spoke slowly in a voice one could scarcely hear.

"What happened to my father?"

"He only had a moment to celebrate the victory. Sadly, one wounded brave launched an arrow before any of us could warn Henry. He was mortally wounded."

Another man stepped forward. "His last words were of you, Jed. He said 'tell Jed he was right. Tell him I love him.' Then he expired."

The first man continued. "We carried him down to the village. He was given a traditional burial ceremony." The man paused. "You may not know but he planned to return with the ship to Scotland. He said he wanted to bring back more settlers to join us. He never made it. The ship sailed the next day to report the sad news to his home."

There was a long moment of silence. Then Jed told them the story of their trip down south and they were solemn when they learned of the loss of Sir Gunn and the other men. The three of them then returned to the village.

The visit with Mali and his tribe lasted four weeks, and during that time the braves exchanged information about their cultures and played some of their common games. There was lots of fun and laughter, and Jed and Martha watched the joy and camaraderie unfold. Finally Jed and Joe decided it was time to return. Jed told Mali they would try to visit again one day.

The next day Jed, Joe, Martha and Joe's braves said goodbye. Jed and Martha hugged Mali and Sam, and they set sail. As they moved slowly out of the Bay, the cries of "Glooscap" echoed across the water. The party sailed south and returned home without incident or bad weather.

Joe and his tribe decided to move further west and Jed, Martha, and Jet went with them. They lived happily and peacefully in the west for many years. Jed built a stone house with a wooden roof for his family to live in and together they developed a thriving farm.

One day Jed pulled out the Merovingian scrolls and the Egyptian scroll he had always kept with him. He reviewed their significance with Martha, and showed her the mark of Dagobert which indicated its originality and said if something happened to him she should guard them with her life. She in turn produced the goblet she had retrieved from the treasure chest and gave it to him.

"I think we should bury them in a safe place," Martha suggested. "One day we should show them to our children when they are older."

"Our children?" Jed teased. "We plan to have more than one?"

"I think it is pretty certain," Martha smiled. "Don't you think so?"

"Yes." Jed became serious for a moment. "Eventually Jet and our other children," he paused briefly and elicited a smile from Martha, "will learn of their importance and inherit them. I have created a crevice in the foundation just for this purpose. I will bury them carefully and seal it up."

Martha nodded her understanding and nothing more was spoken about the scrolls or the goblet.

CHAPTER FIFTY FIVE

The Death of Clotaire

Scotland, Britannia and Francia
756 AD to 771 AD

Jeb turned away from Magda and walked quickly into the night, hiding his own tears. Jerry was asleep, huddled under furs. Jeb headed south toward the sea and their boat. He traveled lightly, carrying a waterproof deerskin sack he could sleep in even when it rained, a day's water supply in a bag of boar's skin which Magda had made, and carried dried deer meat, and a small amount of hard cheese. He found nuts and berries as he traveled.

Jeb stopped by Medcaut on his way, in order to say goodbye to the Abbot before he started his long journey in search of Clotaire. He was surprised and delighted when the Abbot said he would go as far as Glestingaburg with Jeb. The Abbot said he wanted to free the Abbey of the evil that had taken over there.

They traveled very quickly, stopping only twice at monasteries along the way. They gathered a large group of followers from these monasteries who supported what the Abbot intended, which was to roust the followers of the dead Abbot that had imprisoned him. They reached the Abbey in a few weeks. Together they entered and wrested control from the allies of the evil Abbot, then found the large number of monks that had gone into hiding.

Jeb left the Abbot in Glestingaburg and carried on south to the hidden boat. It was still in good shape and had weathered the elements well. The "oven" was also in good shape, so he hunted, stocked up on dried meat and roots, nuts and berries, and water. Jeb was delighted to find he'd not lost his sailing touch. He found favorable winds and sailed in a direct line to Francia, landing on the coast just south of Bononia. He was feeling very confident and spent some time hunting for deer, boar, rabbits, and grouse, then cooked and dried them. Then he hid the boat in a remote thicket of firethorn and hawthorn bushes.

On the outskirts of Bononia he found a stable and traded some of his supply of meat for a horse, saddle, and saddle bags. He also traded for clothes to disguise himself as a lone hunter wanderer.

He first rode west to the castle at Stenay, approached cautiously, and found it deserted. It was desolate and looked as Clotaire had described it after the massacre of his men, although now it was overgrown with tall grass and vines that crept up and covered some of the walls. He found rusty weapons strewn around in the heavy growth. Jeb did not think it had been inhabited since the slaughter. He then went to Romille's farm. She was delighted to see him again.

"My, how you have grown, Jeb," she blurted out. "I hardly recognize you." Jeb hugged her and did the same to Tulca when he came home. They gave Jeb a wonderful meal of mutton, bread, turnips, carrots, onions, and mushrooms. The vegetables were cooked in beer. He remembered all of these vegetables and the meat from before but this time he was offered a big mug of beer.

After listening to Jeb tell of his travels, Tulca said they had seen Clotaire once when he returned the adze he had borrowed, but not since. Romille said she thought he had been on his way to the farm of his kinsman Clothilde. Jeb said he remembered Sarah as well. After resting during the day and feeding his horse, Jeb headed south to the farm of Sarah and Clothilde where he was greeted in much the same way as he had been with Romille and Tulca. Sarah was just as jolly as she was before. They were delighted to see how much older and mature Jeb was. They fed him a similar meal of mutton, turnips, carrots, onions, and parsnips, as well as a mug of beer. Jeb remembered how he and Magda had carried out mugs of beer to the men who had been looking after them. He smiled in recollection.

Again the news about Clotaire was the same: they had seen him only one other time and they were fairly certain he was headed south. Jeb guessed he must have been trying to find other Merovingians around Rhédae. After giving them both a big hug, Jeb rode steadily south. He covered the distance rapidly and had sufficient food and water for the few nights it took. He rested briefly in remote dense thickets of nettle trees, yews, and junipers. He stopped north of Rhédae, tethered his horse in an isolated field, and walked slowly toward the city. He was still in disguise as the rough hunter.

Jeb had a hunch about the whereabouts of Clotaire and searched for the deep cave where he had found Magda. He waited in brush nearby to see if it was in use. After three hours, a slight crackle sounded in the forest, and Jeb kneeled, straining to hear more. A deep-throated human murmur came to his ears. He reached for his dagger and waited. The noise became louder and a group of men led by Clotaire entered the clearing in front of the cave. From in hiding Jeb called out.

"Clotaire, the boat is only made to cross one time."

The men were startled and raised their bows and arrows. Clotaire motioned to lower them. "All right, Jeb. You have proved your worthiness. You can come out."

He and Clotaire hugged in a strong embrace.

"I see you have used the boat more than once, Jeb. I hardly recognize you now. Come join us and meet the others and have a good meal. I assume by now you will join us with a mug of beer."

He asked about Magda and Jeb brought him up to date, telling him about the Abbot and Glestingaburg and the journey north. When it was clear to Clotaire that Jeb had come to help, Clotaire described the situation in the south. He told him the sad news about the death of his father and of many Merovingians but he was optimistic about gathering a force to counter the terrible and evil forces still in control. Jeb was introduced to the several dozen Merovingians Clotaire had gathered under his leadership and was treated as a full-fledged warrior.

Over the course of the next several years Jeb helped Clotaire build up his Merovingian force to several hundred men. Most of them were excellent archers and skilled in hand to hand combat as well. Clotaire was able to drive out the forces of Pepin, who had usurped Jeb's father, and retake the castle at Rhédae but this only lasted for a short time. He had to retreat when reinforcements arrived.

From then on, Clotaire had to resort to guerrilla tactics because he was usually outnumbered. This type of warfare went on for many years and, during this time, Jeb grew in strength, skill, and stature, and was considered a great warrior second only to Clotaire.

And then, in a skirmish on the outskirts of Rhédae, a terrible tragedy occurred: Clotaire was mortally wounded. As he lay dying, Jeb came to his side and Clotaire whispered to him.

"Jeb," Clotaire gasped, "it has been an honor to know you and to teach you. I must now leave this world. It may be the end of the Merovingians but not for the Cross. Protect it."

"Clotaire," Jeb sobbed, "you have always been my idol. I love you."

Clotaire squeezed Jeb's hand and then reached the end of his life.

He was buried high in the hills. Jeb and the others withdrew to the caves where they all agreed to mount one last campaign. On an open plain they attacked a much larger force, out flanked them, and cut them to pieces. Most of the enemy were killed or wounded but Jeb's forces lost many warriors as well. They no longer had sufficient men to continue a prolonged fight. They therefore disbanded. They had won the battle but lost the war. Now, they disappeared into the homes of their kin all across the land.

It was time for Jeb to return to his home far away. He again traveled in disguise on his sturdy horse with enough food and water for the journey. He followed the old Roman roads, still visible but overgrown with wild thyme, mint, and brambles. He traveled east along the Via Domitia until he came to the Via Agrippa, headed straight north to the old hub at Lugdunum, and then it started to rain. Jeb pulled out a waterproof cloak made of deerskin that Clotaire had given to him. As it became a downpour, he reached an old abandoned mansione on the outskirts of Lugdunum, and waited out the storm. When it cleared, he continued on to Bononia and to his boat. It was well hidden and had been kept dry, so that it was still in good shape after all these many years. It was covered over with the growth of time, but he removed the vines of jasmine, blackberry, and thyme, did some minor repairs, and launched it on the familiar route across the sea to his old hiding place.

Clotaire was wrong about one thing: this boat did not take just the one trip across the sea. Jeb was thankful Clotaire had built such a sturdy boat and a fast one as well.

In his disguise as a hunter, Jeb acquired considerable amounts of dried meat and hides which he traded again for a horse. He stayed in disguise and this time used some of the old Roman roads still scattered across Britannia. It had been fifteen years since he left. He rode to the farm and entered the farmhouse where Magda had just finished her work for the day. She was thirty years old and more beautiful than ever. She did not recognize him at first but when she heard him call "Magda" she knew immediately it was Jeb and rushed to embrace him. No words were spoken. They simply stayed in each other's arms.

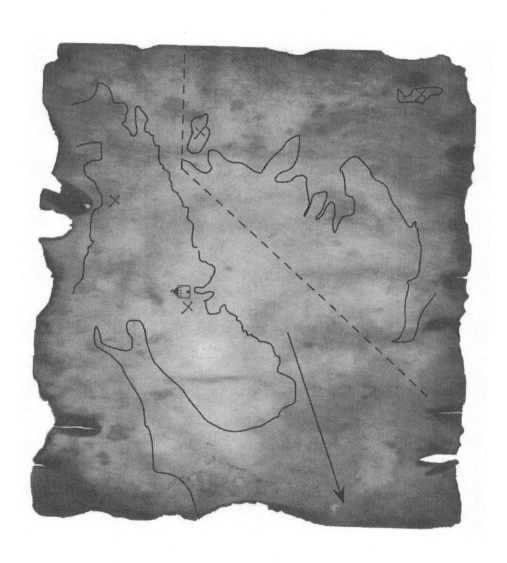

CHAPTER FIFTY SIX

Map and Scrolls

Mahone Bay, Nova Scotia
Summer, 1953 – Early, 1955

After Jes saved him from drowning, the black bearded man underwent a complete transformation. He recovered the bodies of his two cohorts, gave them a proper burial, and stopped his persecution of Jes and Marya. Before he left Mahone Bay, he visited them.

"Only my dead companions and I knew where you were. You saved my life and I want you to know that I will put out a false trail for my organization so that you can relax and not worry about being tracked. I don't know what they will do to me or what they might do in the future but I owe you this much."

. Jes was surprised at this complete turnaround and asked Grandfather why the man would do this and why he was so shocked at being saved.

Grandfather said, "He and the organization he was part of lived by a different set of standards than you and Marya do. He considered you an enemy because your existence and that of the Merovingian Cross posed a threat to the legitimacy of the Church, and therefore to his secret organization. He was sent to kill the two of you or possibly capture you to find out what you knew, and to find the scrolls."

"If he just wants the scrolls, why would he kill us?" Jes asked.

"He assumed you considered him an enemy as well and would kill him if you had the chance. But he forgot that your beliefs would lead you to save a fellow human being, not kill him. When he realized this, he was probably amazed and overcome that an enemy such as you who he was trying to capture or kill on behalf of his immoral organization would spare his life. He knew that he certainly would not have spared yours in similar circumstances. There is good in everyone and you touched the good in him."

"I never thought of Jes as a real Christian," interjected Marya, "he never goes to church."

"It's not going to church that is important," explained Grandfather, "nor are all the rituals and clothing and other symbols of power and authority. The Cathars recognized that the Church had become morally and politically profane, that it sought money and power, that it espoused antediluvian ideas and principles and, worst of all, it used its influence to control and use people more than it ever helped them. In short, it did not follow the teachings and values of the true Christian ideals."

"What do the Cathars have to do with the black bearded man?" Jes was perplexed.

"The organization behind him was formed at the time of the Cathars and Templars and is still in existence to this day. Destroying evidence of the bloodline, finding the treasure, and the relentless pursuit of those incriminating documents and scrolls continue to be the goals of this shadow organization." There was a long silence while Marya and Jes took this in.

"So Jes showed true Christian values by sparing the life of the black bearded man?" summarized Marya.

"Indeed," confirmed Grandfather. "This act by Jes was so unexpected, and so truly Christian, that it caused the man to abandon any idea of harming Jes. Saving the life of one who has been trying to kill you was so alien to the values of the black bearded man and the organization he represented that he could hardly comprehend it. He just left."

Jes and Marya and Grandfather moved back into the huge family house. They believed they no longer had to hide, so they became an integral part of the community. But Grandfather never quite got over the feeling that the organization of the black bearded man would find another man to persecute them eventually. He lived an uneasy life with Jes and Marya and one day suggested that Jes should sell the house and find another, less conspicuous place. With some reluctance Jes agreed but they did not buy another house right away. Grandfather found and rented a small cottage nearby just big enough for them, and held it in a fictitious name to avoid being traced.

They lived peacefully for the next two years, often going out to explore the islands, searching for hidden scrolls and buried treasure, without success. Jes and Marya turned 16 ½ and 15 ½ the summer of 1953. They preferred to fish at night because the fishing was better and they could all see well in darkness.

One warm summer night the three of them were on the water, exploring some of the smaller islands and fishing along the shorelines. Late that night they went to their favorite, Mason's Island. Grandfather sat in the boat with his pole and a thermos of warm soup, a wool blanket on his lap, while Jes and Marya explored. It was getting late and he yelled out to them.

"Time to go. There's just enough time to get back. I don't want to be seen out here in daylight."

"Wait," Marya yelled back, "I see something."

She had shined a light far into a small narrow cave and had seen something wrapped up in linen or cloth. She entered and saw an object wedged into a crevice in the back of the dry cave. She was able to get it out and was astounded at what she saw.

"It looks like some sort of map," she called to Jes, who squeezed in behind her. "It was just wedged in there and not buried."

"Look at this," said Jes, as he pointed to a pile of rocks. "That may not be the only thing hidden here. I wonder if something is buried under this pile." He moved the rocks, dug down, uncovered a parchment wrapped in oilskin, and pulled it out. "It's a scroll. I finally found one. Wait! There are two scrolls, rolled together."

"Bring them with you," yelled Grandfather. "We'll look at them in daylight after we get back."

They marked the place with a cairn and returned to the boat, then were so excited they were talking loudly about their discoveries. Grandfather told them to be quiet as they motored through the shoals and rowed the last mile to shore. They hid the boat just as it was becoming daylight. Once inside their secluded cottage, they looked carefully at both the map and the scrolls.

"Jes, these scrolls are copies. They have probably been buried for hundreds of years until you found them."

"How do you know they're copies, Grandfather," asked Marya, "and not originals?"

"Just a minute and I'll show you." Grandfather retrieved his knapsack from his room. "These are the original scrolls," explained Grandfather, as he produced an old scroll and a set of rolled up scrolls from the knapsack. "I apologize for keeping this a secret but I didn't want it known that I had found the originals." He unrolled the set.

"If you look carefully at the first one you will see the mark of Dagobert on the back of this original. The copy is a very good one. When you compare them you cannot tell the difference. Whoever made the copy did a fantastic job."

"What are all the other scrolls?" Marya asked.

"They are the updates made over many generations. Our ancestors were wonderful. They were true to the Cross and their heritage. It seems they did a complete job of documenting the bloodline."

"How come the map was in the same cave as the scroll? It's kind of strange," asked Jes.

"I can only guess that two people both thought the cave was an excellent hiding place," answered Grandfather, "and the second one put the map in the crevice after the scrolls were buried."

"It looks as if some treasure is buried on Ross Hill," said Marya, as she scrutinized the map, "under something that looks like a castle." Her voice rose in excitement, "so there must have been a castle where the ruins are on Ross Hill!" She continued, "The map also shows treasure buried in the north near Pictou Harbor at Stellarton but it seems kind of vague as if the mapmaker was not sure where. There is also an arrow pointing down south but it's also vague. And then there are two more strange things: it shows Oak Island but it isn't specific; then it points out to the area around Mason but it doesn't say where. It certainly is a strange map. Could there be five different locations where there is treasure buried? I've always thought there was treasure buried on Oak Island and also on Mason Island."

"I think the scrolls are much more valuable than any of the treasure," offered Jes, "especially with that scroll from Egypt. Lots of people would love to get their hands on it. What are you going to do with it, Grandfather?"

"Jes," Marya interrupted, "we should put the copies of the scrolls and the map back in the cave and bury them deep. As long as we have them, I don't think we can sleep in peace and live a normal life."

"What do you think, Grandfather?" Jes turned to him, "Is Marya right?"

He took a long time to answer. "She is probably right, except at this point no one knows you have found the scrolls or that a map even exists. It's strictly a matter of your own peace of mind. Frankly, I don't see the difference whether you bury them or keep them somewhere safe. You still know where they are, so you should do what you think right."

"You didn't answer, Grandfather," repeated Jes. "What are you going to do with the set of scrolls and the original Merovingian scroll and the Egyptian scroll? Is that also the original?"

"I believe it is since it was with the scroll that Dagobert hid," he replied. "Furthermore, I have kept another secret and I will show you." Grandfather reached again into the knapsack and removed a silver goblet. He unwrapped it. In the dim light, its shine was soft, like the inside of an oyster shell. Marya reached out a hand to touch its molded and sculpted sides.

"I believe this is a very important goblet or chalice that was kept with all the scrolls. It is extremely old." He paused and continued in a low voice, "and I believe it is probably sacred and holy. I can only guess at its significance but I believe it tells a story, along with the original Egyptian scroll."

There was a long silence while Jes and Marya slowly grasped the importance of what they were seeing.

"And to answer your question," he continued, "I plan to leave here soon with the scrolls and the chalice and hide them somewhere where I hope no one will find them, at least for many years. I don't know when or if I will return."

"Oh, Grandfather," Marya cried. "Why? Why do you have to leave us?"

"You always come back when you go away." Jes was holding back tears.

"It's time to leave you two on your own. And this is something I must do." Grandfather spoke firmly. They were silent for a moment until Marya spoke up.

"Did you ever think of destroying them, Grandfather?"

"Never," he replied vehemently. "They are definitive proof of the history and progression of the Merovingian Cross from the time of Mary and Sarah to the present. I just don't think the world is ready to deal with the implications of this. And who knows what the future will bring since the Merovingian Cross lives on."

"When will you leave, Grandfather?" asked Marya in a subdued voice.

"As soon as I see the two of you married," he answered. "As Jes said, it's the Christian thing to do."

"It really isn't necessary, though," put in Jes.

"It will be all right with me," replied Marya.

Jes and Marya were married the next day. They wrote their own vows, and spoke them at their ceremony, which was presided over by Grandfather. They were married at the north end of Mason's Island on the edge of the lake, more than half a mile north of the cave where they had found the scrolls and map. It was a lovely ceremony on a beautiful day. There was no church of any kind involved. They had a few friends with them from Mahone Bay.

After the ceremony, Grandfather put his arms around Marya and Jed, and gave Marya a kiss on the cheek.

"I am going to leave tomorrow. No tears. I have my job to do and I don't need to stay here any longer. It's better. The two of you will be fine without me but I suggest you continue to be on your guard just in case some strangers come looking for you. Meanwhile, I have some traveling I want to do, no, that I need to do."

"We will miss you, Grandfather," said Marya. "Please come back."

Grandfather drove away the day after that in his old yellow car. As he disappeared down the road, Jed could not stop the tears and Marya also shed copious tears and did not try to stop them. They hugged each other and spoke no words. They each in their own way had developed a very strong love for Grandfather and they knew how much he loved each of them.

"Do you think he will come back, Jes?"

"I think so. I hope so but I don't really know." They clung together for some time and wiped away the tears.

Two years passed and Jes turned eighteen and Marya seventeen. They'd had a daughter a year before who they named Maeve. She had striking red hair and blue eyes that seemed never to miss anything. She had the Merovingian Cross from birth and no one tried to hide it. As Grandfather had said, the Merovingian Cross lives on and who knows what the future will bring. Jes and Marya found another hiding place in a cave on an island for the copies of the scrolls and map. They did not see any suspicious strangers but lived a circumspect life. They heeded Grandfather's advice and tried to be as unobtrusive as possible. During this time they did not seek out the treasure buried on Ross Hill or the other locations on the map, nor did they talk about the scrolls or map. They had agreed that to search would probably be a waste of time, and would only keep them thinking about "what if" and never about what they had.

But one day Marya broached the subject.

"Jes, I've been thinking. Grandfather has the original scrolls and it's the proper thing to leave the copies where we buried them. But the map and treasure still haunt me. We should at least try to find part of it."

"I found the scrolls but you always did want to find some treasure. What about Ross Hill?" he said. "We can't easily look in the other places, especially since the map is pretty vague, but we can drive up there."

"Oh, Jes. Let's do it. Let's go there one night with Maeve. She'll think it's a great adventure."

"So will you. It's wonderful to see you getting so excited."

Even though they both had great night vision they waited for a full moon. Marya said it would seem more haunting with a moon. They searched until they found the area indicated by the map and saw the outline of a circular stone pattern at ground level of what could have been the foundation of the castle. Grass and shrubs had grown up around the round shape but the pattern seem to suppress growth. Marya's joy and excitement disappeared and she became crestfallen.

"Jes, it was an exciting idea, but if there is buried treasure, it is way belowground and we'll never dig it up."

"Well, then I don't think anyone else has either. Look at Maeve. She's having fun."

Maeve was giggling and running around in the moonlight. Marya smiled and held Jes's hand.

"Let's go home."

CHAPTER FIFTY SEVEN

Sarah and Alaric

Rhédae
Summer, 44 AD

Sarah was now thirteen and a half and Alaric fourteen. After swimming in the slow moving current at the edge of the river, they sat on the bank in the midst of overhanging willow trees shielded from view. The water from their long hair dribbled down their shoulders and backs. They dried off in the noonday sun. It was silent except for the chirping of a pair of sparrows. Sarah lay back on the soft grass and looked up at the clear sky.

"It's so peaceful here, Alaric. I could fall asleep in the warm sun."

"So could I," he whispered. A soft wind blew through the willow branches. "Sarah, you are so beautiful lying there in the sun."

She turned to face him and smiled. "So are you, Alaric." They were quiet for a moment.

"Sarah, we need to decide what we are going to do. Where should we go?"

"I think we should go hide up in the deep cavern on the hill and make a plan," she decided and Alaric agreed.

"Let's go put together a pack," Alaric suggested. "I'll meet you back here at dusk. And find what food you can." They went separately to their dwellings.

When Sarah returned to the hut she shared with Mary, Joshua and Lazarus, she was told that Lazarus was very sick.

"How sick is he?" Sarah asked.

"Very. He might not survive this illness," Mary said. "We don't know what it is."

Joshua came to join them and Sarah ran to hug him. She stifled a sob.

"I think his spirit is broken," Joshua said to the two of them. "I don't think he wants to live anymore. The mind is a powerful thing and when it gives up, the body does also."

Sarah ran in to an inner room to see Lazarus and bent down and hugged him. It was dark in the windowless shack, and the air was oppressive. He responded weakly by putting an arm around her.

"Don't grieve for me, Sarah," Lazarus whispered. "It's time for me to go."

"It's never time!" Sarah was quiet but vehement. As she looked into his eyes, Lazarus's gaze clouded, and he lapsed into unconsciousness and stopped breathing. Sarah wailed. Mary and Joshua came running. Mary closed Lazarus's eyes with her palm, and Joshua bowed his head. Sarah knelt in the dark, clutching the dead man's robe.

They buried Lazarus wrapped in cloth in a small cave with a rock rolled in front of the opening. Sarah went to find Alaric. She said it was too early for them to run away but promised him they would do so in the next couple of days. They agreed on the time they would meet. At home, Sarah quietly packed her rug, an extra set of clothes, a little dried meat, and bread she thought would not be missed. She hid her sack, and when dusk arrived two nights later, stole silently away to the river to meet Alaric. He was already there and they walked quietly up into the hills toward the large cavern. As they approached in the dark it started to rain, soon becoming a downpour. They were sopping wet by the time they entered the cave. They dried off, curled up on their rugs covered with cloaks, listened to the sound of rain falling, and slept fitfully. They woke at dawn. Listening to the sounds of sparrows and thrushes outside the cave's entrance, they ate some of the meat and some bread Alaric had brought.

Just after Mary and Joshua awoke, Alaric's father, the blacksmith, came knocking.

"Alaric's gone," he blurted out. "I think he ran away. He has been behaving strangely lately. Where's your Sarah?"

Mary rushed to look for her and came running back. She could scarcely speak.

"She's gone too," Mary whispered. "Joshua, where are they?"

"I have an idea," he spoke calmly. "We will find them."

"And I have very bad news, Mary," the blacksmith interjected. "That old malicious woman, your former friend, has betrayed you and spread lies and rumors that have reached the Roman authorities. The word is that they will come today to arrest you. They will probably charge you with treason or some trumped up charge. You must leave immediately."

Joshua thanked him and quickly packed up a few things for Mary and himself. He led her away toward the mountains. She was confused. She said they should find Sarah. She seemed to have no concern for her own danger. Mary wasn't herself. He held her hand, and did not let her leave his side. They made their way slowly up into the hills.

"Mary, I don't want to leave you alone in this state so you must come with me. I think I know where to find Sarah." Mary nodded and followed him. Joshua went very slowly, holding Mary by the hand. They climbed until Joshua approached a large cavern and hid himself and Mary in a nearby small thicket of juniper. Very soon, they observed Alaric come to the entrance of the cave. Joshua stepped out and revealed himself.

"Are you and Sarah enjoying your new home?" he said.

Alaric smiled and knew there was no point in trying to hide or run away again. Sarah emerged and Joshua explained Mary's situation and pointed out that they were not the only ones running away. Sarah hugged her mother and said she was sorry. Mary visibly changed and was more like her old self. She forgave her daughter.

Joshua took them back down the mountain and they hiked for a couple of days in the direction of the river where they had hidden the boat. They came to the river bank, found the boat, which was still carefully protected, prepared it, and launched it. Joshua decided to sail back down to the sea. When he reached the mouth of the Tet he sailed back up the coast to a river that was wide at first and then narrowed. He found a secluded spot where they camped in the brush after hiding the boat. When it became dark and the rain started he set up their tent. It was crowded for four of them but they managed for a few hours until it let up. None of them were very hungry but they ate a little meat and bread nonetheless. Joshua talked about the options they had: they could seek another land and leave behind all of their friends and family, or they could go back and do the best they could with the situation. There was no answer.

"We'll discuss it in the morning," he said, "but personally I believe it's better to face one's problems rather than run from them."

Meanwhile, Alaric's father wanted to find them and tell them the news about the woman who had betrayed Mary and Lazarus. She in turn had been betrayed by someone that knew her history from Massalia. She had led a ring of thieves who stole valuable jewelry and sold it in the underground market. Now she had been arrested and jailed and it was rumored that she would probably hang for her deeds.

In the morning everyone agreed with Joshua that they should return and face their problems, and they began sailing back up the Tet. They did not go home directly but instead went to Alaric's home. His father welcomed them with open arms and told them what had transpired. Mary decided it was still a good idea to stay out of sight for a few days so she went to live in the cavern in the hills.

Before she left she came to Sarah and handed her the scroll she always kept with her.

"It is now yours, Sarah, to look after and to protect at all costs." Mary spoke solemnly. "And to update and to pass on to future generations. Take care of it."

"I will Mama," Sarah responded and tucked it away under her cloak.

Before Mary left for the mountain cave, Joshua came to her and said he would join her soon.

"But first I have a duty I must perform."

"Does it have to do with Lazarus?" He nodded.

After Mary left, Sarah stayed with Alaric and his family. Before he joined Mary, Joshua went to the tomb of Lazarus, rolled away the stone and called to him to rise and come forth. Lazarus walked out and was completely recovered. He had no recollection of events after he lay sick in the dark room. Joshua blessed him and told him to live in the house of Mary'

"I will join Mary in the hills. We will return one day." Joshua climbed up to join Mary in the mountains.

Some months went by and eventually Mary and Joshua felt it was safe enough to return to their home and join Lazarus. Sarah was overjoyed that her mother and father came back to their home nearby but she was content to stay with Alaric and his family, and did so for several years. In the summer of 47 AD, when Alaric turned seventeen and she was sixteen and a half, they went to Joshua and Mary.

"Father," Sarah addressed Joshua. "Alaric will be going off to join a group of fighting men next year and we want your blessing and that of my mother to marry before he goes. I will be seventeen at the end of the year and I am ready to be his wife."

"I love Sarah very much and I promise to be a good husband." Alaric spoke softly but firmly. "And I know what you are thinking. I will not be a good husband if I am killed but I am smart and will not be."

"You read my mind, Alaric," Joshua responded with a smile, "something rarely done. I believe you will be correct. Mary and I give our blessing." Mary nodded and stood behind Joshua with her hand on his shoulder.

Alaric and Sarah went to his parents and asked for their blessing. They were not surprised and had been expecting the two of them to marry one day. Sarah had grown into a beautiful young woman with long black hair and no longer asked her mother if she would look like her. Alaric was a tall strikingly handsome man with long blonde hair.

Just before the end of the year on December twenty-fifth, when Sarah was seventeen, the beginning of a fierce winter storm covered the landscape with several feet of snow and the strong winds piled drifts against the sides of the houses and rattled the windows. Inside the house of Mary and Joshua it was warm with a crackling fire and they had a sumptuous feast of wild boar, pheasant, parsnips, onions, carrots, nuts, and berries. Sarah and Alaric exchanged vows in the presence of Alaric's parents, and Mary, Joshua, and Lazarus. They went into the mountains for a week and returned to live for a time in the home of Alaric's family.

Alaric did indeed leave the next year to join a group of men, and within two years became the leader of several thousand skilled soldiers. They fought and won many battles, and Alaric was not killed in battle as he and Joshua predicted.

Sarah and Alaric had many children, and both lived to a very old age. Their children and grandchildren were ancestors of not only the Merovingians, but also the Visigoths.

CHAPTER FIFTY EIGHT

First Grandchild

Scotland
Summer, 771 AD

Jeb held Magda for a very long time and finally released her with tears in his eyes. He told her that he had found their savior, their mentor Clotaire and had helped him build a force of the remaining Merovingians, but then he told her about Clotaire's end. They had both loved him and Magda was silent when Jeb told her about his death.

"He did his best to gather a force of Merovingians but they never had enough men to really win a major war," Jeb said. "The men, and especially Clotaire, were magnificent warriors but it seemed as if they were always outnumbered. There are many Merovingian graves from the southern sea to the northern sea."

He told her about all the many Merovingian tombs he saw in Bononia before he found the boat and sailed across the sea. This last part of his brief story about his travels seemed to make him dejected. He fell silent and appeared to be lost in thought. Magda felt he was just lost and down in spirit and decided she needed to bring him out of his melancholy.

"I have someone for you to meet." Magda said. "Jerry?" she called and a grown man of eighteen entered from a back room. He approached slowly with downcast eyes. "You have arrived just in time. He and Maddy are to be married tomorrow."

It was a little bit awkward at first but Jerry and Jeb hugged each other. Then a vision of beauty appeared. It was Maddy, who was now a lovely young lady almost the same age as Jerry. Her long red hair tumbled down to her waist and her blue eyes seemed to twinkle like stars. She stepped forward and gave Jeb a brief hug. And Jerry put his arm around her.

"We were too young to remember you," Maddy stated, "but do you remember us?"

"Yes indeed," Jeb answered, "as young happy children, and I have had the two of you and Magda and your mother in my mind all the time. It has been what has kept me going."

"My mother passed away two years ago," Maddy spoke softly with downcast eyes. "There are just the three of us now."

"I'm sorry," Jeb responded and gave her a brief hug.

They sat at the table and Jeb told Magda happier details of his travels. She in turn told him about the success of their farm and how Jerry and Maddy had grown up under the tutelage of the monks and been educated by them. Jeb noticed Jerry had a perplexed look on his face but dismissed it as he listened to Magda. Maddy took Jerry's arm and pulled him away. She said they had to visit someone but would return.

After they left, Magda broke down in tears. He put his arm around her to comfort her.

"What's wrong, Magda?" Jeb was confused.

"The truth is, Jeb," Magda said through her tears, "things are not all right. It has not always been successful. It is a struggle night and day. I did not want to say this in front of Jerry and Maddy, but since you left, we have barely survived. Susannah and I have raised the two children as best we could and tried to make a living with the farm but it has been very hard. Look around you. The house needs lots of work. It is becoming dilapidated. We need a barn and a storage building for crops, and we have wanted to raise animals but have not had the money. We did not know what else to do but keep going. And then when Susannah died, well, that was almost the last straw. Jerry and Maddy have been great but they need to lead their own life." Magda started sobbing.

"I'm so sorry, Magda," Jeb said, as he held her in his arms. "I never should have left but I will try to put things right."

They talked more about what they might do and Magda began to feel better. They held the wedding the next day and they made it a joyous occasion. Jerry and Maddy left on a short honeymoon and Jeb and Magda started working with common purpose. They planted winter crops, Jeb built a barn and grew hay, Magda set up a weekly market to sell crops and that led to more customers coming by for vegetables. Jeb worked on the house, which needed many repairs, and then he built a storage shed for crops, for drying corn, and holding produce for sale. Finally they acquired a horse and several cows and a dozen chickens and even a couple of lambs. They approached winter feeling much more secure about the farm. Magda even began to talk about acquiring more land and building a stone house. Their house had a small stone foundation but otherwise was all wood with a thatched roof.

Winter arrived and they watched the snow come down and slowly bury the land in a winter wonderland. They had a fire going to keep warm and enough food to eat and even some beer that Jeb had learned how to make from the monks. *Life is good*, thought Magda. They had made enough money from the sale of crops so that Jeb began to look for land north of where they lived.

He found some fertile acreage for sale five miles north of them and acquired it for a modest sum. When the weather permitted he worked on the stone foundation and gradually built a farmhouse of stone that nestled in a protected valley with lots of oak, maple, ash, and cherry trees. The stone walls rose ten feet, and by end of winter, he had put a thatched roof on it. It was a cozy yet spacious farmhouse with a main room and huge fireplace. Jeb had the help of a local stonemason to build the fireplace of beautiful stone they found nearby. In exchange for his labor Jeb gave him a good supply of food from their storage. The farmhouse had two separate bedrooms, a kitchen, and pantry off the main room. It was a lovely home for Magda and she was eager to move there.

As soon as winter let up Magda and Jeb planted root crops, and early crops such as corn and peas on the new land. Meanwhile Jeb started work on a barn and other buildings. He received help for a couple of months from Jerry. Maddy and Jerry stayed with them until they could acquire their own home. With their help they completed Jeb's new buildings and had their first crops from the winter available in Magda's home market.

When spring arrived they were ready to move to their new home and Maddy and Jerry moved into their old house. That year was a very prosperous one for them. By the end of summer Jeb expanded the farm and added more animals, including pigs and goats. They built up a thriving farm.

And then when fall arrived, Maddy and Jerry had wonderful news. They announced they were going to have a baby. Jerry had a satisfied look on his face but Maddy was beaming as she told Jeb and Magda.

Shortly after that, they received grave news. One chilly fall day, the Abbot paid an unexpected visit. They were surprised to see him, since as far as they knew he was still at Glestingaburg. He had a somber look as he arrived.

"It's good to see you again, sir." Magda said as she welcomed him.

"When did you return from Glestingaburg?" Jeb asked. "We are surprised but happy to see you."

"My work is done down there but it seems I am needed at Medcaut," the Abbot explained. "There are strong indications there that they will face a major invasion in the next few years from the northeast countries. There have already been a few small attacks on the coast north of them and the Holy Island is a prime target. Many of the people there have already fled south along the coast and a few have gone inland."

"We haven't seen any people coming through," said Magda.

"You are probably far enough inland for now," he replied. "But keep your eyes open for signs. There have also been predictions of huge storms and lightning coming from the east and even some dire warnings about famine and strange things that cannot be believed."

"Like what?" asked Jeb.

"Dragons, if you can believe that."

"No, I can't," said Magda. "But famine is always something to be concerned about."

Magda and Jeb gave the Abbot a mug of beer and a warm meal of mutton, turnips, carrots, onions, and parsnips, as well as fresh bread. He remarked that it was a lovely meal.

"I see that you have done well on your farm. Is this your lamb?" He pointed to the meat.

"Yes," said Magda. "It is good, isn't it?" He nodded.

"Magda has had good success selling lamb and chickens and eggs and the many vegetables we grow," Jeb explained and praised her. "People come from miles around. Her reputation has spread."

"And it helps that my prices are quite reasonable," she added with a smile.

The Abbot left and Magda told Jeb that they should take what the Abbot said very seriously and stock up on food. He built an extension to the barn to store hay and added another smaller storage shed. He finished just as the cold winds and heavy snow of winter descended upon them. They were prepared for a very harsh winter with food and firewood and all the buildings in grand shape.

One day, sitting by the fire, Jeb had an idea to share with Magda.

"After the winter, how would you like to hike north with me? According to the Abbot, it's only twenty miles or so from here to the waterway coming in from the sea. Jerry and Maddy can look after things for a few days."

"What a lovely idea, Jeb. It would be wonderful to breathe the sea air again. I love the smells and the sounds of the seabirds."

"We'll travel there as soon as spring arrives and the flowers and trees bloom again." He paused. "By the way, where did you hide the scrolls that I gave you before I left to find Clotaire?"

She said she had buried them in a cavity of the old house but had recently retrieved them. She produced them from a pack where she had put them the day before.

"Where are you going to put them?" she asked.

"I made a special hidden compartment in the stone foundation of the new house when I built it, just for that purpose. I created a hollow space and blocked it up temporarily with a loose stone. I got the idea from the secret compartment in the old church in Rhédae where I originally found them." He took the parchment scrolls from her. After he wrapped them in deerskin and hid them in the foundation, he sealed it up and made it look just like the rest of the wall.

The winter was one of the worst they had seen. The snow piled high in huge drifts from the whirling wind and blanketed the fields and bushes and pushed up against the sides of the barn and nearly covered the small sheds. The rare Eagle Owl that sometimes blessed them with its presence sat high in a tree, hunkered down and protected from the storm but keeping an eye open for a small meal. They seldom saw it but heard its booming 'HOO-o' at dawn and dusk. The livestock were nestled in their warm barn, cows and horses in the high middle part, chickens at one end, and pigs, lambs, and goats at the other end. Jeb and Magda had a crackling cozy fire going in the house, while they waited out the savage winter and prepared eagerly for the birth of their first grandchild. Magda thought they were very lucky after all and Jeb agreed.

CHAPTER FIFTY NINE

Next Generation

Southern New England
Summer, 1404 AD

Jed was now eighteen, Martha seventeen, and their son Jet was three. They continued to live in their stone house near Joe, Jed's friend and brother, and Joe's tribe. Joe and his wife Alia had a daughter they named Sarah. She had long black hair down her back and deep dark eyes. She was a year younger than Jet and they played together often and became very good friends.

Jed and Martha also had a daughter, named Magdalene, who was two years younger than Jet. Her long reddish blonde hair hung below her shoulders and she had striking hazel eyes. Joe and Jed and their families managed to sail up to see Mali and Sam every year or so when the weather was good. Mali's son, Jedi, had a sister named Malia who was born about the same time as Magdalene. Malia had lovely straight long black hair that grew down her back as she grew older. Her dark eyes sparkled and her nature was lively and rambunctious. Magdalene and Jet and Sarah got to know young Jedi and Malia on these trips and all five children became good friends.

The years went by and all the families prospered. Joe had become the Chief of a large and growing tribe which was the result of several tribes banding together to protect themselves against invaders from the north that sometimes attacked their territory. Jed often joined the warriors at their request when a select group of them ventured out to the west and north to hunt and explore. They had an awe and respect of Jed because of his skill and humanity and were honored when he joined them. On one such exploration, the group encountered a battle in progress and realized it was a small colony of Europeans that were under siege from a northern tribe. Their compound consisted of a twenty-foot-square wooden building and three ten-foot-square structures surrounded by a ten-foot-stout wooden spiked fence with holes at eye level. The colonists were surrounded and in dire straits. When Joe and Jed and their band of warriors arrived, the battle was broken off and the attacking braves withdrew. Jed stepped forward so the colonists could see him. He called to them in their European language and one of them, the likely leader, beckoned to Jed to approach.

Jed identified himself, and then learned the colonists had been under constant siege and very close to being overcome and slaughtered. The man was called Henry who explained his group consisted of a couple of dozen men and many women and children.

"It appears you are defending yourself with those slow French guns and a few crossbows," Jed said.

"These are all we have," Henry said. "We found out the guns are almost useless and even the crossbows take time to reload compared to the bows and arrows of the attacking braves."

"It looks like you are in trouble."

"We are, but we have no choice but to do the best we can in defending the compound. It has been very difficult and we have barely survived."

"We'll help."

Jed motioned to Joe and his warriors to join them in the compound. After Jed explained his friendship with Joe, Joe suggested to Henry that perhaps he could have a few of his warriors teach Henry and his men the skills of the bow and arrow. While they were talking, the attacking tribe slipped back through the forest and launched another assault. Their force was three times the size of Joe's group so Jed and Joe created a split flanking movement. While Henry and his men took the center with their guns and crossbows, Joe took half of his men quietly around to the left as Jed took the others to the right. As Henry fired a volley, they attacked from both flanks simultaneously and the tribe was overwhelmed and decimated. The few remaining braves limped away and did not return.

Joe sent a couple of his warriors back to inform his tribe that they would return in a few days after they trained the colonists. Joe and Jed taught them how to make the bows and arrows, how to shoot out in the open, to roll and shoot, as well as some of their attack and defense strategies.

The next time the tribe from the north attacked, Henry and his colony surprised them. They used a few guns, but when the attacking tribe lost many braves to an accurate onslaught of arrows, they kept their distance. The colony would not see another attack for many years.

Henry and his wife Constance had a son named Gerald, or Gerry for short. He was about the same age as Jet and had green eyes. His red hair was disheveled and seemingly out of control. Joe and Jed invited Henry, Constance, and Gerry to visit Joe's village. Gerry played with Jet, Sarah, and Magdalene, and they gradually became friends. The three of them and their parents were also invited to visit Henry's compound where they met other children. Gerry's best friend was a boy named Jimmy, nicknamed Jem. He was about a year older than Magdalene and had long brown hair to his shoulders and deep dark brown eyes.

The years went by and the two groups became very close. Jet and Gerry became thirteen, Sarah and Jem twelve, and Magdalene eleven. They all learned to shoot with bows and arrows as Jed and Martha had done years before. One day in the summer of 1414, the five of them ventured to the west and encountered a broad river. They found a small inlet where the swift current created an eddy where they could swim safely. Jet made sure each had a bow and arrows at hand. Sarah told them to be very quiet just in case someone came along.

As they were about to leave the water and dry off before putting on their clothes, Jet motioned them to be silent and still. A group of five older warriors walked by and were startled to see Jet and the others in the water. They all reached for bows and arrows and Jet, Sarah, Jem, and Magdalene got off their arrows and rolled into the water. The arrows struck home. Gerry was a bit slower, his arrow wounded the remaining warrior who returned fire, striking Gerry in the shoulder before he could roll into the water. Jet came up and fired another arrow at the wounded warrior with deadly accuracy. They dragged the five dead warriors into the brush, and fashioned a makeshift stretcher. Jet and Jem carried one end and Sarah and Magdalene carried the other but the going was long and difficult and the green wood they used for the frame slipped through their hands.

When they became exhausted, Jet decided to send Jem and the two girls back to bring help while he guarded Gerry in thick brush. Jet could not resist repeating his mother's stories about how Mali admonished them about the importance of speed and accuracy: *Shoot quickly and don't miss, and roll after shooting.* A couple of hours later Sarah returned with Joe and three warriors. They swiftly hauled Gerry back to the compound where his wound was treated.

Then Jet and Jem took Joe to find the bodies of the five warriors. The battle had happened near the big river that Joe called the Housatonic. He said it was named by one of the many Mahican tribes that lived along it to the north. Joe searched the area and found two canoes up river hidden in brush. Rather than bury the bodies along the river bank, he put them in the two canoes and weighted their bodies to keep them inside and to give weight and speed to the canoes, then launched them away from shore and into the swift current.

"It is better to have them drift out to sea," Joe explained. "The waves will overturn the canoes and they will not be found, only the canoes."

Joe was very concerned about the killing of the warriors because he recognized that they were from a Mohawk tribe west of the river. The Mahicans and Mohawks were often at war. He realized that if the tribe of the missing men suspected the men had been killed by either the Mahicans or the colony it could spark renewed hostilities.

Another year went by without incident but Joe continued to be concerned about the deaths of the five warriors. He sent out a scouting party every day to make sure they were not surprised by an attack. Jed noticed Joe never was relaxed and this incident continued to weigh heavily on him.

One day in the summer of 1415, Jed suggested that they should get away for a time and visit Mali. The families all thought it was a good idea. Before they left Jed and Martha took Jet and Magdalene aside and told them about the crevice he had created in the foundation of the house, and the hidden scrolls and the lovely goblet and their meanings.

"If anything ever happens to the two of us," Martha said, "it will then be your sacred responsibility to guard the scrolls and to update them and to pass them on to successive generations."

Then Jed and his family, and Joe and his family all prepared to sail north to visit Mali and his family. Jet and Magdalene had asked if Gerry could join them and it was agreed. Then Gerry came to Jed.

"Could Jem come with us?" Gerry asked. "He is part of our group."

Jed talked to Jem's father and he thought it would be a fine idea, and thanked Jed for including him.

"You can thank Gerry for bringing it up."

They packed up as much as they could and located the ship which had been moved further west, closer to their dwellings. Jed and Joe trained all five of the children to handle sails and sheets and taught them the navigational terms.

Again they benefitted from good weather and Jed heard the yells of "Glooscap" as the ship approached Mali's camp. It had been a couple of years since they had visited and all the children were growing up. Jet and Jedi, and of course Gerry, were now fourteen and Jedi had followed in his father's footsteps and become an outstanding young warrior. Sarah was a beautiful thirteen and quite mature. She adored Jet but tried not to show it too much, but it was clear also that Jet was fond of Sarah. Jem had become a handsome muscular thirteen and was very shy. Jedi's younger sister Malia and Magdalene were both twelve and good friends. Jet noticed that Magdalene and Jem had been spending a lot of time talking together during the trip.

"I think Jem is smitten with your sister," Sarah whispered one day to Jet. "Do you think she feels the same?"

"I'm not so sure. It's difficult to tell." Jet paused. "Are you smitten with me?"

She poked him and laughed. "You know I am," Sarah smiled, "and you better feel the same or I will pull your ears off."

"I would look pretty funny with no ears." Jet made a face. "So I better give you a hug." It was a very quick hug.

Malia suggested they go to the pools.

"We go there often. My father and mother and your parents used to go there when they were our age. It is our favorite place too."

They all agreed and followed Jedi and Malia through the woods as silently as they could. As they came to the waterfall they noticed a pile of clothes partly hidden and heard voices.

"It sounds like Mother's voice," Malia said. "They must all still like the pools."

The voices stopped suddenly. No one moved.

"They must have heard us," Jedi whispered. "We better move downstream or we will get arrows flying at us."

They moved quickly and quietly downstream to the lower pools that were deep with little current. The water was nearly silent and allowed them to hear the slightest sound. Malia and Magdalene and Sarah quickly dropped their clothes and slid into the water. Jet and Jem quickly followed. Jedi made sure everyone had bows and arrows at hand and went in. Gerry was shy at first but did not want to be the only one staying out so he joined them. They frolicked in the water and cupped and splashed each other without making noise. A soft rain began to fall and the sound of it splattering the leaves was the only noise they heard. Suddenly there was a rustling in the bushes and the seven of them all grabbed bows and arrows. Then they heard laughter. Voices called.

"Don't shoot!" Jed and Martha and Sam and Mali appeared smiling. They were followed by Joe and Alia.

"You made so much noise we heard you but then you did not hear us," Mali said with a small smile. "You need more lessons."

Jedi responded quickly. "But we heard you first at the waterfall. If we had fired our arrows you would not have been able to sneak up on us, would you?"

"You are right," his father acknowledged. "We take it back."

"Nonetheless," Sam put in, "you allowed us to sneak up on you."

"Enough," Martha jumped in. "Let us leave and let them enjoy the pools." The six parents disappeared into the forest.

A short while later Sarah noticed that Gerry and Malia were very close and talking softly to each other. The rain continued as they played and swam in the pool. Jedi held up his hand for silence. They heard a rustling in the bushes. Sarah was not to be fooled.

"We hear you," she called. "You can't trick us. Come on out."

The rustling became louder and suddenly a large brown bear lumbered into the clearing near the edge of the stream where Malia was splashing Gerry. She screamed and startled the bear. It reared up and leaped into the water. Without hesitating Gerry pushed Malia away and put himself in between her and the bear. He tried to be as big as he could and raised his arms but did not move. The bear was six feet from Gerry but stopped and slowly dropped into the shallow water on its forepaws. He just looked at Gerry who remained still and calm. The bear was no longer startled nor was he intent on harm. He finally moved away to the shore and slowly lumbered off stopping once to look back.

Everyone had frozen although Jet and Jedi had produced bows and arrows ready to fire. When the bear was gone, Malia came to Gerry and threw her arms around him and sobbed. The others came over and told Gerry how brave he was and Gerry beamed and then started shaking.

"It's just a delayed reaction, Gerry," Sarah said as she and Malia took him out of the water and wrapped him to get him warm. "It's a bit of shock. You'll be all right in a minute."

Malia stayed with him and put her arm around him while Sarah and the others dried off and got dressed. The rain had stopped by then. Malia and Gerry got dressed and they all headed back to camp. They were quiet for some time.

CHAPTER SIXTY

Passing the Torch

Southern New England
Summer, 1415 AD

The next day, after the encounter with the bear, Sarah and Jet came quietly up to her father, holding hands.

"Father," she began, "we have something to ask you."

"We would like to marry next year," Jet announced.

"We would like you to promise me to Jet according to tradition. Is that the correct thing? Would you?"

Joe listened and smiled and reached to give Sarah a hug.

"You are sure? You have grown quite a bit and I can understand, but are you sure?"

"We are both sure," Jet and Sarah said together.

"When we return to our village. You will be promised."

Sarah hugged her father and then Jet.

"I will be a good wife, Jet," she said, "not like the women in my tribe, a little bit more modern. All right?"

He did not answer but gave her another hug.

Malia had the same idea and talked to her father, with Gerry at her side.

"Gerry and I have known each other for some time, Father, and we are fond of each other. I am coming of age and don't want to be promised to another man."

"Chief Mali, I love Malia and want her to be my wife. I am learning your culture and would like Malia to be promised to me, according to your wishes. I will be a good husband to your daughter."

Mali maintained a very serious demeanor although his voice was soft. He directed his comments to Gerry. "I have seen the two of you together and understand. I have talked to the father of Jet and Magdalene and we have decided to let Malia return with you under his protection. Does your father know of your wishes?"

"Not yet. We wanted to talk to you first, sir."

Mali smiled. "Not necessary. Jed will talk to him on my behalf when he returns. Malia has much to learn about your way of life. If you both still feel the same in a year, I will promise Malia to you. You will wait another year, and in accordance with our customs, will be married here. That may seem like a long time to you but that is my decision."

They nodded their agreement.

Malia was smiling broadly when she told her brother what their father had said.

"I hope it is all right with you, Jedi, if I go to live with Jet and Magdalene for a year. I need to find out if I could be a wife to Gerry in that world."

"It's all right, Malia. But be sure it is the right thing to do."

Sarah and Jet were married a year later in the early summer of 1416. She came to live with him at the farm until they could find a home of their own. Malia lived a year with Martha and Jed, and during that time, spent a lot of time with Henry, Constance, and Gerry in the colony and adapted very well to their way of life.

Sarah was very helpful on that score in telling her some differences between the European and native customs.

"But the differences aren't really that big," Sarah said. "Just be yourself anyway."

"I think I already figured that out. My mother had a European father and she is pretty modern by native standards."

In the summer of that year Jed and Martha sailed up to see Mali and Sam, and Gerry and Malia came with them.

Malia and Gerry then came to Mali and said they wanted to marry as soon as he would give his blessing.

"You are both very sure about this?" Mali looked very stern.

"Yes, Father," Malia replied quietly. "After a year I know I want to be the wife of Gerry." Mali looked at Gerry who spoke without hesitation.

"I love Malia, Chief Mali, and I promise to look after her and protect her. I may still be a little young but I am ready to accept the responsibilities of being a good husband to your daughter." Mali smiled.

"I have talked to Jed and he told me about his conversation with your father, Gerry. As I promised, you and Malia will return with Jed and Martha. Malia is promised to you according to our customs and will live with your family for another year. Both Jed and your father Henry will look after you. At the end of the year you both will return here, and if you both still want to marry, you will be married here under our tribe's tradition."

Malia and Gerry thanked him and Malia hugged her father. They left, and when they were out of sight, jumped for joy. When they returned they shared their news with Sarah and Jet and in turn Sarah presented their own news.

She and Jet announced they were expecting their first child. They were beaming and everyone congratulated them and hugged them. Malia and Gerry told them of the decision of Malia's father and they were hugged and congratulated.

After returning the previous year, Magdalene had spent a great deal of time with Malia at Gerry's family home in the colony compound. Jem often joined them. He turned fourteen in the spring of 1416, and had developed into a tall, muscular young man with very long brown hair to his waist and deep dark brown eyes. One warm day in the spring Malia suggested they swim in a pond half a mile from the compound. They brought bows and arrows as a precaution. Malia dropped her clothes and jumped in the water.

"Come on in," she called quietly. "It's warm."

Magdalene slid in slowly followed by Gerry. Jem was shy but finally joined them. As Magdalene watched his muscular body slide slowly into the water, Magdalene tingled with excitement she had never had before. After that, they spent more time together just talking quietly.

One day Malia whispered to Gerry.

"I think Magdalene is smitten."

"Just like you were when you met me?" Gerry smiled. She poked him and laughed.

In the next few months, Jem and Magdalene spent most of their time together. She turned a very mature thirteen in the summer of 1416. One day during the visit of Gerry and Malia to New Scotland and Malia's home village, Magdalene asked Jem, "Have you had a girlfriend before?"

"No," he replied.

"Am I your girlfriend?" she teased, and smiled.

"You know you are," he said and tickled her.

She giggled and then hugged him.

"Let's go swimming in the river," she said and they quietly hiked to the big river. They dropped their clothes and slid into the chilly water. Although they hid their clothes under a bush and stayed close to shore, they had forgotten one important rule: Always carry bows and arrows with them. They were playing quietly when Jem heard a sound and pushed Magdalene into the bushes just before a group of warriors came along the edge of the river. They were armed and had war paint on. They stopped some distance away to fill up water bags and to eat briefly. Jem took Magdalene by the hand and brought her behind a bush. He retrieved their clothes, they dressed quickly, and took a path away from the warriors. They raced back to Joe and described them.

"Those are Mohawks judging from the war paint you describe," Joe stated tersely. "We must prepare the colonists and send out scouts to see what they are doing."

Joe and his tribe, along with Henry and the colonists, were ready. The scouts reported the Mohawks were approaching stealthily through the woods heading for the compound. When they were in range the colonists, with some guns and crossbows, but mainly native bows and arrows, stood up and shot through the holes in the spiked fences, while Joe and his warriors attacked from the flanks as they had done once before. The result was a rout. Many of the Mohawks were slaughtered and the rest fled.

"Jem," said Joe, "you were courageous in racing back to us without being detected. We would admonish you both for forgetting your bows but in this case it would not have made any difference."

Jed, Martha, Gerry, and Malia returned a few days later and were told of the incident in the river and the attack.

Sharing this narrow escape brought Jem and Magdalene even closer. Malia observed that they seemed inseparable. They still went swimming in the river now and then, sometimes with Gerry and Malia, and always with bows and arrows.

The months went by and winter came with a vengeance. Jet and Sarah had a baby boy with black hair and beautiful dark brown eyes. When Jem turned fifteen and Magdalene fourteen they announced that each had promised themselves to the other but would wait another year before marrying.

"I think that when I am fifteen," Magdalene said to Malia, "I will know if I will be a good wife and Jem will be a good husband." Malia agreed.

In the summer when Gerry was sixteen and Malia fourteen, they returned with Henry and Jed to New Scotland. As always they sailed into the harbor to the cries of "Glooscap!" Malia and Gerry were married on the shores of the Bay and disappeared into the wikuom they had built themselves. At the end of a week the group prepared to sail back to the south. Gerry and Malia had decided to return to Gerry's compound. With much sadness, as they sailed away, Jed and Henry watched Mali wave and turn away. As the cries of "Glooscap" echoed across the water Jed turned to Henry.

"Henry, I have known Mali for many years and that is the first time I have seen him turn away with tears in his eyes."

In the late summer of 1417, Magdalene announced her intentions to her father, and then they both talked to Jem's father. Both fathers agreed to their plan of waiting two years to marry, when Magdalene would be sixteen and Jem seventeen.

During the two years they became increasingly devoted to each other. Magdalene hugged Jem one day and whispered in his ear.

"We're getting to be an old married couple, Jem."

"Not yet, Mag."

On a beautiful warm summer day in 1419, they were married on the shore of the pond where they often swam together. And they did the same as Jet and Sarah, and Gerry and Malia: they built a stone house much like the one Jed and Martha had.

Martha and Jed decided to entrust the scrolls and goblet to Magdalene. She and Jem buried them in a crevice of the new stone house close to the colony's compound. With the arrival of other settlers, the compound had grown to include twenty homes, several barns to house the livestock, and

338

a communal square, where the families gathered on the rest day to talk and give thanks for their good fortune. A ten-foot-high spiked fence surrounded the compound, the surrounding forest had been cut down, and the land was transformed into farmland.

There were many voyages to visit Mali and Sam over the many years that followed. Joe's tribe and Henry's colony prospered and thrived, and lived in peace and harmony.

One cold winter evening with snow falling silently, Martha and Jed sat around a roaring fire.

"Jed, when you found me curled up in your tiny room on the ship, did you ever imagine this?"

"Never." He smiled. "At least for a few years."

CHAPTER SIXTY ONE

The Future before Us

Southern New England
Summer, 1957

Jes turned twenty and Marya nineteen, and Maeve was a rambunctious delightful three and a half year old with beautiful red hair and blue eyes. They decided to leave Mahone Bay and head south.

"Jes, I'm tired of worrying about what Grandfather said. He said he thought sooner or later they would find a successor to the black bearded man. Let's leave here."

They packed up their belongings, which were small in number, and loaded them into a car Jes had bought some time after he had sold the house. They drove south in the middle of the night to get a head start in case someone was watching them. Once they reached the road that crossed Nova Scotia north to the Bay of Fundy they stopped to rest and continued during the day. They made the trip into an adventure for Maeve, pointing out lakes and trees and anything to pique her interest. They did what Marya always wanted to do: they explored the lovely places she remembered when they had previously driven south along this route from the Bay of Fundy.

They stopped at a lake close to the road and camped during the day and most of the night. They took Maeve into the chilly water and she squealed with delight, and when Marya splashed her, Maeve splashed back and giggled. They had a nice meal of sandwiches, and in the middle of the night drove further up and over the hills to the National Park. They stopped in the tall trees and listened to an owl hooting and later at dawn they heard a woodpecker pounding on a dead tree. Jes thought the owl was a Great Horned Owl from the rhythm of the whoo-whoo-whoos and Marya replied that she was sure the woodpecker was a pileated woodpecker from the heavy drumming.

While they sat silently in their tent eating a light breakfast of ham and cheese and bread, the rain began to come down and they could hear thunderclaps rolling across the land, and in front of them they saw a flash of lightning in the distance. They huddled in their tent until the rain stopped.

"This is what I wanted to do when we were younger and traveling with your uncle and father," Marya told Jes. "I am so happy here with you and Maeve. I want to be at peace and enjoy the sounds and smells of the world. Do you smell the wet pines?" She did not need an answer. Jes put his arm around her.

They reached the ferry and sailed across the Bay of Fundy. Even with more rain coming down they spent most of the time outside on the ship's deck watching the seagulls swooping and flying overhead and listening to their cawing and their cries. Once they landed on the other shore they decided to make good time for the rest of the long day, driving steadily for seven hours. They stopped at a camping area on a lake in southern Maine, cooked hamburgers on a small hibachi, and watched the sun set over the western part of the lake. Once again they took Maeve swimming. She seemed to be at home in the water. Marya was delighted to see her smiling and happy and playing. She thought to herself that it would be nice if she had a friend her age to play with.

The next day they drove steadily south trying to retrace the route taken by Jes's uncle and father. Marya recognized Route Six and they headed west across the Connecticut River and followed it until they reached familiar territory and wended their way to the end of the dirt road and the little house in the woods. It was still the way Marya had left it eight years earlier but the air was a little musty. It was late in the day but still warm. Marya aired out the house and they sat outside on the lawn, eating a small dinner of the remaining bread and meat and cheese. Maeve ate a little bit but preferred to explore the yard looking at every tree and bush and flower. The rain began and a few mosquitoes buzzed around, so they went inside and settled in. Maeve finally ran out of energy and fell fast asleep. Marya and Jes had an early night and drifted off to sleep listening to the rain.

During the next few months they cleaned up the inside and the outside of the house, dusting the tables and chests and shelves, and washing floors and windows. Outside they worked together to mow the lawn and trim bushes and paint the house pale blue and the picket fence a fresh white. Jes bought a chain saw and cut down some trees, trimmed branches, and built up a pile of logs and kindling for the fireplace. Fall came and the leaves turned a golden yellow and bright red and Marya thought it was glorious.

"Jes, I think it is so much more beautiful in fall down here than up in Mahone Bay. I'd forgotten how absolutely glorious it is." Jes nodded his agreement.

At first, they lived a quiet, secluded, and almost isolated life to avoid attention, but during the fall they became acquainted with another young family a few houses down the dirt road. Sandy and Jim were just a little older than they were and they had a little boy about a year older than Maeve named Jeff. Jeff had dark brown eyes and a mop of curly light brown hair. Maeve and Jeff often played together at both houses but Jeff liked to visit Maeve and play in the woods. The children asked Jes to build a treehouse, so just before fall turned to winter, he found the perfect spot, with three trees spaced just right. He built the house with a solid floor and three walls and a roof open on the sides so they could look out or duck down and hide. It had a small ladder with railings on the lowest side so they could climb up and down and not fall off. They played there often and pretended it was their own castle, and Maeve was the queen and Jeff was the king. They even made crowns of flowers and leaves. But even kings and queens became hungry, so sometimes they pestered Marya to make sandwiches so they could have their lunch there. The weather gradually became cold and they played less and less often, and then one day while they were huddled in the treehouse, the sky was filled with dark menacing clouds and a loud thunderclap shook the skies, like a voice filled with anger. The birds stopped twittering, and all around, as though the world stood still, waiting for a sign, the silence was broken by wind whistling though the leaves. Then snow started to fall slowly and quietly. They ran into the house.

"Mama," called Maeve, "snow is coming down. Look!"

Jeff's mother, Sandy, came to take him home when she saw the snow descending.

Shortly after that, Jes arrived home early from his job as a carpenter. He was glad it was a Friday and he did not have to work the next day. He built a fire in the stove, which heated the house, and as dusk came, the wind picked up and the snow came down hard. Winter started off with a fury and the snowstorm was a big one. The snow covered the ground and small bushes. *It is a beautiful sight*, thought Marya.

It snowed all night, and in the morning, Maeve bundled up and went out to play, with Jes keeping her company. They tried to build a snowman but the snow was too dry and light.

And then they had a big surprise.

Walking up the road through the snow drifts came Grandfather.

"Grandfather!" Jes yelled and waved. "Where did you come from? Where is your beautiful yellow car?"

"Stuck down the road in a snowdrift." He smiled and came closer. "That must be Maeve. My, you are a big girl. You were only one year old when last I saw you. How old are you now?"

She held up three fingers and tried to make a half. "Thwee and half," she said.

Grandfather held out his arms to see if Maeve would come to him. She did and he picked her up briefly and hugged her and then put her down. He wanted her to get used to him before he gave her a real hug.

"You are the only one that knows about this house, but what made you think we were here?" Jes asked.

"I figured you might come down here. I was right. And I almost made it before this storm. It's beautiful here, I must say, with the snow drifts all around, and so peaceful and quiet."

Jes brought Maeve inside and Grandfather followed. Marya ran to hug him. They exchanged stories and Marya and Jes together prepared a wonderful meal of leg of lamb, potatoes, carrots, onion, and broccoli, and some of her homemade bread.

"This is a delicious dinner, Marya and Jes," Grandfather said. "I'm impressed with your combined talents."

After dinner they had coffee, and sat and talked while Maeve played at the feet of Grandfather.

"Did you find a place to hide the scrolls and the goblet?" Marya asked, when there was a pause in the conversation.

"Yes."

"And will you tell us where they are?" Jes continued.

"No." Grandfather's eyes flashed.

Jes and Marya had expected this answer. Grandfather had always done his best to protect them, and wasn't going to change now. Keeping the whereabouts of the scrolls and goblet unknown was his way of safeguarding Jes and his family. They didn't continue the questions. Grandfather stayed until he could dig out his old car from the snow. Meanwhile Maeve asked if she could play with Jeff so Marya invited little Jeff and his mother to meet Grandfather. While they were talking, Maeve and Jeff were running around and tumbling now and then. Both of their shirts rose up and the Merovingian Crosses were both visible. Grandfather looked at Sandy and she nodded.

"Yes," she said.

Nothing more was said.

The next day Grandfather drove away, after hugging all three of them. In response to Marya's expectant look he called as he drove away.

"Yes, I'll be back again one day," he yelled. "Do you think anything will keep me from seeing my great-granddaughter now and then? I want to see her grow up to be a wonderful young woman like her mother."

Marya smiled and they waved and he drove away.

"Marya, I wonder where he hid the scrolls and the goblet?" Jes posed to Marya.

"I don't know," she replied, "but I do remember he said something before about doing some traveling. Do you suppose he has hidden them somewhere in Europe? You told me once he had gone there to do some research on books he was working on."

"I think it is more than just a possibility. It would be just like him, wouldn't it?" Jes smiled and put his arm around Marya.

She responded by hugging him. "I believe you may be right. But where, Jes?"

"The question should be: what books? Perhaps he went to look for Rhédae or to visit Glastonbury or Roslin."

"He wouldn't?" They stared at each other. "Would he?"

EPILOGUE

Two hours sitting at a desk answering questions, writing brief notes, and signing my name had left me exhausted and sweating. It was my twelfth book signing in five days and I'd had enough, or so I thought. The crowd was beginning to thin out and suddenly there was no one standing in front of me. But there was one person waiting some distance back from the desk.

For fifteen minutes I had noticed the tall slender woman looking at me. She was neatly dressed in a dark gray suit that fit her well. I had the impression her suit was old and that she was very fit. She held a copy of my book tightly in her hand and waited patiently. When the coast was clear she stepped forward.

"Do you mind if I ask you a question?" she asked in a soft low voice.

"Not at all," I replied, "What's on your mind?"

"How do you know the Merovingians had a birthmark on their chests over their hearts?" Her voice had a little edge to it.

"It's covered in the first part of my book. It's discussed in a number of sources and there is early documented evidence of these birthmarks." I hoped she'd be convinced.

"And the Cross originated with Sarah?"

"It was of divine origin."

"And it didn't exist before her?"

"The cause of its divine nature didn't happen until just before her birth." She was silent. I held my breath.

"And you seem to believe the Merovingian descendants continued all the way through the centuries?" Her tone was not challenging as I expected it to be. I breathed a sigh of relief.

"There is documented evidence of the lineage from the Merovingians onward."

"But not before?" Her voice dropped to an amazingly low level. I barely heard her.

I hesitated. "Actually there is very good evidence but it's not completely definitive and conclusive."

"Yet?" I did not respond at first. She became silent for a moment.

"I think hard evidence will turn up one day," I finally answered. "And it will be convincing. Until then we are left to our beliefs."

"I believe it will." She paused. "And it will be convincing. How do you know the birthmark carried through to the present day?" Her voice had a sharp edge to it, not threatening but with a sense of excitement and tenseness.

"You seem to be asking for proof. I wish I could provide it."

She did not hesitate. Making sure that no one was near enough to us to see, she undid her jacket and then very quickly undid the buttons of her blouse. She was not wearing a bra and opened her blouse without hesitation and without any shyness. Her breasts were still lovely and shapely. Her birthmark was right between them, a small white circle with a red cross in the middle. Just as quickly she pulled her blouse together and buttoned it. We were silent for a moment. Then, as if nothing had happened, she continued in a calm voice.

"Would you sign my book?" she asked and held it in front of her.

"Of course," I answered quickly, "to whom shall I address it?"

"Magdalene." She spoke so softly I barely heard her. This was for my ears only.

"Your last name?" I replied just as quietly.

"Just Magdalene."

I pressed her no further but addressed it to her and signed with no comments. I did not know what to say. She thanked me and disappeared. I hesitated for a moment, then jumped up to go after her, but she was gone. Why hadn't I asked her more? I had so much to talk to her about. How could she leave me with such tantalizing questions? Who was she? Where had she come from?

The signing wrapped up a few minutes later after a late burst of half a dozen people. The mystery would have to remain unanswered. Why hadn't she given me a last name? I realized I already knew the answer.

A year after my round of book signings, I was talked into doing just one more tour, this time in Europe. Four hours sitting at a desk, answering questions, writing brief notes, and signing my name, had left me wishing for an end to the signing and the beginning of a cold beer. I was very tired. It was my sixth day in a row and I needed a long break. I could not help thinking of the woman named Magdalene. I wondered who and where she was.

This book was more popular than I had expected and I should not be complaining, but I was still exhausted. And then I saw her. I was astounded to see her over here in Paris.

The tall slender woman stood there looking at me as she had done a year earlier. She was neatly dressed as before, this time in a light blue suit. I wondered what she would say. She stepped forward holding a copy of my book tightly in her hand. She hesitated briefly and then leaned over the desk.

"Do you remember me from before?"

I nodded. "What brings you over here?"

"I live here in France."

"Where?"

She ignored my question. "I want to ask you more questions, if you don't mind." She spoke in a low voice.

"Please," I replied. "Ask away. I don't mind at all."

"I was glad to read the many ideas you promulgated in your book. They made me feel good." She paused. "And where did you get them?"

"I think I just heard voices." She gave me one of the biggest smiles I have ever seen. She then became serious.

"Sarah and Alaric had many children, you said. Did they all have the birthmark?"

"I'm not sure about that but the birthmark passed on to the Merovingians of royal blood. They intermarried with the Visigoths, fought with them, and eventually conquered them."

There was a moment of silence.

"As I recall, you said your name was Magdalene. Do you use another name, a nickname?"

Magdalene had a very serious look but then it turned to a grin. "I guess we are getting to know each other. How about Maggie, if you must."

I smiled in return. "Maggie it is. Do you have any other questions, Maggie?"

"And what is your name?" I was taken aback and felt my face flush. "Jeff. Any other questions?"

"Many. I would like to know much more about the children and grandchildren of Sarah, Magda, and Martha." She paused, "but that is another whole story, isn't it?"

I nodded.

"I look forward to reading it," she said, and then continued, "And of course Maeve and Jeff fell in love and married."

"What do you think?" She gave me a huge smile. She sat down on a chair facing me across the desk. There was more silence and then she spoke gravely.

"You have some pretty serious implications in your book. Have you had any criticism from the Church?"

"Not yet," I replied, "but I think quiet voices and small movements are not a concern to a massive organization like that." I paused and went on softly, "Besides, it's only a novel." She managed a tiny smile, then pulled her chair forward, looked around, and leaned in very closely to me.

"Have any others come forward and told you they have the Merovingian Cross?"

"Strangely enough," I pondered, "only one other person has. It was a young woman."

"Perhaps the Cross is quite rare, as you seem to imply in your book."

"Perhaps it isn't that rare. You were brave enough a year ago to show that you have the Cross without knowing me very well. Now that we know

each other…" I did not finish the thought. I put down my pen, looked at her directly in the eyes and said nothing. I looked around slowly to make sure we were alone and then opened my shirt from the top to just below my breastbone. My birthmark was right in the center of my chest between my ribs. No words were spoken.

There was a long silence. She looked at me with piercing eyes.

"Perhaps there will be a second coming if one believes in that," she said. "And one day a woman with a Merovingian Cross may start the real Church, one based on the true ideals of humility, compassion, and caring for one's fellow humans. The Cathars drew away from the corrupt Church, the morally bankrupt Church. That is to say, a Church seeking money and power and clinging to outdated trappings in order to control the masses. Perhaps that might occur again in the near future."

There was a moment of silence. I did not know what to say. I was overwhelmed by her passion and the intensity of her conviction. I finally found my voice.

"You seem to believe it will," I responded. "Are you that woman?"

"Sad to say, no." She wilted before my eyes, the energy and passion gone, "If I were only a little younger, perhaps I might be."

"A church does not need to be a building or a set of rituals or a powerful organization." I tried to bring the light back to her eyes. "It can be the passion and ideals and conviction of a single person such as you to start a movement. It's never too late to speak out for what you believe in, to speak against corruption and what it brings."

"I did not tell you before, but my daughter has the Merovingian Cross and so does my granddaughter." The light came back to her eyes. "They have the energy and passion, and time, which I don't have. And they also have the purist of ideals. They live the life of Jes and Marya. Perhaps if there are enough like them we will see the change we need."

We were silent for a moment. "I believe you are right, Magdalene," I said. "At least, I hope you are right."

There was a long silence.

"What is your daughter's name, Maggie?"

"Sarah."

I was speechless. But she had more to say.

"You seemed to imply that the scrolls and goblet might have been hidden here in Europe. Déjà vu, isn't it?"

I smiled.

"And what about the treasure?" she continued, "None of it has ever been found."

"Not yet."

"While you are in Europe, would you like to search for the scrolls and goblet with me?"

I was startled by this proposal. "That's a possibility. Perhaps we can meet and discuss it? How do I reach you?"

She hesitated, then wrote on a piece of paper, folded it, and gave it to me. There was a long silence. She started to leave, then turned back.

"Do you know that they have never found the real tomb of Cleopatra?"

"It is only a matter of time." I shrugged.

"Perhaps. And they have never found the final tomb with the remains of Mary. I hope they never do. It was her wish."

"I hope you are correct on that score as well, Maggie."

"And, finally, Joshua was vehement and he was right. They never found his remains."

"And I don't think they ever will."

I turned away for a moment to reach for a glass of water. When I turned back, she was gone, disappearing as silently as a ghost. I wondered for a moment if she was real. My thoughts were the same as before. Who was she? Where had she come from? Was she serious about searching for treasure? I thought perhaps I had invented her, to speak my thoughts.

Then I opened my hand and unfolded the piece of paper she had given me. I read her writing.

Rhédae.

APPENDIX

ANCIENT NAMES – MODERN NAMES

Aegyptus – Egypt
Agathe Tyche – Cap D'Agde, France
Aquae Sextiae – Aix-en-Provence
Arelate – Arles
Avennio – Avignon
Baranis – Sallum, Egypt
Berenice – Benghazi, Libya
Bononia – Boulogne-sur-Mer, France
Gesoriacum – Boulogne-sur-Mer
Glestingaburg – Glastonbury, England
Hadrumetum – Sousse, Tunisia
Hippo Diarrhytus – Bizerte
Ichnusa – Sardinia
Kerkouane (Site Punique) – Ancient City in Tunisia
Leukaspis – Marina, Egypt
Lugdunum – Lyon, France
Mare Nostrum – Mediterraneum
Massalia – Marseille, France
Medcaut – Lindisfarne, England
Paraetonium – Mersa Matruh, Egypt
Petras Maior – Bardia, Libya
Ra – Saintes-Maries-de-la-Mer, France
Regio Syrtica (Oea) – Tripoli, Libya
Rhédae – Ancient Town near Rennes-le-Château, France
Ruscino – Perpignan
Ruspina – Monastir, Tunisia
Sah – (Constellation) Orion
Tacapae – Gabes, Tunisia
Taparura - Sfax
Tarasco – Tarascon, France
Zygra – Sidi Barani, Egypt

Made in the USA
Charleston, SC
27 March 2016